Scavenger Hunt

"Chad Boudreaux weaves his legal and security expertise into a high velocity tale of counter-terrorism and conspiracy that will grip the reader until the very last page."

—**Michael Chertoff,** Former U.S. Secretary of Homeland Security

"Boudreaux's *Scavenger Hunt* is a page-turning, bone-chilling thriller that challenges the limits of national security, effectively captures the aura of the Justice Department, and takes the reader on a wild ride."

—**John Ashcroft,** Former U.S. Attorney General

"*Scavenger Hunt* brought me back to my days as an idealistic young prosecutor and that sense of the urgency and importance of doing right. This is a novel that reminds us that there are those who make the decision to fight and do so honorably as the guardians of true justice."

—**Frances Fragos Townsend,** CBS National Security Analyst and Former U.S. Homeland Security Advisor

"Boudreaux's storytelling and character development are superb, but it's his first-hand knowledge of the Justice Department's inner workings that really sets this book apart. Strap in for a heck of a fun read!"

—**David Hosp,** critically acclaimed author of the *Scott Finn Series*

"Chad Boudreaux, who has been in and around government and complex legal issues for the last two decades, brings intrigue and page turning drama to this spellbinding fictional story at the nexus of law and national security."

—**Sigal Mandelker,** Former Under Secretary of the Treasury for Terrorism and Financial Intelligence of the U.S.

CHAD BOUDREAUX

SCAVENGER HUNT

A NOVEL

**When justice is blind,
scavengers do the hunting**

NEW YORK

LONDON • NASHVILLE • MELBOURNE • VANCOUVER

Scavenger Hunt

A Novel

Published in New York, New York, by Morgan James Publishing. Morgan James is a trademark of Morgan James, LLC. www.MorganJamesPublishing.com

Proudly distributed by Ingram Publisher Services.

Morgan James BOGO™

A **FREE** ebook edition is available for you or a friend with the purchase of this print book.

CLEARLY SIGN YOUR NAME ABOVE

Instructions to claim your free ebook edition:
1. Visit MorganJamesBOGO.com
2. Sign your name CLEARLY in the space above
3. Complete the form and submit a photo of this entire page
4. You or your friend can download the ebook to your preferred device

ISBN 9781631959431 paperback
ISBN 9781631959448 ebook
Library of Congress Control Number: 2022935936

Cover & Interior Design by:
Christopher Kirk
www.GFSstudio.com

Morgan James is a proud partner of Habitat for Humanity Peninsula and Greater Williamsburg. Partners in building since 2006.

Get involved today! Visit MorganJamesPublishing.com/giving-back

This first book is for my beautiful mom, Tricia Heath (1953–2013).

*She brought me into this world when she was a teenager and, with Churchillian vigor, taught me to never, never, never give up. As a single mom abandoned by those who promised to care, she held me like there was no tomorrow, swaying side to side on that musty-brown couch in that dumpy apartment that had become too expensive. Mascara-laced tears streaming down her face, she whispered to me, over and over, in a resolute cadence, "We are going to make it, Son. **We are going to make it.**"*

This one is for you, Mom, and for all the other moms who never, never, never give up.

*Oh, Mom, one more thing. **We made it.***

PROLOGUE

San Francisco, California

Plunging to the earth, he struggled to control his breathing as his insides clawed through his skin. More than forty thousand people stared at him, the latest *cause célèbre*. The world moved in slow motion, even as he plummeted. The wind whipped around his denim jeans and through his curly hair. As he descended, the explosive roar of the crowd became deafening. Hysterical fans screamed, danced, clapped, and slapped high-fives.

This was it, the moment he'd waited for his entire life; the moment his older, wiser brother had described countless times; the moment when he'd reap the rewards sown over years of discipline, toil, and resolve.

He wiped tears from his eyes and saw Alcatraz in the distance, the abandoned fortress of rock and steel attached to an island floating on the choppy, blue-green waters of San Francisco Bay. He thought about the psychopaths who'd once inhabited the Rock. People portrayed as standard-bearers for civilization believed—actually *hoped*—that some of the Rock's erstwhile denizens had escaped justice—at least earthly justice. He thought about those criminals and their deranged supporters. They had never dedicated their lives to any noble, enlightening cause. They had never experienced the fulfillment he enjoyed.

He focused his attention back on the gathered crowd. Those in attendance had paid hundreds—some *thousands*—of dollars for this show. *His show.* He noticed the multitudes dressed in black and citrus orange. Some had arrived early in anticipation of the once-in-a-lifetime extravaganza. Many brought small children and purchased pink cotton candy, lemonade, and over-priced novelty items to commemorate the day. Those in the most expensive seats, he thought, had invited their agents or perhaps the CEOs of their best corporate clients. Pride overtook him as he witnessed the 46,500 people congregated *en masse* to take part in this moment.

He truly was a star.

He pulled the steering toggles of his parachute, slowing his descent. A high-speed approach was unwarranted. There was no reason to hasten this experience. He wanted to relish it. There was little turbulence. His bright red- and yellow-striped canopy remained stable, so landing wouldn't be a problem. Flaring techniques wouldn't be needed. As he approached his landing zone, he witnessed the rosy faces in the crowd. No empty seat in sight. Making sure not to disappoint, he smiled and waved at the surprised onlookers.

Fighter jets circled for another fly-by. *What a great show!* he thought. As the F-16 Falcons blazed overhead, the crowd started the wave. His older, wiser brother couldn't have planned this event any better.

He tugged on the parachute's toggles once again, further slowing his fall toward the baseball stadium, making him seem suspended in mid-air, suspended in time. As he adjusted his body in the parachute harness, he spied the escort gathering below, beyond the tips of his tattered white sneakers, waiting for his arrival. Right on time. No longer anxious about his magnificent entrance, his heartbeat slowed. Everything was proceeding by design. Nothing would go wrong at this stage.

The parachute's canopy shielded his vision, but he trusted the stand-alone cargo was descending on course. The plan had evolved through several iterations, each relying upon successful landings. The show's success depended on his cohort releasing the cargo at the precise moment so it would land at the precise spot. There was no doubt the calculations would be exact. His older, wiser brother had promised the cargo-carrying parachutes would descend true to course, and his brother's word was bond. The show would prove to be a resounding success.

As he descended closer to the chaos, all sounds faded. His ears enjoyed a blissful silence. He pulled down on the parachute's toggles one last time. The plush green grass and manicured red dirt came into focus. His great moment had arrived. He closed his eyes and meditated on his past struggles. He thought about his childhood and his family. He thought about the woman he'd loved so dearly who'd died not long ago. If she could only see him now. He was a hero. This would be an event for the ages. He would go down in history as the man who changed the world with his rave performance.

His eyes reopened. Home plate was seconds away. He saw the police officers waiting—weapons drawn, handcuffs twirling, scowls pasted on their *pompous American faces*.

A second later, his feet slammed to the ground.

And his world went dark.

SCAVENGER HUNT

A few miles away, the man's older, wiser brother descended in his parachute, wiping away his own tears—tears of joy for the martyr his younger brother had just become.

———

Chevy Chase, Maryland

Images from the high-definition, flat-screen television penetrated the thick cigar smoke billowing throughout the darkened room, but the experienced reporter's words alone betrayed her anxiety.

Chaos descended upon San Francisco earlier today when a suicide bomber saddled with explosives parachuted from an airplane onto the field of Renaissance Stadium. The unidentified terrorist detonated several high-order explosives that destroyed much of the complex and killed what could be, according to first responders, as many as ten thousand people.

Thousands of other innocent victims suffered significant burns and countless physical injuries caused by the explosive inferno. Some were trampled as the crowd, gathered for the first game of this year's World Series, stampeded to the stadium's exits. People unaffected by the initial blast panicked when two box-crates attached to stand-alone parachutes descended upon them, and for good reason. Those crates contained more explosives that killed thousands more.

Authorities believe this terrorist attack—the worst in our country's history—was carried out by a group calling itself al Thoorah, which means "The Revolution." That network was formed just a few months ago after its founder, Omar Saud, was denied the top leadership position in al Qaeda. Although the government will not confirm this, our sources tell us that police apprehended Mr. Saud and another accomplice as they tried to escape the area by boat.

According to eyewitnesses, the plane used in this attack had circled the stadium once before, carrying a large banner that read: "Go Giants!" After it had violated restricted air space, fighter jets were scrambled. Authorities refuse to comment on whether the fighter pilots arrived in time or had the authority to thwart the attacks, but California Senator Miles Hummel has already called for a congressional investigation.

In response to this attack, and to the uptick in terrorist attacks occurring throughout the US, several members of Congress are demanding that President Clements resign, citing his inability to protect the homeland . . .

The meaty, arthritic hand picked up the remote control and turned off the television. It stamped out the stub of a Cuban cigar and picked up the telephone on its third ring. "Yes?"

"Is the line secure?"

"Of course."

"Do you have the list?"

"Indeed. As you know, I'm always prepared."

"Read me the names."

"Jake Reid. Brent Olson. Natasha Hensley."

"Is that it?"

"No."

"No?"

"I wish to talk to you about another who has come to my attention."

BEGINNINGS

1

Washington, DC

Blake Hudson swallowed the final drops of his fourth cup of coffee, grabbed the sports section from the morning paper, and rushed to gather his things after spending too much time engrossed in *The Washington Post*. He couldn't be late. His boss didn't tolerate tardiness or excuses, and after just five months on the job, Blake could ill afford any unforced errors. And to be sure, Blake's participation in today's meeting would be more important than ever. He had learned some shocking information, leaked to him during a phone call with a judicial clerk at 2:30 a.m., that, if true, could upend today's vital courtroom hearing involving the terrorist mastermind Omar Saud. Worse yet, it had the potential to place in jeopardy the already-fragile security posture of the entire country.

It was 6:34 a.m. He didn't have time for the subway, and Uber and Lyft were in short supply. He'd need a taxi.

As Blake scampered from one room to another in search of his wallet, Judge followed him around the bottom floor of the nineteenth-century, two-story row house. The mammoth black dog despised being abandoned. Judge craved to plunge headlong into the wild adventurism beyond the front door. But Blake was dapper from head to toe, dressed in a pinstriped suit and spit-shined dress shoes instead of athletic shorts and sneakers. For the canine, the culmination of context clues was a dispiriting sign that Blake was off again to Nowheresville. Blake realized that Judge's outlook was bleak. Judge's frantic movements in the house evidenced his growing discouragement.

To Blake's knowledge, Judge was the only Great Dane on Capitol Hill. After watching the clumsy beast slip and slide into one wall after another, Blake understood why. The narrow homes in the area, coupled with postage-stamp backyards, were inconducive to pets towering six feet tall on their hind legs. But Blake wasn't complaining. With a huge dog and a modest salary, he was lucky to have found a place to rent in the nation's capital. That his landlord was on sabbatical in Europe for a year and had never laid eyes on Judge only added to his good fortune.

But Blake knew that good fortune came in finite quantities. Another reminder that he couldn't be late to work.

Remembering that he'd left his wallet at the office, Blake tossed his newspaper on the front windowsill and hurried down the long, narrow hallway to his bedroom. The clip-clop of paw-beats behind him sounded like the echoes of a bass drum. Once he reached the bedroom, he sifted through the aged Folgers coffee container that sat atop his hand-me-down dresser, scooping out just enough quarters buried among the sticky pennies, nickels, dimes, and old movie stubs to get him to the office. Darting back toward the bedroom door, he bulled past Judge and raced to the front of the house. Reaching the front door, he patted his pants and coat pockets until he located his access badge and phone.

And then he waited.

The extended hallway allowed Judge ample room to gain momentum. It took a moment for his oversized paws to establish traction on the waxed and worn pinewood flooring. But when that happened, the situation became dangerous. Blake heard him coming—like a runaway locomotive. Judge barreled down the hallway, then slammed on the brakes at the turn, slid, and then . . . a monstrous thud.

"Judge?"

Judge groaned and scrambled to his feet. For five seconds, the two just stared at one another.

"Look, I know we didn't take a *walk* this morning. I'll be home at lunch today. No pet sitter. We'll go for a *walk*."

The trigger-word "walk," amplified by Blake, normally piqued Judge's interest and caused him to scamper to the hook near the back door. That hook anchored Judge's most prized possession—the leash. The leash, in turn, was the instrument of hope, spurring more excitement than a T-bone steak. But there was no excitement now. Judge just gazed at the leash.

It was the guilt treatment.

Staring into the mirror over the fireplace, Blake ran his fingers through his short, light-brown hair and fiddled with the Windsor Knot on his gold necktie. "Judge, don't look at me like that. You know I'm late." Kneeling, he opened his arms. "Come here, boy."

Temptation proving unbearable, Judge lowered his head and waggled toward Blake, his tail flailing from side to side. Blake grabbed Judge's ears and then wrapped his arms around his thick neck. "Remember, you're my best friend."

Judge opened his mouth as if to smile, his thick, pink tongue draped over his lower lip and his head bobbing up and down in rhythm with his heavy, happy breaths.

The cajoling complete, Blake scurried from the house in search of a cab. He was running out of time.

————

Blake's hazel eyes scanned the area for a cab. Exiting his small front yard, he made a right turn on the red-brick sidewalk and marched up East Capitol Street toward the United States Capitol.

The chaotic, bustling DC streets contrasted with the quietude of Blake's home. Stepping outside, he felt like someone had thrown a pail of ice water in his face. Emergency vehicles whined in the distance. Type-A personalities jogged through the streets. Cars honked, dogs barked, commuter and tour buses bellowed, and early rising workaholics teeming with ambition bantered on cell phones.

Blake was six blocks from the United States Supreme Court building. He predicted that the area would be fertile ground for hailing a cab, but he was wrong. Not a cab in sight. Reality began knocking like a pesky neighbor. He was coming to accept that he'd be late, and the dreaded consequences started to sink in. He needed to brief Mize before the court hearing.

That's when he reached Fifth Street and broke into a puckish grin. To his surprise, four houses down the block two black Suburbans with police lights mounted on top were idling at the attorney general's residence. His boss was still home, and the meeting with Mize wouldn't start without him. There was still hope.

But Blake had limited options. Attorney General William S. Kershing's motorized escort never stayed in one place long. The normal practice was "capture and release," as his FBI protective detail called it, then they were gone. The attorney general would be leaving his house soon.

Blake pressed forward, his brisk walk turning into a slow jog with the heavy mound of coins jingling in his pockets and the morning's Sports page tucked in the back of his suit pants. But then, before reaching the curb, Blake heard familiar voices that stopped him cold. He backtracked a few steps and reset his gaze on Attorney General Kershing's house.

The attorney general was coming out.

He saw three men of equal stature, all wearing dark suits, walking from the house with his boss in the middle. The agent to Kershing's right stopped at the front passenger door of one of the Suburbans before turning around to survey the area. The agent to his left waited for Kershing to lunge into the back seat, shielding the attorney general from any would-be assassin. In an instant, both agents climbed in the truck, and before the doors were closed, the tandem of black Suburbans was off—sirens roaring, lights flashing. The agents had "captured" Kershing and were driving him to the Justice Department. They had executed the procedure with such precision that, for a moment, Blake forgot about his quest for a taxi.

Then he saw one coming.

The mustard-colored, late-model taxi had stopped and waited for Kershing's entourage to drive off, and Blake could see that the driver was in no hurry. Blake raced toward the taxi, paying little mind to traffic before darting across the street. He leaped in the taxi's pathway to catch the driver's attention, causing him to jam on the brakes and swerve onto the curb.

"What in the *world* do you think—"

"I'm sorry," Blake said, grabbing the newspaper from the small of his back and plopping down in the backseat, "but I need to get to the Justice Department in record speed. Ninth and Pennsylvania. Do you think we can beat those two Suburbans?"

"I don't need to be playin' no games here," the driver said, mashing the accelerator to the floorboard and speeding past East Capitol, his coffee-stained white T-shirt barely covering his beer belly. "I ain't gonna risk losin' my license because you got up late for work or nuthin' like that."

Before Blake could plead his case, his head slammed against the backseat. To avoid whiplash, he clutched the grab handle with his right hand. With his left, he covered his nose to mitigate the putrid odor of vanilla air freshener mixed with mildew. The driver ran a series of red lights and decelerated to make a sharp left turn, manipulating the steering wheel with only the lower half of his palm. As the cabbie continued to complain over the honking horns of diverted taxpayers, Blake held on for dear life, knowing that this would be his fastest trip to work.

"I mean, you whippersnappers just think you can hop in a man's car and start tellin' people to break the laws and such . . . that just ain't right . . . and I ain't gonna put up with it. I'm a grown man!"

After his taxi zoomed past the Capitol, and with the driver still grumbling objections, Blake looked to his left. Through the naked limbs of Japanese cherry trees, he spotted Kershing and company traveling in the same direction on a parallel street two-hundred yards away. They weren't stopping for traffic. Noticing the whaling sirens and flashing lights, drivers decelerated and maneuvered their cars to the side of the road.

His adrenaline redlining, Blake kept a watchful eye on Kershing. The attorney general had a clear path. The Suburbans were dashing through the streets like thoroughbreds whipped by possessed jockeys in the last lap of the Kentucky Derby.

But Blake's driver *was* possessed. The taxi was blazing through a 25 mile-per-hour speed zone at twice that speed. Traffic signs didn't matter. He blew past Capitol Police officers on horseback. And he disabused cocky pedestrians of the notion they owned the right of way. The cars that Blake's taxi passed looked like they were parked. Blake worried about being pulled over or, worse, having a wreck. It was only by sheer luck that they'd made it this far.

Seven blocks to the Justice Department.

The attorney general's convoy would soon merge onto the street on which Blake's cab was traveling. Their respective roads formed a *V* a few blocks from the building. The first to reach the intersection would reach the office first, the other held up in traffic. That intersection was the critical juncture. As all three vehicles converged on a direct path into one another, none showed any evidence of slowing down.

Blake could summon no words of warning, his tongue buried halfway down his throat. The knuckles on his right hand had turned white around the grab handle. Blake's light was green, but it was evident that Kershing's agents would disregard the rules of the road—red light or not. The collision course had been set. There was no turning back.

Blake panicked, realizing he had forgotten to latch his seatbelt. But it was too late. The cab driver, so immersed in his diatribe of complaints, didn't even notice the Suburbans. As the taxi entered the intersection, the two drivers in the attorney general's entourage slammed on the brakes. Both Suburbans fishtailed out of control. Ducking in the back seat, Blake could smell the burning rubber from tires skidding on the asphalt and hear the pedestrians screaming and car horns sounding off in rebuke.

Blake sighed in relief as the taxi cruised forward, unscathed. He looked back at the mess in his wake and was encouraged to learn there'd been no collision.

"Drivers in this town are nuts," the cab driver said.

Blake looked forward with a devious grin. The Justice Department was dead ahead. Another routine, on-time arrival.

"Nothing to it," Blake whispered to himself. "Now I just need to worry about the court hearing. And Omar Saud."

2

After the cab driver excoriated him for paying with two handfuls of quarters, Blake bolted to the nearest entrance of the Robert F. Kennedy Justice Department building, or Main Justice, headquarters for the Department of Justice. As the sun continued its slow ascent, Blake noticed scores of Type-B—and perhaps a new category of Type-C—personalities in the area, establishmentarians who were mucking about and drudging themselves to work.

He could still see the Suburbans in the distance. Still recovering from the near-collision, the attorney general's agents were obeying the traffic laws and falling in line with the normal procession of automobiles. Blake chuckled as he walked through the towering twenty-foot aluminum doors that provided access to the Classic Revival-designed building. Oh, what he'd pay, Blake thought, to be a fly inside Kershing's vehicle right now. He was certain that a scathing, profanity-laced admonishment from the country's lead law enforcement officer had the FBI agents reeling and lamenting their plans to expedite the morning drive.

Ten armed men guarded the perimeter of the Main Justice building, and several more manned its entry points. Intelligence analysts believed the building was near the top of terrorist targets because, in addition to the attorney general's high profile, the lawyers who worked there prosecuted terrorists, hardened criminals, and "made" mobsters. Passing through the corner entryway, Blake felt the wind generated by the high-powered blowers that prevented the union between air-conditioning and Mother Nature. The hot air attacked his face and rushed underneath his suit jacket, causing a momentary puff in his ensemble. Reaching the interior of the building, he straightened his disheveled hair, pulled out his badge, and smiled at the security guard. As usual, the guard was standing upright with perfect posture at the badge scanner. Noticing Blake, the guard greeted him with a genuine smile and held up his right hand.

"Heard over my radio that the boss almost had a wreck. You know anything about that, Mr. Counselor to the Attorney General?" the security guard asked, slapping Blake a high-five before scanning his badge.

"Of course not, Oscar," Blake said, a smirk pasted on his face.

Blake invested in Oscar Childs, a longtime pro who was flirting with retirement. He would travel out of his way to enter Oscar's corner of the building. On this morning, it just happened to be convenient.

"You see a white dude named Blake Hudson around here lately?" Oscar asked.

Hudson—momentarily confused—stopped and stared at Oscar.

"Yeah," Oscar continued, "he'd come down here talkin' about those Dallas Cowboys, how they were going to whip up on my Washington Commanders. Crazy."

"Oh, I see," Blake said. "Here we go again."

"I guess he quit workin' here 'cause I hadn't seen him for days," Oscar said, a less than subtle reminder that Blake hadn't stopped by to argue about the upcoming football season. "Or maybe he can't defend his team no more."

"Come on! Your team is pathetic. And the front office couldn't even come up with a legit name. Commanders? You kiddin' me? I guess the rivalry is now Cowboys and Commanders."

Oscar laughed, highlighting the wrinkles on his face.

"By the way," Blake said as he walked away, "if the attorney general comes this way, find out every last detail about his ride to work."

That should slow him down, Blake thought.

———

Blake walked through the corridor underneath mosaic ceiling tiles and alongside loggias reflective of the 1930s Art Deco period in which the Main Justice building was built. Robert F. Kennedy's fingerprints covered the building. Before different assassins shot them dead in cold blood, John F. Kennedy had appointed his younger brother the sixty-fourth attorney general of the United States at the green age of thirty-six. RFK had wrestled with gargantuan issues like the Bay of Bigs and the Cuban Missile Crisis, championed civil rights progress, and waged war against the mafia bosses. Decades later, in 2001, President George W. Bush named the building after RFK—the Robert F. Kennedy Main Justice Building—in a successful effort to persuade the youngest Kennedy brother, Teddy, then a lion in the US Senate, to support the No Child Left Behind initiative.

SCAVENGER HUNT

Blake entered the Great Court, the expansive outside courtyard surrounded by the building's four sides. Shadows covered a quarter of the area, and dew protected the vibrant grass not yet exposed to the morning's sunlight. Looking at his watch, Blake picked up the pace. After passing the large, circular fountain in the middle of the Great Court, he entered the opposite side of the building and approached a spiral staircase. He galloped up the worn marble steps until he reached the fifth floor, whose ceilings were much taller than those on the other six floors.

The fifth floor was special. Even those who'd worked at the Justice Department for years lowered their voices when they walked its halls. Blake passed the curved walls that surrounded the wooden doors guarding the attorney general's office and, in his euphoria of beating his boss to work, saluted the life-sized murals of former attorneys general and Supreme Court justices. Once he reached his destination, he noticed the lights were off in the attorney general's historic conference room. Harry Mize had not yet arrived.

RFK's children had left their own marks on the building. Their father had taped their amateur drawings along the walls of his cavernous office, which was now the conference room, and the tape had pulled off some paint. Even more fascinating, inside the attorney general's conference room there was a door tattooed with pot marks—indentations forged by RFK's underaged scalawags firing BB guns.

And more fascinating still, Blake thought, on the far end of the attorney general's conference room was another door. That smaller, more mysterious door marked the gateway to what attorneys general who followed RFK referred to as the RFK "honeymoon suite." The secret room, connected by a narrow staircase to the ornate, exquisite attorney general's conference room, was spartan in contrast. The honeymoon suite contained nothing but a tiny bathroom and a cot-like single bed—amenities more suited to an Army barrack than a perch of power. Dark, wooden walls surrounded the bed without the aid of windows. RFK ordered the building of the honeymoon suite, legend had it, for his dalliance with Marilyn Monroe. History had spilled much ink on *JFK's* affair with Monroe, but few knew that RFK was closer to her than his brother.

Blake opened the door to his office. Technically late, he'd arrived before the only two people that mattered. Walking past his brown leather couch, receiving chairs, and wooden bookshelves, he turned on his desktop computer, plopped in his high-backed leather chair, and waited on the attorney general of the United States.

He wouldn't wait long. Before he could catch his breath, the door flew open without a knock.

"Mornin', Blake."

"Good morning, General."

Kershing held the door open, staring at Blake with his penetrating dark brown eyes, his long arms like tentacles. Blake saw he was rattled and unhappy. The AG's receding hair, Blake thought, appeared much grayer. His eyes exhibited signs of fatigue and age. His fit frame, polished attire, and impeccable posture, however, conveyed a perception of undeniable strength. With one glance at the man, it was clear who ran the place.

"Sorry, I'm late. I had to take care of some personal matters."

"Not a problem," Blake said. The prohibition against tardiness and excuses didn't apply to Kershing.

"I promised the secretary of defense that I'd meet with General Frank Leavitt at the Pentagon this morning at 9:30, but I can't make it."

"Okay."

"Besides, SecDef backed out, so I'm not going to waste my time meeting with his minions. Get the file from Agnes and tell her to inform Frank that you'll be attending on my behalf."

"What's the meeting about?"

"Military tribunals, enemy combatants, and such. You're familiar with the main issues. Did I introduce you to Frank when he was here last week?"

"No, sir."

"High strung but a good guy. Worked with him when I was still with Clements."

The name registered with Hudson. Thomas P. Clements was the president of the United States. Kershing had been his chief of staff for two years before Clements appointed him attorney general.

"Sure you want *me* to attend?"

"You have anything else scheduled today?" Kershing asked.

"After our meeting with Harry, I'm planning to walk with him to the Omar Saud hearing."

"Harry doesn't want anyone there. And our meeting is canceled. Harry and I talked last night. He knows what to do, and he's probably already at the courthouse."

"I was just going to take notes."

Kershing leaned against the doorframe. "Blake, you work in the Office of the Attorney General now. Not many lawyers—especially lawyers your age—get that opportunity. I hired you because the chief justice told me you were his hardest working judicial clerk. I didn't hire you to be a notetaker. Your job is to help me lead this department and to effect change, and today, that change is waiting for you at the Pentagon, not on the backbench of some courtroom."

"Understood, sir. I appreciate you taking a chance on me. I won't let you down. Speaking of courtrooms, though, one of Judge Sandersen's clerks called me early this morning. Woke me up just after two o'clock. Said she had some information."

SCAVENGER HUNT

"Yeah? What was it?"

"She told me that Sandersen was going to rule that Saud should have *unmonitored* access to counsel."

"Unmonitored?"

"Yes, sir."

"Nonsense! Giving Saud unmonitored access to a lawyer is crazy talk."

"I'm just the parrot."

"Harry doesn't need to be bothered with outlandish rumors right now, Blake. He has enough on his plate."

It didn't make sense, Blake thought, keeping this information from Harry. Nor did sending him to the Pentagon square with sound reasoning. He took to heart Kershing's pep rally on effecting change, but Rick Morales and Amanda Gormon—both of whom shared Blake's esteemed title of counselor to the attorney general—knew more about military tribunal issues. Today was not the time to reshuffle assignments to preserve the sanctity of the office.

"You okay this morning?" Blake asked, deciding not to dwell on the attorney general's nonsensical orders. "You seem flustered."

Over Kershing's shoulder, through the opened door, Blake could see two members of the security detail cringe.

"Flustered? Well, let's see. Some deadbeat," he paused, fighting back the urge to curse, "*cab driver* nearly ran me off the road." He pointed his thumb over his shoulder, still looking at Blake. "Starsky and Hutch back here wanted to make record time to work, blaring the siren and flashing the lights. So yeah, I'd say I'm flustered . . . among other things."

Blake could now identify the driver, the agent's face turning Communist red. "I'm glad you survived the commute, General."

"No thanks to these guys," Kershing grumbled as he walked off.

Blake hadn't scored any points with the FBI detail. Kershing had never minded the flashing lights, wailing sirens, and rapid deployment before today. That thought, Blake knew, had to be running through the agents' minds.

Inching his chair toward his computer screen, Blake heard Kershing marching back to the doorway. "By the way," Kershing said, sticking his head in the office, "I almost lost the bet, but I caught myself. Discipline, Blake! Rule your mind, or it will rule you!"

"I wasn't going to charge you, General," Blake laughed, remembering the wager between the lawyers in the office.

The wager was simple. Each person who used profanity in another's presence was docked a dollar, which was then split between the non-offenders. The wager originated at the behest of the attorney general himself, known for his sailor's mouth. He established a system of accountability within the office to satisfy his wife's constant bickering about his foul language. The wager already had buried Kershing in considerable, soon to be insurmountable, debt.

"You're a good American. One more thing."

"Yes, sir?"

"When Frank sees that baby face, he's going to smell blood. Don't let those military generals push you around. They're accustomed to being in command. They've fought battles. They've deployed thousands of troops in the harshest of conditions. They've been nose to nose with the enemy. Yadda, yadda, yadda. Stay tough."

"Maybe I should sprinkle chalk dust in my hair."

"It won't help."

"Don't worry about me, boss."

"I won't. Eye of the tiger."

Blake shook his head and smiled as the attorney general of the United States closed the door. As usual, the forecast called for a wonderful day at the United States Department of Justice.

Unfortunately, the daily forecast would soon change, as would the life of Blake Hudson.

3

Assistant Attorney General Harry Mize winced as the gavel crashed down. It was the first time he'd ever broken ranks with steadfast stoicism in a court of law. His hands were trembling, the pit of his throat desert dry. Under his starched white shirt, the perspiration percolated on the small of his back. At that precise moment, June 23 at 11:36 a.m., he knew things were going to change. He couldn't remember a more devastating defeat in his thirty-three years of legal practice.

He wanted to scream, but instead, he placed his hands on his legs underneath the table so his suit pants would absorb the moisture. He took deep breaths before wiping the beads of sweat from his creased forehead.

He thought about home. He longed to nap on the banks of the Tennessee River. He wanted to bury his face in the palms of his hands, but he couldn't appear weak. Harry Mize was one of the best lawyers in the country. Hardened. Seasoned. And after more than three decades of successful trial work, he wasn't about to let one misguided decision break him. Or was he? As usual, Mize was his own most persuasive adversary.

Mize considered the hordes of onlookers—the voyeurs of this molestation. They arrived early, had filled the courtroom, and had no clue what had just happened. Not what *really* happened. They had no idea of the effect Judge Sandersen's ruling would have on their country. Following the ruling, he had heard the hands slapping, had smelled the pungent scent of drugstore cologne, and had witnessed the supercilious sneering.

If they only knew, he thought.

He could feel the odious breath of reporters on the back of his neck and visualize their snarling, gnashing teeth. He had no doubt that staff writers for the more radical publications would dedicate the afternoon to crafting catchy headlines about the big *win*. They got what they wanted. What they thought they wanted anyway.

If he only could tell them.

He reminisced of his years as a small-town federal prosecutor in Tennessee. His cases rarely had captured the media's attention. He had enjoyed being in front of an audience of twelve jurors who, despite their modest backgrounds, could articulate right and wrong better than society's elite. That was his Roman Coliseum, his platform for excellence. Trial after trial, Harry Mize would lean his tall, distinguished frame over the podium, reading glasses notched just on the tip of his pointed nose, arguing—preaching—in his Southern drawl about the meaning of justice. He remembered closing arguments when jurors nodded in agreement—some even winked—as he told them what *really* had happened.

But his efforts today produced no positive reaction. There had been no jury. Only the judge's opinion mattered, and she wasn't buying his merchandise.

He thought about the judge. Mize, fifteen years her senior, thought about the things he couldn't tell her no matter the outcome. He had misjudged her to his detriment. He thought she would eschew public pressure. Maybe his miscalculated hope sprang from his knowing she was, for all practical purposes, the last line of defense. Perhaps it was some form of childish instinct clinging to the stubborn but often disproved theory that the good guys always win.

Did she realize that what was to come would be traced back to June 23, at 11:36 a.m.? Did she have any idea what she'd just done? Why couldn't he just tell her?

He knew why.

His trademark eloquence had proven insufficient to penetrate the facade she was staging for the national audience. Judge Sandersen had played the role of her life, swallowing Slick Nick's chicanery like a largemouth bass inhales a crankbait. Her performance was so magnificently orchestrated that Mize wondered when she'd found time to rehearse her irrational gobbledygook. He knew for certain it had been before his argument, before he arrived at the Prettyman Federal Courthouse, and before donning her fancy-schmancy lipstick and masking her facial canvas with paint-thick rouge.

He thought about Nick Duncan, his court-appointed adversary, despised by liberals and conservatives but exalted by misfits who were impervious to reality and devoid of ideological mooring. Slick Nick was reveling in his victory, along with his gallery of iconoclastic disciples. His pomp was only outdone by his basking in the career-motivated praise of his brainwashed underlings.

Mize began to fidget, stroking his light-blue Hermes necktie. The courtroom walls started to close in. He felt like the ceiling was going to crumble down—first, tile by tile; then, stone by stone and followed by a climactic avalanche of falling debris.

Long, deep breaths. He closed his eyes and tried not to fret. This wasn't the end, was it? He could appeal the ruling. Yet, without knowledge of what *really* was transpiring, he couldn't be sure that the appellate courts would reverse. Terrorist cases had become so laden with politics that nothing was certain anymore.

Mize knew that the outcome of today's hearing was all about politics. Lady Justice wasn't blind. She was wearing see-no-evil lenses and had been cursed with a more troubling disability—muteness. There existed no doubt in his mind that political machinations had suffocated legal precedent on this day.

After wiping his hands on his thighs, he turned around to face an empty courtroom. He then closed his briefcase, slid back his chair, and stood up. And with a final deep breath, turned to walk away.

As he approached the door, Mize noticed a man sitting in the back corner of the courtroom. Mize tried to break eye contact, but for some reason, the man captivated his attention, his eerie demeanor calling for recognition. The man rose from his seat but refused to interrupt the stare. Mize stopped by the door and waited for him to approach.

"Unfortunate outcome," the man said as he sprang forward, squeezing his short, portly frame between the seats.

"I've never been a good loser," Mize responded, losing interest and leaning his left shoulder into the large courtroom door.

The man was a step from Mize. His rugged face broke into a slanted smile, and he extended his meaty right hand. Mize noted that the man's gnarly teeth were tarred with coffee and tobacco stains.

"I'm Elliot Nichols. It's been a while."

Wanting to escape, Mize shook the man's hand, noticing the weak grip. "Have we met?" He felt obligated to ask the question, though disinterested in anything the man had to say.

"We met several years ago in Nashville. You prosecuted Dr. Barnett—"Doctor Love," they call him now—for sexual misconduct with a patient. I worked for the hospital."

Mize remembered the case well. He had put the scummy obstetrician in jail for fifteen years.

"I wasn't a witness," the strange man said, "just an observer." His assertiveness and clever delivery made it difficult for Mize to leave. Mize, though, was aching to disengage, yearning to return to his office. "What's your reaction to today's ruling?"

"You win some, you lose some." Impatient with the small talk, Mize leaned harder against the door until it creaked open. "Take care," he said, not waiting for a response.

Mize walked on the right side of the hallway, his mind a shambles until he approached a pack of reporters. Its focus was on the victor, each scrivener trying to scream her questions louder than the others as Slick Nick—his morals as solid as melting ice—dictated tomorrow's headlines. Mize bolted past the crowd, leaving little chance for a successful pursuit. He then turned the corner, scurried down the escalator, and rushed by the security guards, never once stopping until the revolving door deposited him into the piercing sun. Shielding his eyes, he noticed, for the first time, verdigris stains that, over the years, had dripped like green blood down the statue of heroes located on the courthouse grounds.

Mize took a detoured route back to the Main Justice building so he could collect his thoughts. He would first tell the attorney general and Blake Hudson. They would brief the White House counsel and the president's chief of staff. The president was taking an extended weekend at Camp David, so hopefully, Mize thought, the briefing would be tomorrow—late tomorrow. He needed time to consider plausible options. He wasn't looking forward to his report. There was no way to polish gritty news.

His mind kept wandering back to Elliot Nichols. Something was disturbing about the man, about the way he looked and what he'd said. What was it? Mize couldn't stay focused long enough to put his finger on it. He struggled to remember their brief conversation.

Mize realized he couldn't prolong the inevitable any longer. He looked at his watch and realized it was well past time to return and deliver the news. Approaching the Navy Memorial on Pennsylvania Avenue, he could see the Main Justice building across Ninth Street beyond the National Archives. A part of him wished it had disappeared. He stopped short of the middle of the memorial's circular fountain to catch his breath. His heart hadn't quit pulsating since Judge Sandersen's ruling, and the walk had only increased his blood pressure.

He drew closer to the cool water and leaned against a mural of fallen sailors etched in copper. The mist emanating from the fountain covered his face before trickling down his neck. He knelt down, set his briefcase on the ground, and closed his eyes.

A minute later, he stood up, raised his head to the sky, and whispered a short prayer.

And then on June 23, at 12:25 p.m., Harry Mize collapsed.

4

Blake Hudson sat upright, his back as straight as plywood, in a conference room on the third floor of the Pentagon, staring at the man across from him at the oval table. Four others dressed in military attire flanked the man in the middle. The general's chest was bedecked with a battery of ribbons, reflecting not only his numerous achievements but, above all else, a recognized lifetime of valor.

"General Leavitt, I understand and respect what you're saying, but—"

"I'm not sure you do, Hudson."

"Look, I'm not here to rehash the problems you've experienced with prior attorneys general and their administrations. Attorney General Kershing's—"

"Son, I can't be hamstrung by conservative legal constraints. I just won't. I've already spoken to the folks over at NSC, and they tell me that your office is the problem here."

Eye of the tiger. Eye of the tiger.

"Sir, with all due respect, the attorney general's primary initiative is to provide for security to its fullest extent within the bounds of the Constitution. That goal, I trust, is shared by President Clements and the secretary of defense and the NSC."

"How dare you invoke POTUS and his cabinet secretaries!? You don't know what their opinions are! I do!"

The stakes were high in this room. Blake knew that Leavitt shouldered the weight of thousands of soldiers—breathing and buried. To Leavitt, even trivial issues carried great significance. The smallest of mistakes often led to many casualties. In his world, unlike Blake's, gray areas didn't exist. No exceptions.

"Sir, I don't presume to know the opinions of the president or—"

"And don't sit there and question my commitment to the Constitution!"

Blake was making zero progress. The Department of Defense thought that the Justice Department was the problem. The military mindset? Destroy the problem.

"Sir, I wasn't trying to—"

"Many of my soldiers have lost their lives protecting the Constitution!"

Blake needed to walk a fine line between establishing credibility and stroking Leavitt's ego. Leavitt was offended that Kershing had sent a tenderfoot. Worshipped like gods on the battlefield, military generals were nothing but mid-ranking bureaucrats at the Pentagon. Blake had to re-instill Leavitt's pride. Leavitt wouldn't negotiate if embarrassed in front of his troops.

"You're right, and I think about their sacrifices every day."

"You don't know what sacrifice is, son."

"I beg to differ, General."

"Ever serve in the military?"

"No, but I'm one of the few in my family who hasn't."

"Your dad . . . Middle East?"

"Yes, sir. And my mother's father fought in Korea and then again as an officer in Vietnam."

"Is that all?"

"No, sir. I have ancestors who fought in the Great War, and their fathers toted pistols and saddle rifles on horseback for the Texas Rangers, where, *I might add*, they spent much of their time chasing cattle rustlers and bandits."

"Pancho Villa?"

"You bet."

General Frank Leavitt stared at Blake before passing on a contagious smirk to his four inferiors in the room. They all returned half-hearted smiles as Leavitt slammed his hand on the table. "Well, package me up, I'm sold, ol' boy! You should've told me all this earlier!"

Blake smiled. *Finally . . . the welcoming party.*

"Look, *Blake,* these detainee issues are sticky as molasses," Leavitt continued, leaning back in his chair and crossing his legs.

Blake waited for someone to pour single-malt scotch and light cigars when he felt his phone vibrate. He pulled it out and checked the number.

"Excuse me," Blake said. "I apologize, but I need to take this."

He rushed out the door and into the hallway, allowing the door to slam behind him.

"Mildred, I'm still meeting with General Leavitt. What's going on?"

"Blake, you need to come back to the office. Something has happened to Harry. They're taking him to the hospital and—"

"What happened?"

"Just come back here, and . . . I need to go."

Blake reentered the conference room, the urgency manifest on his face.

"Gentlemen, I'm sorry, but we'll need to finish this discussion later. Something's come up that demands my immediate attention."

Leavitt appeared concerned but not flustered, trying to glean something from Blake's expression. "All right, then. I think we can revisit these issues early next week." Leavitt's lickspittles nodded in unison. "Blake, you need a lift?"

"No thanks, sir," he said. "I have a car waiting for me outside."

"That car have rotors?"

"No, sir, but my building doesn't have a helipad."

"Everything okay?"

"Not really, but it shouldn't alarm you. At least not yet."

Cabo San Lucas, Mexico

Jake Reid was fishing alone today. He had no customers and had dismissed his crew with pay. Dreams of peace and prosperity on the Sea of Cortez were subsumed by frustration after thirteen months. Instead of fighting billfish, dorado, and yellowfin tuna for wealthy tourists, he was fighting to pay the bills in Cabo San Lucas, Mexico.

As owner and captain of the *Mission Possible*, a thirty-one-foot Bertram deep-sea fishing boat, he had all the tools. He was an experienced angler with state-of-the-art equipment, and he had a reputation for catching a *ton* of striped marlin. And that's what people paid big money to do on the tip of the Baja Coast.

Jake Reid's problem was his refusal to become a team player. And that was unacceptable in Los Cabos, where indigenous anglers-turned-entrepreneurs monopolized the fishing industry. Too stubborn to market his services internationally, or share his profits with the local businessmen, his odds of success were nil. Today that realization was sinking in. Reid was warming to the fact that Mexico never would be his home.

But where was home?

He knew where home *used* to be. Home was where his wife had left him. Home was where his five-year-old daughter, Rebecca Ann, was buried after . . .

Thanks for the entertainment, Mr. Reid.

Home was the one place he wanted to forget, the place from which he'd run away but never could escape. And, yes, home was the place he'd been instructed to leave—the place where the trouble began and the trouble would end.

18

CHAD BOUDREAUX

Thanks for the entertainment, Mr. Reid.

The water was tranquil at dawn, the salty breeze cool on his face. He checked the cooler next to the captain's chair to see if the bottled water was cold. He would need to re-hydrate to neutralize last night's hangover from El Squid Roe, the liveliest bar and dance spot in Cabo, if not the world. Reid couldn't remember the precise time at which he'd passed out, but he was certain that he'd slept alone. And today, he wondered whether he'd chosen to fish alone. He struggled to fight back the obvious questions.

He piloted the Bertram through the marina, rubbing sunblock on his golden forehead and aquiline nose, then on his slender cheeks covered with his furry beard. He'd not purchased a razor since leaving the United States. There was no need. He had convinced himself that appearances meant nothing in Mexico. So far, there had been no arguments to the contrary.

He turned on his CB radio and listened to the Mexican captains contribute to the morning fishing report. Most of the boats fishing for blue and striped marlin would be heading to the south of Punta Gorda, a large mass of crystal-blue water located within the Sea of Cortez. The bigger boats could expect success catching *rayado*, or striped marlin, on the Pacific side of Land's End.

The radio transmissions refreshed delightful memories that pushed Reid to the edge of despair. The CB radio dialogue reminded him of nights when Rebecca Ann was a baby. She would kiss her daddy goodnight before running downstairs. Her mother would then put her to bed in a room at the opposite end of the house while Reid prepared for his next mission in a country at the opposite end of the world. He remembered those static-laden sounds, the purrs and laughs of his daughter coming over the airwaves.

The baby monitor, he now realized, always seemed to be right next to him. He often would smile as his wife and daughter sang "Itsy Bitsy Spider" and read, over and over, the intoxicating words of *Goodnight Moon*. Reid had been most at ease when his daughter was tucked away in her nursery. He wished that he would've invested more time in that special place and capitalized on the ten to fifteen minutes before she fell asleep. That was the invaluable time when she'd displace her rebellion with sincere attentiveness and often wrap her arms around him.

Oh, how Rebecca Ann had loved her daddy, Reid thought. Almost half as much as he still loved her.

Thanks for the entertainment, Mr. Reid.

It took but a second for memories of his child to eat away at his soul; yet, for some demented reason, he welcomed the pain and turned up the radio. Leaning back in his captain's chair, he propped his feet on the steering wheel and turned his New York Yankees baseball cap around like a defiant schoolboy.

SCAVENGER HUNT

The most frustrating thing, he thought, was trying to determine how they'd found out. He had always been so careful, never revealed his true identity. But somehow they'd fingered him, and his life had changed forever—for the worst. He couldn't help but think that someone in the Central Intelligence Agency had turned on him. One of his own. There must have been a mole, someone worried about a mission gone afoul and willing to sacrifice Reid and his family because it was "in America's best interest." The mere thought of that excuse sickened him. It was nothing but a cheap, irresponsible way to avoid accountability, to endanger the lives of those most willing to sacrifice everything for their country.

What would happen if and when he returned home? Were he ever to find the mole, would that person meet the same fate as Rebecca Ann's killer? Those were questions he couldn't answer . . . questions he was terrified to confront.

Thanks for the entertainment, Mr. Reid.

The Mexican fishing report had turned X-rated, which was common for Los Cabos fishermen. The dialogue, as usual, was laden with Spanish profanity and devious laughter.

But the comedy stopped abruptly when an outsider, speaking English, interrupted the conversation.

"Jake Reid, turn your CB to Channel Four. Repeat. Jake Reid, turn to Channel Four."

A chill penetrated Reid's spine. It was a voice he'd heard once before in another place, in another time. A friendly voice, or so it seemed.

It took him a few seconds to regain his composure. He dropped his bare feet from the steering wheel, lunged forward, and fumbled around to find the dial on his CB radio. He turned the manual dial to Channel 4 and swallowed the remaining food in his mouth. And then he waited, reluctant to make contact.

"Are you there, Jake?"

It was enough to force a response. "This is Jake. Who is this? Where are you?"

"Drop three, ten, one," the voice directed.

Recognizing the rudimentary "ping-pong" signal shift, Reid ran the math. From Channel 4, a drop of three would be Channel 1. Adding ten would take him to Channel 11. Dropping one from Channel 11 would take him to Channel 10. He turned the dial to Channel 10 and mashed the lever on the handheld CB transmitter. "Jake Reid here. Who's speaking?"

"My name is irrelevant. All you need to know is that I work for your former employer. You are needed back in the United States. Something terrible has happened."

"What? Why? Where are—"

"I can't discuss my current location or the purpose for my contact over this frequency, but I'll reach out to you again soon—after you reach shore. Your travel back to the United States has been arranged."

"Wait a minute! I'm out here in the Pacific Ocean! I'm not coming back to shore for another three hours! Hello!?"

Nothing.

He sat in disbelief as the *Mission Possible* continued its rocking motion farther out to nowhere. He could hear the metronomic *slap, slap, slap* of water against the boat's hull. He checked his watch, turned his Yankees cap around, and started the engines. Taking one last look around, he turned the bow of the Bertram back toward shore.

Ready or not, it was time for Jake Reid to go home.

5

Washington, DC

Rick Morales consoled Amanda Gormon in the hallway near the wooden doors to the attorney general's office as Blake approached and asked, "Is he going to be all right?"

"He had a stroke, or heart attack, or both," Rick said, his dark-brown eyes canopied under thick, bulging eyebrows and his muscular frame keeping Amanda from falling to the floor.

"So what's his prognosis?"

"Not sure if he's gonna make it."

Now standing in front of his colleagues, Blake shook his head in disgust. "Unbelievable. Where'd they take him?"

"George Washington."

George Washington University Hospital had hosted its share of injured public figures. It admitted its most notable patient with a gunshot wound in 1981. At the time, Ronald Reagan was in good spirits, spewing jovial and memorable one-liners that comforted the nation.

"What are we waiting for?" Blake asked. "Let's get down there."

"We can't go right now," Rick said. "For some reason, Michael wants us to stay here."

Michael Gregg, disliked by most, was Kershing's highbrow chief of staff. He ruled the office like a despot and had the personality of a prune.

Rick Morales, on the other hand, was the most popular lawyer at Main Justice. A seasoned trial lawyer with an uncanny sense of charm, he had a gift of persuasion and a knack for time management. He could prepare a case for trial while sitting in the bleachers at his children's baseball games. And when he wasn't prosecuting Bond movie villains, it was all shenanigans. In high school, he had been both the valedictorian and class clown.

"Something must be in the works," Blake said. "Amanda, you okay?"

Amanda Gormon nodded without much conviction. Her blonde hair was pulled back from her puffy face in a ponytail, her right cheek anchored to Rick's now mucked-up blue Oxford. Blake could see the remnants of mascara that had drained like sewage down her face. Although attractive in a studious way, her features failed to demand attention in a crowded room. But Hollywood looks weren't her strength. She was the smartest of the three counselors, and everyone on the fifth floor at the Justice Department knew it—a true mega-savant.

But her current condition perplexed Blake. Mize's collapse was tragic, but Amanda and Harry Mize weren't kindred spirits. Maintaining eye contact with Rick, Blake pointed to Amanda and, turning over the palms of his hands, made clear his befuddlement.

"The AG couldn't contact Harry earlier," Rick said. "Harry had turned off his phone, so Kershing sent Amanda to find him."

"And?"

"She was the one who pulled him out of the fountain."

"I'm okay, Blake," Amanda said, dislodging her head from Rick's shoulder, her stringy hair sticking to her tear-dampened face. "I just need some time to decompress."

"What do you mean by *pulled him out of the fountain*? What fountain?" Blake asked, frustrated that he needed to excavate important bits of information that Rick and Amanda should've offered.

But Blake never heard the answers to those questions. Amanda's lips were moving, but Blake's brain wasn't processing the sounds. It had just hit him. *Omar Saud and al Thoorah.* Harry must've been walking back from the hearing. Blake had worried about Harry all morning, but now was the first time he'd connected the dots since he learned of Harry's incident.

Blake was almost afraid to ask. "Did Sandersen rule from the bench?"

"Yep," Amanda said, her voice now audible. "The judge granted Omar Saud unmonitored access to counsel."

Blake's eyes glazed over. It had happened. Just like the judicial clerk had predicted. Blake had failed to warn Harry—more precisely, he'd been directed not to—and now it had happened.

"Blake?"

"Has the judge never heard of Lynne Stewart!?" Blake said, opting not to disclose the fact that he'd been pre-warned, referring to a lawyer once convicted of passing along information from a high-profile, imprisoned terrorist to his followers. "Are you kidding me!? That's unprecedented!"

"I didn't know that," Rick said.

"Unreal," Blake said. "To make matters worse, the lawyer he'll hire is a . . ."

"Is a what?" Rick asked.

"I'll tell you later," Blake said, remembering that he was in an area of the building where classified information couldn't be discussed.

"I'll be right back," Amanda said as she walked a few steps to her office.

Blake was paralyzed. The tragic puzzle pieces of Harry Mize's day were beginning to coalesce and form a sensible shape.

"Kershing says the judge's ruling will have disastrous consequences. Is he right?" Rick asked.

Before anyone could speak another word, the FBI agents in Kershing's protective detail emerged from the wooden doors outside of the attorney general's office. Kershing was in tow with his chief of staff walking lockstep at his side. Michael Gregg was briefing the attorney general on the names, backgrounds, and political persuasions of certain United States senators. Amanda emerged from her office at the sound of echoing footfalls.

"Amanda and Rick," Kershing said as he continued marching, "I need you to grab whatever notes you have on the Saud case and come with us. I've requested an emergency congressional hearing to discuss this mess. I'll be waiting for you downstairs."

"Blake," Gregg said, "I'm not going to the hearing. Meet me in my office in thirty minutes. Need to speak to you about something else."

"Okay," Blake said as Gregg disappeared around the corner.

Once again, Blake was perplexed by the delegation of assignments. If the attorney general was to brief Congress on matters related to Harry's hearing, then Blake should accompany him. Blake wasn't a criminal lawyer, but Gregg had asked him to monitor the hearing for the office. Neither Rick nor Amanda knew much about it. Harry was one of the most capable prosecutors at DOJ, so he didn't need an experienced criminal lawyer looking over his shoulder.

"Anyone know what the heck's going on? Why doesn't Michael want me to go?"

"We'll call you and give you an update," Amanda said.

"Rick?"

"Don't look at me, Blake. I can't figure the guy out. Do you have any notes on this?"

Blake threw open his door, walked into his office, and grabbed the folder marked SAUD from his filing cabinet. Rick entered behind him.

"I'll give you this entire folder, which is all unclassified."

"Not going to do me much good at this point."

"Kershing knows the issues," Blake said, handing Rick the folder, "but he may ask for something in here. This is a catastrophe, Rick."

"I'm not sure I understand why everyone is so freaked out."

"If Saud gets unmonitored access to a lawyer, then al Thoorah will learn where he's being detained and bust him out. Heck, he could run the operation from his jail cell. This is the break they've been waiting for. These terrorists are ruthless. They'll stop at nothing to further their cause, which is now to free their leader and continue wreaking havoc on American soil. And we all know what Saud can do when he's unchained."

"But really, Blake, he's surrounded by armed guards. Who cares if the bad guys know where he is? Rarely do we conceal the whereabouts of prisoners."

"This case is different," Blake said, lowering his voice to a whisper. "Here we have classified intelligence that makes it clear that al Thoorah is planning to spring him. These thugs are just waiting for the order, and then they'll try to find him. Right now, he can't communicate with anyone on the outside but a court-appointed lawyer, and we monitor all the coms. Also, we've been moving him from one location to another."

"Does the judge know that?"

"She knows we move him, but she doesn't know that his cohorts are planning a rescue attempt. She also doesn't know that his would-be lawyer is a bona fide terrorist."

"Why don't we tell her? Problem solved."

Blake walked to the television, mashed the power button, and turned up the volume. "The CIA has an undercover operative who's feeding us information. They won't let us divulge to the court the information he provides."

"Makes sense to me."

"This operative walks around in Pakistani caves all day with a long beard and a tattered Koran. If his information leaks out, Saud's men could pinpoint him as the source. Then they'd locate and neutralize him."

"You mean kill him?"

"You got it."

"Then why don't they pull the operative?"

"He's too valuable. You know how hard it is to penetrate an al Thoorah cell?"

"I haven't tried lately. Is his court-appointed lawyer in on this?"

"Probably not. He's just doing his job."

"I need to run downstairs. But before I go, best guess—scale from one to ten?"

"Is ten bad or good?"

"Bad."

"Eight."

"Really?"

"Trust me. I've been reading the intel. Things are about to spiral out of control."

"Katy bar the door."

"Rick, if this doesn't get reversed on appeal, we're gonna need more than Katy."

6

Bandar-e Anzali, Iran

The polluted water of the Anzali Lagoon sloshed around his black Polartec bodysuit as he stood erect and adjusted his custom-made PSG-1 sniper rifle. His formidable auburn eyes squinted as he scanned the darkened shoreline of the makeshift beach. He was the first member of his elite unit to reach the rendezvous point. The waxing moon provided the only source of light, and the salty air impaired his normally 20/10 vision. He didn't know the general location of the others. He prayed they'd return unscathed, accompanied by the living, breathing fruits of the undertaking. If not, he'd search for them, risking everything, including his life, if only to bring back corpses. Such a course of action was never an option but a well-accepted directive that everyone in his squadron followed.

Allowing his rifle to hang from his shoulder strap, he pushed a button on his watch that triggered an orange light.

Two minutes and forty-three seconds . . . and counting.

Where he stood, the murky water rose no higher than his waist. Keeping his feet planted, he joggled his knees, careful not to make significant waves, diverting any unwanted marine life that may disrupt his concentration.

Captains in the Iranian Fishing Company's fleet had long since moored their boats, but the lagoon still smelled like sturgeon flesh. The Iranian fishermen, nestled in their bunks, had spent another day netting fish along the Caspian Sea to satisfy the commercial interests of Mother Persia. After capturing the sturgeon, they'd rip apart the membranes for the roe that would be served in the finest restaurants throughout Europe. Fishermen feeding the caviar industry kept the local fishing economy afloat, but Brent Olson knew that enemy soldiers also populated this area.

CHAD BOUDREAUX

One minute and fourteen seconds.

Olson didn't eat caviar. American chickens raised in the Midwest region of his homeland laid the only eggs he allowed near his mouth. The mere thought of eating caviar, and the pretentiousness that Olson ascribed to it, was a contradiction to his lifestyle. Besides, he thought, mildewed seines and strewn fish entrails aside, caviar was just gross . . . no matter how good it tasted.

Twenty-nine seconds.

As he waited, he thought about his wife. His energy for every mission was fueled by his desire to return to her embrace. Though she never complained, she worried about his missions. The secrecy surrounding his work only increased her anxiety.

Ten seconds.

He was ready to go home. This place reeked. Everything about it stunk. Yet, as he stood in a filthy lagoon thousands of miles from the United States, he was assuaged by at least one happy thought—Molly Olson didn't eat caviar either.

His watch vibrated. His troops were late.

Being late wasn't the end of the world. Unforeseen things often happened on high-risk missions in hostile territory.

Timeliness was a virtue expected of all members of Olson's team, but it couldn't always be achieved. He aimed for perfection, but soldiers had to accept schedule modifications. That didn't mean he had to like it. Unable to make radio contact, Olson could only speculate as to what was taking so long.

He heard the distant sounds of rotor blades chopping the wind . . . and growing louder.

Where are my men?

The men on Olson's team were, in terms of affection, a close second to his wife. He knew more about them than he knew about Molly. That wasn't a negative reflection of his marriage but a realization that grew out of being a part of "A Squadron" of the United States Army's 1ˢᵗ Special Forces Operational Detachment-Delta, or Delta Force. He'd never gone into battle with Molly, never faced near death with her, never done things with her that he did with Delta Force. And that was a good thing. To be sure, he often wondered whether she'd speak to him if she knew the whole story. Olson was a loving, caring, and gentle husband at home, but he was ruthless on the job.

A tactical warrior.

Any guilt borne by the casualties wrought by his hands had long ago been buried by the honor of the cause. That was enough for Olson. He'd been programmed to think about the cause. Nothing else mattered. He knew that by exterminating the bad guys, he was protecting the good guys.

SCAVENGER HUNT

His squadron was the cream of the crop, and none of its members asked questions about the reasons behind a particular mission. Delta Force had recruited Olson while he was an Army Ranger. The Rangers themselves were no slouching bunch, perhaps better than any other country's special forces. Delta Force, however, picked the elite from all the other branches of the US Armed Forces. Unless one had a death wish, he wouldn't mess with SFOD-D. These guys shaved with serrated blades and toasted victories with blood martinis.

Spats of gunfire erupted in the distance.

Without flinching, Olson focused again on the shoreline. A rustling noise located just beyond the water's edge in the brush followed the gunshots. They all came out at once, seven shadows bounding toward him—three figures assisting three others to walk, one returning fire from behind the group. Olson could hear unknown voices screaming cacophonous phrases in a foreign language about three hundred yards away. The seven closest figures said nothing and made no noise.

Finally!

Olson saw the helicopter descending against the moonlight. The men high-stepped through the mudflats toward Olson. The chopping sounds of the blades muffled the angry voices in the distance. But the enemy continued firing a staccato fusillade of bullets. Olson looked up and saw the large mass hovering directly overhead; he could feel the heavy gusts of wind generated by the rotor of the 50,000-pound bird. Enemy fire was zinging by the approaching figures, puncturing the filmy surface of the lagoon, and chinking off the MH-53M Pave Low IV helicopter that would provide the only means of escape for the group.

"Get underwater!" Olson yelled.

Without hesitation, six of the men plunged deep into the lagoon, out of sight. The seventh followed course, but only after firing off some desperate last rounds. The co-pilot of the MH-53 dropped the rope ladder as the lead pilot turned on the helicopter's high beam lights and aimed them toward the foreign soldiers, lighting up the shoreline like a sunbather in a tanning machine.

Olson immediately spotted his targets, who were running toward the water, firing uncontrollably while attempting to keep their footing. Olson neither spared nor wasted bullets, the salvo of shots from his rifle reducing the number of troops in the Iranian military. Each shot right on target.

As he waited for the next group of militants to infiltrate the beach through the brush, a man emerged from the water, gasping for air. The man's lungs had limited capacity; he'd fought off his rescuer to escape the suffocating waters, and he needed to breathe, no matter the cost of the oxygen. Olson swung his rifle to his back and lunged forward to grab the man. Moving ahead, he could see another cluster of Iranian soldiers running toward him.

"Be calm," he instructed, as he picked the man up with his right hand, leaned down, and draped him over his left shoulder. "I've got you."

Brittle and malnourished, the man only weighed about one hundred twenty pounds. Olson looked at the chopper. He saw the others climbing up the rope ladder.

Enemy fire was upon them. Bullets were zinging past them within inches. It was only a matter of time before . . .

Olson began pouncing in the water. He *had* to get to the ladder. *On the double!*

After catching the swinging rope, he stepped onto the ladder's first rung and started his ascent toward the helicopter.

But then it happened. He felt a stinging pain in his right hamstring. He'd been hit!

His right leg dangling in the air, and with the beaten man draped on his shoulder, Olson struggled up the ladder. Reaching the final rung, he lunged into the aircraft as it surged higher into the sky. Three of his men rushed to his assistance—one snatching the hostage from Olson's grasp, one taking his rifle, another grabbing Olson's arm and pulling him to safety.

Once aboard, Olson sat down and triaged his wound. Properly treated, it was nothing to worry about. He'd had worse wasp stings in his native Nebraska. He'd ask the medic to carve out the bullet when he returned to base. Better yet, after a few jiggers of Jack Daniels, he'd do it himself. Not bad for a high-risk rescue mission, he thought. The tally of enemy casualties was usually much higher for similar operations.

A dim green light was aglow inside the helicopter, the outside hatch still open as the chopper gained momentum. Olson looked at the three emaciated men he'd studied for weeks but never met, men who'd been hostages until fifteen minutes ago. They were downtrodden yet giddy, hugging each other with radiant smiles. Olson looked at his men and nodded in satisfaction. He then stared again at the fruits of the mission, captivated by their collective reaction to freedom. These guys were the true heroes, Olson observed. Men of honor and fortitude. He wondered what instruments of torture and levels of abuse they'd endured over the last two years.

One of them gathered the energy to speak over the turbine engines and rotor. "They got surface-to-air missiles in that jungle area off the beach! SAM units all over the place!"

"The SAMs have all been neutralized," Delta Two said. Disabling the missile launchers had been Olson's responsibility. Delta Two needed no confirmation from Delta One. Some things you just knew.

Another hostage, wearing nothing but a burlap cover around his waist, looked around at all his rescuers. When he made eye contact with Olson, tears rolled down his cheeks. He raised his right hand to issue a forceful salute. His hand, which contained only two fingers and no thumb, was trembling. Olson smiled and returned the gesture, waiting for the man to lower his hand first before ending his responsive salute.

"Sir, you saved my life. I would've drowned or been shot dead had you not come back for me," he said. "And I repaid the debt by getting you shot."

"Sir, may I ask for your rank and name?"

"I'm James Washington. I was . . . I *am* a captain in 10th Mountain."

"Captain Washington, you don't need to address me formally. It's an honor to meet you. You're a hero."

"Sir?"

"You're a hero to everyone on this chopper and everyone in America. My job is to get you back home alive. I only regret that I didn't get you home sooner."

As the helicopter soared higher, Olson's thoughts shifted to Molly. As usual, he'd be unable to tell her about the mission. Were she curious, he'd just direct her to the above-the-fold story in tomorrow morning's paper. As for his men, they'd take a few weeks of needed leave after reaching Fort Bragg.

Olson, on the other hand, wouldn't get any time off. He'd been ordered to Washington, DC for an assignment that, for whatever reason, didn't involve the other members of his team. True to course, he didn't know the nature of the assignment; true to course, he didn't ask.

That was probably for the best. Preparation for the Iranian hostage extraction had been difficult, and its execution life-threatening, but that was child's play compared to what was coming.

7

Washington, DC

The attorney general of the United States, normally accompanied by many, sat alone at a table in the most secure area in the Senate Hart Building, facing a group of seventeen curious United States senators. He had no papers or binders at his disposal. He clasped his fingers together in front of him and looked straight ahead with his thin brow furrowed. The members of the Senate Select Committee on Intelligence formed a crescent around Kershing's island with the chairman at its core, each one of them fixated on the man who'd insisted they call an emergency closed hearing.

"If I may," Kershing began, "I will forego the formalities associated with these hearings. Today's circumstances are extraordinary, and time is of the essence." He cleared his throat. "This afternoon, one of the nation's most talented lawyers, Assistant Attorney General Harry Mize, had an apparent stroke. As I sit here, I don't know if Mize is dead or alive. After being pulled out of a pool of water at the Navy Memorial, he was rushed to George Washington Hospital. The last I heard, he was in critical condition."

The chairman intervened. "All of us on the committee offer our deepest sympathies and hope that he recovers quickly and fully."

Kershing issued a nod of thanks.

Before the attorney general could continue, the senator from Kentucky, the oldest member of either house of Congress, reached for the microphone in front of him. His feeble, clammy hands were shaking, his beady eyes almost closed. "Mr. Chairman, I had the honor and privilege to serve alongside Mr. Mize's father for many years in the Senate," the white-haired man said, struggling in a crackling voice to finish his sentence. It obviously caused him physical pain to speak.

31

SCAVENGER HUNT

"The chair thanks the honorable and distinguished senator from Kentucky for his life-time of service," the chairman said before larding on more self-serving blather. "I also had the pleasure to serve with Harry Mize Jr."

Everyone waited for the nonagenarian senator from Kentucky to continue. He was still hunched over the microphone, his light-blue suit—sewn together before the invention of the microwave oven—enveloping his fragile frame.

"If his son is one-half the man he was, then our country . . . then we have suffered a great loss." The elderly man closed his statement with a quick nod of the head, a gesture meant to convey that his words were irrefutable.

"Well said, Senator," Kershing said. "We are all praying for his good health."

The chairman looked at his aged colleague, who, after having said his piece, was slumped back in his chair, away from the microphone.

"Please continue, General Kershing."

"Thank you, Mr. Chairman. Ladies and gentlemen, I didn't come here to discuss the tragedy that has befallen Harry Mize. I'm here to warn of the imminent catastrophe facing the American people absent swift congressional action. Assistant Attorney General Mize lost a hearing today, and the effect of that loss caused him to suffer that stroke or full-scale heart attack, whichever it was. Mize realizes the significance and the credibility of the reports the intelligence community provides to us every day. He knows that al Thoorah terrorists will stop at nothing to reclaim their captured leader and continue their onslaught of attacks. The result of today's hearing may force us to provide the most dangerous terrorist in our custody with unmonitored access to counsel."

"So the record is clear, what terrorist are you referring to?" the chairman asked.

"Omar Saud. The effect of this order will be cataclysmic and could set off a panoply of terror like we've never experienced on our native soil. Now—"

"Wait a second, Bill," the female senator from Ohio said, "Judge Sandersen is a district court judge. Don't you have the right to appeal her decision?"

"Senator, the problem is beyond one bad hearing. Judge Sandersen's ruling was the first of many that will emerge. We are litigating these and related issues in courts around the country. I'm here to ask Congress to pass emergency legislation to create a new legal construct for terrorism-related cases. The existing legal structure—composed of the federal criminal system and military tribunals—just doesn't work.

"Terrorism is often both a federal and a war crime. This poses a problem under the current legal system, particularly as it relates to interrogating those in custody or protecting classified sources and methods that prosecutors must use to establish their cases. We want to make sure, for instance, that our operatives overseas—from the CIA or otherwise—can gather human intelligence without their identities being revealed in a courtroom."

32

"General Kershing, you haven't answered—"

"There are a few ways to solve this problem, but Congress—not the judicial branch—needs to solve it. We can't continue to allow Article III judges, who have no relevant experience in this area, to craft our terrorism laws through criminal or habeas corpus cases. One solution is to create a national security court, where information would be better controlled and the judges would be experts on terrorism issues. We already have specialized courts like tax courts, bankruptcy courts, juvenile—"

"You haven't answered my original question, Bill. I'm not interested at the moment in creating a new court system. We'll consider your radical clarion call in the normal course of business. I'm concerned about Omar Saud. Do you or do you not have a right to appeal Judge Sandersen's decision?"

"Yes, we do. However, there is no guarantee that—"

"Then why did you summon us here today for an emergency session if you haven't exhausted your judicial remedies?" the senator asked. "If the judge's decision is so radical, then it should be overturned."

"Senator, we're not confident that we can win because we may not be able to convince the appellate court of the imminent dangers. The CIA will not allow us to share with the courts its most sensitive information—even *in camera* where only the judges see it—so they will have an incomplete picture. That, in turn, will make it more difficult for the court to draw the irrefutable conclusions."

"Well, General, would you be so kind as to draw those conclusions for us?" the chairman asked.

"Based on the credible intelligence we're receiving, we believe there would be a concerted effort by al Thoorah to bust out Saud if he ordered them to do it, and if they could pinpoint his location. We move him around every few days. The chance that Saud will be allowed unmonitored access to counsel just adds to our nightmare. We've seen before where a terrorist's lawyer acts as a liaison, a conduit of information, between the detainee and his terrorist cell. If, heaven forbid, some of these terrorist leaders were busted out—Omar Saud, in particular—they'd be able to re-establish control over their respective terrorist organizations."

"It sounds to me, Bill," the chairman said, "like you're not confident that our military and your Marshals Service can keep these guys locked up."

Kershing did not respond.

The senator from Massachusetts couldn't hold his tongue any longer. "General Kershing, I can't believe that you—the leader of the Department of *Justice*—are arguing that Mr. Saud shouldn't be entitled to speak with a lawyer without federal investigators listening to their conversation. The attorney-client privilege is crucial to our country's justice system."

SCAVENGER HUNT

Kershing bit his tongue, refusing to address the fiddle-faddle, wondering when the senator had been banished to civilization's intellectual outpost.

"Listen," the senator continued, "I was here when we passed the USA PATRIOT Act, which gave you and your predecessors broad, sweeping power to track down, arrest, and detain those involved in terrorism. I voted for the PATRIOT Act because, similar to what's happening here, it was jammed down our throats—sold to us as the only possible option to protect our country. I regret that vote because the Justice Department has abused our trust with reckless abandon. The PATRIOT Act's been used to suffocate the civil liberties of our great nation. Prisoners are still being rendered to foreign countries to be tortured. Law enforcement officers are infiltrating groups that peacefully question the government's actions and authority."

"Senator, that's not true." Kershing was getting lathered up.

"Now it's déjà vu all over again, or maybe Groundhog Day. The sky turns red, the black helicopters hover, and the attorney general calls an emergency meeting to paint another macabre masterpiece of doom and gloom. Well, I've had enough of it. My colleagues and I have done everything within our power to—"

"With all due respect, *Senator*, the PATRIOT Act has no bearing on rendition, torture, or law enforcement *allegedly* infiltrating certain groups. That's all hogwash. Most of the horror stories people associate with the PATRIOT Act have nothing at all to do with it. It's fiction. If you read the Act, you'll see that—"

"I *have* read the PATRIOT Act!" he lied.

Kershing couldn't take it anymore. Good faith arguments undergirded with papier-mâché were tolerable; strawman arguments constructed for political purposes were not. The nation's security was at stake. "Voice your quixotic outrage all you want! We don't need political rhetoric right now! We need action! And we need it fast!"

"General, I—"

"People, please!" the chairman pleaded, trying to calm the hostilities.

Rick tapped Kershing on the shoulder and then handed him a note that he'd scratched out in pencil on the back of a restaurant receipt. The attorney general's hand shook as he reached for it, his eyes still planted on the senator from Massachusetts. Kershing then shifted his attention to the note, peering down to read it.

REMEMBER WHY WE'RE HERE. DON'T LET THEM GET TO YOU.

The attorney general turned around to Rick and nodded, indicating his agreement and recognizing that he'd made a tactical error by losing his temper.

Kershing continued. "I need to apologize for my temper and sharp tongue. I was out of line."

"Okay," said the perturbed senator from Ohio.

Kershing was desperate. "I have to admit I'm frightened. But I want each of you to realize that I subscribe wholeheartedly to the principle first annunciated by Benjamin Franklin who said, and I paraphrase: 'A country that sacrifices liberty for security deserves neither.' I don't think we're doing that, but I respect the opinions of those who disagree."

The senator from Ohio injected herself back into the discussion. "I appreciate those words, Bill. We all have a right to be oversensitive these days. I have my own historical quote: 'These are the times that try men's—and, let me add, *women's*—souls.' We're all concerned about the recent attacks on the West Coast, not to mention the others that have occurred since 9/11."

Kershing would offer no more substantive testimony. He noticed that, despite the severity of the issue at hand, most of the senators on the committee were losing interest or had already formed immutable opinions. There would be no legislative relief. In fact, the oldest member of the Senate had fallen asleep in his chair, his chin now resting on his polka-dot bowtie.

Before long, the attorney general picked up the receipt and turned it over. He then grabbed the heavy, gold-plated pen from his coat pocket and began writing in small letters as the senators yammered away with their sophistry and word salads. With his glazed eyes still scanning the half-moon of naysayers, he reached behind his back.

Amanda, still thinking more about Harry Mize than the issues before the committee, lunged forward and snatched the note from Kershing's hand. After reading it, she stood up and walked out of the hearing, leaving the receipt on her chair. Rick glanced up as she walked out. Then, he picked up his receipt and read Kershing's words.

GET THE TRUCKS IN POSITION. IT'S TIME TO GO.

8

Beijing, China

Two Chinese soldiers with acne-scarred, sweaty faces and entrusted with guarding the west side of the compound were stationed four hundred yards apart, smoking cigarettes. Antiquated radios transmitted their words over weak frequencies; their Cold War-era machine guns were attached to frayed, army-green straps and hung from their shoulders. The scene beyond the fourteen-foot tall, rod-iron security fence capped with razor wire captivated them. Three drunken American sailors were pawing on the disinterested Yankee woman, tugging on her light-blue sundress like junior-high hooligans coping with the first stage of adolescence hormones. It was erotic entertainment, to be sure, sensationalized by the voyeuristic circumstances involved. Standing on their elevated watch-stands ten feet above the ground, the Chinese soldiers believed they were out of sight, camouflaged in the darkness, the only sign of their existence their small, burning cherry glows from the tips of their cigarettes, which became brighter each time they pursed their lips and took deep, soothing drags.

Their lips tugged on their smokes more intimately as they fixated on the helpless woman below. She had little chance of escape. She'd been forced to parade across the gravel parking lot into the high-voltage beams of a halogen light, stationed thirty-one yards from the fence perimeter. Both soldiers stared through standard-issued binoculars, hoping to get a glimpse of exposed flesh and finding it hard to whisper in their native tongues at the thought of the imminent defilement.

Growing more aggressive, the sailors pawed on the long-legged woman, pulled her red-dyed hair, and tugged on her clothes. She tried to fight them off, begging them to stop in her clear English accent. The two Chinese soldiers started shaking with excitement, standing entranced—knees wobbling—at the scene below, no longer able to speak to one another or even whisper.

Enthralled by the illicit entertainment, they had no idea that a man inside the compound was monitoring their actions—indeed, their every movement—through the infrared lens of a high-powered scope mounted on a custom-made assault rifle. His arms were steady, his resolve certain.

They would never meet the two spies who infiltrated their side of the compound unnoticed. They would never know that while a tawdry woman was seemingly being violated by three drunken sailors no more than a hundred feet from them, another woman was hanging upside down, motionless, from the six-story building 200 yards behind them, staring into an office belonging to one of the intelligence officers they'd been conscripted to protect.

They'd never know the names of the two operatives who'd seal their fate in front of a firing squad of their peers in the next two days.

————————

The Chinese intelligence officer seated at his desk failed to spot the green eyes gazing at him through his office window. It was pitch black outside and, along with the illumination from his computer screen, a substantial amount of light was emanating from his desk lamp. Even if he'd stared outside his large, mirror-like bay window, he wouldn't have seen anything but his reflection peering back at him.

Turning off the inside lights had never crossed his mind. At least not before this night. The area in and around his building was more secure than Zhongnanhai down the road. No one would dare attempt to penetrate the fortress that surrounded the restricted compound for fear of certain torture and death.

The green-eyed woman struggled to remain patient, but that was impossible hanging upside down. To the naked eye, she looked like she was hovering in mid-air, defying gravity. She was trying not to think about the blood rushing to her head or the rope burn and blisters forming on her slender ankles.

Over the years, she had become a nightcrawler, moving around with stealth in the darkness, running from the moonlight—a shadow.

One of the best shadows in the business.

She whispered into a small, state-of-the-art microphone connected to a micro-boom arm that was held in place by a flexible ear hook. "He's encrypting information. I've got the password to access the hard drive. He's using a simple medium for cryptology." She found the officer's actions interesting but not unusual. "Putting the disk in the top drawer of the desk. Looks like . . . yep, simple key lock."

SCAVENGER HUNT

There was no response, but that, too, wasn't unusual. She knew her accomplice wouldn't speak unless necessary. Now, they'd wait.

As she waited, the green-eyed woman thought about her loyal accomplice. He was a master marksman and could be trusted to provide proficient cover in the hairiest of situations. She knew he'd protect her if something went awry. She knew he'd make no mistakes and would ensure her safety at all costs.

After a few minutes, the Chinese intelligence officer walked toward the door. Then the office turned black.

"Lights out."

———

The accomplice turned his attention away from the Chinese soldiers and focused on the office building. He could see the shadow against the building's facade, whipping up her body, grabbing the cord that held her, and climbing to the top of the building.

Then he saw her figure disappear.

Be careful.

He looked back toward the Chinese soldiers, who were getting restless at the decreased level of debauchery beyond the security fence. Once again conversing over two-way radios, they no longer cared to remain unnoticed, frustrated by the drunken sailors' unassertiveness . . . their unwillingness to close the deal.

Returning his attention to the office building, the accomplice's steely, brown eyes widened. He could see a shapeless hue of darkness moving around the third-floor office.

She's in!

Her alacrity was amazing. This would be easier than planned, he surmised.

But then, the accomplice's heart stopped.

Someone had turned on the lights! The intelligence officer had never left the building and was reentering his office!

Had he forgotten something? Had he heard an unusual noise?

The accomplice could see Natasha stationed underneath the officer's desk.

Perspiration flowed from his pores as he watched the Chinese intelligence officer walk toward the window, looking around as if something were out of place . . . as if something was just not right.

Get out of there, Natasha!

But she had nowhere to go. The accomplice tried to stay focused, but he couldn't take his eyes off the desk. He could hear the American woman caterwauling from beyond the fence behind him and yelling obscenities at the sailors. He heard her slap one of them in the face. The two Chinese soldiers were whistling at the up-tick in drama. The accomplice knew, absent some X-rated behavior, they'd soon lose interest in the sailors' lascivious actions. Time was running out. The Chinese soldiers would be making their rounds soon.

But his eyes were locked on the desk. Natasha was in trouble.

The Chinese intel officer was growing more suspicious. He reached inside his navy-blue sportscoat and pulled out a shiny object.

A weapon! More precisely, a pistol likely manufactured off the alleyways of Hong Kong.

The officer began to walk around the desk, still unnerved by his surroundings.

The accomplice checked to make sure his silencer was screwed onto the nozzle of his rifle. He aimed it at the officer, placing the man's head in the scope's crosshairs. Depending on the window's composition, he thought, it may shatter. But that would be a risk he'd need to take. They might have to shoot their way out of the compound. And while that option wasn't ideal, they'd done it before in more dangerous theaters.

The officer was but a few feet away from Natasha. And as he hunched over to peek under the desk, the accomplice nestled his finger on the trigger. One more second and . . .

The officer stood up.

He pocketed his pistol, grabbed his cell phone, and placed it to his ear before turning his back to the large window.

The accomplice pulled his left eye from the scope and stared at the office window, still refusing to release his right index finger from the trigger. He looked back through the lens. The officer had put away his cell phone, walked back toward the door, and turned out the lights.

"Stay put for now," the accomplice whispered. "I'll let you know when he leaves the building."

"Good idea," the green-eyed woman replied.

A few moments later, the officer exited the building, heading down a dirt pathway that led to the other side of the compound, away from the planned escape point.

"Get out of there!"

He watched the shadow emerge from underneath the desk, glide to the door, and vanish.

—————

Natasha Hensley wasted little time returning to the rendezvous point.

"I'm glad you're okay," he said.

"You should be more concerned about this," she replied, holding up the disk.

"Good job," he said.

SCAVENGER HUNT

"Where's our external unit?"

"Gone."

"What do you mean *gone*?"

"They did all they could short of having intercourse."

"Plan B, then?"

"I don't think so. We shouldn't have much problem getting out. The guards will be talking about what happened—or what didn't happen—for hours."

Moving from the dilapidated garage toward the west side of the fence, the American operatives examined the positions and conduct of the Chinese soldiers. As expected, they were yapping on their radios, their weapons disregarded and leaning against the walls of their posts. They had no idea what had just happened. More importantly, they'd have no idea fifteen minutes from now that Natasha and her accomplice would crawl back through the hole in the west fence and scamper away to safety.

While waiting for her accomplice to gather his equipment, Hensley couldn't help but think ahead to her next mission. She hadn't told him. It wasn't a mission for which she'd volunteered, nor a mission about which she knew any details. She only knew that she'd be leaving East Asia for her adopted America. Just like her trek almost thirty years ago, her life would take her from one Communist country to the world's greatest democracy.

9

Washington, DC

Michael Gregg, the attorney general's powerful chief of staff, was scrawny like a starved cat and had thick, bushy eyebrows. That thought roosted in Blake's brain as he entered Gregg's office. Gregg's frame allowed him to wear thick cotton undershirts without increasing the density of his starched dress shirts. He was one of the few people that Blake knew whose belt served a utility beyond fashion. As usual, Gregg refused to look up when a visitor walked in, acting like he must review just one more sentence in just one more paragraph of just one more page before addressing the existence of another human life form.

"You wanted to see me?" Blake asked, noticing the perfect part in Gregg's thinning light-blond hair.

"Yeahhh," Gregg replied, drawing out the word, making it clear he wasn't ready to greet Blake, "just *one* second." After two painful minutes, the chief of staff closed the olive-green, legal-sized folder in front of him. "Have a seat, Blake."

To appear less despotic, Gregg sauntered from his high-backed chair to the couch. Gregg and Blake had spoken countless times during business meetings, but the atmospheric alignment today was different. This marked the first time that Gregg had summoned Hudson for a one-on-one meeting. Gregg was five feet away from Blake, who was occupying one of two leather receiving chairs decorated with brass rivets along the stitched seams. Blake recognized Gregg's gesture, but Gregg's overt act to make his guest more comfortable fell flat. Blake found the close proximity unnerving.

SCAVENGER HUNT

Blake noticed Gregg had abandoned his coffee mug on the desk, the steam from the Jamaican blend rising toward the recessed lights overhead. The conversation, Blake realized, would be brief.

The chief of staff crossed his lanky legs. "Blake, the attorney general thinks you're doing a good job. He trusts you, and we're both pleased with your work ethic."

Where is this headed? "I appreciate those words, Michael," Blake said. "I'm learning a lot from Amanda and Rick—and you—and I'm just happy to be here."

Gregg smiled as if anticipating Blake's response. "And above all else, Blake, we admire your humility and team spirit. Thanks for proving my point."

Blake flashed a disingenuous grin. The room was starting to heat up. He felt his collar grating into the scruff of his neck. He adjusted his necktie and fidgeted in his seat.

"Let's cut to the chase," Gregg continued. "There's a project—a very sensitive project, to be sure—that carries an enormous amount of responsibility, particularly for someone your age. I've struggled with how to staff this. You're obviously not as experienced as Amanda or Rick, but I'm placing you on the team because it requires someone with your personality. It'll require that you obtain access to classified information that none of us at Justice, including the attorney general, has. You've heard of special access programs. Only a few will know about this project. When—"

Gregg's office phone rang.

"Let me grab this."

Blake stood up and walked to the window behind Gregg's desk, overlooking Constitution Avenue. He could see the brightly-clad tourists entering and exiting the Natural History Museum across the street.

"Yeah, I understand," Gregg said. "The AG should be coming back to the office. . . . No, he has a meeting with POTUS. . . . Well, we'll have to see what happens. I've not received any word from the hospital. . . . People from the criminal division are in the waiting room. They'll call me as soon as they know something. . . ."

Gregg slammed down the phone and grabbed his coffee mug from the desk. The two of them returned to their seats.

"Blake, you and I should grab lunch sometime," Gregg said, sipping his coffee. The white, ceramic mug was decorated with indecipherable images and words, a preschool project that had changed hands on Father's Day—the simple craft of small fingers, now a memento for one of the most powerful men in Washington.

"Say when," Blake said.

"You play golf?"

Does he not care that Harry Mize may be dying right now? "Not very well," Blake said, beginning to fidget as the conversation bogged down in digression. "I run the point on the AG's basketball team when we play at the FBI gym. You should play with us sometime."

"Never was any good at basketball. When things calm down, we should play some golf."

The conditional words "when things calm down" were common in Washington. It didn't take a genius to realize that things never calmed down, especially in the Office of the Attorney General. This escape clause allowed people to sound interested without the burden of commitment. Blake realized why few people enjoyed Gregg's company.

There was an uncomfortable pause. "This new project sounds great, Michael, but if I'm the only person at Justice with special access to information, to whom will I report?"

"You'll report to a man named John Smith. He's CIA. He'll stop by your office in the next few days. Don't contact him; he'll contact you. As you might expect, he's under tremendous pressure."

"Fine."

"He'll show up when he has time. Meanwhile, you need to keep this project hush-hush. I considered detailing you to the Agency but ultimately decided against it. You're too involved in day-to-day matters here."

"Sounds fantastic. Will I keep my other responsibilities, then?"

"Just let me know if you need help."

"Sure thing. So what does this project entail?"

"Blake, I don't know," Gregg admitted, a look of embarrassment on his face. A man in his position wasn't shielded from the details of even the most mundane projects. "They wouldn't tell me."

Blake waited a few seconds before asking the obvious question. "Who wouldn't tell you?"

"The answer to that question, Blake, is classified. And, right now, let's just say that you don't have a need to know."

Blake smirked and nodded his head. While there was little room for further descent, Gregg's stock had plummeted.

Some chief of staff, Blake thought, for the first time questioning the attorney general's professional judgment.

———

A torrent of profanity gushed from Kershing's mouth, but no one seemed to mind, especially Rick Morales. Rick remembered the no-cursing wager and was keeping a running tab on each violation. Come payday, Kershing would assert a colorable defense for today's miscon-duct, but Rick nonetheless kept copious mental notes. If Harry survived, Rick would try to cash in later, with emotions on ice. The two FBI agents in the Suburban were just thankful that Kershing wasn't directing his ire at them.

The inundation of vulgarity continued until the group arrived at George Washington Hospital. When the caravan reached the front entrance, Kershing disembarked without waiting for his protective detail. Amanda hopped out behind him and scampered toward the automatic glass doors.

"Amanda," Kershing said as she passed him. "Find out what room Harry's in."

"Sure thing, General," Amanda replied in a respectful tone. She then turned back around, rolled her eyes, and mumbled, 'What do you think I was doing?'"

The attorney general waited for Rick and the agents before walking through the hospital doors. He wanted to make a grand entrance with his entourage in tow. But by the time they entered the hospital, Amanda was exiting.

"General," Amanda said, "Harry's in stable condition, but the lady at the front desk insists that he can't have any visitors."

"What do the doctors say?"

"Well, I—"

"I don't need someone without a medical degree telling me when I can see my men."

Amanda didn't respond as Kershing barged past her. She looked at Rick, rolled her eyes once again, and shook her head. "He's out of control, Rick. I've never seen him like this."

"He's a stubborn old mule. He uttered thirty-three curse words in the truck. In fact, it might've been thirty-five. He said two words that I've never heard before, but I bet they'd qualify as profanity. That's big money."

"Rick, you're hopeless. I work with a bunch of lunatics and one megalomaniac."

Rick heard the megalomaniac's voice escalating inside. "I think the AG has finally met his match," he said. "That woman isn't backing down an inch."

"I'll be in the Suburban. Hiding. How embarrassing. Did you hear him crow? 'I don't need someone without a medical degree telling me when I can see my men,'" she repeated. "He's lost it. He thinks he's General Patton."

Rick pulled out his smartphone and dialed Blake. Amanda sat on the back bumper of the lead Suburban as Rick trailed off.

Three minutes later, Rick returned. "Blake's stewing back at the office. Michael just met with him."

"Par for the course. You tell him what happened?"

"Of course."

The hospital doors flew open. Kershing's temples were throbbing, his face as red as a lobster. "Get in the truck," he demanded. "I decided to wait until Harry gets some rest before we bother him. He's in stable condition."

Amanda rolled her eyes for a third time before climbing in the backseat for what would be an interesting—and for Kershing, an expensive—trip back to the office.

––––––––––

Chevy Chase, MD

A brown phone rang in a quaint study in a red-brick house located just beyond Washington, DC. The narrow beams of sunlight penetrating the closed plantation shutters provided the room's only illumination. The man walked across the ornate French rug toward the wooden table in the corner and picked up the phone on the third ring.

"Yes?"

"It's me."

"I was expecting your call," the man replied, taking a seat in the leather recliner flanked by an audience of dusty, hardback books organized on the mahogany bookshelves that lined the study's walls.

"I guess you heard about Harry Mize and the hearing," the caller said.

"I attended the hearing and spoke to Mize. But I only learned about his incident after coming home."

"I don't think we can wait any longer."

No response.

"What say you?" the edgy caller queried.

"My position hasn't changed."

"You've made it clear that we should've acted earlier. But what about now? These crazy rulings have changed everything. Unmonitored access to counsel?"

"The team is being assembled."

"What else do I need to know?" the caller asked.

"Nothing other than I will handle this problem. Of course, all precautions will continue to be taken."

"And the boy from Justice?"

"I've decided to include him. Other members of the team may not act unless they have legal cover. Or at least the appearance of it."

"Whatever you need," the caller said. "Are you sure the team leader will take orders from you?"

"Why wouldn't he?"

"Government officials don't take orders from those who aren't in their chain of command, much less someone in the private sector. You know that."

"You're questioning my effectiveness?"

"I just want clarity."

"The team leader is already compromised. He'll be my puppet by tomorrow. I'll leave it at that."

"And how do we know the team will follow *his* orders?" the caller asked.

"It has all the trappings of a legitimate interagency operation. They'll believe their actions are sanctioned. If not, then I have ways of dealing with that too. The less you know, the better."

"Understood."

"What about my compensation?"

"You'll be paid through a private donor—a mutual friend who shares our concerns. Our normal practice of laundering classified appropriation funds is getting too risky."

"Fine. Don't make contact with me from this point forward. Assign a trusted advisor to handle direct communications. Someone responsible. Someone expendable, too, but no snot-nosed punk."

"Good idea. When will this get started?"

"It got started before your second vodka martini at lunch today."

10

Washington, DC

Afrer work the following day, Blake, Amanda, and Rick met at the Lincoln House restaurant, across the street from Ford's Theatre and next door to the Petersen House, or as it's so aptly called, The House Where Lincoln Died. Despite its tourist-friendly location, not many tourists set both feet in the Lincoln House. The bright-red awning and dirty paper menu Scotch-taped to the window deterred potential customers. Aesthetics aside, it was the favorite hangout of the attorney general's counselors.

After descending the narrow stairwell, they traversed the dingy Venetian-red carpet to the far end of the room and sat down at the table in the corner. Several mirrors hung at eye level around the walls. Old newspaper articles and neon beer signs covered the area between the mirrors, and out-of-season Christmas lights draped from the low ceiling. The bar was anchored on the opposite side of the room; its stools filled with day laborers, troubled mid-dleclass businessmen, and displaced alcoholics who poured salt in their Michelobs before ordering double Wild Turkeys on the rocks.

Before Blake could sit down, a middle-aged woman with faux blonde hair and sand-paper skin slid three cold Bud Lights on the table. She wore a white T-shirt decorated with avocado stains and diluted tomato paste posing as marinara sauce.

"Anyone heard from the hospital?" Amanda asked.

"Harry is doing much better. He's regained his motor skills. No long-term paralysis. Should be discharged soon."

"That's great!" Rick said.

"Thanks for letting us know earlier," Amanda said, eyebrows raised.

"Sent you an email."

"I haven't checked my email lately."

Blake winked. "Apology accepted."

"When's he coming back?" Rick asked.

"I don't know. Still haven't spoken to him. I plan to do that soon, though."

"Sooner the better," Rick said. "We need more help on the detainee issues."

Blake nodded and made a mental note to return General Frank Leavitt's call.

"How do we fill the void in Harry's absence?"

"I'm glad you mentioned that," Blake said, "because Michael assigned me to a new project."

"Cough it up," Amanda said.

"Don't know a lot right now. Michael said it's highly sensitive, though. Someone from the CIA is visiting my office soon to read me in."

"What's the CIA officer's name?" Amanda asked. "I work with them a lot."

"John Smith."

"John Smith?" Rick said. "I love spooks. Unbelievable, those guys."

"And gals," Amanda added.

"Yeah, whatever. Everything's always the most secret thing in the world. Real name is probably Eugene. A wannabe Jason Bourne—nothing more than a geek pushin' documents around all day. John Smith. Give me a break."

"Tell us how you really feel," Blake said. "Actually, don't do that. Tell me more about the AG's secret hearing with the Senate yesterday."

"Yeah, this is great," Rick said, chugging the rest of his beer. "Our boss—a.k.a., the Angel of Death—demonstrated his stagecraft like Brando in *Streetcar*. He put on one heck of a show. Said we're all gonna die. What were the words he used?"

"Panoply of terror," Amanda said in a goblin-like voice.

"Right," Rick continued. "He told everyone that because of Judge Sandersen's ruling, additional attacks are imminent."

Blake stared at Rick.

"Come on, Blake. What is this: Iraq Redux? We want legislative action, but you gotta admit he's going overboard when he—"

"He's not going overboard. I told you that the intel is troubling. When I first joined DOJ, I was reading some intense stuff. After the West Coast attacks, it's only gotten worse."

"Can you tell us?" Amanda was on the edge of her seat.

"I'd rather the po-po not haul me off to jail for revealing the nation's secrets in the basement of the Lincoln House."

The waitress returned, handed Rick another beer, and glared at Blake. "You gonna eat or just get sloshed?"

"The latter," Blake said.

"Be sure and cut me off after ten," Rick quipped. "All this spy talk is making me thirsty."

"*Please*," the sassy waitress said, "you've never had more than four in one day. You married men can't hold your liquor."

"Very funny, Mrs. Robinson."

"Coo-coo ca-choo," she flirted before turning her attention to Blake. "Wadda ya have, honey?"

"Another beer," Blake said. "I've lost my appetite."

Walking to the bar, she scribbled his order on the notepad she kept crammed in the waistline of her skirt.

"Does she really need to write down one beer?" Amanda inquired.

"Ease up, will you?" Rick said.

Blake was keeping a watchful eye on Rick's aggressive behavior. Normally calm under pressure, Rick had been out of character the last few days. Recent events had rattled his psyche and threatened to short-circuit his coping mechanisms. Alcohol exacerbated the problem, transforming his pleasant balderdash into risqué insults and boastful rants.

"Why am I all of a sudden *persona non grata* with you?" Amanda asked.

"*Persona non grata*?" Rick said. "Amanda, you've been doing that a lot lately."

"Doing what?" she asked, perking up.

"Dropping foreign phrases like stink bombs. It's pretentious."

"Maybe you don't understand what they mean."

"Nor do I wish to, *mademoiselle*," Rick said. "We live in *America*; Americans speak-a-da *English*."

Amanda stuck out her tongue.

"Euro-trash," Rick said, acting like he was smoking a skinny, European cigarette. "And by the way, *mademoiselle*," he mocked, pretending to exhale cigarette smoke, "you're flirting with a middle finger mentality, which could cost you some cash."

"Wrong," she said, losing interest in the haranguing. "I'm not into trashy symbols. I'll tell you what I think."

"We'll see about that."

"Blake," Amanda said, changing the subject, "we haven't even had the chance to talk about the newest counselor."

"New counselor? In our office?"

"Yep. Rick and I just met him. Clarence Niles."

"Never heard of him. Either of you know him?"

"Nope."

"He's Niles from nowhere," Rick joked.

"Really?" Blake asked, ignoring Rick's tomfoolery. "This is the first I've heard about a new hire."

Rick and Amanda stared off into space.

"What? Y'all don't like him?"

"We didn't say that," Rick replied, peeking at Amanda.

"Then what's the problem?"

"Would've been nice to interview him—or at least meet him—before the offer was extended," Rick said.

"You had no idea either, huh?"

"Nope."

"Let me check the internet while you all bicker some more," Blake said, grabbing his phone.

Clarence Niles? Was this person hired to take over his workload? Gregg assured him that he'd maintain his existing responsibilities, but Gregg wasn't known for keeping his word. And why had Gregg not extended him—any of the counselors—the courtesy of meeting Niles before the job was offered?

And why hadn't anyone heard of this guy? Blake typed his name into Google and then rolled his cursor to the box labeled "I'm Feeling Lucky."

Lucky, huh? He clicked on it.

11

Judge greeted Blake at the door at 8:45 p.m. with waning patience and a full bladder. It was a mammoth welcome, intensified by loneliness and physical necessity. The dog voiced his stark disapproval of being held captive by issuing a magnificent bark that, had it occurred two hours later, would have awakened the entire neighborhood. The rebuke caught Blake off-guard.

"Judge, I'm so sorry."

Blake felt an overwhelming pang of guilt rush through him. The Great Dane had been cooped up without relief for several hours. The sight of the home's darkness exacerbated Blake's shame, as did the thought of better-treated dogs dreaming of vulnerable kitties after a long day of scampering in the parks.

"Get your leash. We're going for a *walk*."

As Judge bolted away to snatch his leash, Blake noticed the blinking message light on his answering machine. He had two messages. He pushed the button, not paying attention to the massive hound slipping and sliding into every wall at the far end of the house.

"Blake, this is your grandpa. I looked for you on TV today. Hope you're well. No need to call me back. I know you're busy. Love you."

Message two. Shallow breathing. No voice.

Hudson couldn't hit the delete button fast enough.

"Judge!" Blake shouted. "Jud–"

Judge nudged Blake from behind, his leash hanging from his mouth.

"Oh, there you are."

Judge relieved himself in the communal front yard. Although trading uncomfortable glances throughout the exhibition, both made sure not to stare at one another. It was an unspoken rule.

After Judge marked a spot that would scare off a lioness, the two of them walked up East Capitol Street, past the Supreme Court building, until they reached First Street. The Capitol was beautiful, Blake thought, illuminated like a beacon of freedom. They jaywalked toward the park, which was located across the street from the Capitol under a grove of oak trees. There was a large fountain full of water located in the center of the park in which Judge liked to wade. As they made their way toward the park, Blake pulled out his phone. Before he could dial Grandpa Hudson's number, however, his phone vibrated in his hand.

"Blake Hudson."

"Blake, this is John Smith. Someone should've told you that I'd be calling."

"Yes, or stopping by."

"Will you be around tomorrow?"

"I should be. What time?"

"Sometime around lunch work?"

"I'll be around."

"Great. By the way, do you have any military training?"

"Military training?"

Chevy Chase, MD

Communications traffic had been heavy in preparation for the homecoming. The brown phone had been ringing off the hook.

"Status?" the man said, lighting his fifth cigar of the day.

"Reid almost missed his connection to DFW, but he's in DC now. Olson's flight got in earlier than expected. He didn't check luggage and flew standby on an earlier flight."

"Did you miss his arrival, then?"

"Of course not, sir. I reached out to our contact at the airline. He called me when Olson boarded the earlier flight."

"My apologies for doubting your prowess. I should've expected nothing less from *my* people."

"Thank you, sir."

"And the woman?"

"Hensley touched down in Dulles two hours ago."

"No problems, then?"

"None whatsoever. Everything went as planned."

"Did she . . . how did she look?"

"What do you mean, sir?"

"In your *non-professional* judgment?"

"Well, sir, to be quite honest . . . breathtaking."

The man bit his heinous teeth into his cigar, closed his eyes, and sighed. "That's what I've heard from others."

"Sir?"

"Never mind. Very good work . . . as usual."

"We should be all set with the arrivals. As you know, Smith and Hudson already live here. Do you want us to do anything about Omar Saud? He's probably vulnerable right now."

"He's not the vulnerable one."

"I can put some men on him. Of course, we have great contacts inside the Marshals Service."

"Don't send any men to him. That's not part of our scope of work. Just monitor his movements through the Marshals Service."

"I understand that, sir, but, with all due respect, the government is going to screw this up."

"I'm fully counting on that."

12

Absent the random passersby, there was no foot traffic in the Great Court. The solitude, coupled with the sounds of splashing water emanating from the fountain, was soothing. Blake was relishing the needed break, eating a crunchy peanut butter and strawberry jelly sandwich on staling wheat bread. Reaching for his 99¢ Ruffles grab bag, he noticed a figure approaching. The man, who didn't have a Justice Department badge or a visitor's name tag, pounced up the steps to the marble platform at the base of the fountain.

"Are you Blake Hudson?" the salamander-faced man asked. The dark-brown suit that covered his skinny frame, Blake gathered, had fallen out of style in the early eighties. His tie was an abstract mixture of tortoise-green and gray, and it stopped well short of his generic black belt.

Blake swallowed his food before standing up to greet the man. "The one and only. And you are?"

"John Smith. CIA."

"The one, but *not* the only, John Smith," Blake replied. "Pleasure to meet you in person."

The two men shook hands. Gray eyes met hazel during the exchange. So far so good, Blake thought. His grandpa had taught him that any man who failed to make eye contact while shaking hands would sooner or later, if given the chance, stab that person in the back. Blake knew it was nothing more than an old Texas adage, but Porter Hudson was never wrong.

"How'd you know I was out here?"

"I stopped by your office, and Rick—I think that's his name—told me that, when you don't go home to care for your dog, you like to eat lunch here. Am I interrupting?"

"You're in luck. I was just finishing up my gourmet meal." There was an uncomfortable silence, and then Blake looked back at his visitor. "You haven't seen my waiter anywhere, have you? He's wearing a light-blue tuxedo with a lavender bowtie. Has a speech impediment."

Smith didn't smile but continued to survey the area. "Let's take a walk."

"Sure. Let me just call upstairs and let my assistant know that I'm stepping out."

Blake reached in his pocket and grabbed his phone.

"Were you able to get all the necessary clearances?" Smith asked, still looking around as if someone was following him. The modest breeze failed to displace his short but wavy hair, its jet-black roots giving way to gray tips.

Blake nodded with his phone to his ear and then raised his finger. "Mildred, I'm going to take a walk and get some fresh air. Anything going on?"

"Someone named General Leavitt from the Pentagon left you a message. Needs to talk to you about detainee issues. When will you be back?" Mildred asked.

Blake placed his hand over the phone's mouthpiece. "John, how long?"

"No more than forty-five minutes."

"Mildred, I should only be gone an hour." Blake tucked his phone away and tossed his now crumpled-up lunch bag into the nearby trash receptacle. "Ready when you are, John."

Before walking through the full-height, stainless-steel turnstiles at the building's exit, Blake waved to the security guard watching the surveillance monitor near the doors.

"I have all my clearances."

"No problems?"

"They were concerned about my double-murder conviction, but other than that, everything was kosher."

Smith issued a courtesy smile.

"Speaking of clearances," Blake said, "I see that you don't have a name tag. Not that I don't trust you. Just curious how you got in the building."

"I've worked with Justice in the past. Showed my CIA credentials at the security desk. I know most of the guards."

"Do you know Oscar Childs?"

"Of course," Smith smiled. "Why do you ask?"

"We like to argue over football. I'm a Cowboys fan. He's not."

"I met Oscar when he was a security guard at CIA headquarters," Smith said.

"Interesting. I didn't know Oscar had worked at Langley."

Smith didn't respond.

Blake led the way out of the building. "I'm just walking. Is there anywhere in particular you wanted—"

"Walk toward the White House. Once we get there, we can turn around, come back, and be done."

SCAVENGER HUNT

There was a brief period of silence as they crossed Tenth Street. Smith lit a filterless cigarette and reached in his coat pocket to turn off his cell phone. Blake noticed that Smith struggled when he walked, his gait resembling that of a retired bull rider.

"I just wanted us to meet in person," Smith explained. "We'll be working on some highly sensitive projects." He looked over his pointy nose at Hudson as they passed the IRS building. "You're younger than I expected."

"Yeah, Rogaine and Just for Men hair dye work wonders."

Another long pause.

"Well, I guess I'll start," Blake said, irritated by Smith's comment.

"By all means. Go ahead."

Blake spoke of his family, gave a general synopsis of his educational background, and provided highlights of his high school sports career. When he finished his personal narrative, Smith started asking specific questions.

"So what are your strengths?" he asked.

"I'm able to process information quickly. I can read fast and that helps. But I don't possess the intellectual heft that some of my colleagues at Justice do. Whatever I lack upstairs, though, I usually can overcome with elbow grease."

Smith nodded.

"In short," Blake continued, "I feel confident that, given a problem, I can come up with a workable solution. I don't have much room to brag, but since you asked . . ."

"I don't consider it bragging. I asked you to tell me what your strengths are. I wanted an honest answer. You've given me half of one."

"That's the truth. If you want the whole truth, I'd tell you I can be persuasive at times. I think that comes with being a trial lawyer."

"You're a trial lawyer?"

"Right now, I'm more of a policy wonk, but when I leave this fantasy world, I suspect that Dr. Jekyll will turn back into Mr. Hyde. Gotta pay the bills."

"And what about your weaknesses?"

"Other than being a trial lawyer?"

"I don't want the interview answer."

"I have many weaknesses. Let's see, I start off focused in the morning but, even with a gallon of coffee, have a hard time concentrating after lunch. That's also when everyone wants to stop by my office and chitchat. It usually takes me two hours to regain my pre-lunch momentum."

"I share that weakness."

"What else? I'm young for my current position."

"Robert Kennedy wasn't much older than you when he was attorney general, and they named the building after him," Smith replied, the insides of his cheeks almost touching as he took one last drag of his Lucky Strikes cigarette before flicking it in front of him and crushing it with his next step. "How are your nerves?"

Odd question but not unexpected. "How do I handle pressure?"

"Well, that's part of my question. How do you handle pressure, and how do you think you'd handle making *life or death* decisions?"

Blake stopped walking. They had reached the gate in front of the South Lawn of the White House, but he might have stopped anyway. *That* certainly was an odd question, he thought. "Do you anticipate that I'll be deciding whether people live or die?"

"Perhaps." Smith's hollow eyes widened as he monitored Blake's reaction. "You told me last night that you'd never worked for the military. I assume that you've never been put in life-or-death situations?"

Blake was leaning against the black iron rods of the White House gate. "Except for some minor input on a few death penalty cases when I clerked at the Supreme Court, that's correct."

"I understand." Smith looked around and then walked closer to Blake. "Blake, I've gleaned a lot from our conversation, and I'm comfortable having you on the team."

"All right," Blake said, growing less comfortable with being *on the team*, whatever the team was.

"But there's one crucial question you *must* answer first. It's a question I'll ask everyone assigned to this project."

"If I'm placed in a position where I need to make a decision . . ." Blake said, pushing off the gate and looking at Smith.

"Yes."

"And that decision is one that could result in someone's death . . ."

"Uh-huh."

"Then I'd carry out my duties as directed," he answered. "So long as such direction was in the best interest of my country and within the ethical parameters by which I'm bound."

"Fair enough," Smith replied. "Are you ready to get back?"

"Sure. Can you tell me what all this is about?"

"Not out here."

"I can talk tough all day," Blake continued, trying to clarify his position without vacillating or seeking Smith's approbation, "but I must tell you, your last question doesn't sit well. Chalk up another weakness for me, I guess. That one caught me off guard and is still . . . I don't know."

"Another strength, counselor. It's a difficult question for a civilian to answer. You may never have to worry about it. I will go over the nature of our project when we meet as a group."

"And when will that be?" Blake asked.

"I'm still waiting to meet with the others. They should be in town soon."

"You can at least tell me about them, can't you?"

"In due time. I can tell you that I think there'll be three others besides you and me."

"Trial lawyers?"

"No," Smith smiled. "Respectable folk."

"Right," Blake said. He realized he was being inquisitive, and he understood that Smith was on a tight leash. "Time for you to tell your story."

"The unclassified part of my life is boring, but I'll tell you the interesting parts in a classified setting. I'm going the other way."

"Okay," Blake said, realizing that John Q. Smith looked as uncomfortable on the streets of DC as an American soccer mom would on the streets of Moscow.

"I'll contact you soon. The group will be meeting on the eighth floor."

"The eighth floor of what?"

"Main Justice. Three floors above your office."

"You mean the seventh floor? My building doesn't have an eighth floor."

"You have much to learn, my friend," Smith said, waving goodbye and walking away.

"No, wait."

"I'll be in touch."

As Blake turned around to continue his walk back to Main Justice, he spotted one of the tourists taking his picture. "Don't waste your film!" Blake yelled at the man. "I'm not that important!"

But the $500 stuffed in the photographer's back pocket argued otherwise.

13

The attorney general's suite resembled a stately living room. Oil paintings and photos of Kershing alongside dignitaries and members of law enforcement decorated the wainscoted walls. The hardwood floors glistened and recast the day's sunlight underneath the carved giltwood armchairs that formed a semicircle around Kershing's desk. The entire place evidenced power. The mahogany desk, which overlooked Constitution Avenue, was well worn from hobnobbing with chairs that, throughout several decades, had rubbed against it. There was an antique armoire against the wall adjacent to the desk. The armoire housed a high-definition, flat-screen television and other state-of-the-art electronics. Most days, this was the most serene office in the entire building.

But today was unlike most days.

The wooden office door flew open with the attorney general yelling at his counselors—including Clarence Niles, the newest lawyer in the office. "What do you mean she just went down there and did it!? This is outrageous! I want that lady arrested immediately!"

"General, I don't think that's a good idea," Amanda said, turning her head and rolling her eyes at those behind her. Peering back at Kershing, she continued her warning. "If we go after this woman, it won't do us any good, and our actions will be plastered on the front page of every newspaper in the country. We all need to calm down and focus on prevention."

"What else is there to prevent, Amanda!?" the attorney general asked.

"Well, General, I think that's obv—"

"And why did the Bureau of Prisons let this woman conduct this interview? Somebody tell me that! And how did she find out where Saud was being detained? Wasn't that one of the reasons we were worried about Sanderson's order? Don't you think if a reporter can find him, that the terrorists have pretty good odds? My head is about to explode."

SCAVENGER HUNT

Blake noticed Amanda's mucked-up hair as she engaged the apoplectic Kershing. No one but his wife could placate him any better, and no one in DC had as much credibility with the attorney general as his only female counselor. She was a borderline genius, and everyone knew her brains and good judgment packed a powerful punch.

"General, Omar Saud wasn't in a Bureau of Prisons jail. He was in a facility that's owned and operated by the State of Nevada. The Marshals Service should've prevented this from happening, but something fell through the cracks," she said, fearing the response.

"Well then, somebody better get me the director of the Marshals Service on the line, whatever his name is! We should've declared Omar Saud an enemy combatant and thrown him in a military brig! I'm going to kick myself for not insisting on it! This animal destroys Renaissance Stadium, killing thousands, and we end up accommodating him in a four-star hotel!"

"General," Amanda said, "this jail is not the Ritz-Carlton. I can assure—"

"Agnes!" Kershing, on the precipice of a conniption, screamed toward the closed office door. "Get me the director of the Marshals Service on the phone!"

Blake watched Clarence Niles rush over to the laptop and insert a shiny, metallic drive. Niles, a slim African American of average height with chiseled features, piercing brown eyes, and a shaved head, then turned on the large screen on the wall and readied his assortment of sharpened, number-two pencils and brand new yellow legal pad. Everyone but Kershing took a seat and watched intently. The attorney general was pacing around his office, leaving not one square foot untraversed.

"*This is Jenny Jacobs with Liberty Broadcast News. Today, after months of legal battles and resistance from the Clements Administration, I'm here in an undisclosed detention facility to interview Omar Saud, the purported mastermind behind the bombing at Renaissance Stadium in San Francisco, arguably the worst terrorist attack in our nation's history. Mr. Saud is awaiting trial for his alleged role in the deaths of more than ten thousand people. Notably, Mr. Saud has agreed to conduct this interview despite being refused access to counsel.*"

"She apparently didn't hear about Harry's hearing," Rick said. "He now has access to counsel, correct?"

"Not at the moment," Blake clarified.

"Turn it up, Clarence!" Kershing demanded.

"*Mr. Saud, first, the question everyone wants answered. Were you or were you not an accomplice in the terrorist attack in San Francisco?*"

"*I was, how do you say . . . an innocent bystander. I am not guilty of any crime.*"

"*How can you say that? You were fleeing the area by boat after landing the plane the terrorist jumped from, and the US government is going to argue he was your brother.*"

"As-as-as, I understand your, your legal process, Ms. Jenny Jacobs," Saud stuttered, "I am innocent until proven guilty. So why do you insist on convicting me before I can tell my story?"

"Were you not a passenger on the plane?"

"I was in the-the-the airplane. You see, how do I say, say this? While some of your facts are correct, the conclusions that you draw are-are not. It is not a crime to be a passenger on-on-on . . . sorry."

"Take your time, Mr. Saud," Jacobs said.

"I was saying that it-it is not crime to be a passenger on an airplane."

"That may be the case, Mr. Saud, but would you agree that the circumstances implicate you in the attacks? Let's be honest, why else—"

"Yes," he interrupted. "Let's be honest. One of the pilots was-was shot in the head with a pistol that, according to the . . . how do you say? . . . redacted newspapers they let me read, were-were, I mean was, never found. Why cannot they find this gun? I was left for dead by this madman terrorist you call my brother and who killed all the peoples. I am lucky to be alive, Jenny Jacobs. What other circumstances do you-you imply? That I am not from your country? That I am from a place that your leaders have called 'evil?' Are these crimes in your country?"

"Believe me, your national origin, the place from which you come, has nothing to do with this in my mind. I understand that prejudices exist, and I have spent my entire life trying to help people from other countries who are persecuted. But what I'm trying to figure out here is—"

"Here is what you need to figure out. This is what you are missing. How is your president going to-to-to look if he has no one to punish for these horrible acts done to your peoples? How he's going to-to win re-election if he and his administration, as you call it, cannot put somebody for the people to hate and spit at and call the killer's accomplice? These are the questions you must ask yourself. This is-is-is why I am being held captive like a dirty dog in this cell. This is why I am being kicked and yelled at and-and-and not given enough food to have any energy to defend myself."

"Blake, why is he speaking in broken English?" Kershing asked, talking over the interview. "Wasn't this guy educated at Cambridge? And why is he stuttering?"

"Sir, it could be the conditions in his cell, or he could be experiencing delirium."

"Well, does this freak have any conditions that, to our knowledge, require medication? And would somebody get me the Marshals Service on the phone!?"

Everyone but Clarence turned his or her attention from the television screen. Clarence, with one ear on the sidebar conversation, remained engaged in the interview, scribbling copious notes. Amanda walked out of the office into the anteroom, closing the door behind her.

"General," Blake said, "I read in the file somewhere that his pre-detention medical examination revealed no symptoms or conditions requiring medication or treatment other than a chlamydeous bacterium for which he received a relatively long course of antibiotics. He does have some problems that are common in Middle Eastern—"

"What did you say he had? A chromosomal bacteria?"

"No, sir. He had a chlamydeous bacterial infection. He had chlamydia."

Rick couldn't resist driving home the point and perhaps soliciting a costly curse word or two for good measure. "He had VD, boss."

"I know what chlamydia is, Rick! Not from personal experience, of course. Why am I not surprised that this guy has the funk?" Kershing let out a deep sigh and took a moment to collect his thoughts. "Well, could he be experiencing some adverse reactions to the antibiotics?"

"No, sir," Hudson said, trying his best to respond to Kershing's question without embarrassing him. "The antibiotics were issued several months ago, and it's my understanding that they'd be long out of his system by now."

"Well, unless this butcher has psychosis or head trauma, then he's up to no good, and—" Kershing cut short his statement, losing his train of thought, "Would somebody *please* get me the Marshals Service on the line!? For heaven's sake, how many times—"

"Director of the Marshals Service on line two, General!" Amanda said, walking back into the office just in time to preempt a temper tantrum.

Kershing stomped to his desk, plopped in his chair, and, by duck paddling his feet, rolled himself toward the phone. He then picked up the receiver, shoved it between his face and shoulder, and, before pushing the button to activate the line, tried without much effort to look back at the assembled group.

"His name is Robert Ringold, right?"

"Goes by Bobby," Blake said as Amanda nodded in agreement.

Kershing grabbed the receiver from his shoulder, paused for a moment, pushed the hands-free button, and laid the receiver back in its cradle. The director of the Marshals Service was on speakerphone.

"Bobby, this is Bill Kershing. Why did your people allow Jenny Jacobs to interview this fruitcake!?"

"General Kershing, our folks at the detention center—"

"I mean, do you understand how problematic this is? This is more than bad journalese. Do you know what a mess this is going to become?"

"General, my people at the detention center—"

"This is dangerous stuff, Bobby! This tape is going to be broadcast all over the world if we're not careful! This makes us look like a bunch of buffoons!"

"I understand, General. The reporter presented to the attending marshals an order from a judge in DC. They called me after the interview started, and I told them to shut it down. Unfortunately, it appears they had about ten minutes with him prior to my directive."

"The court order has been stayed, pending appeal, but regardless, it has nothing to do with *reporters*!" the attorney general screamed, hammering his fist on the desk. "It addresses his right to *counsel*! Jenny Jacobs is not his counsel of record! I doubt she's even a lawyer!"

Blake realized that Robert "Bobby" Ringold's day was turning from bad to worse. Kershing didn't even extend the courtesy of telling the director who else was on the call. Such was life. Blake knew this would be Ringold's penultimate, if not final, conversation with the attorney general. At the end of this conversation, or during the next, the AG or his chief of staff would ask him to step down as the head of the Marshals Service. That he was a presidential appointee wouldn't matter. It was an election year. The president wouldn't hesitate to accept the attorney general's strong recommendation that he be sliced. *Bobby? Bobby who?* Then everyone could check off the "we took responsibility and held people to account" box. There would be no opportunity for Ringold to defend his agency's actions. Jenny Jacobs had interviewed the number-one terrorist in the world because of a few indolent guards in his chain of command. Ringold would be held to account for their failures.

"General, I know this happened on my watch, and I apologize for letting you down."

Blake thought about the attorney general's accountability. Just as those US Marshals in the crosshairs were Ringold's responsibility, Ringold was Kershing's. Hopefully, Blake thought, the president would be more forgiving to his former chief of staff. Kershing had, for many years, served the president during difficult times. Would it be enough? Though the two were close, the answer to that question hinged on whether the United States suffered another large attack. Friendships took a backseat to poll numbers in this town.

"Bobby, we made a mistake. Let's not make another one. No one else is allowed to see Saud without my or the president's explicit authority. Clear?"

"Yes, sir. Absolutely."

"If this Saud nutbag requests a pastor, priest, rabbi, imam, or Air Jordan himself, you need to pull that person from our cleared security list. No exceptions. Understood?"

"Understood, sir."

"Keep Michael Gregg updated on the local fallout of this," Kershing said as he pushed the red release button on his phone.

"Well, if it makes anyone feel any better," Amanda said, "we all realized this would spin out of control sooner or later. With Judge Sandersen's ruling, it was only a matter of time before something blew up in our faces. This isn't the end of the world."

Rick lifted his face from the palms of his hands. "It's only a matter of time before we die, Dr. Pangloss, but knowing you're dying early doesn't make you feel any better."

"I'm just trying to put things in perspective, Chicken Little!" Amanda said. "Sitting around pouting doesn't help the situation!"

"I don't have time to listen to you bicker," Kershing said. "Anyway, Rick, she'd knock you out in record time like Mike Tyson knocked out Marvis Frazier."

"Or stick out her tongue," Rick mumbled under his breath.

"We need to take immediate steps to prevent further fallout," Kershing directed. "Does anyone know where Michael is?"

Everyone in the room shook his or her head.

"Clarence, I want you to set up a call with the president. Amanda, you need to call Jenny Jacobs at Liberty Broadcast and tell her in no uncertain terms that if this interview sees the light of day, her career is over. Blake, I want you to contact Judge Sandersen and tell her majesty that we plan to file an emergency motion for an injunction to prevent Liberty or anyone else from broadcasting this interview. Figure out the status of her right to counsel order too. Rick, I need you—"

"General!" Michael Gregg yelped as he charged into the office, scanned the room, and made note of its occupants. Gasping for breath, the chief of staff continued. "General, it's the secretary of defense on line one. Saud doesn't have a stuttering problem—he speaks perfect English. Cryptologists at NSA have analyzed the interview, and they believe that Saud was speaking in code."

"What!" Kershing screamed, lunging to his feet. He placed his hands on his hips and looked at the television screen. The coverage had ended with Jenny Jacobs protesting her inability to continue the interview and arguing that her First Amendment rights had been violated. "Unbelievable. Let me talk to SecDef. Everyone else needs to make sure this interview doesn't get out. Things are going to Hades in a handbasket."

Just then, Agnes strolled into the office. "General Kershing, the president has called an emergency meeting in the Situation Room. Your attendance is required."

"What's it about?" Kershing asked.

"Something about an interview that is currently being aired on Al-Jazeera."

14

"Blake, it's John Smith."

"What's going on?" Blake asked, his phone to his ear as he walked with Amanda, Rick, and Clarence down the fifth-floor corridor.

"We're ready to meet upstairs. I can come down and escort you to the eighth floor."

"Listen, John, something urgent has come up, and the AG needs me to take care of some things."

"Blake, you comin' with me?" Rick asked, not caring that Blake was on the phone, trying to nudge him along as Amanda and Clarence scurried like mice toward their respective offices.

Blake gestured to Rick that he needed another second to rid himself of the caller.

"I know what's keeping you busy today," Smith said. "We'll be discussing the same issue."

"You heard about the Saud interview?"

"We have connections throughout the government providing us with intel."

"Your sources are better than ours. We just learned about this."

"If you're needed to manage a crisis, then I won't interfere. Your chief of staff did assure me, however, that my project would take priority."

"No, I understand. I can ask someone to—"

"And this will be the first briefing with your new team."

"That makes sense. I'll be in my office if you wanna come down." Blake turned toward Rick. "Would you mind calling Judge Sandersen for me? I need to meet with the CIA guy."

"Captain Kangaroo?"

"John Smith."

"Whatever."

65

"He said he's assembled our team, and I need to meet everybody."

"Sure. I wouldn't want to disrupt the spook's schedule when we're facing a national emergency."

"Yeah, I know, but he did say that we'd be working on this same issue."

"Doing what?"

"He didn't elaborate."

"No problem, Blake. I'll debrief you this afternoon if that works."

"*Gracias.* By the way, at some point today, I'd like to talk to you about our new friend."

"Your boy, Smith?"

"No," Blake said, making sure the hallway was empty. "Clarence Niles."

———

Most people didn't know there was an eighth floor in the Main Justice building. This included people who *worked* at Main Justice. The maintenance men who knew of its existence referred to it as the attic. But, in fact, it was a normal floor, serving as a buffer between the seven occupied floors and the roof. Similar to every other floor, it encircled the perimeter of the building like a disjointed Olympic track. Unlike the other floors, it wasn't accessible by the passenger or freight elevators. To reach it, one had to take an elevator or stairs to the seventh floor, and then take a smaller, inconspicuous flight of stairs up one additional level.

Blake followed Smith around the oval corridor, occasionally lowering his head to avoid the hanging chains draped over air ducts and metal pipes. He noticed that the droopy chains appeared to be swinging back and forth of their own volition.

"I remember this place from yesteryear," Smith said. "Before they built Hoover across the street, FBI worked up here."

"I didn't know that," Blake said.

"Yeah, they had shot tanks over there, used for ballistics testing, and crime labs up ahead. After the FBI moved across the street, the entire eighth floor became a utility warehouse, filled with pipes, hoses, electrical substations, water pumps, and chillers."

"Don't forget the spider webs and dead bugs."

"That too."

"Place resembles a movie set for a low-budget horror film," Blake observed. He then whispered to himself, "Or an abandoned mineshaft."

As they continued walking, the roar of antique utility motors and the humming of conveyor belts made it difficult to concentrate. Where there was lighting, it was dim—a few naked 40-watt bulbs dangling from semi-exposed, low hanging wires, placed in unconventional locations. There was just enough illumination to not need a flashlight.

"Legend has it that Hoover hid Hoffa's body up here," Smith said.

"I'm sorry?" Blake said as he leaned his head forward trying to hear over the sound of the motors.

"J. Edgar Hoover hid Jimmy Hoffa's body up here!"

"That doesn't surprise me one bit!"

Soon, the noise pollution began to fade. It was calmer on this side of the building and better suited, Blake thought, for claustrophobics. He didn't mind the challenge of walking this floor, but he began to wonder why Smith had chosen this bizarre place to meet.

"Why don't we just meet in the Command Center?" Blake asked.

The Justice Department Command Center, which occupied a sizable portion of the sixth floor of the building, was a state-of-the-art sensitive compartmented intelligence facility, or SCIF. It prevented even the most sophisticated of communication retrieval devices to penetrate its walls, and it contained secure lines for lawyers and agents when discussing, sending, or receiving highly classified information. It also had secure computers, high-security safes, and detailed maps of the world.

"I considered meeting there," Smith said, "but I want to make sure we're not bothered. We may have some long days and nights ahead of us."

Smith's reasons made sense. Blake liked the pros that worked in the Command Center, but they asked a multitude of meddling questions. That's what happens, he thought, when people spend all day and night cooped up in small areas without windows, isolated from the world but surrounded by the crown jewels of the country's treasured secrets.

They slowed down when they reached a newly refurbished section of the eighth floor. Blake approached one of the few windows in the area and looked outside.

"Any idea why this window is constructed of laminated glass?" Blake asked.

"They don't use real glass anymore. Architects learned their lesson from the Oklahoma City bombing in '95. Most of the victims died from shards of glass that flew through the air like daggers launched from a crossbow, not from the explosion's inferno."

"Really?"

"Yeah," Smith said. "One investigator in Oklahoma found a piece of glass embedded two feet deep in concrete."

Blake continued staring through the window as he reflected on the bombing of the Murrah Federal Building. He'd been in grade school when it happened.

"This way," Smith directed, turning to an opening in the hallway. He walked to a thick, black door, which was ajar. "The others are inside."

SCAVENGER HUNT

Blake entered what appeared to be a new SCIF. The secure facility was not cavernous, but there was plenty of space to operate. Unlike most of the eighth floor—where scattered bulbs provided isolated pockets of lighting—bright, fluorescent tubes illuminated the area. The taxpayers—unknowingly, of course—had spared no expense in funding its construction. As much as everyone praised the Command Center, which was much larger, Blake realized that it paled in quality.

"Blake Hudson," Smith announced, locking the SCIF door behind him, "going around the table, this is Brent Olson, Jake Reid, and Natasha Hensley."

Blake walked toward the end of the table to shake the hands of his new colleagues. "Nice to meet—"

"Have a seat, Blake," Smith interrupted, curtailing Blake's attempts to introduce himself.

Blake nodded at Olson before cutting short his pleasantries and following Smith's curt directive. Not easily perturbed, Blake was taken aback by Smith's abrupt change in demeanor, which Blake attributed to unnecessary posturing.

"Now that we're all here, let's start with an overview of our project. You'll have the opportunity to meet and greet when I'm finished."

As Smith walked to the end of the table, Blake surveyed his surroundings and smelled the new carpet. Everyone but Smith was sitting around the table placed in the center of the SCIF and surrounded by six white leather chairs. Two secure desktop computers sat on an elongated table pushed against the wall. Underneath the table, there were three boxes containing tablets. There was a whiteboard behind the table, where Smith took his seat. There were also stacks of office supplies against the opposite wall, which also served as the backdrop for an electronic map of the world. Television monitors occupied two of the four ceiling corners of the room. One of the two monitors showed a paused taping of the Omar Saud interview on Al-Jazeera. There were four electronic clocks located between those monitors showing the current times in Moscow, Riyadh, Beijing, and Zulu.

Blake wondered if anyone else here knew Smith or had a clue about the project. He noticed the legal-size notepads, boxes of pens, and a list of phone numbers in front of each of them.

"To state the obvious, this is a peculiar assignment. The less you know about things that don't matter, the better. This is old hat for most of you. For the rest of you," he said, eyeing Blake, "I trust you'll figure it out. My purpose isn't to be melodramatic but, rather, to ensure that this assignment is a success. Implementing safeguards and taking precautions are vital to that goal. Okay?"

Everyone nodded, some sooner than others.

"Let me apologize for our meeting place. Understand, though, that it's a necessary inconvenience in carrying out the mission. I trust you'll be satisfied with the equipment available to you here. It is, without a doubt, top of the line."

Blake noticed the alternating description of the undertaking. What started as a project, and then turned into an assignment, was now a *mission*.

"Why are we here? The government needs a rapid, stealth team that can mobilize and deploy to prevent or mitigate future terrorist attacks by the terrorist network al Thoorah. As you know, its leader, Omar Saud, remains in US custody, but that has only increased its members' aggressiveness."

Blake's throat dried up, the moisture in his mouth microwaved. Did he just hear the man correctly? Blake scanned the faces of the other members of the group. The two other men sat stone-faced. The woman glanced at him with a courtesy smile. Was she not listening to this? What did they need him for? He was a lawyer, not an agent or soldier.

Do you have any military training? Life and death decisions . . .

The man who called himself John Smith was starting to sound like John Rambo. Blake stared wide-eyed at him as he continued to describe the mission. "The activities flowing out of this operation will be covert in nature."

Another subtle transition, Blake thought. The mission was now an *operation*.

"Let's first talk about al Thoorah—a.k.a., the enemy. I will use simple social and cultural distinctions to make my point. Understanding differing mindsets is crucial. You were born into a complex but uniform culture. If your parents did their jobs, you were instructed to be accepting to all variations in life, including races and national origins. Our civilized society demands us not to discriminate between Caucasians and African Americans, between Hispanics and Asians, between blues and reds, purples and greens. Furthermore, you were taught not to discriminate based on religion—that is, between having religion or not, or among different religions.

"The enemy, however, was taught from birth that his race, national origin, and religion are all that is good and all that matter. He was taught that every one of you at this table, because you're an American, is evil. Each of you is out to kill him and his family and spread your wicked ways throughout his homeland, infecting his loved ones for generations to come. The enemy was taught that his sole objective in life is to kill you before you kill him and his family. There are very few exceptions. In short, your mindset and the enemy's are polar opposites. Advantage . . . enemy."

Blake's eyes followed his wandering thoughts, which were drifting to the three other people listening to Smith sermonize. He paid particular attention to Brent Olson, a man who would stick out in any crowd. He was a chisel-jawed, mammoth human being. His close-cropped hair and steely eyes only added to his mystique, casting him as a perfect template for a comic book super-hero. His most striking features were his arms, which were bulging out of his short-sleeved shirt. He possessed biceps the size of Blake's thighs. His forearms would make Popeye blush. Olson looked out of place at the Department of Justice, where pale and scrawny bookworms like Michael Gregg could be spotted hugging the walls as they sidled from one office to another.

"One caveat here," Smith said. "One characteristic you share with the enemy. He feels the same emotion you do when he looks into his children's eyes. He feels the same pain you do when his daughter is crying. He feels the same anger when he loses a son in battle. Point being: just because he lives like an animal, don't underestimate his human instincts and emotions."

Olson's impeccable posture and gargantuan girth were in stark contrast to Jake Reid's physical appearance. Reid's lean but unremarkable physique was draped with tanned but not yet sun-worn skin. He looked like a man pulled off the street after months of holding a WILL WORK FOR BEER sign. He had a full, scraggly beard, and his thick, black hair surrounded his face and rested on his shoulders. His hands were calloused, his elbows scab-covered. He looked defeated as he hunched over the table in his chair.

Yet, there was an intriguing quality about Jake Reid. Despite an otherwise hollow face chronicling a history of emotional pain, his royal blue eyes had an unmistakable glint of hope. And Blake was captivated by the man's expression. While everyone else's face in the room was etched in serious uncertainty, Reid's narrow lips were showing the faint glimpse of a smile. For some reason, Reid was happy to be here.

"Let's talk about education. You attended school, studied hard, went to college, and then landed a respectable job. The enemy spent his youth studying asymmetric, unconventional warfare. His schooling focused on the means and methods that would accomplish his sole task—to murder you with reckless abandon. He wasn't in Cub Scouts. He didn't play Pop Warner football or waste time playing the piano. He didn't watch *Sesame Street* or Disney movies. He learned how to shoot and dismantle automatic weapons while you were playing Spy Hunter at Chucky Cheeses. Your education and the enemy's are different. Advantage . . . enemy."

But the lion's share of Blake's attention wasn't focused on the men in the room. He had his eyes on Natasha Hensley. She made it impossible to pay full attention to Smith. Missions and operations sounded treacherous, but she was the primary cause of Blake's fluttering stomach. Risking embarrassment, he couldn't quit gawking. Her face was like a high-powered magnet to which Blake's eyes reacted like metal.

Hensley's figure was seductive, finely sculptured to arouse the attention of all life forms. Her skin was softly textured, her autumn hair pulled back in a ponytail. But it was her piercing green eyes that mesmerized Blake. If she were Medusa, he would have long since turned to stone. In the back of his mind, he hoped that he could find something wrong with her. An annoying accent, a distasteful tattoo, a bad attitude. Like a child, he wished for her to pick her nose or pass wind. Anything.

Get it together, Hudson!

Regaining a measure of discipline, Blake refocused his attention on John Smith, concentrating on the troubling business at hand.

"So what advantages do we have in fighting this enemy?" Smith asked. "Olson, can you help me?"

"Fortitude, technology, tactical innovation, information dominance, and being on the right side of a culture war where good is pitted against evil," Olson said without the slightest of hesitation.

"What other problems do American soldiers face when hunting down these fanatical killers?"

"A person's senses are more acute when being hunted," Reid said. "More adept at avoiding capture."

These guys are good, Blake thought as a bead of sweat trickled down the small of his back. *What have I gotten myself into?*

————

The Hard Times Café was a restaurant that specialized in chili. Replete with Texas flags, bull skulls, and enough "y'alls" to shake a stick at, the joint reminded Blake of home. The food was good, the music even better. The jukebox was packed full of old country hits, not the cheesy new stuff that had rocketed atop the pop charts and brought shame to the Grand Ole Opry.

"We need more wings!" Jake Reid shouted at the waiter, licking the Buffalo sauce from his fingertips, his long hair in a ponytail. "Anyone need another beer?"

"Yeah," Blake said. "Let's get another round."

Blake had recommended that the group meet, without Smith, in a more relaxed environment. Breaking the ice hadn't been easy given the circumstances. But the alcohol had a melting effect, and the group's icy veneer was beginning to thaw.

"So what does everyone think of John Smith?" Olson asked.

"He's pretty uptight," Hensley said. "Jake, you work for the CIA. Have you ever met Smith?"

"To be clear, I *worked* for the CIA. And no, never met him. That's not unusual, though. It's a big outfit, and I rarely visited Langley."

"What are you doing now?" Blake asked.

"I'm a fisherman."

"Really?"

"Yeah. Retired from the Agency several months ago. Trying my luck in Mexico."

"Must be nice," Olson replied.

"It's tough to crack the market down there, but I'm making steady progress."

"So why'd you come back?" Blake asked.

"They asked me to return for this operation."

"Are you married, any children?" Hensley asked.

Thanks for the entertainment, Mr. Reid.

"I'm not married," Reid replied, his limited answer conspicuous. He stared at everyone, looking as if he wanted to supplement his response. But he couldn't summon the words. He gulped down his beer before changing the subject. "What about you, Brent? Any family to speak of?"

"Got a rockstar wife," Olson replied, easing Reid beyond his awkward moment, "and we're trying to have kids. It's difficult with my schedule."

Blake noticed everyone's caution in asking follow-up questions. They had just learned that Olson was a member of Delta Force. They didn't know, though, how much of his job was off-limits. Observing the group's hesitancy, Olson steered the conversation elsewhere.

"Natasha, you work for NSA?"

"Technically, but I'm detailed to DIA right now."

"Defense Intelligence Agency. That's interesting," Reid said. "Are you doing any cryptology?"

"I was a cryptologist at NSA. That got pretty boring, so I . . ."

"Say no more," Olson said, signaling that Natasha's job was as clandestine as his own. "Love the work that DIA is doing. They're becoming more effective than our friends at the CIA. No offense, Jake."

"Agreed. The CIA has become an entitled, dissenting body with a life of its own, and it tends to leak information to suit its own agenda."

Thanks for the entertainment, Mr. Reid.

"Natasha," Olson continued, "you from this area?"

"California."

"How about you, Blake?" Olson asked. "You said you were a Texan, but I can barely pick up the accent. When did you leave the Lone Star State?"

"Couple of years ago."

"I hear that's a great country," Natasha quipped.

"Yep," Blake said chuckling. "There's a rebel force back home that still pushes for secession."

"Lawyer?" she continued.

"Try to be."

"So what's your role working for this group?" Reid asked.

"Good question, Jake, but I don't know the answer. Honestly, I'm confused about the whole thing."

"Didn't learn much this afternoon, did we?" Olson mused.

"No," Reid replied, "and I agree with Natasha. John Smith is a ball of nerves."

"He'll be all right . . . hopefully," Olson said. "It's not my style to question orders, but I'm accustomed to having a clear plan. And this guy didn't give us much today. I have an idea of the nature of our mission, but there remain many unanswered questions."

"So what is it?" Hensley asked.

"What is what?" Olson said.

"The nature of our mission," Blake interjected, "as you understand it?"

Olson looked at Reid and then leaned forward, prompting everyone else to do the same. "To disrupt al Thoorah attacks," he whispered.

"I know *that*," Blake said, "but how?"

"Sounds like a good old-fashioned scavenger hunt to me," Reid said.

"Good point," Olson said, not wanting to extrapolate in a public area. "Maybe that's what we should name the operation—Operation Scavenger Hunt."

Blake took a gulp of beer and stared at the large Texas flag hanging from the ceiling. He was ready to go home.

15

Blake stood at the corner of Ninth Street and Pennsylvania Avenue, his dark suit and silver necktie flapping in the wind. Waiting for the walk signal, he checked his watch and sipped his dark roast coffee. After the interview with Omar Saud, coupled with its subsequent broadcast, the energy level in the city and at the office had skyrocketed. Justice Department employees—even those with no counter-terrorism responsibilities—adopted an increased sense of urgency and accountability for protecting the country. Blake didn't need the caffeine to keep him awake, but the stroll to and from the Starbucks allowed him to clear his head.

Once the walk signal flashed, and the hybrid cars, SUVs, and lone minivan slowed to a stop, he continued his stroll across Ninth Street toward the J. Edgar Hoover Building, headquarters for the FBI. Reaching the other side of the street, he waited once again—this time to cross Pennsylvania Avenue.

Before he could continue, he heard a chorus of screaming sirens. Startled by the deafening sounds of approaching motorcycles from the direction of the White House, he jaunted forward to the median and waited. Blake watched the drivers of the white and black police-model Harley Davidsons, speeding in all directions, divert the traffic. A procession of black vehicles followed. It was the presidential motorcade, and it had caught Blake right in the middle of it.

"Stay where you are!" one of the motorcycle officers directed, yelling at Blake before flying by.

"I'm not going anywhere," Blake said under his breath.

Another officer decelerated, stopped at the intersection of Ninth and Pennsylvania, right behind Blake, and climbed off his bike, using it as a barricade to block traffic traveling down Ninth Street. The remaining motorcycles zoomed by, paying no attention to Blake, clearing the way for the president of the United States.

CHAD BOUDREAUX

It was, Blake thought, both an effective and a grand exercise in protection. As the bikes traveled closer to the United States Capitol, he could see the most important armored vehicles in the motorcade: two black Suburbans followed by three black limousines. The windows in the Suburbans were rolled down, revealing members of the Secret Service dressed in commando-style clothing. The agents searched every rooftop of every building, as well as all onlookers, as the motorized cavalry surged ahead. Blake glimpsed into the backseat of the second Suburban, where he spied two gunmen holding assault rifles and eyeing the crowd. Given his current location, they kept a watchful eye on him.

The limousines, with dark tinted windows, followed the Suburbans. Blake knew the president occupied the one in the middle, and that's where he focused his attention. As President Clements's limo sped by, Blake witnessed the silhouette of the most powerful man in the world, sitting alone in the backseat.

Two more black vehicles followed the presidential limousine—customized vans with satellite dishes and other mechanical and electronic devices mounted on top. An ambulance, acting as the caboose, followed the black vans. Once it passed, Blake exhaled, realizing that he'd held his breath throughout the entire episode.

"Amazing experience, huh?" a man said as he joined Blake on the median.

The coast clear, and the sounds of sirens and roaring engines fading, the two men walked across the street toward the Main Justice building.

"Sure is," Blake said. "I've never been caught up in the melee like that. That'll scare you to death if you're not expecting it."

"The fear factor is their goal. And you just know they love *legally* breaking all the traffic laws."

"Teenager's dream, I guess," Blake said, extending his hand. "I'm Blake Hudson."

"Glad to meet you, Blake," the man said. "Rex Levine."

"Nice to see you, Rex," Blake said, shaking the man's meaty, limp hand.

"You work around here?"

"I work *right* here—at the Justice Department," Blake said, stopping at the sidewalk kiosk to purchase a pack of gum.

"Lawyer, huh? Interesting. What division?"

"Attorney general's office."

"So you basically run the place," Levine said with a chuckle.

"Hardly. I do as I'm told. How about you?"

"I'm a government contractor, specializing in telecommunications. I just returned from a meeting at the FBI. Working on a few projects for the director and the chief information officer."

"Oh, yeah?" Blake said, attempting to appear interested. "I know some folks over there."

"Yeah, I met with Sally Jenkins."

"Don't know her. Where does she work?"

"Nice lady," Levine said, smiling and failing to answer the question, his stained, crooked teeth catching Blake's attention. "You know, I had a friend who worked in your office some time ago. He worked for then-Attorney General Ashcroft. Let's see . . . that would've been what administration?"

"Bush 43," Blake said, pocketing his gum and now continuing his walk toward the corner entrance of the building.

"Right. George W. Bush. Not to be confused with Bush 41, George H.W. Bush. People would call 43 'Junior.' He wasn't a junior, you know."

"I remember that. He also wasn't the forty-third person to be president."

"How's that?"

"Well, Grover Cleveland was elected to two non-consecutive terms."

"That's right."

"Useless trivia, free of charge."

"Anyway, my friend used to tell me that he did some exciting work. But I guess you know all about that. You're likely involved in some high-level and secretive stuff yourself, huh?"

"Mr. Levine, is it?

"Rex."

"Rex. I'm a paper-pusher, a carriage horse if you will."

"Sounds to me like self-deprecation. I don't guess I need to worry about the country being attacked again, do I? I trust you're doing things to protect us?" he prodded.

"That's what I hear."

"What are some of the steps y'all are taking these days?"

"Doing everything within our power. I do my part, which, like I said, is pushing paper. It was nice meeting you, Rex," Blake said. "This is my entrance."

"Nice meeting you, too, Mr. Hudson."

Blake walked through the large doors and flashed his badge to Oscar Childs.

"Looks like the Washington Commanders overpaid for questionable talent again in free agency, Oscar."

"We'll see, Blake. You should be more concerned about the convicts the Cowboys signed."

"Low blow, my friend," Blake replied. "Low blow."

Blake took another sip of his coffee and smiled as he walked to his office. He didn't see Rex Levine stop at the end of the block and reach for his phone. He didn't hear the strange man's ensuing conversation. And he had no idea that he'd meet Rex Levine again.

Next time, the conversation would be much less amicable . . . the circumstances much more direful.

OPERATIONS

16

Bethesda, Maryland

"I thought you were dead, old man," Blake said as he entered Harry Mize's sun-kissed bedroom. Harry, dressed in button-down pajamas, had propped himself against the headboard of his king-sized bed and, before he noticed Blake, had been devouring legal briefs. Frank Sinatra was crooning throughout the spacious bedroom, which smelled like chicken noodle soup.

"Blake!" Harry exclaimed, setting his reading glasses on the nightstand. "Take off your jacket and pull up a seat. I need your thoughts on our appeal in the Saud case."

"Harry, you must be joking," Blake responded, walking over to shake Harry's hand. "You were just discharged from the hospital after knocking on death's door, and now you're already helping with the appeal?"

"What else can I do? Watch the soaps? Judge Judy? I can't sit around and twiddle my thumbs. Besides, I probably don't have much time before the president declares Saud an enemy combatant and throws him in the brig."

"I apologize for not stopping by the hospital."

"Not at all," Harry said. "I've had enough people waste the government's time trying to make me feel better."

"I was encouraged to learn that the stroke didn't affect your motor skills. Looks like you've already whipped it."

"Probably wasn't even a stroke. Doctors always exaggerate to scare you into eating healthy. I would know. I married one. How are you doing?"

"Good. Michael has me working on some terrorist-related matters," Blake confided, "so I'm sharing my other oversight responsibilities with Clarence Niles. Otherwise, not much to report."

"Where is Clarence from?"

"Southern District of New York. First I've worked with him. Had to look him up on the internet."

"SDNY, also known as the *Sovereign* District of New York. They don't like Main Justice in their britches."

"They don't like anyone in their britches. Clarence is Main Justice now, so we'll see how he fits in. So far, so good."

"How's the attorney general holding up?"

"He's trumpeting calls for a legal revolution, scaring people to death about Sandersen's ruling. We'll see how well that goes over with Congress. Ironically, Jenny Jacobs's interview with Saud is helping the cause. That didn't go over too well."

"I'm dying to hear your thoughts about that interview."

He told Harry everything he knew about the interview and the subsequent broadcast, making sure to amplify Kershing's vehement reactions throughout the process.

"What about the coded language Saud was using?" Harry asked.

"They ruled out Morse code, although they suspect it's something similar. Experts familiar with his profile are worried. They say he doesn't do anything without a reason."

"That's what I've heard."

"Some believe, though, that the intelligence community is exaggerating his potential. DOD and DHS say it was a botched attempt at communication."

"Let me get this straight. They don't know what he said, but they're comfortable dismissing it as a red herring?"

"That's what they're telling *us*."

"Sounds fishy to me. I bet they're holding something back. What else are we doing to prevent another attack?"

Blake paused and considered how much to tell Harry about Scavenger Hunt. "People are following the normal precautions," he demurred. "Extra security where Saud is being detained, increased awareness in analyzing and filtering intelligence related to al Thoorah. They're reassessing the threat level for the first time since the San Francisco bombings. The attorney general is talking with ministers of justice around the globe. Of course, the secretary of Homeland Security is taking the lead."

"Sounds right," Harry said, exuding a large sigh. "Don't guess we can do much more."

"Need anything before I go?"

"Yeah, grab that bottle of Blanton's bourbon on the dresser and pour me a little nip."

"Sure thing."

"Like Davy Crockett, this Tennessean is due a little intemperance now and again."

Blake uncorked the bottle, waited for Harry to drink the water from his soon-to-be bourbon glass, and then poured.

"Much obliged," Harry said, holding out his glass. "Oh, one more thing. Something that's been bothering me since I left the courthouse. You have two seconds?"

"Of course," Blake said.

"After the hearing, some rough-looking guy approached me and introduced himself. He told me his name was Elliot something-or-other, and that he'd met me several years ago. I had prosecuted some slimy doctor who'd taken liberty with some patients while they were under the gas. Elliot said he'd worked for the hospital."

"Okay."

"Maybe I'm losing my memory, but that man's face was unforgettable. And I interviewed nearly everyone who worked at the hospital. It was a high-profile trial for me, so I remember it like it was yesterday." Harry paused to sip his whiskey and then was aroused by his recollection. "Elliot Nichols! Got it."

"What can I do?"

"Just let me know if he tries to contact anyone else. Like I said, I think he was fibbin'—likely after some privileged information. I suspect he's a freelance reporter after the latest scoop. But in retrospect, my conversation with him was disconcerting."

"Elliot Nichols?"

"I'm sure that's what he told me," Harry said, grabbing his reading glasses from the nightstand and writing the name on a nearby napkin. "Here you go."

Blake took the napkin, read the name, and placed it in his coat pocket.

"One more thing, Blake."

"Yes, sir?"

"Be careful and watch your back."

Blake stared at his bedridden colleague. "Why would you say that?"

"These are troubling times. *Very* troubling times."

17

Washington, DC

Blake walked into the eighth-floor SCIF studying his handwritten notes. He was surprised to see Natasha Hensley already sitting at the table, tapping her pencil on a closed notebook pad. She had the look of a teenager forced to attend defensive driving.

He had hoped she'd somehow appear less attractive today, but those hopes were dashed. She looked mesmerizing.

"Hi, Natasha. How's it going?" he asked, confirming that she wasn't wearing a wedding band.

"It's going."

She smiled at Blake, but he acted as if he didn't notice. Her response was straightforward and natural, he thought, but it came across as seductive.

He placed his notes at the head of the table and tossed aside his navy-blue suit jacket.

"Did you go home after dinner last night?" he asked as he sat down.

"Yeah," she said, continuing to tap and rotate her pencil. "You?"

"Yep. I'm getting too old to stay out with the dry cows."

"Dry cows?" she giggled, crossing her legs, putting down her pencil, and giving Blake her full attention.

"It's a Southern saying, I guess. Wet cows stick around the barn after sundown and nurse the calves. Dry cows wander off into the pasture and try to stir up some . . . mischief."

The two stared at one another and then laughed as Brent Olson and Jake Reid entered the SCIF.

"Hello, team," Jake said.

"Gentlemen," Blake said.

"Whoa. What do we have here?" Natasha asked, surprised to see a clean-shaven and shorthaired Jake.

"Decided I needed to grow up," Jake said. "So what have you all been up to?"

"Just got here," Natasha said.

"What was so funny when we walked in? The way Natasha was laughing, I thought Blake might have proposed," Jake jabbed.

"Easy, killer," Blake said, exhibiting an embarrassed cough, now afraid to look at Natasha.

An uncomfortable silence fell upon the room, one full of potential energy. Jake had hit a nerve and appeared ready to exploit it. Blake's defensive response only made things worse. Men were ruthless when they smelled third-party infatuation because it made them nervous. The best way to clear the air was to expose it. Emotions didn't matter. If you couldn't take the heat, too bad.

"Don't turn red, Blake," Jake said.

"What do you mean?" Blake asked, trying to clean up his mess. "I'm not turning red. I just didn't want to offend Natasha."

"I wasn't offended," Natasha said, twisting the screws into Blake even tighter, making him walk the plank.

These people are ruthless! Blake thought.

"Let's get down to business, shall we?" Brent said, not in the mood for levity. "Blake, what do you have for us?"

Blake had spoken to John Smith and would be briefing the group on its first assignment. "Before I get started, I'm curious if anyone's spoken to John Smith since our initial meeting."

"Not me," Brent said as the other two shook their heads.

"First of all," Blake continued, "does anyone believe that John Smith is his real name?" All shook their heads again.

"Well, I spoke with what's-his-name a few minutes ago over a secure line. He understands that the circumstances surrounding this operation are 'vague and cryptic,' to use his words. He reiterated the importance of our work and said that if everything goes as planned, we'll be commended for our service."

"Not sure how reassuring that sounds," Reid said.

"I agree," Blake said, but I've been confused ever since I met Smith."

Everyone continued looking at Blake without saying a word.

"Our conversation contained little substance," he said, "and didn't last long. Forty-five minutes tops."

"Is that it?" Jake prodded. "No discussion about how we're supposed to thwart terrorist attacks?"

"No discussion whatsoever of the specifics. It wasn't for a lack of me asking; I guarantee you that."

"How long have you known Smith?" Brent probed.

"I met him a few days ago. The next time I saw him or heard from him," Blake said, "was right before he escorted me to the eighth floor—to *this* room—to meet you. I didn't hear from him again until a few minutes ago."

"How did you know when your conversation today would take place?" Natasha asked, her question prompting nods from the other two.

"He called me out of the blue, just like he always does."

The others glared at one another. Blake, realizing an uncomfortable intensity had sabotaged the light-hearted atmosphere, knew he had to make a better case. Inquiring minds wanted to know.

"Look," he said, interlocking his fingers in front of him on the table, making eye contact with his new colleagues. "Absent what I gleaned from my conversation with Smith this afternoon, which I plan to describe in a minute, I don't know any more about this operation than you do. I was hoping one or more of you could shed some light on this for *me*. I see that you're just as clueless as I am about things."

"Blake," Brent said, "don't take offense to our being skeptical. Smith obviously has tapped you as his point man. I think it's reasonable to assume a person in that position would know more."

"I agree with you. And if there's anything we lawyers do well, it's ask probing questions. But Smith is keeping things close to his vest."

"This isn't business as usual," Natasha said, "so the lack of detail shouldn't surprise us. Most of the intelligence missions I've worked on are cryptic or vague up to a point. At least we know the goal: protect the country from al Thoorah terrorist attacks."

"Agreed," Jake said. "I didn't intend to trigger an inquisition. Let's hear what you've got from your conversation today with our boy, John Doe."

"John Smith," Brent corrected.

"Him too," Jake said, smiling at Brent's rigid personality.

"Go ahead, Blake," an impatient Brent directed.

"As for roles and responsibilities, I hadn't thought of myself as Smith's point man. But whatever works. What I do know is that I'll serve as legal counsel to the group."

"That's all fine and dandy," Jake said, "but I'd be surprised if we need much legal guidance given the clandestine nature of our undertaking. Every assignment worthy of a paycheck, it seems, is conducted outside the black letter of the law. Always with Uncle Sam's imprimatur, of course."

"You're wrong, Jake," Brent countered. "Given the uniqueness of this group and the challenges al Thoorah poses, we'll need Blake's advice more than ever."

Natasha nodded in agreement.

"Natasha," Blake said, aching to regurgitate his information and move on, "you'll handle the logistics and coordinate the planning for the group. You'll also oversee electronic surveillance and intercept, whatever that means."

"Sounds about right," she said.

"Jake and Brent, you'll handle all ground operations. I asked Smith what that entailed, and he told me you'd know once we had our first assignment."

Blake stood up and walked to the door, pulling it shut and locking both locks. He then walked back to his chair. Natasha, he noticed, began tapping her pencil again on her notebook that she'd yet to open.

"Natasha has the hardest job of all," Jake said.

"My job sounds like a walk in the park," Natasha said.

"I'm glad *you* think so," Blake said, "because all this sounds difficult and sketchy to me."

"Welcome to the real world," Jake said. "You can't always fight terrorism by filing documents in a court of law."

"Maybe you're right," Blake conceded, "but whatever happened to traditional intelligence, law enforcement, and military channels?"

"That's easy," Jake said. "Too much bureaucracy. And those within the bureaucracy don't trust one another."

Thanks for the entertainment, Mr. Reid.

"So how do we work outside the bureaucracy?" Blake asked.

"Lady and gentlemen," Jake said, "like we said last night, what we need is a good, old-fashioned, Cold War scavenger hunt. Plain and simple."

Blake didn't know how to respond. Until now, he'd been unwilling to accept the inevitable truth about the group and its purpose. But Jake had hit the nail on the head, and Blake knew it. He had no idea what lay in store for them in the coming weeks, but he knew it wouldn't be business as usual. At least not "business as usual" as normal citizens like Blake would define the phrase.

"Which brings us to the first assignment of Operation Scavenger Hunt," Blake said, hoping that the more he repeated the name of the operation, the more he'd grow accustomed to it.

Hensley uncrossed her legs, pulled up her chair, and for the first time during the meeting, opened her notebook.

It was time to get to work.

18

Chevy Chase, MD

The cabinets near the leather recliner were special. They housed a high-end humidor that contained several boxes of cigars. Adjacent to the humidor, but located in the same cabinet, were plastic baggies that contained bands for various brands of Cuban cigars. More than a few of those cigars were nestled in an opened and half-empty cigar box that sat atop the small, round, and otherwise unremarkable table.

The man waited until the sixth ring to pick up the phone. "Yes?" he asked in a deep, resonant voice as he cradled the phone's receiver between his face and shoulder, his attention more focused on the unlit cigar in his hand than on the caller.

"What did you find out?" Peter Karnes, the cigar-smoking man's new point of contact, asked.

"The news is much worse than expected."

"Give it to me. I'm sure you won't sugarcoat it."

"No, I'd never do that." The man emitted a specious chuckle as he slid the MADE IN THE DOMINICAN REPUBLIC label off his 1993 Siglo I cigar and replaced it with its original SIGLO label, with the appropriate place of origin—Havana, Cuba—prominently noted.

"Well then?" the young Karnes inquired.

"We believe that Saud's attempts at some type of quasi-Morse code were successful. He probably set something in motion."

"You're kidding."

"Oh no, my friend. I do not kid about such things," the man said as he grabbed the matches from the table. There was nothing but silence as the man lit his cigar, and smoke began to billow toward the ceiling. "Still there?"

"Yeah, but I'm confused," Karnes said. "Our intel folks tell me not to worry about the broadcast interview. They hear there is little chance Saud could've described his current location. They don't think he knows where he is. He was hooded in transport and hasn't been allowed outside."

"I bet Ms. Jenny Jacobs could find him. Seriously, can you hear what you're saying? You're dismissing as uneventful a broadcast of a captured terrorist leader. Think about it. The broadcast itself is enough to trigger a terrorist attack. That he issued a message only increases the probability. You shouldn't be worried about people finding out where he is. You should be worried about another terrorist attack within the continental United States."

"You think the intelligence community is composed of a bunch of idiots?"

"That's not what I said, Peter. I think the national intelligence director is playing politics. He knows November is approaching. The last thing he needs is another threat of an attack looming before the election. He knows some perceive the president as weak on terror. The polls show him behind Senator Cummings by *fifteen points* on terrorism issues. That's a huge margin on issues that, as recent history has illustrated, will no doubt resonate with the American people."

"I think you're blowing this out of proportion."

"I have more faith in my men—men who get paid handsomely to provide me with unbiased analyses. In this case, I also have the added luxury of common sense, something you seem to be lacking."

"Don't turn this around on me! You told my boss you were certain that Harry Mize would win that hearing!" Karnes said. "Wasn't this guy supposed to be the—"

"He's the top criminal lawyer in the country, and nothing's certain in life but that you and I are getting older!"

"Right! So what happened!? There has—"

"It had nothing to do with Harry Mize," the older man said. "His argument was flawless and persuasive. I was there to witness it all. The judge had made up her mind before the courthouse opened for business. She's in the special interest groups' back pockets, and they came out in droves for the hearing. Mize is nothing short of—"

"Mize had a stroke after the hearing! We have lawyers here that would eat him for lunch!"

"Mize would trample your lawyers! They're a bunch of bookworms, and he has more trial experience than all of them combined!" the man countered before taking a long drag and breaking his often-violated rule against inhaling. After a long exhale, he felt a wave of relaxation rush through him and continued. "Listen, we're arguing over the past. I'm not going out of my way to defend Mize. There's nothing in it for me. I just know that he did a fine job."

"Then why the stroke?"

"Good question, but it didn't affect his argument, and it doesn't affect where we go from here." The man looked around his office and focused on the eleven-antlered deer head across the room, hanging over his desk. "Besides, I don't have any control over who the Justice Department chooses to argue its cases. Not yet."

"No, you're right. I'm just frustrated by all this. It makes no sense to me."

The man chuckled again. "We're taking steps to keep this under control. It'll take some time, but you can tell your boss that I'm *hopefully optimistic*."

"Can you tell me more about this group you've assembled? I read about Blake Hudson. What about the others?"

"They're all perfect. Natasha Hensley. She technically works for NSA but has been on detail to DIA. She's an inspiring young operative. She's been involved in a few recent operations and garnered accolades for her performance."

"Good."

"Then there's Brent Olson."

"Wait a second. *The* Brent Olson?"

"The one and only," the cigar-smoking man said proudly.

"You were told no golden boys. I thought my boss's instructions were clear."

"Golden boy? Olson? Far from it, friend. If anyone is a golden boy, it's the boy from the Justice Department. Not Olson. But remember, *your boss* agreed to bring on Blake Hudson."

"Hudson is different. He's not a national hero. He's clueless. And he won't be running operations off our radar screen."

"Hudson can turn against this operation just as quickly as our operatives."

"*You* recommended him!" Peter Karnes exclaimed.

"He's needed to provide legal cover to the team. I met him a few days ago," the cigar-smoking man chuckled, "and he told me he's nothing more than a paper pusher. He's in over his head but discreet."

"Whatever," Karnes said. "I'm not worried about Hudson, golden boy or not. From what I hear, he'd just as soon lose his life than his job. After the first operation is up and running, he's on the hook, like everyone else."

"So why the anxiety over Olson?"

"Two things. First, I often interact with DOD, and I know that Olson is a goody-two-shoes. He'll never buy into this project. Second, can you imagine what would happen if Olson were killed? The military brass would hunt us both down and spare no method of torture."

"*First*," the cigar-smoking man replied, "to answer your stupid question, Olson is the last person who's going to be killed. You are without a doubt the only person *ever* to call him a 'goody-two-shoes.' You're just showing your ignorance. The guy is a killing machine. He'll snap your neck in a New York minute. There is not an assignment that he can't handle, and the stakes are too high to rely on anyone but the best. Period. *Second*, he's already knee-deep in this operation. Animals like Olson can't turn down an assignment like this. It's in their blood. It's what they feed on."

"Did you just call me stupid? I'm growing tired of your attitude."

"Easy, good friend," the man said, inhaling a little more of his cigar and then gritting his teeth. "I called you *ignorant* and merely alluded to your *stupid* question. Remember who I am. I can be a nice guy, but I'm not going to sit here and take a bunch of disrespectful backtalk. If you need my services, you'll learn to respect your elders. Is that understood?"

"Who do you think *you* are talking to? Do you know wh—"

The man reached over, placed his cigar in the ashtray, and in the same motion, slammed down the phone. The call had ended. He rocked back and forth in his leather chair to gain momentum for standing up. Once he stood up, he walked over to the opposite end of the room and grabbed a blue folder from his desk. Then he returned to the chair, tapped the ash from his cigar, placed it between his teeth, and sat back down.

As he waited, he thumbed through his notes. He had no doubt the irritating call would resume within minutes. Peter Karnes just needed his superiors to educate him—someone to let him know what a big mistake he'd just made. Though it was in his client's best interest, he hated working with underlings. And he couldn't tolerate snot-nosed punks like Peter Karnes.

After seven minutes, the phone rang. The man let it ring only twice this time before picking it up. No need to humiliate the child any further. He would deal with his disrespect-ful caller in due time. "Yes?"

"Sir, I apologize for my behavior. I was out of line."

"Think nothing of it," the man said, smiling at the palpable shift in power.

"I didn't realize that—"

"I'm quick to anger but quicker to forgive," he said, telling what he knew to be a half-truth.

"Please continue, sir."

"Ah, yes. As I was saying . . . then there is Brent Olson."

19

Washington, DC

John Smith burst into the SCIF with Natasha Hensley in tow. After acknowledging Blake's presence, she walked to one of two adjacent computer terminals in the room and entered her password. After that, she entered a second password that gave her access to a secure portal, which included audio and video capabilities. This would allow her to collaborate in real-time with the two absent members of the group. After locking the SCIF door, Smith hovered behind her, and then paced back and forth as she made the appropriate connections.

"What's going on?" Blake asked.

"Natasha intercepted a communication from Jenny Jacobs to two men in eastern California. As expected, Jacobs told the men where Saud is being held. They're planning to bust him out this afternoon," Smith responded, never taking his eyes off the computer screen. "See if we have audio," he told Natasha.

Blake stood up and rushed to the computer terminal, looking over Natasha's shoulder as she was typing. "What? Jenny Jacobs is conspiring with terrorists? Wow."

"Sit down, Blake," Smith directed.

"Did we figure out how Jacobs could track Saud's whereabouts?" Blake asked as he sat down.

"She's sleeping with someone in the Marshals Service," Natasha said.

"Excellent. Never a dull moment around here. Where are Brent and Jake?"

"Sacramento," Smith said, not wanting to be bothered.

Blake could tell by the smell in the room that Smith had just smoked more than a few Lucky Strikes before entering the building.

"Audio's up and secure," Natasha said.

"Brent? Jake? This is John. Can you hear me?"

"Loud and clear. Is everyone else there?" Jake asked.

"Yeah—Blake and Natasha. What's your twenty, and what's the status?"

"We're just leaving the airport. Brent is driving to the motel. We should be ready for engagement in less than an hour."

"Good," Smith said. "Did you get what you needed?"

"Yes, we did. Good equipment. The vehicle was ready for us right where you said it would be."

"Jake, any sense if they'll still be at the motel?" Natasha asked.

"No, but they'd be foolish to leave early. It only heightens the risk of getting caught. If they're Middle Eastern, that makes it even riskier."

Blake started to grow concerned as he heard the correspondence unfold. "Wait a second, what are we planning on—"

"Jake," Smith said, "the intercept recorded Jacobs speaking to a man who likely is American. No foreign accent whatsoever. There appeared to be another person with him . . . speaking Farsi. Probably all al Thoorah recruits. Wouldn't be surprised if one of these guys is a domestic sympathizer, born and bred in the United States, and the other from Saud's inner circle."

Neither Jake nor Brent responded.

"Hello?"

"Yeah. We hear you. Judging by Brent's face, I think we're thinking the same thing: how much angrier that makes us."

"It shouldn't," Smith said.

"You're right. Shouldn't make any difference, but for some reason it does. The John Walker Lindhs of the world are difficult to figure out."

"Just get in that room and confirm the targets," Smith instructed. "I have a cleaning crew on-site. They'll check the parking lot and identify any vehicles containing explosives."

"Are we supposed to meet up with them?"

"No," Smith said. "If all goes as planned, you won't see them until you're leaving. They'll neutralize any explosive devices and clean up your mess when you're done. These guys are elite. They'll be watching your back when you enter the motel room so no one sneaks up behind you."

Blake couldn't hide his concern. He, like Smith, started pacing the floor. He knew the Bureau of Alcohol, Tobacco, Firearms, and Explosives, known as ATF, or the FBI explosives teams would be in charge if explosives were involved. Those two components within the Justice Department arm-wrestled over explosives jurisdiction. For some reason, though, neither agency was involved in this operation, a fact that left Blake perplexed.

"Has anyone notified the detention facility in case we fail or there is another group of terrorists we don't know about?" Jake asked.

Blake stopped pacing and stared at both Smith and Natasha. That same question was on the tip of his tongue.

"Yes," Natasha responded. "I called and left an anonymous threat. I wouldn't be surprised if they've already transported Saud from the facility. The place is on heightened alert in response to Saud's interview."

"After the AG screamed at the director of the Marshals Service," Blake said, "I guarantee you they're at DEFCON 1." Then it hit him: Natasha had placed an anonymous call. Why not just ask him or the attorney general to call the director of the Marshals Service and warn everyone of the rescue attempt through proper channels? He looked at Smith and said, "You haven't told the AG about this?"

"Jake and Brent, we'll be here if you need us," Smith said, ignoring Blake, failing to answer his question. "Make contact when you get close."

"Aye, aye, Captain," Jake said. "We'll have video up by that time. We're out."

"So far, so good," Natasha said, leaning back in her chair and then swiveling it around toward Blake, staring up at him with a smile of satisfaction.

"You had a huge breakthrough this morning," Blake acknowledged, walking toward the computer terminal. He then turned back to Smith. "But I don't understand why no one has told—"

"Sit down, Blake," Smith interrupted. "Let's talk about that."

Smith and Blake sat down at the table while Natasha kept her seat just a few feet away.

"This is critical," Smith said, "so I want to make sure we're crystal clear on how this operation must work."

"I couldn't agree more. Makes no sense to me why the attorney general of the United States is unaware of an operation being run out of his building."

"Blake, once Michael Gregg became aware of this operation, he knew that AG Kershing couldn't be involved."

"I don't understand," Blake said. "Kershing is a sponge for information. Why couldn't he know about this? It's happening three floors above him in his own building."

"For one, he doesn't have access to the information required, and Gregg didn't want him to have access. You'll need to ask Gregg why."

Gregg was no dummy, Blake thought. And it didn't take a genius to realize that intelligence operations could be toxic career killers. A chief of staff's duty, at the Justice Department or elsewhere, was to protect the principal, in this case, the cabinet secretary. Gregg knew if Kershing were never read into the operation, then he could claim ignorance when things started to blow up. That would be harder to do, though, with operations being run out of Main Justice.

"And the operation is moving forward this way," Smith said, "because when we presented the case to the FISA court, the judge denied our application for a wiretap. She ruled we didn't have probable cause to tap Jenny Jacobs. Given that Her Highness Jacobs had not only located where the US Marshals were detaining Saud but also interviewed him, that was a terrible decision. Getting the wiretap should've been a perfunctory exercise."

Blake wasn't a criminal law expert, but he was familiar with the Foreign Intelligence Surveillance Act, or FISA, court. The chief justice of the United States assigned certain judges from the federal district courts to the FISA court to hear matters concerning foreign intelligence surveillance. The FISA court, which issued electronic surveillance orders, conducted its business in a highly secure, windowless room on the seventh floor of the Main Justice, one floor down. To the chagrin of government skeptics nationwide, FISA judges conducted their cases in complete secrecy.

"Bad decision or not, a ruling to deny your application stands subject to appeal to the Review Court. So what's our legal basis for tapping Jacobs?"

"Blake, you must understand what we're up against. We're at war with al Thoorah."

"You're telling me we have no legal basis," Blake said, stunned. "Zero. Squat." Smith had just revealed to him that the group was violating the law and that the country's top law enforcement officer was being left in the dark. "Why didn't someone tell me the FISA application was denied? For that matter, why wasn't I told anything about our marking Jenny Jacobs?"

"Blake—"

"No one even told me we filed a FISA application. There are other ways to do this without violating the law." Blake couldn't keep his primary concern muzzled or his emotions under control. He stood up and, with the back of his legs, slammed his chair against the wall. "I don't want to be implicated in this!"

Smith eyed Blake closely, his mind calculating how to respond to the outburst. "The alternatives take too much time and carry too much risk, as evidenced by what's transpiring right now. Terrorists are hours away from busting Saud out of detention. No telling what else they have planned or who else is involved."

"Yeah, but—"

"They could bomb a building or another stadium. We just don't know. These animals are ready, willing, and able to kill innocent civilians. Right now, they're locked and loaded and don't play by your rules. If we aim to stop them, then we must take extraordinary measures."

"The cliché 'if we don't play by the rules, then we're no better than the terrorists' has never been more apropos," Blake said.

"It's also never been so foolish and naïve!" Smith snapped, standing up, his finger wagging at Blake. "Preach that gospel to the dead victims' families after lunatics blow up a shopping mall. Tell that to the lady who'll have her arms and legs blown off, confined to a wheelchair for life with a colostomy bag nestled by her side."

"Look—"

"Carry your righteous soapbox to the little boy with third-degree burns covering his entire body. Communication may prove difficult, though, because—"

"Give me a break, John!" Blake said, no longer withholding his emotions, tired of being interrupted and treated like a blind pacifist. "I realize there'll always be extreme illustrations one can manufacture to justify unlawful, extra-judicial actions. But in the end, without law, there is always more chaos than order. We obviously must do everything within our power to combat terrorism. But we can think outside the box *and* within the Constitution."

"Listen, Blake. I understand your concerns," Smith said, "and this will be the last time we'll resort to these inordinate measures, I'm sure. We just had a bad ruling at a time when we were in desperate need of immediate surveillance."

"Who at the Bureau is involved in this operation? And how do they plan on making the arrest?"

"No one at FBI is involved," Smith said.

"So this is just a military operation or, should I say, a joint CIA and military operation? You don't need a law degree to predict how this is going to unfold, John. You know as well as I do that these potential arrests will *not* hold up in a court of law."

"Fine by me. If everything goes as planned, these terrorists will never see a court of law."

"What other options do we have? Enemy combatant status?" Blake asked, shaking his head.

"It's a clear-cut case. They should be tried in a military tribunal."

"Well, there are some seminal Supreme Court rulings that may say otherwise. And besides, if you haven't noticed, President Clements is highly allergic to military tribunals. That's why Saud's not in DOD custody. If anyone should be an enemy combatant, it's him. That he's not is one of the main reasons we've had so many legal problems with him."

Blake looked at Natasha, who was staring back at him, a glare of uncertainty blanketing her face. His face twisted and his temple throbbed as his mind churned the myriad legal scenarios and consequences. As he processed the influx of shocking information, no clear path emerged. And as he sorted through the immediate issues, he couldn't quit worrying about his own criminal culpability.

"Blake," Smith said, "this group wasn't established to do business as usual."

"Well, at least we agree on one point."

There was a long pause as the two men studied one another, both second-guessing the accuracy of their initial assessment of the other.

"Who established the group?" Blake asked, cutting to the heart of the matter. Smith had crossed the line, and there were now no holds barred.

"I take orders from the director of CIA," Smith said. "Ask *him*."

"I'll be sure and do that the next time he comes over for dinner, *John*!" Blake said. "Come on! You know I don't have the cachet to dial up the CIA director."

"Blake," Smith snarled, "we're charged with creative thinking, and creativity becomes crucial when threats are imminent. Right now, we have a terrorist death squad within our borders that plans to strike at any moment. It doesn't get more imminent than that."

"Doesn't answer my question. I asked you a simple question, and you give me another lesson from Sun Tzu."

"Blake, why don't you just leave? You need some time to yourself."

Blake took a deep breath. He needed to bring this dispute to a peaceful, diplomatic resolution. Backing Smith into a corner was counterproductive. "Look, I'm no idealist, and I don't do everything by the book. But we're staring at unspeakable violations of federal law. This isn't a covert operation overseas; this is, in essence, an unsanctioned military operation on American soil."

"I hear you, Blake. And believe me, if we could've done this by the book, we would have. You have to understand, though, that when slight departures from the law are weighed against innocent lives, tough choices must be made."

"Slight departures? John, I know you're frustrated with me, but understand this whole thing has me baffled."

"You've made that clear. And I've made it clear that I'm doing the best I can."

"There's no way to sugarcoat this. We could all go to jail."

"I don't need your approval," Smith said matter-of-factly, without any hint of hostility. "I have a job to do, and your objections are duly noted. All I'm asking is that you remain focused and give more thought to the consequences of doing nothing. We have less than an hour before this goes live."

Blake noticed that Natasha was staring at the computer monitor, her attention now back on the operation. "Natasha," Blake asked, "what are your thoughts?"

She took a deep breath, spun her chair around, and clasped her hands together. "I'm not sure what else you expect us to do."

Blake was ready. "Set up a roadblock a few miles from the jail, stop these guys, and act surprised when we find explosives in the car. Several scenarios come to mind that would produce effective, legally acceptable results. The scenario being considered flies in the face of the law. It creates significant legal liability for us and gives the ACLU enough ammunition to set back law enforcement for generations."

"That's why we're lucky to have you on our team," Smith replied.

"Uh-huh," Hudson said, smelling the sulfuric odor of snake oil. He knew what Smith was thinking. They were wasting precious minutes debating a moot point. Someone already had placed the wiretap. Conversations were recorded. Brent Olson and Jake Reid were en route. The most pressing concerns for the group were in California, not in the revamped Justice Department attic.

"But you can't just stick your hand down the rabbit's hat and—*presto!*—problem solved. You just made up those scenarios; you haven't done your homework to measure their effectiveness. On the other hand, I've had the most time to evaluate the options, and I believe this is the safest. I'm confident the course we're taking provides—by a substantial margin, I should add—the least risk of casualties."

"Well," Blake argued, "I—"

"Let's take your example," Smith interrupted, determined to put the issue to bed. "Say we set up a roadblock. Makes sense, right? Set it up, surprise the enemy, and toss everyone in the paddy wagon. Isn't that the way it's done in the movies? But here's the problem: this *ain't* the movies."

"I'll take your word for it, John, but I'm not sure any of us knows what they'd do."

"I'll tell you what *I'd* do, and I'm not as brazen as a terrorist. I would try and bust through the roadblock, go around it, or turn around. Whatever their choice, they'd be running scared at a high rate of speed with a trunk full of explosives. We already know that these people will conduct suicidal bombings even when undetected. Do you think that'll change after they've been spotted . . . their capture imminent?"

"Well, I—"

"Not likely. And there may be others involved in this plot. What then?"

"We've exhausted this topic for now," Blake said, growing agitated by Smith's high-horse lecturing. "I'll take your advice and think more about the arguments you've presented."

Blake rose from his chair and walked out of the room. Leaving the door cracked, he stood still upon hearing Natasha's voice.

"He's really shaken up, John. Do you think he'll talk?"

"No," Smith sighed. "I wouldn't have let him go if I had any doubts."

———

Blake stood in the darkness of the eighth-floor hallway, staring through cobwebs and out the dusty window overlooking Pennsylvania Avenue. There wasn't a cloud in the sky, and he could see the heat emanating from the street as cars and pedestrians passed in and out of his line of sight. Beads of sweat percolated on his forehead as he analyzed the current situation. He could smell the pungent odor of WD-40 used to keep the antiquated machinery on the floor chugging along. The group's rash decision-making, he thought, had placed everyone in a sticky wicket. He was troubled by how long it took Smith to get him involved. Smith's band of brothers had already flown across the country and was now driving to its destination with approved operational plans. He didn't even know of Jihad Jenny Jacobs's involvement or that Natasha had set a wiretap. Before he knew anything, agents had prepared a FISA application, presented it to the FISA court, and *voila!* Application denied.

Blake was curious why Smith hadn't told him of the operation earlier. Did he know the FISA application would be denied? Is that why Blake was cut out of the loop?

What's more, if he wasn't needed earlier, when crucial legal decisions were being formulated, then why bring him in at the eleventh hour? And for that matter, he mused, why was he—a lawyer with scant experience in criminal law—even chosen to participate in the group? Little made sense at this point.

Wasn't Blake the point man, the liaison between John Smith and the rest of the team? If so, Smith had undermined his role. But that was small potatoes at this juncture. Was Smith simply a poor manager, acting haphazardly and fumbling around under herculean time restraints? Blake didn't know many people who worked for the CIA, so he refused to guess whether poor management was emblematic of the agency itself.

Hundreds of questions rushed through his mind, but he needed to focus on one: What now?

Options were limited; the hovering prospect of prison too frightening to contemplate. He realized his objections, even if argued with increased vigor, wouldn't affect the current assignment. The locomotive had left the station and was carrying two armed, trigger-happy commandos with a voracious appetite for action. That wasn't to say that a more forceful, if not a written, objection was not warranted. Such an approach might help to prevent future indefensible decisions. At the very least, it may prove beneficial in a future criminal investigation or trial. Maybe his own. Blake was struggling to determine just how much his opinion mattered within the group. He was also hindered by his limited experience dealing with the intelligence community. Was this business as usual for spies? Surely not.

He could run to Attorney General Kershing and seek clarification or even cry foul. He didn't know how much, if anything, the attorney general knew about Operation Scavenger Hunt. From all accounts, Gregg had kept the AG shielded. The more Blake thought about it, though, the more he was convinced that Kershing's fingerprints were all over this; that Blake's participation was just a front-seat reminder to the spooks that the mighty Department of Justice must play a role. That theory was consistent with Blake's perfunctory role and his being cut out of key decisions.

Talk of the attorney general being unaware of Scavenger Hunt was probably a lie, nothing more than prophylactic deception. Why tie a Cabinet-level official to illegal activities, especially in an election year? You had two willing scapegoats—Brent Olson and Jake Reid—who, if ever caught, wouldn't even be slapped on the wrist. Olson didn't exist, and Reid was, for all intents and purposes, a Mexican citizen. If things got bad, he'd be back at Cabo Wabo or El Squid Roe singing "Mas Tequila" while everyone else tried on orange jumpsuits.

No, Blake thought. Going to Kershing wasn't the answer. Not now.

There existed but one viable option at this point. As Blake walked back to the secure room, he knew he'd have to accept it, at least this *one* time.

He only hoped it wouldn't be one time too many.

20

When Blake reentered the SCIF, the assignment was underway. Smith was hunched over Natasha's chair like a defensive end ready to rush a quarterback; her back was as straight as a board. Video was up, audio down.

Blake stood behind Natasha where he had a clear view. A small video device was attached to either Jake Reid's or Brent Olson's shirt—he couldn't tell whose. He could see a large pizza box, and the person holding it was walking up a flight of stairs.

"Where are they?" Blake asked. "And who's carrying—"

"Shhhh," Smith hissed. "They arrived early," he said, not sparing a glance from the monitor's four corners.

Then Blake saw Brent walking in front of Jake, who was carrying the video transmitter. Brent was dressed in a white, short-sleeve, collared shirt; a pistol was nestled in the back of his black linen pants, the butt of the weapon positioned in the small of his back. Brent diverted from Reid's pathway and took cover on the second-floor breezeway of what appeared to be a low-budget motel.

———

Sacramento, California

The room number was 213. Jake nodded to Brent, who took his position. Jake shortened his steps, his destination two doors to his left. He surveyed the parking lot to his right, scanning for hoodlums and wondering where Smith's "clean-up crew" was hiding. It likely was monitoring Jake's every move. No matter. That was the least of his worries. He would have to trust Smith's crew to remain hidden until needed.

Noticing nothing suspicious in the parking lot, he took a deep breath and walked a few additional steps before turning toward the weathered-blue door marked 213.

A heavy, harvest gold-colored curtain hanging inside the room covered the window adjacent to the door. This made it difficult to gauge who was inside and what he, she, or they were doing. Jake took one final peek toward Brent.

Brent gave Jake a thumbs up.

No one was coming. The coast was clear.

Jake turned his attention back to room 213 and knocked on the door.

"Dave's Pizza Express!" he yelled.

And then he waited. His heart pounded, his armpits drenched.

There was no response.

Jake waited twenty seconds and then rapped on the door again. "Dave's Pizza Express! I've got an extra-large burning through my hands! Half pepperoni and mushroom, half supreme! Get it while it's hot!"

Jake almost stepped back as the curtain moved an inch. Luckily, his feet stayed planted. It could've been a fatal error. Any hint of timidity, any slight fidget, could cost him his life or doom the mission. His role was that of a disinterested, disgruntled pizza deliveryman, who, in his mid-forties, didn't care much about anything but handing off yet another pie to another stranger. He had almost blown his cover.

The curtain returned to its original position.

Still no response.

Jake peered at Brent, who just stared back at him. Jake then knocked on the door once again, this time without saying anything. Ten seconds later, a voice called out from inside the motel room.

"We didn't order a pizza! Sorry!"

Jake gleaned several things from the response. At least two people were inside, and one of them was an American male. The voice came from at least five feet from the door. That the room's inhabitants refused to open the door was probative, but not proof positive they were terrorists. People feared opening their motel room doors in high-crime areas. And for all Jake knew, the man inside could be hiding from his assistant's husband.

"I'm sorry, sir!" Jake exclaimed. "I didn't hear you! I've got your pizza here! Extra-large!" Silence.

This was a crucial period. Jake was at a crossroads. He could fall back and knock on the door to his right—room 215—feigning confusion. This would lend more credibility to his pizza-man charade but likely wouldn't extract the guests from room 213. Or he could remain persistent and grow more aggressive. If the terrorists were inside, they'd become impatient with a stubborn pizza deliveryman drawing attention to their room and may try to quell the distraction. With no more thought, he increased the pressure.

"Listen! I didn't hear what you said, but you owe me seventeen and change for this pie! I took this order myself, so I know this is the right room number! I don't appreciate—"

Jake stopped yelling when he heard the sound of a deadbolt unlock from inside. The door cracked open a few inches, chain-lock still attached. An American man stared back at him with cold, bloodshot eyes and a crew cut. Jake could feel the rush of frigid air and smell marijuana escaping the darkened room.

"I told you we didn't order no pizza. Here's twenty dollars for your troubles. You can keep the pizza or give it to someone else. Now, please, leave us alone."

Jake, trying to gaze inside the room, accepted the money, noting that the man had no tattoos or other identifying marks on his right hand or forearm. He did have grime underneath his fingernails, but so did others who stayed at roach motels.

"Sorry if I bothered you, mister."

Jake realized that, without further evidence, he and Brent would need to implement Plan B, which involved waiting in the van until someone emerged from the room. But that plan carried more risk and increased exposure.

Jake had never liked Plan B, so he decided to give Plan A another try.

"Appreciate the twenty bucks, man. Tough times, you know. Can't wait to get chewed out by the dude who ordered this pizza. *Sure* you don't want it? You paid for it."

The man shook his head and began to close the door.

Jake was despondent. The occupants in Room 213 were nothing but a bunch of potheads, it seemed. Before the door shut, though, he heard another voice.

And instantly made the connection.

Dropping the pizza box, he grabbed the suppressed firearm from his back. Before the doorkeeper could re-bolt the lock, Jake kicked open the door with all his might. The door flew off its rusty hinges and came crashing down on the doorkeeper, who was lifted off his feet from the impact. The .45-caliber Llama in the doorkeeper's left hand fell to the floor.

Aided by sunrays penetrating the doorway, Jake surveyed the room and leveled his gun. In addition to the doorkeeper, he saw one American and three men of Middle Eastern descent. All four were huddled together in shock, staring at the silencer at the end of his pistol's barrel. There was a rifle and two sawed-off shotguns on the bed. Those weapons were surrounded by an assortment of ammunition and at least five grenades. Before a word was uttered, one of the men raised what appeared to be a Glock 9mm and aimed it at Jake.

But the man never fired a shot. He was no match for Jake's quickness.

Thanks for the entertainment, Mr. Reid.

Jake's bullet was right on target, propelling the man's now limp body into the wall.

Another man rushed to the bed, toward the weapons cache. But the second shot from Jake's firearm hit its mark before the man could take two steps.

The other two darted away. One dove between the bed and the back wall; the other scampered to the bathroom. Jake noticed the doorkeeper's handgun had vanished, most likely carried off to the bathroom.

Jake heard a noise behind him. The doorkeeper had rebounded from his devastating crash and launched the door from his body.

Jake turned around, his homemade silencer leading the way. The doorkeeper, showing incredible quickness, already had jumped to his feet and lunged toward Jake. Jake fired another shot, this time at point-blank range. The doorkeeper's eyes stared into Neverland before he fell to his knees and curled to his side, departing the world in the same fetal position from which he'd entered.

Before he could turn around, Jake heard the remaining American nearest the bed engaging a shotgun shell in the chamber. He whirled around but, in that split second, knew it was too late. The American had risen from the side of the bed, grabbed one of the sawed-off shotguns, and had Jake dead to rights.

Jake had no play. Game over.

But then Jake heard a bullet zing past his ear. He saw the American's eyes go black. Jake then fired his own shot to neutralize any additional threat. The man's shotgun fell to the ground, and his body soon followed course.

Brent emerged from behind Jake. "That was close!" Brent exclaimed.

"There's one more in the bathroom. He's armed."

"Shotgun?"

"Pistol . . . I think."

"You think?"

"Too many guns in here, and I'm rusty."

"A few dead bodies beg to differ."

Jake pointed his gun toward the closed bathroom door. They had the man trapped. Brent hoisted the front door from the ground, leaned it against the doorframe, switched on the lights inside the room, and then turned back around toward Jake.

"Don't get too close to the bathroom door," Brent whispered.

Jake stood still, thinking about what to do next. Brent was right beside him, the two men flanking both sides of the door about fifteen feet away.

Before they could make a move, they flinched as the man holed up in the bathroom fired a shot. Surprisingly, there was no hole in the bathroom door. They stared at one another—confused—and then heard a pistol drop to the floor. Jake then moved closer to the door . . . still hesitant.

"Be careful," Brent warned. "Could be a trap."

Then they both witnessed it: blood oozing underneath the door, draining from the bathroom tile into the living-area carpet.

"Should've anticipated that. No honor in being captured," Jake said.

Jake pushed open the bathroom door. The man lay in a pool of his blood, eyes wide open, peering into space. "Dead," Jake said. "Classic self-execution. Barrel in the mouth, exit wound through the back of the—"

"Jake!" Brent exclaimed. "We're not out of the woods yet! We've got three suitcases full of explosives!"

Jake rushed from the bathroom to the bed. "Any set to timers?"

"I'll know in a few seconds!" Brent said, inspecting the large explosive devices hidden next to one of the dead bodies. "Keep your fingers crossed!"

Jake pointed to the dead American. "Our friend here didn't have much time to trigger a device, but I can't rule it out. He was next to that luggage for a few seconds."

"Jake . . ."

"Oh, no! Don't tell me!"

"I think we're okay," Brent concluded, looking back at Jake.

"Let's scoot. Cops will be here before long."

Jake and Brent didn't waste any time. As they hurried to their vehicle, they noticed a nondescript van idling in the parking lot. Several men and one woman exited the vehicle, marked ABC Custodial Service, and strode toward them.

The driver of the vehicle, a large man with milky eyes, a thick neck, and a black jump-suit approached Jake with purpose.

"You gentlemen done stayin' with us?"

"Yes, but we had some unexpected guests. They left the place a mess."

"How many garbage bags will we need?"

"Five. There's also some interesting luggage. I'm sure you'll be familiar with it. None of it needs immediate attention."

"The front door also flew off its hinges," Brent added.

"How many shots were fired?" the man asked, abandoning the cryptic dialogue.

"Six," Jake said.

"One stray round?"

"We shot one guy twice. All the rounds hit their targets. One suicide."

"Thanks for staying at the Sunset Motel, gentlemen. We'll take it from here."

"What about the police?" Brent inquired, thinking about the suicide shot in the bathroom. "One shot wasn't suppressed."

"We've already contacted our friends at SPD dispatch. We have fifteen minutes. Plenty of time."

"Great," Jake said. "And by the way, the pizza is yours if you want it. Bought and paid for."

Brent hopped in the driver's seat of their vehicle. As Jake climbed into the passenger seat, he took a deep breath. "Nice job, my friend. You saved my life."

"Not at all. You had the hard part. Impressive work. By the way, how'd you confirm that 213 was the right room?" Brent asked.

"Mostly luck. As the door was closing, one of them said something in Farsi. Remind me to thank John for the good intel when we reconnect the audio. The rest of the team probably saw everything. Looks like video is still up."

"I'm just glad we didn't need to switch to Plan B."

"Yeah, but I should've confirmed the room sooner. Still a little rusty."

"What do you mean?"

"They turned down the pizza."

"I still don't follow."

"Some normal dudes smoking pot at a roach motel and not looking for trouble would've never turned down a free extra-large pizza."

Washington, DC

Smith glanced at a dumbfounded Blake when the assignment ended. No one had said a word throughout the entire series of events.

"Well," Blake quipped, "I guess we don't have to worry about these arrests holding up in a court of law."

Without uttering another word, he dropped a folded-up note in front of Natasha on his way out of the SCIF.

21

The following evening, the windows facing the small backyard were open, and the cool night air and the charcoal smoke from the grill wafted inside. Blake, clad in worn blue jeans and a white T-shirt, was standing barefoot on the kitchen's linoleum floor. He was chopping cucumbers on the countertop, listening to the political debate being waged in the background on cable news. Judge was sprawled out nearby, his body swaying during each humongous breath, his tongue hanging out with contentment and anticipation.

After what had transpired, Natasha likely had been surprised when she'd read his note. But that was his intent. Blake needed to talk with her . . . alone. Asking her to dinner would provide him the opportunity to speak candidly about the clandestine group. The note made it clear that she didn't need to RSVP. And she hadn't. But Blake was betting on an acceptance. She was a spy, after all. How could a spy refuse such a cryptic invitation scribbled on a note dropped in her lap at an inopportune time?

In keeping with tradition, Judge barked and wagged his tail when the doorbell sounded. The bark was half-hearted, more the product of habit and excitement than concern.

"Get back, boy," Blake demanded as he approached the door, stopping to check his look in the mirror above the fireplace mantle. "Get back. Sit!"

Blake unlocked the deadbolt without unlatching the security chain and glanced through the spy hole. Judge was sitting behind him, waiting to catch a glimpse. Blake cracked the door open and peeked outside.

"Can I help you?" he asked with a straight face.

"Actually, you can," Natasha said without hesitation in a thick, Irish accent. "It's been thirty days since I got off the boat. I'm down to three shillings and in desperate need of some warm porridge to satisfy my palate."

"Go sell crazy somewhere else," he replied in a respectable Jack Nicholson imitation, closing the door to unlatch the security chain. When he reopened the door, the two chuckled at one another's antics. "Come on in. I didn't know you were Irish."

"Thanks," Natasha replied as she walked through the door. "I didn't know you were a Hollywood impersonator."

"You think I could afford this place on a government salary?"

"I should've known you were moonlighting. Sorry I'm a little late, but it was difficult finding a parking . . . oh my goodness!" she said, mesmerized by Judge who was sitting in front of her.

"Natasha Hensley, meet Judge Hudson. My pride and joy."

Judge, on his best behavior, remained seated, but his tail was wearing a hole in the rug. He couldn't restrain his excitement, needing physical contact.

"Blake, he's simply gorgeous!" she said, kneeling and opening her arms. "Come here, Judgy Wudgy."

Blake stood entranced in disbelief as Judge lunged forward and snuggled into Natasha's embrace. That she approached the enormous beast without hesitation spoke volumes. Not even the burliest of men ventured upon such bravery.

"Consider that a hero's welcome," Blake said. "He's not usually so accepting of first-time visitors. Then again, most first-timers are afraid of him."

"Nonsense," she replied, rubbing Judge's ears until his right hind leg started gyrating in spastic reflex. "He's incredible. And he smells like . . . vanilla extract?"

"He just had a b-a-t-h," Blake spelled out. "Best not to remind him."

Natasha stood up and smiled at Blake, who failed to smile back before she looked away. Once she turned her head, he grimaced, knowing that she'd caught him gawking. It was a weak moment, he thought, and she'd noticed. Not good. He would be lucky if he had any cards left in his hand after that gaffe.

Don't be such a sucker, Hudson!

Before he could recover, the phone rang. He walked toward the kitchen, not intending to answer it.

"Want me to get it?" Natasha asked.

"No, wait!" Blake shouted from the hallway, sticking his head back in the living area where Natasha was standing. "It may be General Leavitt from the Pentagon."

"Who?"

"Some flag officer who's pulling me into an issue that'll ruin my career. Sound familiar?"

"Sounds like we're all out to get you," she laughed.

"Good guy, but I'm not ready to talk to him. Let's go outside."

"What about the food?"

"We'll get it later," he said, slipping on his sandals.

Chevy Chase, MD

"It's me," the man with gnarly teeth said as he smashed out the remains of his Cuban cigar.

"Yes, sir," Peter Karnes said. "I wanted to apologize again for the way I treated you the other day. I was out of line. It will never happen again."

"All good. If we could turn the page now?"

"Please."

"Our team just completed its first mission, which I'm happy to report was a success."

"Okay."

"I need to brief you in person."

"Sure," Karnes responded skeptically.

"Check your schedule. Let's meet at the same place."

"Korean War Memorial?"

"Right."

Washington, DC

Looking down, Blake observed that Natasha had no problem scaling up the wooden ladder that led to the rooftop of his row house.

"You good?" he asked.

"Piece of cake. Glad I wore jeans and tennis shoes. This would've been tricky in a dress and heels."

"If I thought you'd wear a dress and heels to a cookout, I would've never invited you in the first place."

When Blake reached the roof, he walked the tray of steaks over to a plastic table placed in an area unexposed to the wind. He then set the table with old plates he'd purchased at a garage sale before his freshman year in college. He also laid down cloth napkins, his mother's hand-me-down silverware from her previous marriage, and champagne glasses. The bottle containing the convenience-store-quality sparkling wine was nestled in a silver bucket.

After taking meticulous care to position each item, he scampered back to the ladder to assist Natasha onto the roof, the worn and soggy shingles creaking underneath his feet with each step. As he grabbed the salad bowl from her with one hand, he simultaneously pulled her up with the other. Once she was safe on the roof, he released her hand and measured her reaction to the scenery.

"Wow, cowboy!" she said. "You outdid yourself. This is extraordinary. And look at that spread. Nice! Not too shabby for a Texan."

"Thanks. This view is amazing, especially at sunset. There's a fantastic glow over the Capitol. Look," Blake said, pointing west.

"You're right, Blake. It feels like the Capitol dome is sitting right on us; like we can reach out and touch it. And look at how the majestic white color of the dome is set against the sky of blue and orange. It looks like a digital painting."

Blake waited for her to sit down before opening the bottle and filling the two long-stemmed glasses. He then passed around his butter-drenched ribeye steaks.

"Blake, this looks really good. I'm impressed."

"I saw your order at Hard Times Café, so I figured you weren't vegan or vegetarian. The oversized mutt helped me cook the meat."

"I bet he did," she said smiling and then taking a drink.

"So," he said, changing the subject, "tell me about your career in espionage."

His seemingly innocuous statement about her career was, in reality, a probing question about her personal life. The espionage community had evolved over the recent past. Large-scale terrorist attacks had initiated rapid change in the way it operated. The least publicized change, however, was the new vanguard of spies. They were much younger because their targets were younger, especially in Eastern Europe. And they were more aggressive because the stakes and the rewards were higher. Taking these factors into account, the new age of cloak-and-dagger gave birth to spies willing to forego families for extended underground service and to engage in sexual promiscuity and moderate drug use to get closer to their targets. To the extent he had control over the matter, Blake didn't want to invest his time or emotions in an aggressive female spy.

"How do you define espionage?"

"Sure you're not a lawyer?"

"I'm not trying to parse words, but I want you to understand what I do."

"Just tell me," Blake said, cutting off a piece of his steak.

"I'm usually called in for a quick strike."

"Meaning?"

"Meaning tapping a phone or computer or heisting a medium of information."

"I thought there was more to it than that."

"Oh, I think I know where this is headed."

"What?"

"Hate to burst your bubble, but I don't use sex or engage in parlor tricks to get intel."

"Bygones," he said, raising his hands. "I didn't mean to ruffle feathers."

"Listen, Blake, I know you're upset about the wiretap and the last assignment."

"I'm not upset with you," he said. "You did what you were told to do. Nothing more. Let's just leave it at that."

"I want to talk about it. I share your concerns about what we're doing."

"All right. Should we talk about this out in the open?"

"What do you mean?"

"We're on the roof. It won't be hard for someone to capture what we're saying."

"NSA has bigger things to worry about."

"You're the expert."

"So talk to me, cowboy," she said before filling her mouth with salad smothered with Italian dressing.

"My concerns are obvious. We unleashed two trigger-happy G.I. Joes—whom I personally like, by the way—on a covert mission to arrest a handful of terrorists. They didn't have the authority to arrest any of them. Brent and Jake aren't even law enforcement. How could they be? They don't know anything about the law. Seems they don't respect the law. And why should they? They've never had to play by any meaningful rules."

"Well, Blake, to be fair—"

"And I'm not blaming you for this, Natasha, but there was a *clean-up crew* standing by at the Hotel California. *Clean . . . up . . . crew.*"

"Yes, I heard you the first time," she said smiling.

"I know, Ms. Moneypenny," he quipped, returning the smile, "but I just can't believe that I'm saying it. Excuse me for being naïve—I'm still hoping to wake up from this nightmare—but you don't send in a covert *clean-up crew* when the purpose of your assignment is to arrest a few guys. To cut to the chase, we both know that Brent, Jake, and what's-his-name knew these folks wouldn't turn themselves in. One need only look at the assignment plans to understand that their death was a *fait accompli.*"

"I don't think that's right. We always plan for the worst-case scenario," she said.

"Brent and Jake aren't FBI agents; they're not California state police; they're not city or municipal law enforcement. They have *zero* authority to make an arrest. But even now, we're jumping ahead of ourselves. Even if the FBI or another legit law enforcement agency was instructed to make the arrests, it doesn't matter. The wiretap that put us on those guys was illegal."

"It could've led to their arrest."

"Arrests certain to be tossed out of every courthouse in the country. And that's my point. This was all a ruse. Smith didn't send our guys to make arrests. He sent them to *neutralize* their targets. The same way Jake has neutralized foreign operatives for the last twenty years. And the same way Brent has neutralized insurgents ever since he graduated from college. I'm not accusing them of killing for sport, but they work from the same survival handbook. They take their cues from Chuck Norris, not Congress . . . certainly not the Supreme Court."

"The plan was to have FBI, through the local Joint Terrorism Task Force, make the arrest. The original plan envisioned the judge approving the FISA application and the wiretap producing fruit. The backup plan, implemented after the judge denied the FISA application, was to have Brent and Jake apprehend those guys and turn them over to military authorities. Had either plan worked as conceived, the terrorists would've landed in a court of law or military tribunal."

"With all due respect, that logic fails on many levels," Blake argued, polishing off his first glass of sparkling wine and reaching for the bottle, noticing that Natasha also needed a refill. "*First*, the judge didn't approve the wiretap. There were other legal alternatives available. We could've appealed the FISA ruling, for instance. That assumes that our arguments passed the laugh test."

"In hindsight they sure did."

"*Second*, the backup plan was illegal on its face. It's never been done, but lesser actions have been ruled improper. Any hope for judicial sympathy on that score was wishful thinking. At the very least, it was a reckless interpretation of separation of powers, giving the executive branch a veto on virtually any terrorist-related judicial decision. I've read some favorable state secrets decisions that—"

"You're being a dork," she said playfully, taking larger sips of champagne.

"What?" Blake chuckled.

"I feel like you're reading me a legal brief or arguing your case in court. You're being a huge dork."

"*Finally, Your Honor* . . ." Blake continued, acting like a clown.

"You make me laugh. Of course," she said before taking another large sip, "I shouldn't be laughing. I'm obviously in complete denial. And you're obviously headed that way."

"Wouldn't have mattered, but I regret not standing my ground. I was too caught up in the moment and Smith's rhetoric. Next time, I'll know better."

"You would've just dropped the matter altogether, then?"

"No, but . . ."

"But what?"

"I would sleep easier if we'd had a valid search warrant to account for the new residents of the Sacramento morgue."

"Well, me too."

SCAVENGER HUNT

"Can I just say something else? I don't want to ruin our dinner, but . . ."

"Sure," Natasha said, presenting her now-empty champagne glass to Blake for a refill. "Shoot."

"I have other concerns," he said, pouring sparkling wine into her glass and then his own. "I don't understand, for instance, why I'm even involved with Scavenger Hunt. I wasn't brought into this first assignment until the last minute, but I'm responsible for providing legal advice. To be clear, I'm not an expert on criminal matters. But you don't have to be Atticus Finch to discern that every facet of our first assignment was unlawful. Why bring me in at the last minute when I have nothing to add?"

"Because you're a good lawyer."

"But now I'm backed into a corner. This California assignment could cost Attorney General Kershing his job. I'm at a loss what to do, and I can't unsee what I saw. Do I tell Kershing and implicate him in this boondoggle? Or do I keep it secret, and hope this just goes away? I won't even mention how this affects *my* career. For now, that seems minor in the grand scheme of things."

"Blake, the attorney general doesn't have a need to know. You're not allowed to tell him. As I understand it, if you told him you'd be violating other laws."

"I'm waiting for the punch line, Natasha," he said. "Seriously, are you kidding me? Five people are dead. Four of them shot to death by our associates during an illegal assignment. And the fact that the AG doesn't have the need to know of a mission that directly involves DOJ is a joke."

Natasha didn't respond.

"It is what it is," Blake continued, "but that won't protect my boss if this gets out. And if I've learned one thing from living in DC, it's that *everything* gets out. Plain and simple. Beyond that, it's always the cover-up rather than the actual mistakes that brings you down."

"Good point, Nixon."

"This makes Watergate look like a white lie."

"Yepppp," Natasha said, staring at Blake with puckered lips.

"You're getting drunk."

"Yepppp."

"We're going to jail."

"Yepppp," she repeated as they broke out into delirious laughter.

"Look," Blake said, trying to be serious. "You did what Uncle Sam trained you to do. It's history, and we should thank our lucky stars that Saud is still detained. If he were to break free, I'm convinced—"

"Blake," she interrupted, polishing off yet another drink.

"Yeah?"

She put her finger to her puckered lips. "SSSHHHHHH."

Blake's heart once again started pounding as he stared at the gorgeous, green-eyed woman across the table.

Remember the rules, he reminded himself, *or this could get ugly . . . fast.*

22

The following day, multi-colored flags hanging from downtown buildings whirled and popped in the wind. Remnants of newspapers and candy bar wrappers whisked along the streets and sidewalks. With storm clouds squatting over the skyline, Uber and Lyft customers peppered almost every block of sidewalk.

One of those customers was a middle-aged administrative assistant who'd worked for the Federal Trade Commission for twenty years. She was escaping the commissioner's office for a late lunch with her new friend-with-benefits at a popular restaurant near the White House. Running ten minutes behind, she remained determined to keep her appointment. She had wasted most of her day neglecting her boss's phone to prep for this lunch, but there was more to do. She needed to mask her freckles and apply a coat of lipstick that matched her bright-red hair. The short car ride, she thought, would provide ample opportunity to make her adjustments.

As the metallic-blue Toyota Corolla approached, the woman stepped toward the street, careful not to buckle under her three-inch espadrilles. Impatient and perturbed, she held up her phone and flashed her red-polished fingernails as the vehicle stopped.

She noticed the brake-dust-pasted wheels before the passenger side window descended. "Sorry," the unshaven driver with hollow eyes said, but you'll need to find another Uber. My GPS is not working."

"I'm just going to Old Ebbitt Grill," she said, opening the door and climbing in the backseat. The smell of armpits and cheap cologne, absorbed into the cloth seats, filled the air like exhaust. "You have change for a twenty?"

The Uber driver didn't respond, befuddled by her question.

"Did you hear me? You have change for a twenty-dollar bill? I'll give you ten bucks. It's just a few blocks away."

"No," he said, frustrated that he'd stopped, "you will have to find another ride."

"I can find enough in here," she said, digging like a ferret in her fake Prada purse, which she'd purchased yesterday from a street vendor for today's lunch. Before leaving her house, she'd tossed in all of her necessities, including change, tissues, lipstick, her compact, a hairbrush, and a few Milk Duds. "You're not being very helpful," she said, her rebuke tapering off into a disgruntled whisper as she closed the door. She then raised her voice again. "Well, are we going to get there or not!?"

"I do not know where the place is you want to go!" the man replied in a thick accent, looking in his rearview mirror.

She looked up from her purse, noticed his serene face through the reflection, and huffed. "You don't know where Old Ebbitt is? It's one of the most popular restaurants in the city." He didn't respond, and she noticed his eyes had moved on to other cars driving on Pennsylvania Avenue. "Fifteenth Street. Take your next right and work your way down Constitution. I'll tell you where to turn when we get close."

She opened her compact and huffed again as the driver shook his head and drove off.

———

Rick Morales had missed five straight "free throws" from ten feet away, but he wasn't keeping count. He was too engrossed in his conversation with Blake to care. As the two spoke, he walked to and from the wastebasket located in the corner of Blake's office, tossing and then retrieving from the floor a wadded-up piece of paper, each time reshaping it to improve the accuracy of his next shot. Blake was ensconced in his chair with his feet on his desk, an atomic-blue Nerf football in his hands.

"Dude, I think Clarence is fitting in just fine," Rick said.

"Maybe so, but doesn't it strike you as odd that we never even had the chance to interview him?"

"Not really. You know how Michael is."

"I don't have a problem with the guy, Rick. I just find it strange that one day, he just shows up out of nowhere."

"Well, the Southern District of New York isn't nowhere. In fact, to New Yorkers, it's everywhere. For those wanting to cut their teeth on the best financial cases, prosecuting Wall Street is not a bad gig."

"Do I need to drop it, then?"

"Drop it. We have bigger fish to fry. And I'm not talking about a five-pound bass; I'm talking about blue whales."

SCAVENGER HUNT

"Not a fish."

"Octopus then."

"Still not a fish."

"Thousand-pound bass?"

"Brilliant."

As Rick exited the office, Blake heard the heavy rain pelting his window. His feet fell from his desk as he swirled his chair back toward his computer screen. He had forty-four unread emails.

He wadded up the cellophane wrapper that had once surrounded his lunch and tossed it in the wastebasket.

Two points!

———

"I didn't tell you to turn here," the red-headed woman bellowed, frustrated at the driver's inability to follow simple directions. "Why did you turn here!?"

"Get out!" the driver insisted.

"It's pouring down rain! What's your problem?"

"You! You are my problem!"

"I'm not getting out!"

"Suit yourself!"

"What's going on here? I'm already late! Why are you turning in front of the Department of Justice?"

The driver was no longer listening, maintaining a steady focus on the police cars parked across the street at the FBI building, delighted to see the mail truck bearing down behind him. He mashed his right foot on the accelerator as the nuisance in the backseat whined like a bloodhound with its ears tied together.

"You're going the wrong way!"

———

Blake exited his office and walked down the fifth-floor hallway. As he passed Amanda Gormon's office, he heard Rick complaining about the Congress. Unable to focus on work, Rick was in a chatty mood and strolled from office to office. Once Blake reached the water cooler, he bent over, placed the mouth of the bottle under the spigot, and was about to pull the blue lever.

But then it happened.

The explosion lifted Blake's body from the ground and thrust him into the concrete wall. The force had been fierce, the entire building had been rocked.

Moments later, Blake rubbed the back of his head and looked around. Surprisingly, there'd been little structural damage to his part of the building. He didn't know if other parts of the building were affected—if anyone was injured.

Then the silence ended. He could hear screams of despair coming from outside and then inside the building, like the sounds a baby makes moments after emerging from its mother's womb—first a growl, then waxing to a piercing shriek. He flinched as the fireproof doors at the end of the hallway slammed shut with a thunderous bang, the magnet that held them open having been neutralized.

Then he heard the programmed voice amplified over the loudspeakers in the corridor, speakers he didn't know existed until today.

ATTENTION! ATTENTION! AN EMERGENCY HAS BEEN REPORTED IN THE BUILDING! PLEASE CEASE OPERATIONS AND LEAVE THE BUILDING, USING THE NEAREST EXIT OR FIRE EXIT!

Blake gathered himself, stumbled to his feet, and ran to Amanda's office.

"You okay!?"

Amanda was against the back corner of her office, her hands covering her mouth. Rick was on the floor, stunned.

"What just happened!?" Amanda asked.

"We're under attack!" Rick screamed, jumping to his feet, grabbing Amanda by the arm, and pulling her away from the window.

Amanda was shaking, not knowing what to do or where to go.

A siren started wailing throughout the building, spreading pandemonium. Assistants ran helter-skelter for the exits, screaming indecipherably.

ATTENTION! ATTENTION! AN EMERGENCY HAS BEEN REPORTED IN THE BUILDING! PLEASE CEASE OPERATIONS AND LEAVE THE BUILDING, USING THE NEAREST EXIT OR FIRE EXIT!

"I don't know what to do!" Amanda yelled. "This may not be over! But if we go outside, there could be people waiting to . . ."

Amanda's fears reminded Blake of the concerns White House employees experienced after the attacks of September 11, 2001. They'd been instructed to evacuate the West Wing and the adjacent Eisenhower Executive Office Building before being cattle-driven to a park south of the buildings. Once corralled, however, they were told to disperse out of concern that they'd become easy targets.

"FBI is across the street!" Blake said. "Agents will come to our aid! We need to get out of here! Now! There's no telling what kind of damage was done to the lower floors!" Images of the collapsing World Trade Center towers flashed in his brain. "The whole building could come down!"

"I agree!" Rick said. "Let's get to the courtyard!"

As they passed the fire doors and approached the stairs, they witnessed colleagues falling or being pushed down the treacherous marble stairwell. Normally polite and dignified lawyers were trampling each other as they rushed to safety. It was everyone for himself, with the less aggressive curled into balls on the steps, too afraid to move.

"Come on!" Rick yelled. "Let's go! Let's go! Everyone outside! You can't just sit here! Keep moving!"

In just a few minutes, Blake, Amanda, and Rick filed out of the building into the Great Court.

"My goodness," Rick said, his throat sore and his voice faint. "Look at that sight."

Through the billowing smoke, they observed that the explosion had destroyed much of the first two floors facing Pennsylvania Avenue. If that weren't enough, there was a gaping hole allowing people inside the courtyard to see outside the building.

And the bodies.

"Amanda, don't look!" Blake instructed. "You need to stay in the courtyard and look away."

"Oh, my!" Rick gasped.

The torrential downpour was unyielding, and the sounds of thunder and cries of agony filled the air. The three of them huddled together, drenched with rain, waiting for someone to come and get them . . . and explain what had just happened.

But no one was coming.

Blake and Rick sprinted to the front of the building, where the explosion had inflicted the brunt of the damage, sidestepping people without any hope of survival. Hudson knelt beside a now-disfigured woman and screamed, "We need an ambulance!"

Blake witnessed the maimed bodies that lay dead under the rubble of what remained of the building. Other victims were screaming. Many of them were in dire need of immediate medical attention. Many were stomping around in the rain like zombies, mumbling curse words and indecipherable questions.

He could hear the sounds of blown radiators from the three car wrecks that occurred after the explosion. Bloodstained windshields and motionless figures evidenced that two of the drivers had reached their final destination. He saw that Amanda failed to follow his advice and now, in shock, was walking around in circles trying to figure out where she should go, whom she could help.

There appeared to be three general groups of people: those huddling across the street in fear, those rushing to help victims, and the victims themselves—some breathing, others not.

The heavy rain had no effect on the two fires that engulfed much of the Pennsylvania side of the building. Blake noticed the burning frames of what once was a four-door sedan and a mail truck, both buried into the building, both covered with its remains. An American flag being consumed by flames had fallen nearby. There were two toppled crash barricades, the dirt that had weighted them down turning to mud. Justice security guards had positioned the barricades—nothing more than oversized, fortified flowerpots—around the building to prevent such an event from happening. But somehow the sedan had plowed through before making its way to its ultimate target. The mail truck had followed course. As the wailing emergency vehicles and the chopping helicopters echoed in the distance, FBI agents sprinted across the street to help manage the unspeakable chaos.

Blake continued to petition for an ambulance, even though a part of him realized that his pleas were unnecessary. Emergency vehicles were coming.

"Blake!" Rick yelled, tearing off his shirt to use as a tourniquet for a man with a gaping wound to his leg. "Be careful when the ambulances and fire trucks arrive!"

"Roger that!" Blake said, thankful for the reminder. Terrorists knew hordes of people amassed around tragedies. They knew that emergency vehicles would arrive to help the injured and carry off the dead. It provided a golden opportunity for a suicide bomber to drive up in an ambulance or other emergency vehicle full of explosives or biological weapons and inject into the scene an extra dose of horror.

Members from the FBI's bomb squad ran past Blake and the assembly of the wounded to the point of detonation. They made no attempt to assuage the victims. Blake knew that wasn't their job. They had two primary tasks—make sure there were no more bombs and secure the area.

Amanda was still ambling from one body to another. She settled over a woman sprawled out on the sidewalk who was soliciting help. Amanda knelt down, grabbed her hand, and tried her best to console the lady.

Blake walked toward Amanda, knelt down beside her, and continued to process the scene unfolding around him. Though he'd heard the sounds of emergency vehicles his entire life—and, indeed, every day since moving to Washington, DC—he'd never experienced a situation where they were coming to *him*.

Amanda flinched and then focused her attention back on the victim beside her when she felt the woman's grip loosen. "Ma'am! Ma'am! You're going to be okay! Just stay with me! Keep your eyes open!"

Noticing the extent of the woman's injuries, Blake turned his head. There was nothing he or Amanda could do. Even with the best medical care, survival was out of the question.

It didn't take a doctor to make that macabre diagnosis. She would die right here, holding Amanda's hand. The woman struggled to breathe. The sight of her blood, draining with the rainwater across the sidewalk into the grass, had lost its shock value. Her nervous system had shut down; all feeling of physical pain . . . gone. Her time on earth was coming to an end.

"What's your name?" Amanda asked in a whisper. She was squeezing the woman's hand like a vice-grip.

"Mary. . . . Mary Thomas."

"Mary," Amanda said, trying to provide hope, "the medical team will be here . . ." She couldn't complete her sentence, fighting back a vicious onslaught of tears. Blake put a hand on his colleague's shoulder. Amanda covered her face with her free hand, trying to hide her shame for failing to appear strong in front of the dying woman.

"It's okay," the woman said, turning to look into Amanda's eyes. "I know I'm going to die."

"You're not going to die," Amanda said, trying to convince herself more than the woman, grasping with both hands the woman's left arm.

The woman moaned and tried to capture the strength to continue talking. Only a few grains of sand remained. "When this is over, please find my daughter. Her name is Audrey Thomas. She is only nine years old. We exchanged some harsh words this morning when I dropped her off at school. She's in the third grade." The woman stopped talking and smiled, but then her smile morphed into an expression of serious concern. "She's going to be scared. We live alone. When you see her, whenever you meet her, please tell her that I'm sorry I yelled at her . . . I'm sorry I wasn't there to pick her up at school today . . . and that I love her . . . that I love her very much."

Amanda waited for more, but there would be no more. The woman's eyes went blank. She had uttered her last words.

"Who did this!?" Amanda screamed at the top of her lungs, placing both hands on the top of her head, rising to her feet. Stunned and realizing she should've heeded Blake's instructions to remain in the courtyard, she stormed off.

Just then, three fire trucks and two ambulances arrived on the scene within seconds of one another. Before the vehicles stopped, emergency workers and medics leaped onto the soggy, puddle-soaked ground and rushed to distinguish the salvageable from those with no hope.

Rick jogged to Blake and stood with him to survey the wreckage. "This is a nightmare," Rick said.

"The most horrible thing I've ever witnessed," Blake said, eyeing the rescuers, making sure that no one looked suspicious.

"What's Amanda doing out here?"

"She just had a bad experience with one of the victims," Blake said as he and Rick walked toward her.

"Amanda, you shouldn't be out here. We asked you to—"

Rick stopped in his tracks before grabbing Amanda's shoulder. She was on her knees in the grass, swaying back and forth in grief, hemorrhaging sorrow, hovering over one of the many victims. Neither Blake nor Rick could say a word. They just stared in disbelief, not able to take their eyes off the body of Chief of Staff Michael Gregg.

23

Chevy Chase, MD

"I assume you were planning to call me soon. Tell me if my understanding is incorrect," the man said through heavy breaths over the phone.

"I'm sorry," John Smith replied. "It's been a rough two days. I'm trying to get my footing over here."

"Do you think al Thoorah learned where your team is working?"

"No. I've ruled out Sacramento as its motivation. That was a clean operation. Al Thoorah doesn't know we exist."

"Their attack on Main Justice was just a coincidence?"

"It's not a coincidence at all. Main Justice always has been a terrorist target for multiple reasons. It's where the high-level counterterrorism lawyers work. The attorney general works there, along with other officials who jailed and will prosecute Saud. The building is a symbol of American justice."

"Your orders were to stop al Thoorah attacks, and al Thoorah just attacked the building where your team meets, a building you're telling me was a top target for terrorists. I can't think of a more disappointing showing."

"I'll re-examine our intelligence, but I'm not in charge of DOJ security guards or flowerpot positioning."

"Is it true that the department's chief of staff was one of the casualties?"

"Yeah, he was attending a meeting in a room on the first floor that faces Pennsylvania. Everyone in that room died."

"Is that going to pose any problems?"

"It shouldn't. He'd long since served his purpose."

"And your team?"

"Blake Hudson's been a problem, but I think he'll come around. I wasn't expecting so much pushback, but he's still preferable to a seasoned bureaucrat looking over my shoulder."

"Should he be removed from the operation?"

"No, we need a lawyer for cover, and most lawyers are high maintenance. I'll manage him. He's just a kid with a high-ranking position trying to play Honest Abe."

"Having to deal with snot-nosed punks seems to be our lot in life. Is he providing aggressive legal advice?"

Without thinking, Smith chuckled out loud.

The heavy-breathing man bit into his cigar. "Do you think this is *funny*?"

"No, but if you think we're doing things by the book—"

"How about this? How about you laugh when you learn how to do your job? I like to laugh. I like to be happy. But right now, I'm stranded on the North Pole, and happy is on the other side of the world. Do you understand me?"

"Yes."

"Yes, what?"

"Yes, sir," Smith said, swallowing his pride. "I hear you loud and clear."

"What do I tell my client when he calls? I want you to pay close attention to me. I don't care about you. You mean *nothing* to me. I've dealt with people much more important than you in the past. I *own* you. Do you understand me?"

"Yes, sir." Smith's response was hesitant but certain.

"If you embarrass me again, it will be the last time. For your sake, you better dial this in and get your act together. We wouldn't want certain things to be made public, would we?"

"No, sir. We would not want that to happen."

"Back to Hudson. I understand that you need to bend the rules—that's why the group was formed—but the operation needs to appear legit. If Hudson adds no value or proves to be a blithering idiot, then let's take him out and add someone else."

"To be clear, the problem with Hudson is *not* that he's an idiot; it's that he's smarter than we anticipated. He's light-years beyond his age and experience, and he doesn't even know it. I've never met anyone like him."

"I'd rather have a useful idiot. John, listen to me carefully. We cannot—I repeat, *cannot*—tolerate any mistakes on this one. If something goes wrong, the clean-up would be nasty . . . even for my taste. And if Hudson goes rogue, I'm holding you accountable."

"I'll watch him closely. Terrorists just blew up his backyard and killed his colleagues. He's not going rogue anytime soon."

SCAVENGER HUNT

Washington, DC

"Nice of you to join us, Ms. Hensley," Smith said, looking at his watch like an impatient professor.

"Is it safe for us to be here?" Natasha asked as she walked into the SCIF. "There's a crater in the building the size of the Jefferson Memorial."

"The structure of the building is sound," Smith said as he removed his reading glasses and closed the classified folder. "Take a seat."

"Blake," Natasha said as she sat down, "are you okay?"

Hudson nodded.

"How many people were injured?"

"Twenty-nine dead, forty-four injured," he mumbled.

"I'm so sorry," she said, shaking her head in disbelief. She struggled to formulate her next question. "Did you . . . were any of the people who . . ."

"Our chief of staff, Michael Gregg, is one of the twenty-nine," Blake said.

She placed her hand on his arm. "Not sure what to say."

Blake shrugged his shoulders. "Nothing you need to say. Not your fault."

Smith shoved the classified folder to the middle of the table. "I hope everyone at this table understands that we must redouble our efforts. The Department of Homeland Security isn't the answer. The FBI, the DNI, and the NCTC aren't the answer. As good as they are, the Joint Terrorism Task Forces aren't the answer. And, as we all know, state and local law enforcement can't stop this onslaught of terror. There are too many bureaucratic hurdles, too many people worried about legal ramifications to protect us from the threats we face."

"To that point," Jake said, "I was thinking that—"

"I wasn't finished, Jake," Smith interrupted.

Jake's furrowed brow betrayed his feelings for Smith's boorish behavior. Blake too had grounds for objection. He knew—everyone in the room *had* to know—that Smith had aimed that powerful *legal ramifications* upper-cut at him. But like Jake, Blake knew that returning a punch after one snide remark wasn't worth the energy. Smith was upset, and Smith's boss, Blake speculated, probably bit his head off for allowing the Main Justice attack. But who was Smith's boss? Was it really the CIA director as he'd mentioned?

"We must be more proactive. This team was created to stop al Thoorah, and we're the last line of defense. Existing agencies can't collect information fast enough, can't assemble fast enough, and can't react fast enough. Though DHS has demonstrated improvement in recent years, the CIA still doesn't want to share intel with DOJ. FBI doesn't want to share it with state and locals, et cetera."

Blake scooted his chair back and stood up.

"You goin' somewhere, Hudson?" Smith asked, irritated by the interruption.

"I haven't slept in two days, John, and my legs are killing me." There was a palpable tension in the room as the two men stared at one another. "I'm listening to you," he added, no longer willing to hold back punches, "but I'm not in kindergarten, so get off my back."

Blake no longer cared what Smith thought of him. Smith's rhetoric was nauseating, especially when blended with the ripe smell of carnage several floors beneath them. Not only had Blake barely escaped the attack, but also he'd witnessed the dead and mutilated bodies of his co-workers. For everyone else in the room, disaster, chaos, and death were familiar foes. But not for him. If the onery CIA spook was girding for battle with him, then Smith better be loaded for bear.

"To be more proactive," Smith continued, ignoring Blake's machismo, "I want us to start meeting here every morning at seven o'clock. I'll brief you on the daily threat reports, and we'll devise ways to gather our own intelligence."

"What about planning our own assignments?" Brent asked.

"We'll do whatever's necessary—everything in our power, domestic and abroad, to snuff out and take down these fanatical killers." He focused his attention on Blake. "Counselor, you got a problem with that?"

Blake refused to answer, his temples pulsating.

"The information here," Smith said, patting the classified folder, "prepared after the attack, is an interesting read. I want each of you, beginning with Natasha, to look through it."

"I don't need to read it," she said, pushing the folder toward Brent, her eyes beginning to water.

Everyone but Smith seemed confused at her reaction. "Natasha," Smith said, "I've seen that look on too many analysts' faces in the past. I will *not* accept it here . . . *not* now."

"That's easy for you to say, John!"

"I'm the one in charge here. I take personal responsibility for everyone's actions. If I thought you'd screwed up, I'd tell you. Now, shake it off!" he said, his voice escalating with each sentence.

"What's going on here, Natasha?" Blake asked.

"Correct me if I'm wrong, John, but that folder likely contains reports that draw conclusions about the attack on this building." She turned and looked at Blake. "When you read it, you'll see that we—that *I*—should have anticipated the attack. I should've known it was coming."

SCAVENGER HUNT

"Come on, Natasha," Blake said. "John just said that the reports were prepared *after* the attacks. Hindsight is 20/20."

"You're right," she said, her voice quivering, "the *reports* were created after the attacks. The raw intelligence used to create those reports, however, was available in advance. I read the raw intel several days before the attack that killed your friends."

"Natasha, I read the same intel," Smith said. "I didn't put the pieces of the puzzle together either. There wasn't enough there. No time, no place, no identities. Blake is right. You can't punish or blame yourself."

"You're wrong! I knew what happened once I learned of the attack," she replied. "I remembered the conversations between Omar Saud's two cousins, who spoke of 'blowing up the infidels' lawyers.'" We should've taken out those al Thoorah thugs before—"

"We still don't even know their *names*!" Smith said. "Saud's cousins are somewhere in Yemen. We have no intelligence that shows *any* communications between them and sleeper cells in the United States. Let's be realistic here; use some common sense. For all your talent, you're not Nostradamus. No matter how prescient you strive to be, there was little you could've done with the information we had."

"Wrong again. I could've put the Main Justice guards on alert."

"Guess what? Someone already had. Washington, DC has been on heightened alert for over a year. Main Justice has always been high on the list of potential targets. These guards have heard their government cry wolf countless times. Believe me, they weren't going to do another Kabuki dance. What could they have done? Erected a concrete wall around the Justice Department? Not gonna happen. It's not your fault. There's nothing that you could've done to prevent the attack. Nothing."

"We should've gone after Saud's cousins long ago."

"That's my fault, not yours. And by the way, that's the perfect segue," Smith said. "Brent and Jake, you'll need to pack your bags. You're leaving for Yemen first thing tomorrow. Your objective is to capture Saud's two cousins and render them to an outpost on Socotra Island in the Arabian Sea."

They both nodded.

"Blake and Natasha, take the weekend off. Get some rest. We'll meet here first thing Monday morning."

"Michael Gregg's funeral will be sometime next week in California," Blake said. "They haven't set a date yet."

"Come back when you're ready. Jake and Brent will need a few days to travel and prepare for the next mission. Meanwhile, I may need help tweaking the plans, but it's more important that you and Natasha get prepared mentally for what lies ahead."

Of all the questions Blake had concerning Operation Scavenger Hunt, clarity of mission would no longer be one of them. After the latest attack, Smith would pursue al Thoorah's leaders with reckless abandon in an attempt to shut down their network. And although the nature of the group and its tactics still raised a host of legal problems, Blake was less concerned about missions conducted overseas. That said, if someone or some group ever captured Brent or Jake—overseas or otherwise—then chaos would ensue. Blake decided to worry about that later.

"Let's pray that our federal government does its job in the coming days," Smith continued. "With Independence Day approaching, there'll be an increase in chatter and threat warnings."

"When do you expect we'll be ready?" Brent asked.

"We'll be up and running again on the Fourth of July," Smith said. "It's time we reversed the tables and gave al Thoorah a dose of its own medicine. I'm talking about a lightning strike. We're gonna give them a little Independence Day surprise on their home turf."

"Great," Jake replied. "Bolt from the blue!"

"Until next time," Smith said, signaling the end of the meeting. "Natasha?"

"Yes?" she said, as she gathered her things.

"Stay behind. I need to talk to you for a minute . . . alone."

———————

"Are you going to be alright?" Smith asked her after the others had exited the SCIF. "I know how you're feeling; been there myself countless times."

"I'll shake it off. I'm more embarrassed than upset. Let my emotions get the best of me."

"We're all human."

"I'm learning that the hard way."

"Listen, there's something I want you to do for me on Monday. I think you'll find this assignment fulfilling."

"Sure. What's up?"

"Before we get to that, you must know that it carries a lot of risk. And you'll have to go this one alone."

"I'm all ears."

"You'll need more than that."

24

San Diego, California

After Michael Gregg's funeral, proven to be as difficult an event as expected, the wheels of the FBI's Gulfstream V, or G-5, jet lifted off the ground at the same time Blake's head sunk into the leather seat. Kershing was seated across from him, reading a newspaper.

Blake gazed at the sunset until cumulous clouds blanketed his oval window like thick cotton. He then focused his attention on the back of the plane where Rick and Amanda had fallen asleep. *Lucky dogs*, he thought. Kershing had requested that Blake sit next to him on the return flight, and the attorney general didn't nap.

Kershing's armpits, Blake noticed, were drenched with sweat, but every gray hair on his head remained dry. He revealed his beleaguered face as he lowered the newspaper. "It's going to be tough, you know, running the office without Michael," he said.

"I suspect so."

"He was a good man," Kershing said, looking out his window, the mutinous tears working in his eyes trying to infect and betray his steely veneer.

Kershing grabbed another section of *The Los Angeles Times* from the unoccupied seat beside him and scanned its contents, once again shielding his face from Blake's view.

"General, I didn't know him well."

Kershing dropped the newspaper in his lap. "The guy had a gift for organization and an incredible mind. And he was a great father and husband. Good man, all around."

"How did you two meet?"

"I hired him when I was at the White House. Needed an experienced lawyer to help me implement the president's agenda. Michael was the most qualified applicant. He had graduated from Harvard Law School; editor of the law review. But I was struck by his candor and self-confidence.

"So you hired him?"

"Hired him hours after his interview. He worked out great. Saved my butt lots of times. Someone like that is . . ."

Kershing didn't finish. He shook his head and continued looking out the window. The plane ascended above the clouds, revealing a universe of baby blue.

"We're all sorry that Michael is gone, General."

"Maybe we should change the subject. My blood pressure is starting to rise. Or maybe my blood is just starting to boil. Can't tell which. I'm ready to kill something . . . or somebody."

Blake understood but didn't respond.

"I shouldn't say things like that," Kershing continued. "How are you holding up?"

"I'm doing fine . . . considering," Blake said. He thought hard before continuing. "I've been working on that *project*."

"The detainee issue with Frank Leavitt? Don't let those generals push you around. They're all egotists. Eye of the tiger."

"It's actually the *other* project."

There was no response. Kershing once again was looking out the window.

Blake elaborated. "It's a project that . . . that Michael told me was important . . . very secretive."

"How's it going?" Kershing asked.

"I have many concerns with it."

Kershing finally looked at him. "Blake, I trust your judgment, and I'll need you to take up the slack now that Michael's gone. Especially until I hire or promote someone for the chief of staff position."

After an uncomfortable pause, Blake said, "Yes, sir," closed his eyes, and wondered whether Kershing had any idea about Operation Scavenger Hunt.

Washington, DC

Peter Karnes—heretofore a snot-nosed punk—sat on a stone bench at the Korean War Memorial staring at the ghastly faces of the nineteen soldiers, each one over seven feet tall. The stainless-steel soldiers, he thought, knew nothing of the recent bombing downtown. They hadn't heard the emergency vehicles whining from the streets behind them. They were stuck in another perilous place and time. Karnes, on the other hand, was stuck in the here and now. And it was proving equally dangerous.

His disgruntled contact—the man who called himself Parker Johnson—was thirty minutes late.

The young man stared at the Pool of Remembrance, constructed of the finest of Canadian black granite. He remembered the happy times, like the night he proposed to his beautiful girlfriend-cum-fiancée. He wished he could be transported back in time to that moment.

But time moved in one direction, and for Peter Karnes, it was the wrong direction. He had grown more worried about his fiancée in recent days. She was all that mattered. He had to protect her. He was responsible for two people now.

Not a tree leaf danced, and the searing sun penetrated his clothing. His red and white necktie was choking him as his starched shirt irritated his skin. Dehydrated and hungry, he longed to go home to South Carolina. Anywhere out of Dodge. He wanted to forget that he'd ever set foot in the nation's capital. There was something wrong with this place. Something evil.

He wished he'd never become wrapped up in this. Any of this. He should've quit the executive branch or tried to convince his boss to pursue an alternate course. He could've proposed that someone else do the dirty work. But he didn't. And now he'd have to live with the consequences.

He regretted being disrespectful to Parker Johnson. Everyone was under so much pressure, and he'd crossed the line. His reckless hubris had bested him. His heavy-breathing, cigar-smoking contact had hung up on him. Karnes had gone to his boss, who had instructed him in no uncertain terms *never* to be disrespectful to Mr. Johnson again.

But now enough was enough. Main Justice had been attacked. Karnes was in over his head.

People in authority had hatched Operation Scavenger Hunt with good intentions. But something about the operation had always alarmed him. With this freak Johnson calling the shots—someone no longer in government—it was impossible to control.

Karnes realized that people would blame him if something went wrong. After all the service he'd invested in this country, his life would be ruined. And so would his family's. The anxiety had become so acute that Karnes had discussed the operation several times with his fiancée. In doing so, he'd unlawfully revealed highly classified information, but it had been well worth it. She had convinced him to do the right thing. Her compass was rightly calibrated.

Consequences notwithstanding, he would go to the FBI and report his involvement in the operation. It was time to come clean before things really got out of hand. The alternative would prove much worse, he thought. He was scared to death of going to jail.

But as he reflected on this saga, another thought popped into his head. A more frightening consideration. He found himself staring at one of the stainless-steel soldiers, the one with a horrified look on his face. Had Johnson and his henchmen learned about his unsanctioned conversations? Had they wired Karnes's house? Is that why Johnson was a no-show today? Meditating on those questions caused him to shiver.

Karnes stood up and began walking from the Korean War Memorial. When he spotted his parked car, his walk turned into a jog and then into a full sprint. He had to get out of town—*fast*.

25

The next night, Blake sat under the stars with Rick, Amanda, and thousands of others on the United States Capitol grounds, watching and listening to the tenor sing Franz Schubert's version of "Ave Maria." Songs with a religious flavor—presented in a foreign language or not—weren't easily digested at public events. But tonight, Mother Mary was on display, front and center, and even the most zealous of atheists, agnostics, nominal Christians, and Kool-Aid drinkers didn't seem to mind. The fear of terrorism had heated up the melting pot and forced the diverse populace to coalesce in the same broth.

Ave Maria . . . Gratia plena . . . Maria, gratia plena . . . Maria, gratia plena . . . Ave, ave dominus . . .

US Coast Guard helicopters hovered over the city, their searchlights exposing otherwise dark neighborhoods adjacent to the Fourth of July festivities. Sirens from emergency vehicles howled in the distance during the softer notes in the song. The intense fear, pain, and chaos were palpable within the crowd.

. . . Ave Maria . . . Ave Maria . . . Mater Dei . . . Ora pro nobis peccatoribus . . . Ora pro nobis . . .

And then, as "Ave Maria" came to a close, the final chorus being stretched as far as it could, Blake checked his watch. It was 4:45 a.m. tomorrow in the Arabian Peninsula. Thirty minutes before sunrise.

. . . Et in hora mortis nostrae . . . Et in hora mortis nostrae . . . Ave Maria.

When the tenor stopped singing, the searchlights dimmed, and the helicopters moved out of the area.

And the fireworks show began.

The first wave of fireworks included simple, stand-alone streamers. Launched in sporadic succession, each one ascended high into the sky before blasting into a falling shower of light—green, then blue, then red. The Washington Monument was set aglow by a kaleidoscope of bright colors. Once "Ave Maria" ended, the thousands of onlookers began to sing along to "God Bless America," this time well-versed in the words.

————————

Sana'a, Yemen

Brent Olson and Jake Reid were dressed in black Kevlar bodysuits and wearing bulletproof helmets. Their electro-optical surveillance goggles assisted their navigation through the light foliage, guiding them to their targets. Two other men accompanied them. One was leading the way, the other walking in tow and occasionally turning around to survey the area behind the group. All members of the makeshift unit were brandishing firearms.

They didn't have much time. The early-rising sun would soon awaken.

Once he recognized the surroundings, Brent charged ahead, taking the lead and setting a rigorous pace. He directed his team to the shanty depicted in the photographs they'd all reviewed. Fifty yards away, he held up his hand. The others stopped in their tracks on cue. After signaling coast clear, Brent charged ahead with Jake. The others stayed behind to provide cover.

Brent took position underneath the front window, crouching down to avoid detection. Jake darted to the front door, awaiting Brent's orders. Brent rose and peered through the uncovered window. He then crouched back down and turned a knob on his surveillance goggles before attempting to sneak another look.

Night vision off.

What he saw inside surprised him. One of their targets and two accomplices were sitting at a round table, playing cards. A dim light hung over them. Brent noticed the many empty bottles of cheap liquor. The team's job would be easier than expected. He then made a *V* with his fingers and pointed it toward his eyes, signaling Jake to take a peek. Jake moved with stealth to the window, turned off his night vision, and looked inside the house. Without a word or additional signal, the two made their way to the front door. Then they turned the knob on their surveillance goggles.

Night vision back on.

————————

Washington, DC

The next wave of fireworks was more intense. Several fuses ignited at once. One after another, the rockets launched into the dark and vast atmosphere before exploding and lighting up the sky as they cascaded down into a plume of majestic beauty.

Blake wrapped his arms around his colleagues, who sang at the top of their lungs. He then forced a smile, trying to enjoy the visual and auditory grandeur and attempting to block out concerns of what was happening thousands of miles away.

The NSA had intercepted communications from Omar Saud's known primary cousins. It was clear that al Thoorah was planning attacks on America from within Yemen. The CIA had located them in Sana'a and learned from informants that they'd taken control of Saud's terrorist network. The CIA, in turn, apprised trusted Yemeni officials of the situation, and the Yemini president sent a personal note to President Clements, making it clear that he'd do everything in his power to capture and detain Saud's men. But that note never reached the president of the United States. In fact, the president didn't even know about Saud's cousins or their presence in the country. John Smith had made sure of that.

Smith was no longer interested in diplomatic channels or international cooperation. He wasn't going to be a party to any deal. He had called in some high-level favors and plucked the president's communiqué right from the golden satchel.

There would be no safe haven for Saud's men.

Sana'a, Yemen

Jake busted the lock on the front door. He and Brent charged inside the house. A loud blast from Jake's M4 carbine extinguished the light above the table where the targets were seated.

"Be still and remain calm!" Jake demanded in Farsi, seeing three men illuminated in green through his goggles. The two men facing him had their hands in the air, trying to decide whether to run, attack, or surrender. The man seated at the table had his back turned to Jake and Brent and remained motionless. "We're not here to harm anyone! Put your hands on the table!"

Sharp pleas by Jake fell on deaf and drunken ears. One of the standing green men reached for his sidearm. But he was too slow. Before he could draw his weapon, another shot from Jake's assault rifle decreased the world's population by one.

Without hesitation, and with his weapon's nozzle leading the way, Brent inched toward the man sitting at the table. Trying to limit the number of casualties, Brent hoped to obtain a hostage. But when the man at the table sensed someone approaching him from behind, he made a move.

It would prove to be his last.

His attempt at retaliation in the dark was made in vain. Before he could lunge for the shotgun resting at his feet, Brent made sure only one live target remained.

The remaining man stood in shock in the darkness. His fear was evident even through the electro-optic lens.

"We don't want to hurt you!" Jake said, hoping that he and Brent could avoid yet another casualty.

The man screamed, ostensibly in fear but actually to warn others in the house. Thereafter, a woman rushed from the bedroom and made her way to the back door. Then a small child appeared. Before Brent and Jake noticed him, the child turned on the overhead lights to the living room.

Brent and Jake discarded their surveillance goggles and stood still. They hadn't expected this, and they had no idea what to do next.

Washington, DC

And the last wave. The climax. Technicians launched fireworks like ballistic missiles in an all-out war, filling the sky with sizzling color.

People on the Capitol grounds jumped in the air and screamed—some in unison with the song, others just bellowing random noises and indecipherable words. Blake, Amanda, and Rick stood up and held one another like there was no tomorrow. Their throats were hoarse; their shirts wet with perspiration.

Blake was becoming dizzy worrying about the Yemen operation. Everything was on the line. He tried not to fret over what would happen if the mission went awry, if Brent or Jake were captured. Their safety aside, it would be a diplomatic nightmare. Everyone in the group would be exposed. Muslim nations would drop all support for America.

The stakes had never been higher.

Sana'a, Yemen

The child was eerily calm. He didn't need to speak. The semi-automatic weapon in his hands said it all. The weapon was leveled at Jake, the child's hands as still as a cornered possum.

Jake dropped his M4 at the same time Brent raised his rifle, aiming it at the child's head.

"If you move," Brent said to the man whose back was against the wall, "the kid dies."

SCAVENGER HUNT

"Drop the gun," Jake directed, moving the palms of his hands up and down. "I dropped my gun," he continued, pointing at his weapon on the floor. "You can drop yours. No one will be hurt."

But the child was resolute. He stared at Jake with his wiry eyes and bushy hair. The predicament had turned dire. The woman who'd escaped from the house would assemble a sympathetic militia to surround the area. Members of that militia would, in turn, punish those who'd broken into her home and killed several of its occupants.

Brent and Jake had to act, but the cards were stacked against them. It was unclear whether those guarding the house could hold the line. It depended on the numbers. Although highly trained, the two soldiers had little hope of fending off a militia bent on third-world, mob justice. Exceptional training most often lost out to superior numbers. Ironically, after years of fighting some of the most adroit criminals, terrorists, and soldiers in the world, a small child had them—at least one of them—at his mercy.

The man standing against the wall began to weep uncontrollably, heightening the intensity of the moment.

"Shut up!" Brent yelled before turning to Jake, trying to decide on the next move. Brent knew he could end the standoff with one pull of the trigger. He could drop the kid before a shot was fired from the semi-automatic weapon.

Jake, noticing that Brent was glancing at him and getting anxious, turned and stared back at him.

And shook his head.

The signal was unexpected and striking. Jake was willing to sacrifice his own life for that of a child who was not only unknown to him but threatening his existence. Brent, troubled by the decision, had miscalculated the heart—if not the judgment—of his friend. Yet he knew Jake's decision wouldn't further endanger Brent's own life. If the child chose to pull the trigger, Brent would make sure it would be the last decision he'd ever make.

One way or another, he could deal with the final target in the room, who was unarmed, trapped, and panting in fear.

Jake took a deep breath. It was clear that diplomacy had failed. Others would soon arrive. Despite his age, even the armed child knew that the longer he held strong, the better his chances of survival. Someone had to make a move. Brent knew his friend's life was hanging in the balance . . . and so he decided to do the unthinkable.

The child's eyes, and soon the barrel of his gun, moved toward Brent's carbine as it fell to the ground. Not missing a beat, Jake lunged to the floor and rolled toward the child, cutting out his legs. The child tumbled forward onto his stomach. A shot was fired from the semi-automatic.

The bullet missed its mark.

Jake climbed to his knees and catapulted onto the child's back, wringing the gun from his tiny, calloused hands. Meanwhile, Brent, re-holstering the pistol he'd just drawn, chased and then tackled the man trying to escape, pulling his head back by his hair and lunging his knee in the small of his back.

"Jake! You good!?"

"I'm fine! Let's get out of here!"

"You're coming with us," Brent told the man underneath him, punching him in the back of the head for good measure before binding his wrists with flex-cuffs. "You have some questions to answer."

"Get out of here, kid," Jake said as he climbed off his would-be killer. "And remember that an American spared your life."

———

Washington, DC

His body drenched with sweat, his legs trembling, and his heart pounding, Blake plunged to his knees and buried his face in his hands.

And then it was over.

———

Langley, Virginia

The dossier was highly classified, so they wondered how it could've been so easily compromised. The thief had entered the facility, somehow obtained access to the secure storeroom, thumbed through some of the CIA's most sensitive physical files, and then vanished into the night. He had presented an identification card that had fooled both the computers and the security guards. To make matters worse, he'd tampered with the video camera in the storeroom. The picture frame was stilled at 10:05 p.m., showing an empty room at 10:30 p.m. The Agency had spent millions of dollars to prevent such a breach of security. Yet, in just under thirty minutes, under everyone's nose, the dossier was gone.

Luckily, the cameras at the entrance and in the parking lot had remained functional. Security guards were in hot pursuit of the thief. All was not lost. The thief had exited the building and driven from the facility without interference before they knew what had happened. But it had taken only a few minutes to locate his vehicle on its way toward Washington, DC. Two officers were hot on his tail. They were just waiting for him to reach his destination. Then they'd apprehend him. If they were fortunate, he'd lead them to his co-conspirators. They could then round up the whole bunch. They were confident that he wouldn't escape.

The thief surprised them, though, when he exited George Washington Parkway miles from DC and drove to a convenience store.

"Bad time to need cigarettes, huh?"

"Yep. Even geniuses make mistakes."

"What do you wanna do?"

"Let's stay in the car and wait for him to come out. Then we'll grab him."

"Alright."

The CIA security guards watched the figure step out of the burgundy BMW and walk toward the entrance of the convenience store. He was of average height for a man his age. His mustache was dark and bushy. He wore a black hat better suited for the mid-twentieth century. The two officers in the black, unmarked car drove into the parking lot just before the thief walked into the store.

"Did you get a good look?"

"That's him. Same guy we picked up on the exterior cameras. This is too easy."

"Yep."

"You wanna grab him when he comes out, or should we see if he leads us to the others?"

"There may not be any others, and I don't want to risk it. Let's just do this now. An effective interrogation will lead us to any others."

"You wanna get the file from the car while we're waiting?"

"No, let's catch him red-handed."

"He might have the file with him, though."

"I doubt there's a paper shredder in the store. We'll find it."

"Well, he could be going in there to read it."

"So what? He may have already read it. We'll have him in custody soon, so it doesn't matter."

"And what if he makes a pass?"

"Well, that's a good point. Make sure you check anyone who comes out. Like her, for instance," the driver directed, pointing to the slender, blonde-headed woman exiting the store, making her way to the shiny red Porsche parked three cars to their right. "You'll probably want to pat this one down."

"I love my job," the passenger replied, opening his door and then approaching the woman. "Excuse me, ma'am?"

"Yes?"

"I'm with the CIA," he said, showing her his badge. "I'm sorry, but I'll need to pat you down. We have a suspect inside the store, and we need to make sure that—"

"Do whatcha gotta do," the woman replied in a thick Brooklyn accent. "I'm in no hurry."

"Thanks," he said, gingerly patting down the woman. Finding nothing of professional interest, he said, "Can I check your purse?"

"What? It's a crime now to buy a pack of gum?"

"Yes or no? We can do this the easy way or the hard way."

"Do whatcha gotta do, I said."

"Sorry for the hassle," the security officer said, checking the purse and finding nothing but a few cosmetic products, gum, and some knick-knacks. "Have a good night."

"Whatever."

The passenger made his way back to the black car.

"Lucky dog," the driver said as the Porsche drove away.

"Membership has its privileges."

After a few more minutes, the driver became antsy. "Not sure we can wait any longer. Go in and get him. I'll wait here."

"10-4," the passenger replied, preparing his pistol.

"Be careful, though. This guy has proven his—"

"I'm no spring chicken myself. I'll holler if I need backup."

In less than a minute, the passenger ran from the store.

"That's just great!" the driver huffed. "And the dossier?"

"The trash can in the bathroom is on fire."

"Of course."

"So let's go find the Porsche," the passenger replied, still holding the singed hat and fake mustache in his hands."

"By now, she's already ditched the Porsche. Do me a favor."

"What?"

"Go back in there and buy me some cigarettes. I want to enjoy my last ride back to Langley."

Several miles away, after switching automobiles one last time, Natasha was driving home in a black Chevy Tahoe. She removed her wig and pulled the micro-camera from the hidden pocket within her red purse. She then grabbed her cell phone and dialed the number. "I've got what you asked for . . . and I've read some of it."

"Is everything okay?" John Smith asked.

"No, not really."

26

Washington, DC

His eyes bloodshot, Blake stood up when Smith and Natasha stepped into the SCIF. Blake had arrived an hour early. "What happened?" he asked.

"The Yemen assignment was a success," Smith said. Unlike Blake, Smith was clean-shaven and appeared well-rested. "I spoke with Jake after they left the Peninsula."

"Our guys are safe? They captured Omar Saud's cousins?" Blake asked, noticing that Natasha was refusing eye contact.

"Brent and Jake are fine," Smith replied. "There was a brief moment when some kid pulled a gun, but they easily disarmed him."

"But to be clear," Natasha added, "they didn't capture Saud's cousins."

"What do you mean?"

Natasha turned to Smith, whose eyes expressed displeasure at her critical tone. "They killed one cousin in self-defense. The other wasn't there."

Blake sat down but kept his eyes focused on Smith. "So what now? Al Thoorah still has the means to mobilize and continue plans for attack."

"Blake, that's always going to be the case. That's the world we now live in."

"Then why the mission to Yemen?"

"This snake has regenerative power. Cut off its head, and it will grow another one. Our goal is to spur a regressive regeneration of leadership."

"I don't speak spook, John. Please explain."

"Simple. Each time you cut off the snake's head—each time you neutralize or eliminate a leader—it's likely that a less credible, less effective leader will take his place."

"So what's our next move, if any?" Blake was optimistic that the "if any" part would find traction.

"Jake and Brent captured another al Thoorah operative, worked on him through the night, and obtained a credible lead."

"Please do *not* explain what 'worked on him' means in spook. My draft indictment is already longer than St. Nick's toy list."

"Suit yourself."

"What did they learn?" Blake asked, prying for answers.

"Saud's other cousin is in Pakistan," Natasha said, unable to keep quiet.

"Great," Blake said facetiously. "Motion that we rename the effort Operation Globetrotters."

"I'll be in charge of coordinating the next mission," Smith said, ignoring Blake's remark. "I need both of you back here tomorrow evening. Seven o'clock sharp."

"Where are Jake and Brent?" Blake asked.

"They're en route to Pakistan," Smith replied.

"Imagine that."

"Blake, I told you to get some rest."

Chevy Chase, MD

"We agreed that we wouldn't speak until the operation was over. Peter has been briefing me."

"I'll address Peter Karnes in a minute," the cigar-smoking man replied, "but I wanted you to know that I might terminate the operation soon."

"Oh," the client said, the anxiety in his voice palpable. "Are you telling me that al Thoorah is no longer a threat?"

"They'll always be a threat, but we now have them playing defense. Our elite unit wasn't created to last forever. The longer it exists, the greater risk of exposure."

"That's obvious," the client said, "but I remember agreeing on a November disbandment date."

"The team's engaged in a high-risk overseas assignment. The potential for failure is significant. Of course, I have anticipated everything, but we may not make it to election day."

"What else do you need from me? I trust you've received your money."

"I received my handsome payment. Just realize that if something goes wrong—someone gets captured, someone goes AWOL, or heaven forbid, some agency finds out about this and starts an investigation—I'm shutting it down."

"Any clean-up required?" the client asked.

"Hopefully not much. But it depends on what happens. If something goes wrong, do I have any limitations on measures I can take?" the cigar-smoking man asked, not caring what the answer would be.

The client didn't flinch. "No."

"Good. Can we talk about Peter Karnes?"

"I warned him not to be disrespectful. He's just nervous. Handle him with kid gloves."

"That's not the problem. I've lost contact with him. A few days ago, we were scheduled to meet, but he never showed. He's not answering his phone. Any idea where he may be?"

"Come to think of it, I haven't seen him around this week. He was about to get hitched, so maybe they eloped. I'll call and check on him."

"Interesting."

There was an uncomfortable pause, during which time the cigar-smoking man decided not to reveal to his client that Karnes had disclosed the entire operation to at least two people and had decided to run to the FBI.

"Hey, Peter's not one to squawk or go AWOL. You concerned?"

"Of course not," the caller replied, crushing out his cigar. "He seems like a great kid."

"I'll find him and have him call you. Anything else?"

"No, sir. Pleasure doing business with you."

The phone call ended. The man hung up the brown phone, stood up, and walked to his desk. "And it was a pleasure doing business with your snot-nosed punk," he mumbled. "When you find his body, maybe you'll think twice about whom you assign to me."

Western Pakistan

A small unit of soldiers armed with machine guns and rifles sprinted toward a primitive mountain community composed of rudimentary tents and labyrinthine underground caves. Three hundred yards away, they stopped and established a broken perimeter behind three soft-top Jeeps and a neutralized piece of mobile artillery.

It was there they waited.

"Base, this is Squad 5 Leader. We're in position and awaiting aerial support. Over."

"Roger that, Squad 5 Leader. Confirm no women and children in the area."

Squad 5 Leader looked at the others and shrugged his shoulders while lifting his palms in the air. The gesture was not something he learned by way of military training, but its meaning was unmistakable. Three others, including Jake and Brent, replied with similar gestures. The remaining person in the cluster of soldiers and operatives was eyeing the tents through large, camouflage binoculars. He then turned toward Squad 5 Leader before indicating his own uncertainty.

"Cannot confirm there are no women and children. Repeat *cannot* confirm. Allowable perimeter still several hundred yards away from target. Please advise. Over."

There was no immediate response. The five men stared at one another, waiting for what appeared to be a crucial decision that was out of their hands. And then they heard a voice over the transmitter.

"Roger that, Squad 5 Leader. Two UCAVs on the way."

It was hard to spot the small planes flying overhead through the clouds. Both had been airborne for several hours. Their pilots, joysticks in hand and sitting in front of a television monitor in a portable box miles from harm's way, were awaiting orders for a precision attack.

The UCAVs, or unmanned combat aerial vehicles, resembled the Predator drones used by the CIA in Afghanistan after the September 11, 2001 attacks. These UCAVs, however, were much faster, stealthier, and more capable. Their underwing pylons, designed to carry sophisticated weapons, easily supported precise GPS-guided bombs. With their coordinates set, they were but a few minutes away from their target.

"It's game time, boys," Squad 5 Leader announced. "Lock and load."

Brent and Jake stayed behind as soldiers from all around the perimeter charged forward. The UCAVs were in sight and approaching.

The missiles fired toward the encampment. Each one hit its mark, the sound deafening. The ground shook underneath them.

The soldiers began to yell in an effort to frighten the hordes of insurgents fleeing from the tents and tunnels within the impacted area. Brent and Jake began scanning the area, looking for the new most important man in the entire region, the heir apparent to al Thoorah.

Washington, DC

In the SCIF, Smith picked up the phone before the first ring had ended, placing the caller on speakerphone so Blake and Natasha could hear.

"Group 1, this is Eagle . . . mission accomplished!"

There were three sighs of relief around the table. Blake looked at Natasha, who had grabbed his arm underneath the table, and smiled.

"Good work, Eagle!" Smith said, running his fingers through his greasy hair and slamming his fist down on the table in jubilation. "Do you have the target?"

"The target has been taken alive! Repeat! The target has been taken alive!"

SCAVENGER HUNT

There was a roar of excitement in the SCIF. Blake, Natasha, and Smith all stood up and slapped each other high-fives, the esprit de corps palpable.

"That's great news, Eagle! Great news! Once you get back to base, call me, and we'll discuss next steps. Tell Bloodhound we're all proud of you guys."

"Will do, Group 1. Eagle is out!"

Smith disconnected the call and, with a banana-sized grin, addressed Blake and Natasha. "This is a great day for America!"

"Nice work, John," Blake said. "Masterful job putting this together. Not sure how you did it. To be clear, I *don't* wanna know. But you made a difference today."

"No doubt," Natasha added. "Those guys never cease to amaze me. Brilliant."

"We have a solid team," Smith said, trying to catch his breath. "Can't thank you enough for your sacrifices."

Natasha and Blake smiled, something they'd almost forgotten how to do.

"Listen," Smith said. "I'll wait here for the guys to call me. Go, celebrate, and we'll meet again tomorrow morning."

Thirty minutes after Blake and Natasha left the SCIF, Smith had finished reviewing the latest intelligence reports and was still expecting Jake's call. He leaned back in his chair and reflected on the successes over the last few days. Despite a rough start, the group's work was producing much fruit.

The phone in the center of the table finally rang.

"Hello, Eagle?"

"Group 1, this is Squad 5 Leader. Something terrible has happened."

QUESTIONS

27

Riding the DC Metrorail had become a gamble. Terrorists had inflicted significant damage to the nation's subways over the last few years, and rail security was proving to be an impossible goal. Lunatics would carry a bag of explosives onto a subway car and leave it behind before exiting.

As he stood inside, near the subway car door, Blake couldn't help but notice the three drunkards standing across from him, still floating in what smelled like Seagram's Seven.

Not wanting to be bothered, Blake pretended to read the classified section of a three-day-old newspaper he'd snatched from an empty seat. Unfortunately, that didn't inoculate him from the drunkards' aggressive meddling. One of them approached him and asked for money, indicating that he was just short of a dollar and needed *eighty* cents. Blake, intrigued by the inebriate's creative economics but wanting to be left alone, reached for his wallet and handed over a dollar bill.

Blake was startled when someone slapped him on his shoulder from behind.

"I never took you for a philanthropist, Hudson."

Blake turned around and, seeing a familiar face, smiled. "What's up, Henry?"

"You can never be too cautious riding Metro. You never know who you'll run into," the barrel-chested Henry Dalton said, scratching his black, chin-strap goatee while keeping a watchful eye on the gaggle of drunks. When they spotted him, he pulled his suit jacket to the side to reveal the FBI badge affixed to his snake-skinned belt. No one would be approaching Agent Dalton for money.

"You still at headquarters?" Blake asked.

"Right across the street from you. Very sorry to hear about your chief of staff. I was out of town when it happened, but I've been meaning to call you."

"Thanks, Henry. It's been a rough slog. He was your chief of staff, too, you know."

"No disrespect to Michael—and may he rest in peace—but the FBI likes to maintain its independence from Mother Justice."

"Until the FBI needs money or screws up, of course," Blake said before unleashing a playful jab that landed on Dalton's right bicep. "Then you come home crying to Big Momma."

"Leave the trash talk on the basketball court," Dalton teased, his slender athletic face and sharp eyes animated.

"What's keeping you busy these days, Henry?"

"Counterterrorism, mostly. You?"

"Same," Blake said. "Working on a crazy project that's eating up my time." The door slid open at the Federal Triangle Metro stop. "You walkin' my way?"

"Headed to La Casa Blanca for a meeting with NSC. Big tournament at the gym this weekend. You in?" Henry asked.

"Probably not. Need to get my head above water."

"Bummer. I'll give you a buzz soon."

Blake bolted to the escalator and, on his way to Main Justice, reflected on his conversation with Dalton. It had shown a blinding light on Blake's new normal. He hadn't thought about playing basketball in weeks. Operation Scavenger Hunt was monopolizing his time, and it was starting to take a toll. He reminded himself, though, that yesterday's successful mission in Pakistan was a triumphant game changer. With al Thoorah's leadership crippled, he'd be back on the basketball court in no time, and Scavenger Hunt would be nothing more than a brief detour—a fleeting nightmare—from an otherwise successful career and normal life.

———

When he realized that Natasha was ten minutes late to his office, Blake walked over to his coat rack, grabbed his suit jacket, and decided to walk upstairs to the eighth floor without her. Perhaps she'd forgotten to meet him.

Humming the tune from the *Lone Ranger*, he trotted up the final set of stairs and through the darkness of the hallway on his way to the SCIF. He was curious to learn more about yesterday's capture and hopeful that it would lead to the group's winding down. Despite its recent success, he still wasn't comfortable with the group's mission. The spy world remained an enigma to him, but logic dictated that the group couldn't exist much longer.

His interest was piqued when he saw the SCIF's door ajar. That door was *never* open, he thought. He also noticed that the lights were off inside. Another rarity. Before continuing forward, he stopped to check his watch.

SCAVENGER HUNT

Smith and Natasha should've already arrived. The SCIF was covered in darkness, and Blake walked in and flipped the light switch.

But the lights didn't come on. And he couldn't hear the usual hum of computer hardware in the facility. Perturbed, he walked twenty-five yards past the SCIF to an aged, dilapidated file cabinet containing tools, flashlights, wires, and tape. He grabbed one of two plastic flashlights, turned it on, and then returned to the darkened SCIF.

Shining the flashlight beam at different areas within the facility, he couldn't believe his eyes. *Everything was gone!* The chairs, the tables, the clocks . . . *gone!* The computers, the maps, the monitors. *Vanished!* Even the overhead lights had been removed. Nowhere to be found.

The place was empty.

Shocked, Blake scrambled to gather his thoughts. Had the group finished its work? He couldn't think of better news, but that didn't make any sense. For one thing, it was too good to be true. Practically, though, if the group had completed its mission, then why had Smith scheduled a morning meeting? And why hadn't anyone told Hudson? He pulled his phone from his pocket. As expected, no messages and no calls. He'd been home with Judge all night. No one had tried to contact him there. *What was going on?*

Other theories made less sense. Had Smith moved the group's meeting place, Smith would have notified him. And why would Smith choose another place? Had Smith quit? Another encouraging thought. But if Smith wanted to quit, he wouldn't have removed all the furniture and equipment and lights and maps and clocks from the SCIF.

It made no sense.

Had something gone wrong? That, too, made little sense given the successful mission the night before. If there was ever a time to meet and reflect on progress—or to celebrate—it was this morning.

Blake was befuddled. Seeing no more clues, he walked back down the hallway, toward the stairs. He needed to make some calls.

––––––––––

Blake grabbed a sheet of paper containing the group's cell numbers from the top drawer of his desk and dialed Natasha.

We're sorry, but you have reached a number that has been disconnected or is no longer in service. Please check the number you dialed or try again later.

He tried the number again and heard the same recording. Why was Natasha's cell phone disconnected?

Next up, John Smith. After three rings, someone picked up.

"Hello, John?"

"Yeah."

"Hey, it's Blake. Don't we have a meeting this morning? I went up to the SCIF, but no one's there."

"Who's this?"

"Blake. Blake Hudson. What the heck's going on?"

"I don't know a Blake Hudson."

"What do you mean you don't know a Blake Hudson?"

"Who are you looking for?"

"*John Smith*," Blake said, now realizing that he wasn't speaking to Smith.

"Well, this is John *Turner*. I don't know a John *Smith*. Sounds like a made-up name."

"Is this 2-0-2-6-3-6-1-2-3-9?"

"Yeah, but there ain't no John *Smith* here. Just got this number this morning. I bet the John you're after had it before me."

"Sorry to bother you, mister, but tell me something. Doesn't the phone company wait a while before they transfer numbers? And don't they have some recording that provides forwarding information? You know, 'Please make a note of the new number.'"

"You got me, pal. I don't work for the phone company. I wish I did. They pay more."

Blake hung up the phone and worked his way down the list. It didn't take him long to realize that Brent's and Jake's phone numbers had also been disconnected. Was he given bad numbers? Other than Smith, he'd only called Natasha, but her number had worked before. Now there was nothing. He sat in his office and waited for someone to call him, for someone to tell him what was happening.

As he waited, he dialed his cell number from his office phone.

Once it rang, he began to pace his office floor.

28

Weeks later.

The passage of time only nurtured the anxiety. Blake's office had become a Petri dish for outlandish speculation. He thought about different scenarios, none of which made sense outside of Bizarro World. Presumably, everyone had received the same list of cell phone numbers. His phone number was accurate on the list. Someone should've called him. And they knew where he worked. Why hadn't they stopped by his office?

He could understand why Brent or Jake may not call him. He thought they'd all become friends one day, but he knew those renegade cohorts were a shade of a different color. Life to them was all business. They were not of the "call and chat" ilk. Smith, on the other hand, had an obligation to call. He was the ostensible leader of this mess. If he'd chosen to close shop, he should've let Blake know.

But Natasha caused him the most concern. Why hadn't *she* called? She knew where he lived. Why hadn't she stopped by his house? Blake believed that Natasha had become more than just a professional colleague. They certainly had become friends, unless that had been a facade. But people didn't fake friendship unless they had something to gain in return. And Blake couldn't fathom any benefit Natasha could derive from pretending to be his friend . . . or more. Like everything else at this point, it made no sense.

The more he thought about Natasha, the more he realized he must take action. Her conduct pointed toward a more ominous and sinister theory. Perhaps even a set-up.

He approached his computer and opened his contacts list. He clicked on the letter *R* and moved his cursor over several names until he found the one he needed. He stared long and hard at the name, questioning whether to make the call, wondering if such a call would spawn more problems than solutions, and knowing that the questions he must ask would be out of bounds. After much thought and hesitation, he realized he had no choice. He picked up the phone and dialed the number.

"FBI personnel."

"Blake Hudson for Clyde Rothman."

"One moment please," the woman replied. After a few seconds, she was back on the line. "Patching you through to Agent Rothman."

"*Blake Hudson*. The man, the myth, the legend," Clyde said with false but good-humored exaltation.

"I trust you're doing well, my friend," Blake said in a colloquial tone reflecting familiarity.

"I do well. And how's my counterpart in crime across the street?"

"Surviving."

"Yeah. Sorry to hear about Michael and the others. That attack is cause for a complete call-to-arms."

"Thanks, Clyde. Things could be better, which is why I'm calling you. You have a few minutes?"

"What's on your mind? I haven't heard from you in a while."

"I was hoping you could pull a few files for me," Blake said.

"What kind of files do you need?"

"Well, I need some background files on a few federal employees."

"Whoa!" Clyde said. "Sounds like an interesting project."

"You can say that again."

"Well, as you probably know, *Mrs. Clinton*, I'll need a written request from your office containing a legal authorization before I can hand over files on Justice employees."

Blake understood Clyde's reference to the infamous Filegate debacle. "I'm not familiar with the procedure, Clyde. What do you need?"

"Just a letter requesting the files and referencing the Privacy Act exception that gives you legal authorization to obtain them. I assume you have a legitimate, legal purpose. The letter needs to be authorized by the attorney general, but now that I think about it, I think he's delegated that authority to everyone in your office."

"Okay," Blake said. "Can I just give you the names, have you start pulling the files, and then send you the written request later? I'm in a rush and needed this information yesterday."

"I can do it this one time, I guess. I know you're good for it."

"I really appreciate it. One other thing . . ."

"I should be so lucky. Shoot."

"You referenced Justice Department files, so I just want to be clear."

"Clarity is always good in this business."

"Clyde, I need files for people working in other federal agencies too."

"Sounds like you need some *strings* pulled as well as files."

"Yeah, maybe," Blake said. "I need background files on some folks from CIA, NSA, and DOD Special Ops."

There was a lengthy, uncomfortable pause. Blake could hear nothing but the sounds of traffic down below.

"You're joking right?"

"I don't think so."

"Well, even if you aren't joking—which you *are*, obviously, for everyone listening—I don't have access to those files. The CIA does its own background investigations, and the Defense Investigative Service handles most military investigations. Going along with your *joke*, I might be able to put my hands on the NSA file because we often coordinate with NSA on such matters, but CIA and Special Ops information would be almost impossible to retrieve."

"*Almost impossible*? That doesn't sound impossible."

Blake had taken an aggressive step in pushing his request, but he believed it was necessary to emphasize the need for the files.

"Well, anything's possible, I guess. Running a forty-yard dash in three seconds flat is possible . . . no human has ever done it to my knowledge. You know what branch of Special Ops this person—or persons—is in?"

"It's one guy, and he's Delta Force."

"Good grief, Hudson!" Clyde let out a pessimistic sigh, calling Blake by his last name to accentuate his angst. "*Delta Force*? If he were Rangers or 10th Mountain, it would be possible—*theoretically*, of course—to pull background information. But Delta Force? Those guys don't even exist . . . at least on paper."

"But you and I both know they *do* exist," Blake said with an air of exasperation. "And there must be a paper trail reflecting the vetting that's done on them."

"FBI certainly doesn't have access," Clyde replied almost as an afterthought. "Why do you need it?"

"I wish I could tell you, but—"

"Yeah, yeah," Clyde interjected. "Save your breath. Everyone's need-to-know comes with an order of close hold, jumbo fries, and a biggie-sized classification. Blake, I need a legitimate, legal reason to obtain the files. Period."

"Can you just see what you can come up with? The names are as follows—"

"Whoa, whoa! Don't give me their names. Absent good reason, I don't have the authority to get this information for you. Let it go."

Blake had pushed too hard. He took a deep breath and thought better of trying to manufacture a "legitimate, legal reason," as Clyde had described it. He would need to find another means to obtain the information. This way, he recognized, wasn't fair to Clyde.

"Sorry, Clyde. I know I'm acting out of character, and I didn't mean to back you into a corner."

"No problem, *amigo*. Look, I don't want this to affect our friendship, so why don't we grab some food tonight and discuss old times? I've wanted to talk to you about your sister, Sharon, anyway. I know she's still single, and I want your blessing to ask her out."

Blake paused for a second and then smiled. Clyde was married, and Blake didn't have a sister named Sharon. Their discussion had risen to a level unfit for government phone lines. Clyde wanted to meet in person.

"Deal. Once again, I'm sorry I brought up this mess," Blake said, trying to rehabilitate the appropriateness of the conversation and quell the concerns of any uninvited, third-party listeners. "As usual, I'm probably just blowing things way out of proportion. I don't want either of us to do anything improper."

"I knew you were joking. Some people never change."

"As for my sister, Sharon, you'd better have a legitimate, legal reason for wanting her company. I don't need access to your background file to know what a dirty, rotten scoundrel you are."

Clyde laughed and said, "Pizza at your house then?"

"My house may not be clean. Let's just grab some bar food at The Exchange. How does eight o'clock sound?"

"Perfect."

"See you there," Blake said, hanging up the phone, wondering whether Clyde Rothman had picked up on his double entendre.

A somber atmosphere hovered over Main Justice. The vicious attack on the building and the loss of the agency's chief of staff, among many others, cast a palpable gloom over the department.

Blake rarely thought anymore about Gregg or the attack. He had new burdens to bear. And despite being told not to document the activities of Scavenger Hunt, he was preparing a cryptic timeline—vague enough to elude classification requirements—for his own reference.

When Rick, accompanied by Amanda, opened his office door, Blake flinched like he'd been caught with his hand in the cookie jar.

"Blake with his bright autumn tie. Nice," Rick said, noticing that he and Amanda had startled Blake. "What's going on? Surfing porn sites?"

"I see the circus is in town," Blake quipped.

"So," Rick said, "to get our minds off the doom and gloom around here, I was telling Amanda about *Natasha*."

"What about her? You never told me that you'd met her."

"You want me to tell you every time I go potty too?"

"You already do that," Amanda interjected.

Rick ignored her. "Blake's been occupied the last few weeks, and now I know why."

"You didn't answer my question," Blake said.

"We met on the eighth floor."

"What?"

"Yeah. I couldn't resist the temptation. I had to check out your new home away from home. It's pretty lackluster up there if you ask me. Looks like a maintenance shop."

"What were you doing up there?" Blake asked.

"What? Did I trespass on Area 51? Give me a break."

Blake nodded his head but didn't say anything.

"Look, Inspector Clouseau," Rick continued, "I didn't realize we had an eighth floor. I was curious. End of story."

"So what's this about a Natasha?" Amanda prodded. "What's her last name?"

"Hensley," Blake said.

"Natasha is smokin' hot," Rick said, "and I could tell by looking and talking to her that she could whip Blake at *Trivial Pursuit* and *Twister*."

"Rick, you drank too much coffee today," Blake said. "Natasha is only a colleague. Nothing more. In fact, we haven't spoken in several weeks. I'll leave it at that."

"Okay, changing the subject," Amanda said, "did you ever touch base with that general at the Pentagon about the detainee issue?"

"Ouch. I forgot about General Leavitt," Blake said, turning toward his office phone. "I better call him. It's been weeks. You sure you don't want to handle this, Amanda?" he asked. "Rick?"

They were gone.

"Exactly," he mumbled. At this point, though, what did he care about diving headfirst into career-ending issues? General Leavitt was the least of his worries.

Calling Leavitt would be his last action item at work for the day. Then he would rendezvous with his old friend Clyde Rothman. If that meeting failed to produce any fruit, then he didn't know what he'd do.

29

To the casual passerby, The Exchange was a semi-upscale bar, upstairs from another bar that was hipper but too tawdry. Truth be told, the only thing distinguishing the two was that the customers on the second floor were required to wear "appropriate clothing," whatever that meant, and to pay more for their drinks. At closing time, patrons on both levels acted like fools during the run-up to elections.

Clyde Rothman and Blake took up their conversation in the back, an informal area replete with broadcloth couches and soft leather chairs.

"Here's the deal," Clyde began. "The attorney general can request the interagency information you need. But his authority can't be delegated to you or others in your office. It has to come from Kershing to the FBI director herself. The director, in turn, must convey the request to at least a deputy-level official in each agency, who then will authorize the request. Normally, though, the AG wouldn't even go through FBI to get interagency materials of this kind."

"Why would he?"

"Exactly. There's no need unless there's an ongoing FBI investigation that implicates the requested information. In most circumstances, that's not the case, and going through the Bureau becomes an unnecessary, wholly unorthodox, extra step."

"Understood," Blake said.

"But because we're sitting and discussing this issue in a dimly lit area of a bar that we know won't break even tonight, I expect you to tell me the procedure I just outlined won't work for you."

"Do I need to say it?"

"If you want to continue this discussion, Blake, then you need to tell me what's going on. I need more."

Blake stared at the floor. He'd known Clyde since college and trusted him as a friend. Could he trust Clyde with this radioactive information? On the one hand, Blake would be breaking the law by outlining the specifics, or perhaps even the existence, of his highly classified operation. On the other, he'd be breaking the law anyway if he continued to pursue the files he needed. There also was a sporting chance that Clyde would get caught helping Blake and be forced to testify against him.

He decided that was a risk he'd need to take. He had to trust Clyde. Besides, he'd been bending laws ever since Operation Scavenger Hunt started. What's a few more?

"I can't tell you everything."

"Fine."

"The project I'm working on started in June after a court issued a terrible ruling in a case involving access to Omar Saud. Everyone freaked out. We were worried about more terrorist attacks. Eventually, someone—somewhere—came up with the idea of creating an interagency team to shut down the al Thoorah network."

"Who was it?"

"I don't know."

"I guess the team includes the guy from Delta Force?"

"The group consists of me, a woman from NSA—apparently detailed to DIA—two guys from the CIA, and, yes, a Rambo-like soldier from Delta Force." He stopped and looked the pudgy-faced, balding Clyde straight in his narrow eyes. "Some of what I'm telling you may be classified. It's hard to tell. But I've never known of such a random assortment of federal employees composing a group with such a limited function or . . ." his voice trailed off as he added, "what I thought was a limited function."

"So how does such a group go about stopping al Thoorah?" Clyde asked.

"I can't tell you that—not yet anyway. At this point, I want to minimize our exposure. I can tell you that everything we did was covert—we carried out several dangerous and troubling assignments, foreign and domestic."

"Domestic? Isn't that FBI's job?"

Blake didn't respond.

"You still haven't given me enough. What more can you tell me about why you need those files?"

"Everyone in the group has gone AWOL. I can't find anyone, and no one will return my calls. That's not technically correct. Everyone's phone number is disconnected or transferred to another customer."

"Interesting."

"You're telling me. I fear they may have turned against me. I don't know. I've tried to contact two of these folks by more traditional means, such as by calling their agencies. But no one knows where they are, nor do they seem to care."

"Why only two?"

"Come again?"

"Why have you only contacted the agencies for two of them? I thought you said there were four, not including you."

"Because I'm not sure one dude even works for the government anymore. He's former CIA, but I think they just brought him out of retirement. The guy was fishing down in Cabo to pass the time. That's what he told us anyway. Come to think of it, he's pretty young to be retired."

"I see."

"And who do I call to see if someone from Delta Force is reporting to work?" Blake asked.

"Right. Good point."

"But if the circumstances of their joining the project are like mine, this all makes perfect sense. Someone would've told their bosses that they'd been detailed to a classified project, and no one would know to hold them accountable. A part of me worries they're in trouble. I just don't know, but I need to find out."

"That's a troubling set of facts, Blake, but you haven't given me cause enough for circumventing FBI regs. Normally for DOJ and FBI requests alone, I'd need to fill out a log sheet that includes the name of the person from your office making the request. With the others, I'd also need to list the nature of the request."

"So?"

"So you're asking me to skip that process, which will put my career on the line. I risk going to jail. That's why I need something more tangible."

"What if I told you that, once the project started, the mandate had changed? What if I told you, speaking hypothetically, that what started as a charge to monitor and interdict certain terrorists turned into a directive for extrajudicial killings in the name of homeland security? What if, after several killings of terrorists, something went terribly wrong and members in the group ceased communication? And what if I told you, Clyde, that I am scared to death that I'm caught in the middle of some maelstrom of illegal activity that is spiraling out of control without anyone but me around to take responsibility?"

Clyde's eyes glazed over, his face turning ashen. "Blake, what have you gotten yourself involved in?"

Blake didn't answer, continuing his rhetorical list of descriptive questions. "And what if I told you that I believe—at least something in my gut tells me—that I can learn something from those files? They'd be helpful if only to confirm the truth of what these people have told me about themselves."

"Other options?"

"You tell me. I can't go to the attorney general. I'm told he doesn't know anything about this project. He's been shielded from it, and it doesn't take a genius to understand why."

"Really? Who, then, established this group and created this project?"

"I don't know. I'm not even sure my understanding is accurate. The person at Justice who got me involved in the project is dead."

"Michael Gregg?"

"Yeah, but I'm not sure he could have helped me figure this out. It's all troubling. I wouldn't ask you to access those files if I had another alternative. But I won't press the issue if you believe you'll get into trouble. Believe me."

"I believe you. Do you think you're being followed?"

"Good question. Haven't thought much about it. I wouldn't be surprised if someone has tapped my phones and bugged my house. I've just been trying to stay busy at work on unrelated, less important matters . . . waiting for someone in the group to contact me . . . trying to appear casual."

Clyde nodded his head. "Well, I don't know how the files are going to help, but I've always trusted your intuition."

"I appreciate that."

"You know that if I get caught and questioned, I'll be forced to reveal your participation in all of this."

"I understand."

"Do you understand the consequences?"

"I think so. But the consequences of doing nothing, I fear, are worse. I wouldn't be here making this request otherwise."

"I can't promise you anything, Blake, but I'll get a feel for how much my back-channels are willing to cooperate. They owe me a few favors, and they have an incentive not to expose me. Let me sleep on it, and we'll see what happens."

"I'll respect whatever decisions you make. I have to ask you, though, why are you considering this? What changed your mind?"

"Something you said."

"What?"

"You told me the attorney general was shielded from the operation."

"Someone told me that."

"But after you and I spoke this afternoon, I checked our log sheets related to background file requests. I learned that Kershing himself requested background files a few months ago, just before you say your operation began."

Clyde took a drink of his draft beer, which had warmed up during the conversation. "Yeah? So?"

"So one of the files he requested, the only one I was able to pull . . . was yours."

Blake's body went numb. He was speechless.

"Now give me the names," Clyde directed.

––––––––––

"Well *that* certainly was an interesting meeting," Blake said as Amanda and Rick followed him into his office.

"Understatement of the year," Rick said.

After everyone found a seat, Blake and Rick stared at Amanda.

"Sorry," Blake said.

"I'm fine with it," Amanda replied. "Really. I'm sorry you guys didn't get it."

"I'm *shocked* you didn't get it, Amanda," Rick said. "As much as you drive me bonkers, there's no one more qualified for the job."

Blake sighed and stared at the ceiling. "Chief of Staff Clarence Niles. I didn't see that one coming."

"He must have dirty pictures of the AG. Nothing else explains it."

"Look," Amanda said, "I like Clarence, and I'm sure he'll do a great job. Besides, to the extent I was considered for the position, I would just as soon stay engaged in the legal issues. I'm not suited for management."

"He'll be fine," Rick concluded.

"We all need to support Clarence," Amanda said. "He has a difficult job ahead of him and will need our help. On the bright side, the president's poll numbers are up."

"Yeah," Rick noted, "despite the recent attack, the president's numbers on terrorism are improving."

"That's strange," Blake observed.

"Not really," Rick said. "Americans coalesce around their leader during times of national tragedy."

"It won't last long, though," Amanda said, walking out of Blake's office.

"We don't have much longer to go," Rick said, following her out. "We just raised the flags from half-staff, and the election is around the corner."

Blake leaned back in his chair after his colleagues exited. *Chief of Staff Clarence Niles?*

30

Mindlessly tapping his keyboard, Blake thought about his conversation with Clyde Rothman. The attorney general *himself* had requested Blake's background file. Why? He'd already cleared a thorough background investigation. Nothing made sense anymore, and recent events were driving him insane. He took a deep breath, trying to remain focused. His thoughts continued bouncing between the members of his group—Natasha, in particular—and now, Attorney General Bill Kershing.

He turned his attention to his office phone. It hadn't made a peep in days. He picked it up, held it suspended for a moment, but never placed it to his ear. Were his calls being monitored? He placed the phone back in its cradle and removed his cellphone from his pocket. He needed to call Grandpa Hudson. If not for advice, then for therapy. He needed to hear a friendly voice, someone to tell him he was doing right no matter what. He needed unconditional support when everything appeared conditioned on something else.

He dialed the number without hesitation, his fingers punching the keys without input from memory.

"Grandpa?"

"Hey there, champ!" Porter Hudson exclaimed. "How are ya?"

Talking to Grandpa was like visiting a shrink without being on the clock, a form of psychotherapy unknown to published psychiatrists. "Surviving the rat race," Blake said, his phone pinned between his shoulder and ear as he stared at his computer monitor and re-entered his password. "How's everybody down there?"

"Fine, I reckon. Been looking for you on CNN."

"I stay away from the cameras. How's Grandma?"

"She wants to know when you're coming home to see us. She's been dealing with . . ."

Blake quit listening. He could see the cursor moving on his computer monitor. Something or someone else was controlling it. Someone was opening his files!

He sat motionless in his chair, not believing what he was witnessing. Then, his back straightened. He stood up, thrusting back his chair with his legs, while his eyes remained locked on the screen.

Calm down, he thought, *there must be an explanation for this.*

The cursor stopped. Whoever was controlling it just learned that Blake had logged on.

"Grandpa," he said, his voice escalating, "I need to call you back."

"All right, champ." The response was sullen.

Blake tossed his phone on his desk. He sat down, grabbed his computer mouse, navigated the cursor to the icon marked "OSH," and double-clicked.

Empty!

Everything in the unclassified "Operation.Scavenger.Hunt.doc" file, including his cryptic timeline, was gone!

He opened the right drawer of his desk. He could see that someone had accessed his files. Someone had been in his office; someone had been looking for something.

He rushed from his office and bolted down the hallway. The thought of someone rummaging through his desk and erasing his files without permission caused him alarm. His gallop turned into a full sprint before reaching the stairs. He grabbed the aluminum railing and proceeded downward, his feet landing on every third marble step of the spiraling stairwell. When he reached the first floor, he turned toward the IT office. Then he froze and thought for a moment.

Have they been to my house?

He reversed course and sprinted outside in search of a ride home.

———

For the first time ever, Judge failed to greet Blake at the front door. Random papers were strewn around as if an F-4 tornado had touched down in his living room. Seeing the back door open, he grabbed the iron stoker lying near the fireplace and walked toward his bedroom.

"Judge?"

The place was quiet. Whoever had broken in had no interest in being covert. Perhaps it was a message. Except for his personal laptop, nothing of value in the living area appeared to be missing. They had wasted their time, he thought; he'd not stored any work-related documents or financial information on his laptop.

And then he heard it.

SCAVENGER HUNT

Heavy gasping coming from the back of the house!

He rushed forward without hesitation, his heart pounding with fear and uncertainty. When he reached his bedroom, the iron stoker fell from his hands and crashed to the floor.

Blake's hazel eyes welled up with tears. Judge lay in a pull of blood, his long, prodigious face bludgeoned. His once-powerful legs contorted in a manner that opposed the laws of nature. His rib cage was exposed, revealed through the deep gashes. Judge didn't look at Blake, but his eyes were wide open, staring into nowhere as he heaved for air.

"No, No, NO!!!" Blake screamed at the top of his lungs, his voice reaching a crescendo, echoing throughout the row house. He tore off his necktie as he fell to his knees. He then cradled Judge's head and checked the dog's pulse.

Blake lost control.

"No! No! Why!? Why!? Why!?" he recited in a spastic cadence. He pulled Judge to him, trying to caress his face without inflicting more pain, his tears splattering to the ground and colliding with the immense maroon puddle. "Judge!" he cried. "What did they do to you!?"

Judge was unresponsive, too enfeebled to moan in agony, and too incapacitated to move any part of his mangled body.

Blake wailed, slipped his hands underneath Judge's bedraggled frame, and, in one swift and powerful motion, leveraged his weight and heaved the dog over his shoulder, nearly two hundred pounds of seemingly lifeless flesh and bone. Judge was still breathing. That faint glimmer of hope, coupled with uncontrollable distress, amplified Blake's redlining adrenaline.

With an unparalleled sense of urgency, he bounded outside of the house, carrying Judge to the sidewalk. Blake's white dress shirt was soaked in blood. His distress morphed into an unprecedented, wicked rage. Blake's chest contracted as he marched down the sidewalk, the hatred mounting.

"I'm going to *kill* whoever did this!" he yelled at no one in particular as he walked across the street, gurgling with froth, not even bothering to check for oncoming vehicles. "Do you hear me!? I'm going to rip your blackened heart out!"

He began to scream curse words, shouting at the top of his lungs words not sanctioned at anytime, anywhere. He had lost all sense of his surroundings, unable to hear any sounds, and everything around him became a turbid blur.

Still sobbing, Blake charged down East Capitol Street, Judge's front paws limp and bouncing off Blake's back after each step, his hind legs dangling below Blake's waist. Blake couldn't appreciate the weight he was bearing. It was a non-factor. Judge needed immediate medical attention to survive. There was a veterinarian near Eastern Market, several hundred yards away.

Pedestrians on the street stopped in their tracks at the grotesque sight. One man grabbed his child and pulled him to the side, getting out of Blake's path. Others huddled together, trying to decipher the scene. One woman wearing a pink hairnet ran to Blake and then began walking in stride.

"Oh, my! What happened!?" She put her hands to her mouth in disbelief. "Oh no! Where are you taking him!?" She couldn't help herself. "What have you done!?"

"Get away from me!" Blake rebuked. "Go!"

Blake soon began to falter under Judge's load. His arms were shaking, his knees buckling. Adrenaline waning, the animal hospital was still blocks away.

"Judge, don't you close your eyes! Don't you leave me! You can't leave me!"

A silver BMW drove up behind him. The driver reached across the passenger seat and opened the door as the car decelerated to coincide with the pace of Blake's walk.

Blake turned to her, his lower lip throbbing; his now hollow eyes swollen, gushing tears. "He's a good boy," Blake said to the woman with an eerie calmness. "I love him *so* much. . . . He didn't do anything wrong."

"I know he didn't, sweetheart," the woman said. "Get him in the car."

———

Ninety minutes later, Blake's hair was tousled as he stood on the concrete pavement outside the animal hospital. He'd thrown away his bloodstained dress shirt and acquired, free of charge, a scratchy navy T-shirt promoting the latest, scientifically formulated dog food. He lingered in a daze, trying to manage his emotions . . . to contain the rage.

The prognosis wasn't good. Judge was in critical condition and would need to remain at the animal hospital indefinitely.

Blake didn't hear the obnoxious bell chime when the smudged, glass door to the animal hospital opened.

"There you are," said one of the vet techs.

"I needed some air."

"They'll call you with any change." She noticed Blake wasn't paying attention. "This is just the worst day," she said, fidgeting her short, brown ponytail, holding back tears, trying to console him.

"I can never repay you for your kindness. Just help Judge," Blake said, turning to look at the woman charged with consoling him.

"We will. I called the police like you asked. They should be at your house by now," she said, placing her hand on Blake's shoulder. "Any idea who could have done this?"

"No idea. But I can tell you this much: I won't rest until I find out who."

"And I thought this neighborhood was getting safer. I guess I was wrong."

"I doubt today's events had anything to do with your run-of-the-mill, neighborhood crime."

"In any event, I hope you find the people who did this."

"Me too. Thanks again for your amazing help. You have a huge heart, and if Judge survives this atrocity, we'll owe his life to you."

"Not at all."

After hugging Blake and before disappearing back inside, the vet tech stopped and turned around. Her jaws tightened, tears of anger rolling down her cheeks. "Find them."

"Trust me. I will."

———

When Blake reached his house, he saw his nosy, retired neighbors huddled on the sidewalk. He wondered where they'd been hours ago when Judge needed them. Most looked away upon witnessing Blake's steely, bloodshot eyes as he walked by.

"Where are the police?" Blake barked without breaking stride.

"Not here yet," an elderly man answered. "You call 'em?"

"Long time ago," Blake said. "This is outrageous."

He hopped up his front stairs and entered the ransacked home, noticing the trail of splattered blood that traced his prior steps and provided a gruesome reminder of his recent experience. The scene being too much to stomach, he turned back around.

As he walked outside, he watched the late-arriving police officers step out of their cars . . . laughing and carrying on. His calming walk from the vet would prove useless.

Things were about to get ugly.

31

Blake's army-green Land Rover Defender was old but fast like Grandpa Hudson's mind. Grandpa had outfitted it with a custom high-powered engine before transferring the title. Driving toward the US Capitol en route to the Main Justice building, Blake dialed a number that he'd memorized his first week on the job.

"Justice Command Center."

"This is Blake Hudson in the Attorney General's Office. I need to speak with one of the security guards, Oscar Childs."

Blake winced right after uttering his name. Someone had erased his files at the office and may be after him. He had no idea how concerted the effort was. He regretted not using another name. He needed to be more careful.

"Where are you, sir?" the man asked.

Blake paused. Why did this person care where he was? They'd never asked him that before. "On my way out of town," he fibbed.

"Is this an emergency, sir?"

What's with the twenty questions? Blake thought. "No, it's not."

"Oscar retired last week."

"What do you mean he retired?" Blake asked.

"Just that, sir. He retired."

Great, Blake thought. Oscar had been the only Main Justice security guard he could trust. "You know how I can reach him? You have his address?"

"Sorry, sir, but I can't give out his address. Rules are rules. But I can connect you by phone."

"Good enough."

SCAVENGER HUNT

The man dialed Oscar's number and then dropped from the line. The phone picked up after two rings.

"Ma'am, my name is Blake Hudson. I'm a colleague . . . I'm a *friend* of Oscar's. Is he around?"

"No, but he'll be back in about ten minutes. Give me your number. I'll have him call you back."

"May I just come by and see him?"

"What did you say your name was?"

"Blake Hudson."

"And you know Oscar from where?"

"From work, ma'am. I won't take much of his time."

No response.

"It's a very important matter," Blake continued. "He'll want to speak to me."

"Suit yourself."

"Great. What's your address?"

———

Blake had never been to Anacostia, which was due east of the US Capitol. Not far in terms of miles, it was worlds away in terms of socio-economic status. Truth be told, Blake had never heard a good word about the place. By all accounts, including Oscar's, Anacostia was a rough area of town. And it had the violent-crime statistics to back it up.

After crossing the Anacostia River, Blake noticed a black sedan behind him, two cars back. It caused him little alarm at first. The more he thought about it, however, and the longer the sedan remained in his rearview mirror, the more anxious he grew. This area didn't see many sedans. Opting not to forsake his hysteria, he turned into a convenience store, acting as if he was stopping to pump gas. The sedan, meanwhile, passed without incident.

He waited a few minutes before continuing toward Oscar's house. Driving the Defender back onto the road, he reflected on his bad day. In the last few hours, someone had erased the files from his office computer, pilfered through his office desk, broken into and ransacked his house, stolen his laptop, and butchered his dog.

He couldn't expel the visions of Judge from his mind. The canine had relied on Blake to protect him. But Blake wasn't around when his best friend had been sliced up and beaten to a pulp. He wasn't there now as Judge fought for life. He hoped against the odds that Judge would be there when he returned. He tried to suppress his guilt and seething anger and focus on protecting his own life.

Blake knew that action fueled by adrenaline was reckless, if not dangerous. He needed to be smart. He needed a plan. He needed to analyze the problem and search for answers. He had to start somewhere . . . with someone. That somewhere was in Anacostia and that someone was Oscar Childs, the unassuming security guard.

John Smith had indicated that he knew Childs from the CIA. That wasn't much to go on, but it smelled like a lead. Blake needed to ask Childs whether anyone at DOJ had suspiciously mentioned Blake's name. It was a long shot, but without solid leads, he had to follow his instincts. And his instincts told him that Oscar could help.

———

Oscar was wearing a white T-shirt and rocking in a squeaky wooden chair on his front porch when Blake arrived. Nighttime had set in, but a naked porch light surrounded by passive mosquitoes illuminated the front of the dilapidated, wood-framed house and its owner.

"Say it ain't so, Oscar," Blake said, ascending the three steps to reach him.

Oscar stood up to shake Blake's hand. "Afraid so."

"Retired?"

"Gave it up."

"You're kidding," Blake said, noticing for the first time the gray streaks in Oscar's short but full head of hair. He looked smaller and frailer without his security uniform.

"With my pension, I can sit on this porch and earn plenty of money. Besides, my wife begged me to quit after the terrorist attack on the building."

"Well, I'll miss having you around. You're the only one who knows football."

"Appreciate that," he said, "but something tells me you didn't drive out here to talk about my retirement or sports. You shouldn't be out this way, anyhow. These are rough parts . . . especially for a white boy."

"If someone gives me any trouble, I'll just drop your name."

Oscar chuckled. "No one around here cares about Oscar Childs. The only names they care about are Jackson and Franklin, and they'll shoot you in the head to take all the Jacksons and Franklins you got stuffed in your wallet. They may kill you for a few Lincolns."

"You're right. I didn't come for small talk."

"Have a seat. Can I get you anything to drink?"

"No, thanks," Blake said, sitting in the rocking chair adjacent to Oscar. "I was wondering if, before you left, my name ever came up among the guards?"

"What do you mean?"

"Anyone ever tell you to watch out for me or stop me? I don't know. This sounds silly, but I think someone at DOJ is after me."

"What? Never heard anything like that. We had meetings where people talked about suspicious activity or specific threats against the building. Didn't do much good. But no talk about any DOJ employees. My main job was figuring out whether the badge reader beeped green or red."

"I see."

"You in some kind of trouble?"

"I shouldn't be," Blake said. "But strange things are happening to me. Don't repeat this, but someone erased some files on my computer."

"Erased your files?"

"Someone broke into my house, ransacked the place, and—"

"My word."

"Yeah, beat my dog. His prognosis is still uncertain."

"Oh, my! I hate to hear that, Blake. What in the world? You think all that's related?"

"Not sure, but I think—"

"Too much to be a coincidence."

"Exactly. Besides, they stole nothing of value from my house except for my personal computer. I own other things that a common thief would want. These deadbeats wanted information—work-related information."

"Whatcha gonna do?"

"Figure out what's going on. That's all I know to do right now."

"You're welcome to stay with us, but I doubt your truck would be here in the mornin'."

"Thanks for the offer," Blake said, considering now whether it was even safe to return home. "I'll get a hotel room."

"Hate to see you like this. You look tired."

"It's been a long day, Oscar. Listen, I have one more thing to ask. Did you ever meet a man that goes by the name John Smith?"

"Sure did."

"When was the last time you saw him?"

"Several weeks ago. He was working at Main Justice."

"After July Fourth?"

"I don't recall."

"He told me y'all met at Langley. Is that true?"

"Yes. Long ago, I worked as a security guard at the CIA. He was an agent, I believe, or officer—whatever they call them there. I saw him now and again."

"Any idea what his real name is?"

"His real name is John Smith, best I know. I used to kid him about that all the time. Why do you ask?"

"Interesting," Blake said, more to himself. "I just assumed that *John Smith* was an alias. You sure that's his real name?"

"Pretty sure. Don't see why he'd use an alias at CIA headquarters. He's not foolin' anybody there. How does this affect you?"

"I've been working with Smith for a few months. But now, I can't find him. He doesn't return my calls, and I need to speak to him. I'm hoping he can answer some questions for me."

"Well, I do know this *for sure*. He ain't gonna be returnin' no more calls, and he ain't gonna be answerin' no more questions."

"Why not? What do you mean?"

"John Smith is dead."

"What!?" Blake asked in a loud whisper, lunging forward in the rocking chair. "How do you know that?"

"I read about it in the Metro section of *The Washington Post* a few days ago. They had his picture and bio in the obits. Talked about his CIA days and everything. Didn't say how he died, though. When you get old like me, you read the obits first thing in the morning. You start seeing friends you . . ."

Blake leaped to his feet and shook Oscar's hand. "I'll stop by again, my friend. Tell your wife that I'll meet her next time."

"You be careful, my man."

As Blake drove off, Oscar realized that he'd never see Blake Hudson again.

32

The short turning radius on Blake's Defender allowed him to whip around on Oscar's street in one swift move. In just a few seconds, he was off, traveling back to Capitol Hill. Thinking ahead, he wanted to ditch the Defender near his house, but he'd need another place to sleep. Calling Rick or Amanda crossed his mind, but he worried about risking his friends' lives. He had no idea what had happened to John Smith, but the myriad coincidences were congealing into a macabre mosaic of uncertainty and danger. He needed to catch his breath and clear his mind. Only one thing was evident at the moment—his life was spinning out of control.

The possible causes of Smith's death flashed in Blake's mind like cards turned over in Solitaire. The man could've died of countless natural ailments, Blake thought. Smith was a rabid smoker and well past the prime of his life. But it was hard to leap from the blade of Occam's Razor, and the most likely cause of death was also the most troubling. Someone had probably murdered Smith, Blake gathered; perhaps the same henchmen who had broken into Blake's house; perhaps the same person who had deleted his files at the office. Without knowing much, he couldn't rule out anything, and with his life at stake, it was better to be cautious than dismissive.

But the real question was *why*. Why had the members of Scavenger Hunt disbanded? Why had all of their phone numbers been disconnected? Why had no one in the group contacted him? His phone numbers—home, office, and smartphone—were still active. Every group member knew where and how to find him. Why would someone rummage through his house and office and erase his working files? Why had the attorney general himself requested his background file? And perhaps the biggest why of all—*why* would someone *kill* John Smith?

CHAD BOUDREAUX

The other questions were *what* and *who*. *What* had happened since the mission in Pakistan, and was the answer to that question driving the sudden unraveling? *What* was he going to do now? *Who* was causing all these problems? Blake didn't know the answers to any of those questions. But he was convinced that if he could find the answer to "who," the answers to "what" and "why" would fall into place. He hoped that a pot of strong coffee and a quiet night in a secluded hotel room would allow him to decompress and sort through it all.

Blake shifted the manual transmission into second gear and, noticing the green light, turned onto East Capitol Street. He could smell fried food and exhaust as he shifted into third and fourth gears, accelerating past the fast-food chains that peppered the strip malls on either side. He glanced at the passenger seat, grabbed his phone, and pressed the icon to open his music app. As Elvis Presley's "Promised Land" filled the air, Blake took a trip down Memory Lane and thought of his Great Dane.

But his rendezvous with relaxation was short-lived.

A vehicle was approaching at a high rate of speed. Blake's neck straightened, and his body snapped to attention. He mashed the gas pedal as he witnessed two headlights bearing down on him from a side street on his right. He swerved the Defender into an oncoming left lane to avoid being hit. A car collided with another as it veered to its right to escape a head-on collision with his vehicle.

Panic setting in, Blake could hear over Elvis's crooning the cacophony of crashing metal and car horns blaring past him. Maneuvering his vehicle back into the right lanes, he looked into his rearview mirror and spied the wrecked cars and the vehicle that had nearly rammed into him. It was fishtailing as the unidentifiable driver tried to maintain control.

It was the black sedan. And it was racing toward Blake!

He floored the accelerator once again. Everything around him was a blur, the sedan in his rearview mirror the only recognizable image. He noticed his pursuer gaining ground. Fast. It wouldn't take long for the vehicle to catch him. He had no idea what would happen then.

The black sedan was behind him. It bolted from its drafting position and around to his left. Blake could hear its engine roar as it accelerated forward.

He swerved to his left, preempting the driver's move. After falling back a few car lengths, the driver of the sedan tried to draw even with Blake once again, this time on the right side. Again, Blake maneuvered the powerful Defender in front of the sedan and then into the right lane, preventing it from pulling next to him.

But he couldn't keep the cat and mouse game up forever. His evasive measures were only temporary solutions. Looking ahead, he was fast approaching a red light. His eyes focused back and forth from his rearview mirror to the light ahead of him.

SCAVENGER HUNT

The light turned green just in time. Blake breathed a sigh of relief and checked his mirror once again. This time, however, he couldn't see the black sedan. He checked his passenger side mirror, but the car had vanished. Then he heard the roaring sound of an accelerating vehicle on his driver's side.

The sedan was in his blind spot, inching its way forward. It was too late for Blake to head the car off. He looked out his driver's side to see the sedan's tinted passenger side window descending. He caught a glimpse of his pursuers, noting the passenger and driver were wearing ski masks.

The passenger raised his arm, leveling a handgun at Blake's head.

Blake jerked the steering wheel hard to the left. His Defender collided with the sedan, causing the passenger to be thrown about the car. The driver of the sedan then returned the favor, slamming the car into the Defender, causing Blake to veer into a parked van on the right side of the road.

The Defender sideswiped the van, sparks flying everywhere.

Before Blake could maneuver his vehicle back into his lane, it clipped the back bumper of a car parked in front of the van.

After the collision, the Defender spun around one hundred and eighty degrees.

Blake tried to catch his breath. His vehicle had stopped, the motor stalled. Smoke from his tires filled the air. He turned around, looked out his back window, and saw the black sedan's brake lights. The car was slowing to turn back around.

The would-be assassins had unfinished business.

Blake shifted the Defender into neutral and tried to restart it. But it wouldn't turn over. He checked his rearview mirror as he turned his key. The sedan was coming his way. He could see the small barrel of the passenger's gun jetting from the car's window, with a silencer mounted at the end. His heart began to pound against the cavity of his chest as he pleaded for the old Defender to start.

"Come on. Come on!"

And then, it caught.

Blake shifted into first gear, his tires leaving ten-foot rubber marks on the asphalt. He was traveling the opposite way, down the wrong side of the road. He shifted into second and then third gear, honking his horn to prevent a collision with oncoming cars, hoping the approaching drivers would slow down the killers on his tail.

But the sedan was gaining ground, undeterred by the oncoming traffic.

A moment later, Blake jolted in his seat as the sedan rammed the back of his Defender. Before catching his breath, the sedan once again crashed into him, causing his head to fly back into the seat, challenging his ability to maintain control. Blake maneuvered the

Defender into the two right lanes and focused on the upcoming yellow light. He then checked his mirror in anticipation of another devastating blow from behind.

But the sedan was holding back.

Blake looked again at the traffic light. It had turned red, and a few cars were making their way from side streets into the intersection. From his vantage point, he couldn't tell whether more cars were coming, whether the intersection would be clear when he arrived.

But he couldn't slow down. He had to risk flying through the intersection. It drew closer . . . then was upon him.

He mashed on the accelerator.

As he'd feared, a pick-up truck was coming right for him from his left. He could hear the horn and the squealing tires as the truck's driver slammed on his brakes. Blake closed his eyes, clenched his teeth, stiffened his arms, and held on to the steering wheel with white knuckles as he blazed underneath the red light. The driver of the truck turned his steering wheel hard to the right, causing the vehicle to spin out of control and roll over into the intersection.

The calamity was deafening. The toppled, skidding truck slammed into the black sedan, lifting it from the ground and into the wooden utility pole on the corner, which tumbled toward the intersecting streets, suspended only by chords of telephone lines attached to other poles in the near distance.

Hudson took a deep breath and peeked behind him. He was out of harm's way . . . for the moment.

33

The next afternoon, a mild mid-September day, election day around the corner, President Abraham Lincoln, Emancipation Proclamation in hand and clad in his famous frock coat, stared down at Detective Frank Rolly. Blake could see from a distance, however, that Rolly wasn't paying attention to the statue above him. He was too busy checking his watch, wondering why he was standing alone in the middle of Lincoln Park.

It was the largest park on Capitol Hill, and its seven acres were ten blocks east of the US Capitol. With its towering, wide-assortment of aged trees and plush green fescue, it was a place where urban dwellers congregated after work and on weekends to escape the confines of cookie-cutter office cubicles and stacked row houses with little or no yards. Though much smaller than Central Park in New York City, it had a similar vibe. It possessed the serenity of being removed from the hustle and bustle of the political capital of the world while, at the same time, being smack dab in the middle of it.

It was 3:03 p.m.

Walking toward his contact, Blake was wearing a Beastie Boys T-shirt, faded blue jeans, and a rugged pair of brown working boots, apparel that he'd kept in a duffle bag on the passenger-side floorboard of his Defender.

As Blake approached, the unkept, out-of-shape Rolly checked his watch several times. The gesture wasn't lost on Blake.

"Detective Rolly?"

"That's me," Rolly replied in a raspy voice, neglecting to shake hands before wobbling like a wombat to the nearest park bench. "You Blake Hudson? You're late."

"Yeah, sorry about that."

"I've got several other appointments after you," Rolly fibbed, sitting down. "I won't cut into their time."

"No problem," Blake replied, sitting next to Rolly. Rolly's sunglasses had left indentions etched into his sandpapery face, which framed his washed-out, disinterested eyes.

"Shall we get down to business?" Rolly asked.

"Sure. What did you find?"

"Well, I interviewed a few of your neighbors."

"And?"

"They didn't see anything."

"Not surprising."

"Of course, you can't trust everyone you interview," Rolly said. "And a lot of people won't talk because of the 'no-snitch' rule—one of the few rules people don't break in this town."

"Meaning that people don't rat out their friends?"

"They don't rat out anyone—friends, enemies, strangers. Most times, they're scared of the perps. Other times, they're just too lazy to testify. That could be a full-time job in your neighborhood."

"Didn't think my house was in a high-crime area," Blake said.

"You may be right . . . but it *used* to be," Rolly deduced, lifting his pudgy finger to accentuate the last point.

Blake bit his tongue, repressing his intense desire to parse through the detective's questionable logic. That this guy was in charge of the investigation gave Blake limited confidence in its ultimate outcome.

"Point being, your neighbors are zero help."

"I understand."

"The only people around were old timers. Legally blind, probably. I wouldn't be surprised if the perps picked the pockets of those geezers after they ripped you off. Most of your neighbors work," he said, examining Blake's casual clothes, picking up his small stack of papers, and reviewing the incident report. "I see here that you have a work number listed on our report. You between jobs or somethin'?"

"No."

"You work nights?"

"I took the day off," Blake said. "I check voicemail, though, so you can call my office number if you need to reach me."

"You work in an office?"

Blake grew frustrated. "I work for the government."

His answer was intentionally vague. Blake had learned soon after taking his bar exam that lawyers were public enemy number one with many law enforcement officials. For the most part, beat officers and detectives had an indiscriminate abhorrence for attorneys, blaming them all for the rigorous procedures law enforcement officials had to follow to execute a search warrant or make an arrest.

Blake also had learned that Justice Department lawyers were not given special treatment. Quite the contrary, DOJ meant FBI in the minds of local law enforcement officials. FBI, in turn, meant a stuck-up bunch of feds who loved to assert jurisdiction over the best local cases.

"For the government, huh? What is it that—"

"Let me stop you there," Blake interrupted. "You implied a second ago that I was burglarized. Have you come to that conclusion? Because I don't think that makes sense."

"I haven't come to any conclusions yet, pal. We may never figure out motive. But you told the officer on the scene that you had a laptop stolen, correct?"

"That's right, but—"

"But what?" Rolly interrupted. "Last I looked, stealing computer equipment was burglary."

"I don't disagree with that. Maybe I wasn't clear. Other clues lead me to believe that whoever did this had another motive. My files and personal documents, for instance, were scattered all over the floor."

"You think they wanted something off your computer, a file or somethin'?"

"Exactly. Also, there were more valuable things in my house that weren't stolen."

"Rich boy, huh?"

There was an uncomfortable pause. "What?"

"I see your point," Rolly continued, jotting down a few notes on the back of a well-worn piece of yellow notebook paper. "But laptop computers are easy to heist and easier to sell. It's still burglary."

"I understand that the *perps*, as you call them, committed burglary. I'm just saying that they had another motive."

"For all I care, pal, you can speculate all day long—without me here."

"Please continue."

"Says here you had a dog in the house."

"Yeah. They beat him to a pulp. Not sure he's going to survive."

"Sorry to hear that, pal. Really am. But the fact you had a dog means they didn't have much time to pick and choose what they wanted to steal, right?"

"If we're talking burglary, I think that means they would've chosen another house."

"Good point. You a lawyer?"

"I saw the jimmied lock on my back door. Judge would've seen him, her, or them through the back door, which is mostly made of glass. More importantly, they would have seen him."

"Judge?"

"That's my dog's name."

"You *are* a lawyer."

"Nice work, detective. What does that have to do with anything?"

"More than you know," Rolly said under his breath.

"Look, I defend law enforcement officials. I work for the good guys."

"Uh-huh. Well, what if Judge was asleep when they broke in? I saw that you had an enormous pillow in your bedroom. I'm assuming that's where he slept?"

"Correct."

"But if he would've been at the door, or even if he'd rushed to attack them, they would've pummeled him right then and there."

"His food and water bowls would've been plainly in sight, but your point is well taken."

"That's why they pay me the big bucks. That's a joke, of course."

"Judge always sleeps on his pillow on my bedroom floor. And he sleeps often. Two things you should know about Great Danes, though—Judge in particular. First, while he always makes a fuss when he sees a stranger, he also craves attention and doesn't have a vicious bone in his body."

"You didn't tell me he was a Great Dane."

"You didn't ask. Besides, there are pictures of Judge throughout my house."

"All you lawyers are alike."

"Would you give me a break? I'm the victim here."

"Did you have a second point?"

"Yeah, he was an absolute sucker for Pop-Tarts. Even the crinkle of the wrapper caused him to lose his mind and forget everything else around him."

"So what?"

"I keep a hefty supply of Strawberry Pop-Tarts in my kitchen cabinet, and *as I'm sure you saw*, there was an opened Pop-Tart wrapper next to his pillow. I didn't give it to him. I have little doubt that whoever broke into my house lured him into the bedroom with it."

"Why would they do that? If he wasn't bothering them, and he was busy eating his Pop-Tarts, then they would've left him alone, right?"

"If we're talking simple burglary, then I'd agree with you."

"But even if they were looking for documents or files, the same is true. Why beat the dog if he ain't causin' no problems?"

"To make a point," Blake said.

"Interesting."

Elementary, Blake thought. "The second thing you keep implying is that there were more than one of them. Is that what you think?"

"I don't know if that's the case. That's just the way I talk. You know, you see so many robberies and murders, et cetera, that after a while you just start grouping them all together. The fact is, without eyewitnesses, we don't have a good sense of timing or number of perps."

"You find any fingerprints?"

"Yeah, I almost forgot the most important part. Got some hits on prints lifted from your house. You know a Natasha Hensley?"

"Yes. Well, at least I thought I did. She was at my house not long ago."

"Think she could've done this?"

"I'm not ruling out any*thing* or any*one* at this point, but I doubt Natasha is involved." *Even if she was*, Blake thought, *you'll never find her*. "Like I said, she visited the house. I would have expected her fingerprints to be there."

"Okay. Let's see here," Rolly said, thumbing through his file. "Then I guess you also know a John Smith?"

"Why do you ask?"

"Because his fingerprints were all over the joint too."

Blake, rendered speechless, stared paralyzed at the detective.

34

Detective Rolly had told Blake, "I'll get back in touch with you." But having dealt with the Washington Police Department the day before, Blake could read between the lines. That translated, "Don't call me; I'll call you." Blake would never again hear from Rolly. In the detective's mind, there was nothing else to see here. Burglary 101. A dead man had broken into Blake's home, so the box had been checked.

Case closed.

Blake didn't care that Rolly was out of the picture. Right out of the box, he'd lost all respect for the slipshod investigator. Rolly was nothing but a washed-up gumshoe with a chip on his shoulder the size of the Rock of Gibraltar. Blake could've benefited from a thorough investigation, but he'd learned enough from Rolly to keep himself busy. And as he opened the door to the motel's front office, he'd convinced himself that he was making progress.

"I'd like to stay another night," Blake said, tapping his room key on the green Formica front desk, smiling after reading the woman's SORRY, NOT SORRY T-shirt.

"Okay," the overweight, auburn-eyed motel clerk responded. "That's Mr. McCallum in Room 167."

"That's correct."

"And how you gonna pay for this, Mr. McCallum?"

"With cash," Blake replied, "like before."

"Uh-huh. Cash it is," the woman said, giving Blake a skeptical look.

"Something wrong?"

"Ain't nuthin' wrong with me. If I was you, though, I'd be careful."

Blake tensed up, now much more cautious. "What do you mean? Has someone been looking for me?"

"Not yet. But you ain't hard to find."

"I don't understand," Blake said, confused.

"I know what's going on. You come in here. Late last night. No car. Dressed like Justin Bieber. Payin' cash. I didn't ask for no ID. I know you're old enough to get a room."

"What are you talking about?"

"Young guy. Got a *girl* that ain't really his girl. Hey, it ain't none of my business."

"Wait, I haven't been with anyone, including any girls. Have you seen a woman in my room?"

"I'm not lookin', and I don't know where you're hiding her. I just say: Be careful. That's all. I know how this works."

Blake tried not to laugh. "Listen. You've got this figured out, except for a few things. Her boyfriend is no good, and she needs out of that relationship. She's been hit too many times."

"Too many times!?" the woman roared, waving her hand around for added emphasis. "Once is enough! I know what she's been through!"

"That's why I'm here. To make things better." Blake reached for his wallet and pulled out one hundred and sixty dollars. "Look, here's sixty dollars for the room. And here's another hundred for someone who'll watch my back—someone who'll let me know if anyone is snooping around and looking for Justin Bieber."

"I ain't never seen your face, Mr. McCallum."

"Thanks."

"I know what's up! You take care of that girl, now," the woman said, organizing the bills like a deck of cards as she stared at eight green faces of Andrew Jackson. She put three in the cash register and shoved the remaining five in her brassiere. "And spend some of that money on some clothes . . . Bieba Baby," she whispered under her breath after Blake was out of sight.

Blake locked both deadbolts before turning on the lights and plopping face down on the bed. He needed to collect his thoughts. Several pressing questions remained unanswered. And each time he sought conclusive answers, his brain only processed more haunting questions. For example, what role, if any, did the attorney general play?

For now, he thought, he needed to look beyond Bill Kershing. After the meeting with Detective Rolly, all signs pointed to John Smith. He was the leader of the group. He had full access to Main Justice. His fingerprints were all over Blake's house. He was an enigma, a man who had led a life in the shadows. The guy had lived for the cause, whatever the cause de jour was in any given day, week, month, or year. He hadn't agreed with Blake's cautious approach to certain missions, and he likely had thought Blake was or would be betraying the operation behind Smith's back.

It was all cut and dry. Smith had to be the person most responsible for Blake's current misery.

But it was just *too* cut and dry. Smith was smarter than that. Why would he leave fingerprint evidence all over Blake's house? Smith had spent his career in the CIA. He knew better. He would've known how to cover his tracks. If Smith had wanted to check up on Blake, couldn't he—indeed, wouldn't he—make sure his efforts had gone undetected?

And why now? Smith had appeared pleased with Blake's attitude and work after the attack on Main Justice. After the attack, Blake had remained critical of the group's assignments in private but supportive in the company of Smith. Smith would've noticed Blake becoming more hawkish as the days progressed. That is unless Natasha had told Smith otherwise. Even then, Blake hadn't voiced any dissent with respect to the most recent missions. In fact, he'd grown more supportive of the operation after the attack on the Main Justice building and the increased focus on overseas assignments. Of course, rationalizing that overseas assignments posed fewer legal problems was like hoping that the Son of Sam would have his traffic tickets expunged, but Blake clung to silver linings.

Beyond the shiny surface, the circumstantial evidence pointing to Smith just didn't add up; and that included the troubling circumstances surrounding Smith's death. According to a phone message from Clyde Rothman, Smith's death was being reported as a suicide. But in the weeks that he'd come to know Smith, Blake never perceived the man as a candidate to take his own life. And to make matters more suspect, the timing was all too coincidental.

Blake flopped on his back and pulled a pillow over his head as he sorted through all the conflicting circumstances. Maybe he was thinking too much. Maybe the answer was right in front of him. Maybe John Smith was the answer to all of his questions: Smith's leadership role, the tension between their opposing ideologies, the fingerprints.

Once again, the fingerprints. Maybe that's all he needed.

He pulled the pillow from his head and grabbed the phone from the nightstand. He needed to check his phone messages at work. After he dialed the number and entered his ten-digit password, the computerized voice indicated that he had four messages.

"*First message*: Blake, it's Clyde. I have what you requested. Very interesting stuff. Hope you got my earlier message regarding Smith. Let's meet tomorrow at the time and place we discussed previously. Later."

"*Second message:* Hudson, it's General Leavitt at the Pentagon. This is perhaps the most frustrating game of phone tag I've ever played. Thanks for calling me back the other day, but

I was traveling. Let's set up a meeting soon to put this detainee issue to bed. Appreciate your patience. Talk soon."

"*Third message:* Mr. Hudson, you don't know me, but I need to talk to you in person about an important matter. I've left you a written message at Mason's Pawnshop on the corner of Tenth and Pennsylvania, Southeast. Just show your driver's license to the man behind the counter, and he'll give it to you. Also, you'll want to leave your cell phone number with him."

Blake pressed the number nine to save the message, and before he had time to ponder its implications, the fourth message had started.

"*Fourth message:* [Pause] Blake . . . it's Natasha."

Blake hopped to his knees. His back straightened.

"I don't know what to say . . . but I have to say something. I wish you would've been honest with me. I can't believe you betrayed us—betrayed *me*—like you did. I thought we were friends, maybe something more than that. [Pause] I guess I was wrong. It wouldn't be the first time. In the end, I hope you realize the damage you've caused. Though I hate giving you the satisfaction of hearing this . . . you really broke my heart. I hope it was worth it. If you're able to live with yourself, I hope you have a good life."

Blake was stunned. *Devastated!*

He'd been sold out,

Natasha, of all people, blamed him for the group's dissolution. To make matters worse, she left no number, no means by which he could contact her.

But at least one piece of the puzzle was set in place. He was the scapegoat. Someone had told the members of the group—at least one of them—that he was to blame.

To blame for what? He only hoped that his meeting tomorrow with Clyde would prove beneficial.

In the meantime, he needed coffee. It was going to be another long night.

35

The next morning, Blake sat with his hands clasped between his legs on a park bench behind the Smithsonian Institution Museum of Natural History. Heavy clouds blanketed the mid-morning sky, and high winds squalled in cycles over the National Mall. Blake envied the loud, jovial kids riding rainbow-colored horses on the Mall carousel, but not so much the exhausted tourists with pale legs and new blisters on their feet. It was just another day in the nation's capital.

Blake stood up when he spied Clyde Rothman walking toward him. He brushed off the seat of his khaki pants, and then greeted his FBI confidante.

"You look awful, Blake."

"Thanks."

"I'm not kidding. I'm worried about you. Are those new clothes?"

"Yeah, I had to go shopping because I don't want to go back to my house."

"You might want to pull the price tag off the back of your pants."

"And I haven't been sleeping much."

"You look like you've lost weight."

Blake returned to the bench, and Clyde followed course, sitting down and leaving a space between them where he placed a small stack of manila folders.

"Tell me what you've got, Clyde."

Clyde patted the stack of folders. "It's all here, but you won't need to see it."

"Why not?"

"I'll summarize it for you, and I suspect my summary will reveal some clues."

"Were you able to get all the information? Even the harder stuff to access?"

"I think so. Once I started reading the stuff that was easier to access, I was motivated to track down the rest."

"Good . . . I think."

"And during the process, I learned we share another mutual friend."

"Really? Who?"

"Henry Dalton. He said he knew you."

"Yeah, I know Henry. We play basketball together. I saw him on the subway the other day. That reminds me . . . I need to call him."

"Good guy. True believer in our country."

"Agreed. So what did you find?"

Clyde scanned the area and leaned his balding head closer to Blake. "Most of your friends, I'm afraid, have considerable baggage. Marks on their record that would raise a flag in their employment vetting process."

"What do you mean?"

"Jake Reid, for instance," Clyde said, pulling out Jake's file. "This guy was told to leave the CIA after he *murdered* the hoodlum who killed his little girl."

"Whoa!"

"Tell me about it."

"Not sure why I'm surprised. I've only known the guy a few months, and he's already killed at least four people."

"Retribution aside, Reid's methods were brutal. It's unclear from his file, but the Agency would've forgiven him had he remained quiet. The CIA doesn't air its dirty laundry. And retaliation for the death of one's daughter, while not sanctioned, merits a sympathetic look—especially in an operational environment where remission is the general rule."

"So what happened?"

"Reid wouldn't stop yapping. From what it says here, he went crazy, alleging that someone in the CIA had revealed his identity, which, he claims, led to his daughter's kidnapping and death."

"Wow," Blake said, his fingers embedded in his hair. "He never once spoke to us—at least to me—about any children."

"According to his file, Jake Reid hasn't worked for the CIA for over a year. Like you said, he was somewhere on the Baja Coast, no longer someone Uncle Sam employed. The file says he purchased a boat and is a fisherman by trade. This all confirms your understanding."

"But that could be a cover, right?"

"It could be, and because he believes someone inside the CIA exposed him, it's not beyond reason. But these files usually don't lie. Having read hundreds of background reports,

I have no reason to believe this one is inaccurate or misleading. I think Langley booted him from the country."

"But he's still nuts."

"Would your head be screwed on straight if you found your little daughter like this?" Clyde asked, handing a photograph to Blake.

After seeing Rebecca Ann Reid's naked, mutilated body, Blake closed his eyes, grimaced, and returned the photograph to the FBI agent. "What's the meaning behind the note pinned to her body?"

THANKS FOR THE ENTERTAINMENT, MR. REID.

"I think it's obvious."

"That's . . . Clyde, that's the worst thing I've ever seen."

"Evil manifested. You want me to continue?"

"What about Natasha Hensley?" Hers was the most important background file to Blake.

"You mean Natasha *Loginov*?"

"What!?"

"Her picture's in here, so I know why this one interests you," Clyde said, thumbing through the stack of folders and pulling out Natasha's. "Citation for public intox when she was seventeen; other than that, no criminal record. She has other problems, though."

"Like what?"

"Her mother died of cancer when she was ten, and her father was declared a 'missing person' soon thereafter. She was orphaned before age twelve. And I bet you can't guess what her father did for a living?"

"I take it he wasn't a shoe salesman."

"FBI. He was a special agent in the FBI, so I pulled his file. This one is interesting," Clyde noted. "Nikolai Loginov, also known as Roger Hensley, turned CIA agent prior to the Berlin Wall coming down. When things cooled down in Moscow, the CIA pulled him out and relocated him to sunny California. After working a few more years for the Agency, he landed on FBI payroll; looks like we asked him to infiltrate local Communist groups in the area. A few years later, though, he just disappeared. There's no mention in the file about leads or anything else. There was an investigation, but it produced no fruit. The front page of his file is now stamped PRESUMED DEAD."

"She's Russian?" Blake asked, miffed.

"Unclear how much she knows about her father, but it's not for a lack of trying."

"I don't follow."

"She doesn't accept his death. Since changing her name to Hensley, she's been looking for him. Early in her career at NSA—I suspect before she realized how closely those positions are monitored—she used her position to further her crusade. That's a no-no."

"What did she do?"

"She made phone calls and had meetings with people at the FBI to solicit clues regarding her dad. Sound familiar?"

"This is different."

"Why? Because we're meeting on a park bench like a bunch of morons instead of at headquarters like the pros?"

"Go on."

"Anyway, she was either slapped on the wrist, feared she was about to get caught, or just figured it was of no use. Either way, she ended her crusade, and no formal action was taken."

"Anything else on Hensley, or Loginov, or whatever the heck her real name is?"

"The rest is all positive."

"May I see her picture?"

"Here you go. Meet your Mati Hari. A face like that is worth more than gold when you're job is gathering intel from human sources."

"Even a still photo captures her alluring stare."

"The term 'femme fatale' comes to mind. As you may know," Clyde continued, "she made straight As in college at Pepperdine and has an IQ that's off the charts. NSA recruited her for her brain, but then, as you pointed out earlier, detailed her to the Defense Intelligence Agency. Not uncommon for five-tool analysts. I don't know if DIA has a separate file on her."

"This is enough," Blake said. "By the way, I got your message about John Smith."

"I have Smith's file here. At first, I tried to get it through my CIA contact when I requested Jake Reid's file, but he told me the FBI had it."

"You know why?"

"Like I said in my message, the dude committed suicide. Slit his wrists. Did you know any of this?"

"I knew he was dead. Nothing more."

"The CIA asked us to investigate, and so we grabbed his Agency file. Nothing peculiar about that. But by the look on your face, I'm guessing you don't believe he killed himself?"

"Let's just say I'll need the investigators' names."

"No problem. I can get those for you."

"Clyde, my predicament has gotten worse since we last met."

"Your office, your house, your dog. Armed hooligans with ski masks trying to run you off the road like your Mad Max. The AG checking your background files. Smith's fingerprints everywhere."

"The list keeps growing."

"I trust you'll tell me what I need to know, Blake, but I'm worried about you."

"I'm working through my problems, but I need more information first. I'll leave it that."

"You have my number," Clyde said, opening Smith's file. "John Smith is—sorry, *was*—a career spook at Langley. And from his file, an effective one at that."

"Still have a hard time believing that's his real name."

"Believe it. He carried out all sorts of successful counterespionage operations and was promoted often."

"So he's clean?"

"Far from it," Clyde said. "Our old friend Mr. Smith was under CIA internal investigation."

"Why am I not surprised?"

"That explains why they outsourced to the Bureau the investigation into his death. They didn't want people to perceive that the investigators were biased against him."

"What did he do . . . allegedly?"

"You won't believe this one. He was accused of stealing money—large sums of money—from the Agency."

"From the taxpayers, you mean."

"Right. I've worked in government too long."

Blake shook his head. "Incredible. Well, that supports the suicide theory."

Clyde summarized select portions from the file. "Deposited money into foreign bank accounts established to pay off foreign informants. Caught red-handed several months ago. Negotiated a lower price with the informants than he requested from the CIA."

"I don't understand."

"For instance, he'd tell an informant he'd pay him $15,000 and then tell the Agency that he needed $30,000. Fifteen thousand then goes into a Swiss bank account under an assumed name. *Voila!*"

"What a loser."

"These are allegations, mind you. But he was required to pay his ex-wife and children a lot of dough each month for alimony and child support. That's tough sledding on a government salary, especially since he never worked in the private sector. No nest egg."

"Anything else on Smith?"

"I shouldn't editorialize."

"What about Olson?"

"Total stud. This is the guy I want my daughter to marry."

Blake gave him a curious look. "Isn't Emma a toddler?"

Clyde smiled. "He's the exception to the rule for this bunch. He's a G.I. Joe—the best in a group that is considered the best of the best. No baggage. Nothing but one medal and one commendation after another. If this guy was working with you, then whatever you were working on was top priority."

"That doesn't provide me much comfort, Clyde."

"He's done it all. Granted, Delta Force doesn't have many rules to follow, but still. His report is glowing. He gets the job done every time."

"Almost every time."

"Sadly, yes," Clyde said, packing up his files. "And that's all I have for you."

"I can never repay you, Clyde."

"You should thank Henry Dalton. He leveraged a contact at DOD to get Olson's file. And they keep Delta Force's background info *very* close hold."

"I will do that," Blake promised.

"Thoughts?"

"What jumps out is that, of the five of us associated with Scavenger Hunt, three have questionable pasts—although Natasha's infractions are small potatoes when compared to Smith's."

"Agreed."

"But Natasha never told me she was Russian or that her parents were dead."

"She believes her father is still alive."

"True, but she could've told me that."

"Good point."

"Let's face it . . . Jake's retribution was diabolic. But after seeing that photograph, I can't blame him. Law or no law."

"So what's your plan?"

"I'd like to figure out where these people are, and how they were recruited to the Scavenger Hunt team. Right now, I don't see common threads, except that we all have ties to government employment. That isn't enough to draw meaningful conclusions. The one conclusion I have drawn is that someone—inside or outside my group—has set me up as a patsy."

"Did you find this information helpful?" Clyde asked.

"Absolutely. Listen, these files are crucial to the extent they explain what motivates people."

"Meaning?"

"At least three in my group were vulnerable to extortion. Smith, for instance, could've been dragooned to undertake the leadership role. No telling how venal he was or what actions he'd taken to clear his name. There's also no telling what dials those behind the curtain were turning as leverage against Jake or Natasha."

"Makes sense."

"On the other hand, if Brent's files are complete, then we know they have nothing on him. Look, if anyone's trying to blackmail me, then I'm too stupid to notice; but my past is squeaky clean compared to some of these folks."

"So where do you go from here?" Clyde asked.

"To Mason's Pawnshop on the corner of Tenth and Pennsylvania."

"What?"

REVELATIONS

36

Charleston, South Carolina

This King James Bible had sat in the same motel drawer for decades. Like countless glossy-black, leather-bound Bibles sitting in motel drawers, it had gathered its share of dust. Once or twice a week, a curious guest or diligent housekeeper would open the drawer, allowing a faint glare of light to break and enter, but otherwise, this Bible had existed in complete darkness.

But then, many years ago, a small Baptist church plant opened about the same time the motel closed. The young, red-haired pastor with boyish looks beseeched his modest flock of stubborn Christians to ante up funds for new Bibles. When the tithe fell short, the congregation resolved by a vote of twenty to nine that used—or as the deacons called them, *pre-owned*—Bibles would serve the Lord's purposes. The church submitted a reasonable bid for the Bibles, and the motel accepted without hesitation. The unexpected windfall the motel made on the transaction helped facilitate its bankruptcy proceedings. The church, for its part, was ecstatic and commenced its spiritual edification.

Now, the seasoned and aged pastor of the 8,483-member congregation, his once-red hair now grayish, his once-boyish face now lined with the wrinkles of thousands of sermons and baptisms, was walking with that now faded King James Bible in his hand. The pages of the Old and New Testaments—once pasted together from neglect; now dog-eared and filled with underlined text and margin notes—cut through the cool air with each step and sway. God's Word was making its way down the bright hallway of Cell Block C in the fortified brig.

"He just wants to make fun of you . . . of your beliefs," the guard warned, escorting him down the hallway. "He's not interested in spiritual guidance. He's met with reverends, priests, palm readers, charlatan faith healers, you name it. They all left in a huff."

189

"Thanks for the warning," the pastor said, increasing the pace of his steps.

"Another man of the cloth to see you, Omar. I told him he was wasting his time—that you'll only mock him. Still not sure why the attorney general allows preachers in here to see you, security clearance or not."

"How dare you insult me in front of my guest!?" the terrorist Omar Saud said in perfect English, his black, curly hair falling below his hypnotizing brown eyes.

"The devil has a special spot for you," the guard said.

"Get out of my sight. Allah will judge us both."

"Good riddance, murderer. Keep the venomous spit in your mouth this time, or you'll be back in solitary confinement."

"You infidels are all alike," Saud said, directing his words to the pastor, the terrorist's jawbones protruding from his slim, dark face.

"You called for *me*, remember?"

"I asked for a preacher of the Protestant faith. I didn't ask for you by name. Had I known that you would come here dressed like a filthy pig, I would've asked for anyone *but* you."

"These are the best clothes that I own."

"If that's true, then your god doesn't think much of you."

"He provides everything I need."

"You are weak!" His scream was followed by a maddening laugh that could wake the dead. "I expected someone armed with fire and brimstone!"

The preacher smiled. "How can I help you, Mr. Saud?"

"You can humor me with your beliefs. I wish to hear more about them."

The preacher began to thumb through his Bible.

"Please sit down on the floor," Saud said. "I apologize that I have no chair or bench to make your stay more comfortable. My accommodations are, as you can see, less than satisfactory for company."

The pastor eyed Omar Saud and was reluctant to sit down alone with him in the small cell. Saud sat near the back wall, between the metallic toilet and small washbasin, only the cold, polished, concrete floor separating the two men.

"What?" Saud continued, noticing the pastor's anxiety. "Will your god not protect you?"

"*Our* God expects me to use the brain he gave me."

"Then have no fear," the terrorist said, holding up the shackles that bound him to the wall, the veins of his thin, toned arms revealed. "I'm not going anywhere."

"Thanks."

"Do not thank me, coward. You were about to tell me about your beliefs."

"I believe this book in my hand reveals the answers to the greatest mystery of the world."

"Now *that* is the best hook I've heard so far," Saud said. "I only wish we had popcorn."

"I believe in the Gospel, which means Good News. That is, the triune God—Father, Son, and Holy Spirit—is sovereign, perfect, and holy and that He created the universe and the earth and everything in them. He created Adam and Eve to worship Him in the Garden of Eden, but they rebelled against Him and brought sin into the world. Since that fateful day, mankind has lived in a fallen world and has been separated from God because of our sins."

"So much for your good news."

"Yes, you're right. We're left with a huge existential and eternal problem. Nothing good about that, and it gets worse before it gets better. God must punish us for our sins because He's holy, and the Bible says that the 'wages of sin is death.' What's more, we, being unrighteous sinners, can't do anything ourselves to satisfy his righteous wrath and judgment."

"I'm still waiting for the good news, preacher."

"So here it is. God, in His infinite grace, love, and mercy, provided his only begotten Son, Jesus Christ, as a substitute for our sins. Jesus was born of a virgin and lived a perfect life only to die as a substitutionary atonement for our sins."

"Jesus and his exclusivity. Your beliefs are discriminating and evil."

"Jesus," the preacher continued, "by living a perfect life and dying on a cross, paid the debt we owed and satisfied the covenant we couldn't on our behalf. He was persecuted, mocked, tortured, and crucified, but he finished the job he set out to accomplish, crushing the head of the serpent, conquering sin, and saving His people from God's wrath. For those of us who are justified by His blood, He gets our sinful record and we get his spotless record."

Saud spat at him.

"And here's the best part," the pastor continued, unfazed. "Jesus was raised to life three days after death and ascended to heaven to sit at the right hand of the Father. Now, all who believe in the Christ and repent of their sins will be reconciled to God and saved."

"I've heard this superstitious rubbish before. It's all nonsense."

"That's exactly what Jesus's brother, James, thought. James had grown up with Jesus. He knew him. But he didn't believe what Jesus was preaching. He didn't believe that Jesus was the Son of God. Everything Jesus was selling must've been embarrassing for James. Jesus and James shared the same home . . . the same mother. But *after* Jesus died and was resurrected, James experienced a radical change. He began preaching publicly—in hostile, life-threatening environments—that Jesus was the Christ. But there's more. The mobs killed James for arguing the case for his brother. His actions make no sense whatsoever unless he was convinced of Jesus' resurrection."

"James was a lunatic like his brother."

"So, too, then, were Jesus's apostles, his primary followers. They were convinced that he'd never die on earth. Yet, though they gave up everything they owned to follow him, they were still known for their many doubts. But once again, after Jesus died, there were *zero* doubts. They claimed the risen Lord had come to visit them. They had *touched* him. They spoke of his resurrection with great specificity and without fear. Their actions made no sense unless they personally witnessed a dead man walking. They knew they'd die for their preaching, and eleven out of twelve were brutally murdered for proclaiming Jesus as the resurrected savior."

After being interrupted numerous times in more than an hour, the pastor finished proselytizing. Saud sneered at him. "Leave your Bible, Preacher. And get out of my cell. You are lucky that my arms are shackled. You make me sick to my stomach, and like Jesus' apostles, I hope someone kills you for your lies."

Washington, DC

Blake picked up the phone and dialed a number he'd memorized.

"FBI personnel."

"Blake Hudson for Clyde Rothman."

"Who is this?"

"This is Blake Hudson in the Attorney General's Office."

"Oh, this is Special Agent Richard Andrews. I didn't realize the attorney general had a direct interest in this matter. You want to speak to Agent Rothman's supervisor?"

"No," Blake said, "I just want to speak to Rothman."

There was no response.

"Hello?"

"Yeah, Mr. Hudson? You didn't hear?"

"Hear what?"

"Clyde Rothman died in an automobile accident last night. We're in his office gathering his personal items for his family."

Charleston, South Carolina

Omar Saud was in tears and couldn't sleep. Throughout his reading, he'd torn pages out of the Bible and tossed them about his cell. Now, he was attempting to reassemble it. The food the guard had left for him was cold, but Saud had inhaled it.

"Guard! Come here!"

The guard walked over to Saud's cell. "I'm glad to see you ate your food, murderer."

"I need to see the preacher again . . . the mighty soldier for God. I need to speak with someone. I need to speak to my people."

"You won't be speaking to anyone else, Saud."

"I need to tell my people they must stop the jihad. I need to tell them that I was wrong."

Saud's throat started constricting. He couldn't breathe, now gasping for air.

The guard reached underneath the bars and snatched the empty plate. His captive had eaten everything . . . including the poison.

"It's a pleasure watching you die."

Saud fell to his knees. "I need to . . . I need to call off the . . . please . . . they will listen to me . . . I can end this."

"I'll see you in Hell, Saud."

"No," he gasped. "I will not be there."

As the guard walked off, Omar Saud spent the last seconds of his life praying to God, through his new savior, for the man who'd just killed him.

37

Washington, DC

Clyde Rothman was dead. That was all Blake could think about on Halloween night as he watched trick-or-treaters walk by from his basement window. He couldn't expunge that awful fact from his mind. The special agent had told Blake that it was a traffic accident. But was that true? Another coincidence in a long and growing list? He hoped that his problems hadn't led to Clyde's death.

From his new rented basement apartment, he had logged hours eyeing the sidewalk. It was a limited view. Between the heavy golden curtains, embossed with white fleur-de-lis, and through the thin security bars, he could see as high as a passerby's belt-line; but no matter how low he crouched, he couldn't see any adult faces.

He turned his attention to the small living area where a Halloween episode of "The Office" was on the TV. The flat-screen TV provided the only lighting in the otherwise obscure basement, making it easy for him to see outside. The small opening at the bottom of the window allowed him to hear the distant sounds of automobiles and laughter throughout Capitol Hill Southeast.

The owners of the English basement, a retired couple who'd spent their lives in the Foreign Service, had decorated it with items long ago abandoned from the primary part of the house, which consisted of the two floors above the basement. The basement walls were composed of red, exposed brick. The Berber carpet in the living area was brown, but not as brown as the couch, the recliner chair, the marred coffee table, and the fake bearskin rug that, for some reason, was hibernating on the kitchen floor. An antique white refrigerator, sitting on a patch of pink linoleum, hosted pictures of a younger, more dynamic duo working throughout the world for the US State Department.

Blake almost fell backward once he refocused his attention outside.

Two large, black rain boots were positioned outside his window.

He had not witnessed their owner's approach. Someone was standing six feet in front of him, facing the house, possibly looking at the basement.

Blake ducked below the window ledge, worried that someone had spotted him. He couldn't hear anyone talking, nor could he discern whether the person outside was just waiting for others. His back was up against the interior brick wall. He focused his eyes on the plaster ceiling. His heart was pounding, and he could feel the sweat starting to accumulate on his scalp and forehead.

He searched the room for a weapon—a knife, a baseball bat, anything. But he'd brought little with him to the basement, and the knives in the kitchen drawers were made of plastic.

He'd never before needed a weapon. Judge had always provided adequate protection. But his four-legged friend was still struggling at the animal hospital several blocks away. Months later, he still was fighting to survive his savage beating. But maybe Blake didn't need Judge tonight. Maybe he didn't even need a weapon. Maybe he was just overreacting.

It was, he reminded himself, Halloween. Trick-or-treaters often contemplated whether to knock on doors hidden in the darkness. Was this nothing more than a responsible parent waiting for his kids? Blake wasn't sure, but he continued to play it safe.

He scooted along the interior wall until he reached the side of the window. Once there, he peered between the curtains.

The boots were walking away.

But as soon as he exhaled there was a loud ringing noise.

Blake lunged for his phone, grabbed it from the coffee table, and turned it off before the second ring. Then he retreated to the window and peeked through the curtains once again.

The person wearing the black rain boots had stopped. Blake watched the boots turn and start back toward the basement.

His heart sank as ominous thoughts filled his mind. This person wasn't panning for free candy. The ringing phone had evoked a reaction uncharacteristic of a normal pedestrian, diligent parent, or trick-or-treater. He continued to watch until the unknown figure changed course again and continued on his way down the sidewalk.

Blake turned on his phone to learn the caller had left a message. Caller ID didn't reveal a name, but it produced an unknown number. This was his guy. Without listening to the message, he walked to the kitchen and hit the send button, which rang the last caller.

"You called?" Blake asked.

"I did. I'm glad you decided to visit the pawnshop."

"So what's next?"

SCAVENGER HUNT

"I just left you a message to meet me in thirty to forty minutes at the second place I described in my note."

"I'll see you there."

Blake rushed to turn off the television and collect his things.

————

Blake walked out his front door, his black raincoat zipped to his neck. Low-lying rain clouds were clearing out, but the sky was ominous, and more precipitation was in the immediate forecast.

Jack-o-lanterns protected by covered porches littered many Capitol Hill doorsteps. Yet there was little movement throughout the city blocks. No cars. Few kids in costume. Not even anyone smoking on a porch. Blake could hear traffic noise in the distance, but there were no sounds in the immediate vicinity except for the humming of electricity used to illuminate the century-old street corners in the area.

He picked up the pace, not only to meet his deadline but because he was afraid of being followed. Marching forward, he decided to take the subway rather than walk. Walking would take too long and lead him down darker streets. He wanted to avoid shadowy places on this night. He had first contemplated driving. But he didn't have access to his Defender, and hailing a cab or trying to find an Uber or Lyft on Halloween in DC would be a fruitless effort. While little sugar-bloated monsters and superheroes were preparing for bed, a larger number of grown-ups were searching for rides to take them bar hopping. Halloween was a lucrative night in the District for those serving up spirits.

Blake walked up Sixth Street and turned left on North Carolina Avenue, making his way to Eastern Market. Eastern Market was the oldest continually operating farmers' market in the city, and it attracted a great number of residents and tourists. People would come from near and far to purchase a wide assortment of meats, poultry, fish, and novelty items.

Eastern Market also boasted other services—namely, an animal hospital. Blake couldn't help but stop and look inside the dark building. He leaned forward, placing his hands on the door, his breath causing condensation to form on the glass. The latest prognosis wasn't good. Judge was dying. Blake wished more than anything to be bedside with his best friend, but he was fighting for his own life.

Be strong, Judge. I'll visit you soon. I promise.

The rain failed to derail the "Howl-o-ween" festivities. Hundreds of people dressed in costumes celebrated the event in the blocked-off street adjacent to the marketplace. College students, for the most part, guzzled cheap draft beer out of plastic cups. Children and youthful parents climbed aboard the hayride, mesmerized by the size of the towering brown and white Clydesdales pulling the load. As Blake waded through the crowd, he heard bits and pieces of gossip, anecdotes, and political power plays being hatched. Each snapshot of normalcy troubled him. It made him wish more than ever that his current trials would end.

After breaking from the bustling marketplace, he noticed a homeless man sitting upright on a tattered, food-stained blanket near a crate of pumpkins and a mound of hay. Before Blake could avoid him, the homeless man made eye contact and flashed Blake a toothless smile. Well adapted to Washington, DC, the man was holding a cardboard sign that read: RE-ELECT PRESIDENT CLEMENTS AND HELP THE HOMELESS.

Blake continued walking. A few months ago, he may have stopped and shot the breeze. Now, he needed to hasten his journey. He checked his watch before approaching the man and, when he looked back up, was surprised to see that the man had turned over the cardboard sign. It now read: ELECT SEN. CUMMINGS AND HELP THE HOMELESS.

"Will you help the homeless tonight, sir?" the man asked.

Blake scooped some change from his pockets and jingled it in his right hand. "I liked the sign a lot better when it was turned over," Blake said, handing over the change without breaking stride.

"I'll turn it back around for a dollar," the shrewd man replied.

"Turn it around when I come back, and we'll see," Blake said over his shoulder. "Better yet, just keep it turned to Clements all night. Cummings isn't going to help you."

"Thank you, sir!" the man yelled. "I'll turn it around right now! Go President Clements!"

Blake was only a few hundred yards away from the subway when he crossed the street and picked up the pace. Reaching the other side, he heard the homeless man's voice again in the distance.

"Will you help the homeless tonight, sir?"

Blake stopped for a moment and looked back toward the marketplace. A man walking in a black trench coat and wearing a *Phantom of the Opera* mask was walking his way, passing the homeless man without acknowledging his existence.

"I see how it is! Thank you anyway, sir! You have a good night!"

As Blake continued walking, he peered over his shoulder again. The Phantom had on black rain boots and was coming right at him.

Once he reached Pennsylvania Avenue, Blake jaywalked through light traffic, eluding fast-moving cars driving toward downtown. No longer worried about appearing conspicuous, he began to jog until he entered the Metro station. He then bolted down the escalators so fast that he needed to grab the moving handrail to keep his balance. When he reached the bottom, he pulled out his wallet and retrieved his subway card. After confirming that he had enough credit to pay the fare, he dashed toward the turnstiles. The electronic turnstile swallowed his card and then spit it back out as he gained access. Blake scurried down another set of smaller escalators until he reached the platform.

There were two families and a group of college students waiting for the train. That gave him a sense of immediate, albeit negligible, security. Anyone after him wouldn't want to confront or attack him with witnesses around. But the would-be passengers were waiting for the subway train traveling in the *opposite* direction. That wasn't good news. If their train arrived first, then Blake may need to board with them to avoid the Phantom. And if he were forced to do that, he'd be late to his rendezvous with his potential informant.

Blake noticed the Phantom had descended the first set of escalators, purchased a subway card, and was making his way to the turnstile. Blake positioned himself in an area of limited visibility. He could see the Phantom, but the Phantom couldn't see him. At least for now.

Blake was elated when the lights started flashing on his side of the platform.

His train was coming.

He looked again at the Phantom, who'd just passed through the turnstile.

But then something unexpected happened. A woman's voice blared from the overhead speakers, echoing throughout the subway platform. *Attention all Metrorail passengers waiting for the Blue Line train to Franconia/Springfield. Your train has been delayed. We apologize for any inconvenience, and thank you for using Metrorail.*

The message was repeated as the lights on the other side of the platform began blinking. The train traveling in the opposite direction was arriving. To add to his frustration, Blake could see the front lights of his would-be train. But it wasn't moving. So close, yet so far away.

Blake saw the Phantom approaching the second set of escalators. He was drawing near. He would soon find his likely target.

Blake had to make a quick decision as his would-be witnesses' train arrived, and the doors opened. He hoped that some of those standing near him were waiting for the Orange Line train instead of Blue. But that hope was short-lived. He noticed that no passengers were getting off the train, and all those waiting with him were boarding. He would be left all alone to face a potential assassin.

This is the Blue Line train to Largo Town Center.

Three seconds to decide. The doors on the train were about to close, he was all alone on the platform, and the Phantom was fast approaching.

The Phantom looked around the platform. The masked man was peering through the windows of the passing train leaving the station before putting his hands in his pockets and shaking his head. Blake watched him turn and spy him as he ascended in the elevator. Without hesitatioh, the Phantom rushed toward the escalators, barreling up the moving stairs to the second station level.

"Come on!" Blake exclaimed as the glass-covered elevator groaned upward. The doors of the elevator opened and Blake sprinted to the escalators, hurdling the turnstile.

As the Phantom made his way through the turnstile, Blake galloped up the long flight of escalator stairs, jumping three stairs at a time with each motion. When he reached the ground level, he rushed down and across Pennsylvania Avenue, back toward the Capitol. And then he saw an unoccupied cab waiting at a red light. Without hesitation, he climbed into the backseat.

"Take me to the Capitol! Fast!"

Blake stared through the back window of the taxi as the light turned green. The Phantom was glaring back at him, his hands in the pockets of his black trench coat . . . the light from the streetlamp glistening off the steel-plated handgun attached to his hip.

38

lake hopped from the cab and treaded up the steep incline that defined Capitol Hill proper. With a break in the heavy cloud cover, lunar illumination provided a well-lighted pathway. The moon, full and prodigious, had little trouble penetrating the moving clouds. Trying not to dwell on his Phantom encounter, he forced his mind to analyze the risk that accompanied his imminent rendezvous with the mysterious caller.

Was this man a legitimate informant, or was he an assassin?

Blake continued around the Senate side of the Capitol. Walking downhill, his pace increased. After passing the dome-topped symbol of representative democracy, he diverted his path from the sidewalk and traipsed across the grass to the meeting place.

The Summer House on the West Front lawn of the Capitol reminded Blake of a hexagonal fort. On the outside, the myriad non-native shrubs largely secluded its brick structure, and three of its six walls contained arched doorways sporting wrought-iron gates. Tourists and other visitors could hear the running water from the nearby grotto. Inside, stone bench seats with armrests were attached to the red, weatherworn bricks that composed its inner walls.

The Summer House was built just in time to witness the raucous inauguration of President James Garfield and to hear the gunshot a few months later that—along with the infection precipitated by three months of medical malpractice—caused his death. A smattering of eccentric historians believed that Charles Guiteau, the slighted madman who assassinated Garfield, hatched his plan within the Summer House walls.

Blake walked down four steps on the east side of the Summer House, opened the wrought-iron gate, and walked inside. The place was empty. He checked his watch. Fifteen minutes late. His circuitous, evasive route had cost him precious minutes. He sat down on the stone bench, facing the National Mall in the distance. He looked around again, but there was no one in sight. Had the mysterious caller come and gone, thinking Blake was a no-show? Had the man lost his nerve? Was this all a hoax?

After ninety seconds, he looked up and was startled by what he saw—a tall, thin man wearing a fedora and a dark overcoat was no more than twenty yards away, standing just beyond the west entrance. Blake hadn't heard the man arrive. He turned and peered at Blake while lighting a cigarette. The flame from his gold-plated Zippo lighter revealed the man's face for an instant, but Blake struggled to discern his features. Struck by the uncomfortable, bilateral stare, Blake gazed down, waiting for the man to approach him.

During his short cab ride to the Capitol, Blake had pondered this moment. He knew that meeting a stranger who'd called from out of the blue was an enormous gamble. Those intent on harming him could've staged this rendezvous. He couldn't rule out the possibility that the goon at the pawnshop—the one who'd passed on the meeting information—was privy to the plot, a co-conspirator. Blake had no idea who'd called him . . . had no reason to believe the mysterious caller was credible. But before he'd reached the Capitol, Blake had convinced himself that someone bent on setting him up would have arranged things differently. The mysterious caller's plan was so immersed in unorthodoxy that it dripped with trustworthiness.

For this reason alone, he was confident the mysterious caller—his would-be informant—was on his side. Now that the moment of truth had arrived, however, his mind was entertaining second thoughts. But despite the tall, thin man's peculiar behavior, Blake remained steadfast. He was tired of running away, tired of being bivouacked in low-budget motel rooms and confined to a dark basement stuck in another generation. And as he weighed the potential consequences against the likely advantages, his adrenaline gave him increased confidence.

He was ready.

Blake decided to wait no longer and make the first move. But just as he was preparing to rise and address the man, a young couple entered from the east gate, holding hands and kissing each other. As they walked by him, Blake put his head down in disgust. He'd waited too long. The rendezvous would be delayed if not postponed. He remained patient, trying not to appear frustrated. He peeked at the west entrance. The tall, thin man was still standing in the same spot, his cigarette halfway smoked. Blake shook his head in disgust as the silly lovebirds sat down against the north wall to his right.

"Johnny, you're so sweet," the young woman purred.

The young man, Blake realized, wasn't shy. It was clear he was proud of the attention he was garnering and was eager to escalate the public display of affection. "That party was a joke," he said. "What a bunch of losers. Did you get a look at some of those costumes?"

SCAVENGER HUNT

"I couldn't peel my eyes off you," she said, giggling with excitement.

As the couple kissed, Blake wondered whether she'd made that sappy comment with a straight face. He couldn't believe it. And he was growing uncomfortable with this dime show, knowing the lovebirds relished people watching them swap spit, stimulated by the voyeuristic atmosphere. One thing was clear. Casanova and his squeeze, Blake gathered, were either drunk or new acquaintances.

At the risk of being declared a Peeping Tom, Blake raised his head again to see that the tall, thin man had nearly finished his smoke. If the impetuous exhibitionists continued their sensual sideshow, Blake thought, he, too, might need a cigarette. But he had to remain focused. He knew time was running out; he had to find a discreet way to approach the bizarre man. Before he had time to concoct a strategy, however, he heard the woman slap the young man's face.

"How dare you!?" she screamed. "Get your hands off me!"

"What? What was that for!?"

"You're a pig! I can't believe you thought you could do that!"

"Be quiet. Don't make a scene," he said, reaching for her arm as she stood up and started walking toward the fountain. "I didn't do anything wrong," he pleaded.

Blake focused on the fracas with half-hearted interest. Absent walking off, there was no way to avoid it. Feigning total disinterest, moreover, would've been the most conspicuous, suspicious conduct imaginable. He noticed that the tall, thin man had stepped on the remains of his cigarette and had now decided to engage in the domestic squabble.

"What's going on here?" the tall, thin man asked. "Are you all right, ma'am?"

"I didn't do anything. She—"

"I wasn't talking to you, son!" the tall, thin man exclaimed, pointing his finger at the young man. Blake was beginning to wonder whether he was invisible, for no one had acknowledged his presence.

"Mister," the woman said, "can you please walk me home?"

"Absolutely," the tall, thin man replied. He sneered at the young man. "You better hope I don't see you again."

The young man didn't respond to the tall man's threat, probably knowing that any rejoinder would incite increased verbal conflict if not a physical skirmish. Instead, he voiced his disgust that a total stranger was escorting her home. "You don't even know this guy!"

"After what you pulled," she cried, "I don't even know *you*!"

"Whatever. You're blowing this way out of proportion. All I did was . . ."

Blake remained seated in sheer disbelief. His would-be informant had just sauntered off with what appeared to be a damsel in distress. Blake was trying to digest the remarkable turn of events. It seemed the closer he came to learning valuable information, the further removed he was from finding answers to his questions.

He buried his face in his hands, thinking about the lost opportunity to learn more about those chasing after him. He mumbled under his breath and lunged forward to stand up.

And at that point, the young Casanova, whose face was still concealed from Blake's view, spoke.

"Blake Hudson, I presume."

39

Blake perked up at Casanova's statement.

"Look away," the young man ordered. "There's no need for you to see me, and there are at least three ways into this place. I want us guarding all entrances. I've got your back covered; you cover mine."

"All right," Blake said, still confused and in no position to negotiate more suitable terms of communication. "I have to be honest. I'm baffled. Who were those other people?"

"I have no idea who the man was, but based on his overreaction to what just happened, we know he's not important to us."

"What do you mean?"

"He wasn't anyone after you or me. Had he been, we'd both be dead. He would've eliminated us on the spot. The persons who concern me—and who should concern *you*—wouldn't waste time saving a girl from possible date rape."

"*Eliminated us?*"

"You have no idea what you're up against, do you?"

"Apparently not. That's why I'm here."

"I understand. Although, if you knew what I do, you probably wouldn't have come. You don't even know who I am."

"I've measured the risks."

"Have you?" the young man asked.

Blake paused. "And the girl?"

"She's a friend of mine . . . actually, a friend of a friend."

"She seemed like more than that to me. You practically had your tongue down her throat."

"Were you followed here?"

204

"I was followed to the Eastern Market Metro station but, with a little luck, escaped when I found a cab."

"I hate to hear that someone was following you, but it's not surprising."

"I don't know what's going on. Somebody ransacked my house, beat my dog, tried to run me off the road and shoot me, and now, I have strange men in masks following me around."

"You need to lower your voice."

"Sorry," Blake whispered.

"Did anyone follow you to this spot after you left the cab?"

"I don't think so."

"Okay."

"Maybe I'm just being paranoid. I've lost my mind."

"Well, let me help you find it. First, you can never be too careful. I don't doubt cold-blooded killers are targeting you. And we're not talking about street thugs and guttersnipes; these are pros. Second, you're involved in a hot mess that implicates matters well above your pay grade, and the people tracking you are ruthless."

"How do you know all this?"

"I'll get to that."

"Please do."

"I'll start from the beginning, but let's be clear—I'm not comfortable, at least at this point, telling you who I am. Once you hear what I have to say, there's no telling how you'll react or what you'll do to find the information you need. I can tell by now that you don't know squat."

"It's not for lack of trying."

"I'll tell you how I know what's going on . . . how I found you. But nothing more. That's for my protection and for the safety of the brave young woman you just saw. We're placing our lives in further danger by reaching out to you. Those are my terms. Agreed?"

"Agreed."

"I know that you're part of a covert group engaged in an operation that, shall we say, takes certain matters into its own hands. How am I doing so far?"

"I don't know what you're talking about."

"Listen!" the young man exclaimed in an angry whisper. "We don't have time to play games! If you're unwilling to cooperate or you're not the person I think you are, then I'll walk away right now!"

"How do I know I can trust you? I don't know you from Adam."

"I gain nothing but further exposure by being here. I'll be content to leave this behind altogether and go about my life. I'm not asking anything of you."

"No, wait!" Blake pleaded as the young man began to stand up. Silence followed his pleas as he strove to make a decision.

"You've already told me somebody ransacked your house and beat your dog. You've also told me that strange men may be following you, trying to kill you. What do you have to lose by trusting me?"

Blake didn't respond. He looked overhead, through the tree's branches and leaves, being ravaged by the high winds, to see that heavy clouds had moved in and were attempting to cover the moon.

"Think of it this way," the young man continued. "Given what you've been through and what's going on, what purpose would I serve against your interests? If I were one of the bad guys, I could've taken you out long before. So let me ask you again. How am I doing so far?"

"You skipped cold and warm and went straight to hot."

"That's more like it. Here's the deal. I worked with a guy several years ago on the Hill."

"What's his name?"

"Just listen. After two years of working together, we became close friends. When our career paths diverged, he remained a loyal employee to my old boss, and I sought different opportunities in the private sector."

"I don't know where you're going with this."

"Although I left the Hill, we still spoke on the phone at least every other day. We would talk about sports and politics mostly, but other subjects were free game. Girls, for instance. About five months ago, however, my friend stopped calling me. When I'd call him, he'd act frightened and clearly wasn't himself. I had a hunch something was wrong, but he assured me he was just stressed out and mired in his work. It was understandable—the nature of the business."

"Whatever business that is."

"Bear with me, and keep your voice down."

"Right," Blake whispered.

"Not long after his unusual behavior started, my friend came to my house in a panic. He told me that he'd been asked to help establish an unorthodox, presumably illegal, operation. It was staffed by a diverse cadre of people who carried out missions—or attacks if you will—against suspected terrorists. It was all underground and riddled with legal problems. Run out of the Justice Department, of all places. Is this hitting close to home?"

"I'm still here. Go on."

"It wasn't the nature of this operation that concerned my friend. He wasn't thin-skinned, and he was privy to highly classified intelligence and threat information. Rather, he was bothered—visibly shaken—by the fact that he had to coordinate all this through a guy named Parker Johnson."

"Parker Johnson?"

"Parker Johnson, he told me, is an intimidating, demanding, and secretive man. He only met my friend in person on one occasion, but they communicated by phone regularly. Johnson would provide him with updates on your operation."

"Did your friend tell you what Parker Johnson looked like?" Blake asked.

"He did. He gave me a detailed description the last night I spoke with him. That night, my friend stopped by my house on his way out of town. He'd just returned from the Korean War Memorial where Parker Johnson was supposed to meet him."

"Why?"

"I don't know. It doesn't matter. What matters is that Johnson was a no-show."

"So? People miss meetings all the time."

"It was a *sign*. Johnson had severed their communication. My friend was afraid for his life. He told me that Johnson's whack jobs were following him. He feared the operation that he'd helped create was coming unraveled. People were becoming afraid of leaks, and your group's assignments were becoming riskier. He told me that if something ever went wrong, all loose ends would be severed. Parker Johnson, he said, would clean up his mess to protect both himself and my friend's boss. Honestly, at the time, I chalked it all up to hullaballoo. I thought he was freaking out over nothing, but it wasn't like him to jump to outlandish conclusions."

"Where's your friend now? Or can you tell me?"

"My friend is *dead*. That's why I'm here talking to you. He told me that if he ever disappeared I needed to find you and tell you what was going on. He also told me that he thought there was someone on the inside."

"Did I know your friend? Who is he?"

"You didn't know him, but he knew of you. He told me how to find you."

"What was his name? I need more. Who is it working on the inside?"

"One question at a time. I don't know what he meant by there being someone on the inside. Maybe someone in your group knows what's going on behind the scenes. But back to your first question. My friend's name was Peter Karnes. They said that he died in a car accident, but that's a lie. He was murdered."

"How do you know?" Blake asked, thinking about Clyde Rothman, who had met a similar fate.

"The girl you just saw was with him the night he died. They both were in Greenville, South Carolina—Peter's hometown. He'd left Washington to escape this Johnson fellow. But Johnson or his whack jobs followed him there. And they *killed* him."

"How do you know he was murdered?"

"Because it was reported as a drunk-driving incident. Peter hadn't been drinking that night. He and his girlfriend—his fiancée—had spent the evening together watching movies. She is from Greenville too."

"She told you this?"

"Yeah. He dropped her off at her parents' house just after midnight. He told her he was going home. His car was found in a ditch less than two hours later. He was miles away from his house. His blood-alcohol level was more than twice the legal limit."

"Maybe he hit the bars on his way home."

"Give me a break, man! Did you hear what I just said!? He hadn't been drinking the whole night. He'd just dropped off his fiancée. He was found less than two hours later in the middle of Nowhere, South Carolina, zip code E-I-E-I-O, with enough alcohol in his system to—"

"So what do you believe happened?" Blake interrupted.

"They found him. That's what happened. We'll probably never learn the details, but there are several plausible scenarios. They could've run him off the road, into the ditch, and then poured Jim Beam down his throat. They could've stopped him and made him chug a bottle and then get back in his car, only to run him off the road. They could've liquored him up, killed him, and then put him back in the driver's seat after they totaled his car. The possibilities are endless."

Blake couldn't quit thinking about Clyde. Clyde had been murdered. And Blake couldn't help but remember the sedan that had tried to run him off the road; the gun pointed at him through the passenger side window. "I don't guess there were any bullet holes in the car?"

"I don't know. I never asked his fiancée about it."

"Did she go to the police?"

"Are you kidding? She's not going anywhere. At least not yet. She's scared to death that she may be next. We both are."

"Maybe the girl is trying to protect herself, protect Peter's image."

"Believe that if you want—at your own peril. I never knew Peter to drink and drive. If you're going to be skeptical of everything I'm telling you, then you're in worse trouble than I thought."

"Calm down. I'm just . . . I'm just trying to make sense of this. You said Peter gave you a description of Parker Johnson. Tell me what he told you."

"Short and stocky with the face of someone who has spent many nights in a smoky bar room. He has gray streaks in his otherwise black hair, just above his ears. Dark eyes."

"Anything else?"

"Yeah. Peter told me he had gnarly, stained teeth from always smoking cigars."

Blake's eyes lit up. He had seen this man before. The strange man who had approached him during the presidential motorcade. It had to be him.

Parker Johnson. Rex Levine.

"I need to know who your friend worked for," Blake demanded.

"When I tell you who he is, you'll be able to tie all of us to him, at least eventually. You have to promise me that you'll keep our identities secret. You have to give us time to—"

The young man stopped short of finishing his statement. There had been a crackling noise from the bushes in the nearby grotto. Somebody had stepped on a stick.

Blake whipped his head around toward the noise. "Quick!" he whispered, standing to his feet, his eyes focused on the small window overlooking the grotto. "Tell me who Peter worked for!"

He snapped his head back when he heard footsteps running through and out the west entrance of the Summer House. His informant was gone.

Then, he heard more rustling in the bushes. He panicked, not able to move a muscle. He hoped the intruder would flee, hoped he wouldn't meet his end right there, right then. In shock, he stood entranced, his mind telling him to run, his shoes embedded in the bricks below him.

But then there was nothing—nothing but the sound of rustling leaves, running water, and crickets chirping in preparation for a hard rain. Nothing but the whites of Blake Hudson's eyes illuminating the inside of the otherwise dark and secluded Summer House.

40

The next day, Hudson returned to work. Those in the office, his nosy assistant included, were attributing his long absence to the Coronavirus. What started in the office gossip pool as "probably just a sinus infection" had evolved to "definitely COVID-19." Blake had to return to the office before the rumor mill diagnosed him with Ebola. Not only did he not want his colleagues curious by his absence, but he also needed access to information.

Back in the office, he almost fell out of his chair when Amanda Gormon barged through his door like a rhinoceros.

"There you are!" Amanda said. "Are you okay!? Where have you been!?"

"Fine now. Just a little bout with Madam Influenza."

"You look skinny, and you have bags under your eyes. You're not contagious, are you?"

"Probably."

"The water cooler gossipers say you had COVID. Did you go to the doctor?"

"I tested negative for COVID. I went to the clinic . . . near my house. I asked for a Z-Pak. The doctor told me antibiotics didn't work for the flu virus."

"Or the Coronavirus, for that matter. Rick and I were worried about you. We went to your house, but you weren't there."

"To my house?" Blake asked, his mind rushing to manufacture more white lies. He would apologize and come clean later when he could put everything in context. In the meantime, he needed to fend off the impending inquisition . . . from the master inquisitor.

"Yeah," she said, rolling up her sleeves, getting warmed up. "Where have you been staying?"

"Well, I've got an aunt and uncle who live in Annapolis. And, uh, they have a house. And, uh, there's another little house out back. You know, right by the water." *I should also mention my papa, Geppetto.*

"Okay," she said skeptically.

"Yeah. . . . And I thought it would be good to get away and rest. To fight this cold."

"You must have been violently ill, Blake. How did you get to Annapolis?"

He waited to respond for a moment. Wasn't the answer obvious? She knew he had a vehicle. She'd ridden shotgun several times.

She continued before he answered. "Rick and I both saw the flat tires on your Defender. Rick thinks someone slit them with a knife. Both side doors are crushed in. The front bumper is dented. What happened to you?"

Blake tried not to act surprised. "I haven't talked to you since my wreck?"

"I guess not."

"I was sandwiched between two cars . . . hit the one in front of me. Some drunk caused the whole pile up."

"Where?"

"Alexandria. King Street. Wasn't my fault. Nobody was injured."

"And the tires?"

"That happened after I parked the Defender on the street. Somebody slit the tires of several cars on my block. Teenagers, probably. It's been a rough few days, Amanda. But as luck would have it, my aunt and uncle were in town when I learned that I was sick. They took me to Annapolis and were kind enough to bring me back."

"I hope you didn't get them sick."

"They seem to be healthy. By the way, where's Rick?" Blake asked, trying to change the subject. "I stopped by his office earlier and his lights were out. His secretary is also gone."

"Administrative assistant."

"Whatever. We call Cabinet-level officials 'secretary,' so the title shouldn't offend anyone."

"You can call her Michelle. That's her name."

"Fine. Michelle."

"Rick went on vacation. Took his family to see his in-laws in Puerto Rico."

"That's right. I kept wondering when he was leaving. Guess he ran out of excuses."

"Apparently so," she replied.

"I'm going on vacation too," Blake said. "Tomorrow, in fact."

"Sounds like you just got back from one."

"What are you talking about?"

"Be careful about abusing your sick leave. You know how Kershing gets when he thinks people are fudging."

"Thank you, Amanda, but I wasn't fudging."

"I didn't say you were."

"You implied it."

"Wrong. You inferred it. Get over it."

"I'm over it. What's up with the cross-examination?"

"Who's cross-examining you? I'm just asking routine questions. I think that's expected given that you've been out so much. Where are you going on vacation?"

"Austin. Need to visit my mom."

"Is she sick too?"

Unrelenting! "No, she just misses her son. By the way, have you been hanging out with that woman's little girl? The woman who died during—"

"I see Audrey three times a week."

"And?"

"She's doing much better, thanks. Although, she still doesn't understand why this happened to her."

"That's very noble of you, Amanda. You're awesome to assume that responsibility."

"Least I can do. Hey, on another topic, did you ask Clarence to help with any of your work while you were out?"

"No. Why?"

"Because two days ago he was trying to get into your office."

"What? Why?"

"I don't know. That's why I asked you the question."

"You didn't ask *him*?"

"No. He's the new chief of staff. He can do whatever he wants. Besides, I didn't want it to sound like I was implicating him. You know how some people *infer* certain things from what I say."

"That's strange," Blake said, gazing at his walls, thinking about Clarence Niles. He then turned and looked at Amanda. "Did he get in?"

"Don't know. Didn't ask him. . . . But *you* can."

"Right. Listen, I need to get back to work so I can get outta town."

"Well, I just stopped in to make sure you were still alive," she sighed, upset that Blake was dismissing her. "I hope you feel better."

"Amanda?"

"What?"

"Will you have lunch with me when I get back?"

"I don't know," she said, walking out of his office. "You may not be forgiven by that time."

"Wait. Forgiven for what?"

She stuck her face back in the doorway. "By the way, your beautiful hazel eyes—as persuasive as they are—betray you when you're lying."

"Amanda!"

"They wander off to the right."

"Amanda, I'm sorry. I can't explain everything right now."

"I'd be happy to have lunch when you return. Maybe by then you'll have kicked this unrecognizable flu virus, moved from your uncle's house in Annapolis, and returned from holiday in the Lone Star State. Meanwhile, tell your mother I said hello. You can talk to my *secretary* about getting on my schedule."

"Ugggh," Blake said, disgusted with himself as he watched Amanda walk away. "When it rains . . . it really rains hard."

———

Blake marched down the hallway, through the Main Justice library, to the other side of the building. The library was cavernous, and it occupied a good chunk of the fifth and sixth floors of the building. Every legal book, pamphlet, periodical, newspaper, supplement, addendum, or annotation was represented beneath the sky-high ceilings and murals and among the leather chairs and couches and within the vast, wooden bookshelves that surrounded the area. Since the advent of electronic research tools, however, lawyers at the Justice Department rarely set foot in the place. The aesthetics of the library were no match for the convenience of a computer terminal, and today was no exception. Not even the librarians were at their centralized station.

After exiting the library, Blake approached the freight elevator bank, pushed the "down" button, and waited. Once the doors to the elevator opened, he moved inside and pushed the "B" button for the basement. Soon after the doors slid together, the elevator made a groaning sound as it plunged downward. Blake could smell cleaning chemicals and body odor in the air. The walls in the dimly-lighted freight elevator were padded with a gray cover, the steel texture of the flooring resembled the tire tread on an off-road vehicle. In all, Blake thought, it looked like the perfect place for a hitman hired by the mob to whack a fink.

When the elevator doors opened, Blake walked to the basement corridor, passing the large metal trash bins and blue plastic cylinders full of soon-to-be recycled paper. When he reached the corridor, he looked both ways before inching forward. His head on a swivel, he checked the hallways for unwelcome visitors, moving toward room B-216, labeled Micro-form Reading Room. Hudson entered cautiously.

SCAVENGER HUNT

The room was filled with at least fifty file cabinets—some black but most a faded manila color—housing the articles and editorials of the last half-century or more. It was all here.

Once he shut the door, he could hear coffee brewing. He followed the aroma of roasted beans to a small cubicle camped in the middle of the room. He peeked over the walls. The room's caretaker had left her reading glasses on top of the "Classifieds" section of the morning paper, which covered most of the otherwise tidy, efficient workstation fabricated of pressed wood. The standard-issued, government clock hung above the cubicle, ticking loudly and almost in cadence with the drips falling from the hoary coffee maker into the brown-tinged carafe—the chorus of cacophony unrelenting.

Justice Department lawyers were encouraged to scrounge through the contents of the room's file cabinets, but Blake's anxiety nevertheless began to mount. He wished to avoid taking any haphazard chances. This place—even more so than the library—was rarely occupied by anyone but its caretaker, who waited, day after day, for someone—any sign of life—to walk through the reading room door, champing at the bit to instruct any patient of the computer-infected generation on her pure form of research. Blake didn't want her asking questions or looking over his shoulder. He needed to be careful, and—after being broken by Amanda's tortuous interrogation—he wasn't comfortable crafting any more white lies on the spot.

He didn't have much time. The cubicle troll would be returning soon.

As the clock continued to tick, he scurried to the file cabinet marked "W" at the back of the room. He first needed to learn more about John Smith's death. Pulling out the drawer, he noticed the archived publications of *The Washington Post*. His fingers skipped along the top of the files until he found what he needed. He pulled out the small microfiche and walked to a station in the back, right corner of the room that housed a desktop microfiche reader, which would provide a blown-up picture of each page. He turned on the machine, waited for it to warm up, and inserted the microfiche. As he viewed the contents of the microfiche, scanning through its many pages, he occasionally switched from low to high magnification lens to examine the typeface in more detail. The machine hummed along while Blake labored in his research.

In less than two minutes, he located the obituaries. And there it was. The article he had expected.

John Smith. Age fifty-nine. Dead.

There was no mention of the means or cause of death, but there was a picture of a younger-looking Smith. No doubt. Same guy. He had worked for the CIA for more than thirty years. He had served his country with distinction. He was a hero of sorts, depending on how one interpreted the text. Although its time was undisclosed, it was clear that his funeral service had already occurred. The want of information wasn't surprising, Blake thought. Most everything about this man was undisclosed. But there was one piece of potentially useful information: the name of the funeral home. That was a start. Blake pulled out his small notepad and pen from his pants pocket and jotted down the name of the mortuary.

Now, Peter Karnes.

Blake had gleaned a few things about Karnes from his brief conversation with the informant at the Summer House. Peter was from Greenville, South Carolina. He had worked in Washington, DC for some time. He may have worked for a member of Congress.

Before fleeing the Summer House, the informant had mentioned that Karnes had obtained access to classified terrorism information. Most people with access to classified information of that sort were in the executive, rather than the legislative, branch of government. But that didn't rule out the theory that Karnes's boss worked for Congress. Karnes's boss, for instance, could've been on the Senate or House Intelligence Committee, and Karnes could've been cleared because of his "need to know" the information—that is, his need to advise his boss on certain secretive matters.

Blake had learned other notable clues. He learned, for instance, that Karnes had died in his hometown just a few weeks ago. Based on his informant's description of that event, and notwithstanding the conspiracy theories, it would've been a newsworthy death in Greenville, South Carolina. The town wasn't small, but it couldn't be mistaken for a metropolis.

Blake walked back toward the rows of file cabinets and approached one marked "G." There, he found a small section devoted to the *Greenville News*. It was amazing, he thought, that any facility in this part of the country had copies of a newspaper from the Palmetto State. But here it was. He pulled several microfiches from the file and walked them back to the microfiche reader. He inserted the microfiche from June and looked through it, but there was no mention of Peter Karnes. Grabbing another microfiche from July, Blake realized that searching for Karnes on LexisNexis or Google would be much more efficient. But he remained uncomfortable researching sensitive matters electronically. After his recent experience, he was well aware that someone, somewhere, was monitoring his computer activity.

Blake's eyes lit up when he inserted the next microfiche. There it was. The story of a boy from Greenville, South Carolina who'd made it big. But his end was tragic. He had received his diploma from Wade Hampton High School. He had attended and received his bachelor of arts degree from Furman University before traveling to the big-top circus in the nation's capital. He had worked for a representative from South Carolina. He'd then worked for Senator . . .

SCAVENGER HUNT

Blake leaned forward to where his eyes were but an inch from the reader's screen. It couldn't be. The contents on the microfiche had to be a misprint. Otherwise, things had just become more problematic . . . more serious. The article indicated that Peter Karnes had been a staffer to Senator Andrew Roberts, the senior senator from South Carolina.

Most notably, Peter Karnes had subsequently become the senior advisor to *former* Senator Andrew Roberts, for whom he'd worked at the time of Karnes's death.

Andrew Roberts, once the hawkish chairman of the Senate Armed Services Committee.

Andrew Roberts, currently the vice president of the United States.

———

Blake was juggling a thousand different thoughts but knew he had to find one answer at a time. The vice president's apparent involvement was disheartening, and it raised the stakes. But there was more to it. If the VP was involved, he wasn't carrying out operations on the ground. There had to be an intermediary.

Blake skirted through the folding chairs of the Great Hall, a large auditorium where notable figures, including the vice president himself, often gave speeches. After checking his watch, Blake jumped on the Great Hall stage and made his way to the stairwell leading to the second floor. In less than two minutes, he'd reached his destination.

"Hi, Greta. Is the assistant attorney gen—"

"He's on the phone. You're welcome to have a seat in his office."

Portraits of past attorneys general from pre–World War II administrations watched Blake as he passed through the majestic conference room en route to Harry Mize's corner office. At the end of the room, beyond the twenty-foot, mahogany conference table, was a sitting area surrounding a fireplace that, because of modern fire codes, had nothing but an aesthetic purpose. Just to the left of the fireplace was Mize's door.

Blake entered through the opened door, the creaky wooden floor announcing his presence, and spied the distinguished Tennessee lawyer looking right at home in his high-back, leather chair, arguing trial strategies over the phone as the Capitol glowed through the windows behind him. Mize gave a thumbs-up and expressed pleasant surprise as Blake sat down in one of the two brown leather sofas at the far end of the office and picked up a legal magazine on the coffee table. Before long, Mize hung up the phone.

"Another boring day at the office, Harry?"

"They're hammering us on this Saud incident. The human rights organizations are peppering us with lawsuits. Investigative reporters are scurrying around like hungry mice. The civil division will need to hire thirty more lawyers just to keep up."

"That's to be expected," Blake said. "Sounds like a guard murdered Saud. I'm glad he was transferred out of Marshals custody after the attacks on Main Justice. Otherwise, the president would be firing another director."

"Well, if that's what the investigators conclude, then that guard will be tried for murder. I'll try the case myself."

"Good."

"But the pendulum continues to swing in the wrong direction. We're lucky Saud's men never succeeded in busting him out of prison. I have no doubt that, in that interview he gave a few months back, he was sending signals. I finally saw the tape. What has the judicial branch come to?"

What has the executive *branch come to?* "You tell me."

"Bunch of lunatics. Whatever happened to separation of powers?"

"You tell me," Blake repeated.

"I'll tell you what happened. The Department of Defense happened. The SecDef needs to get his troops under control, or we'll be forced to send these terrorists to Disneyland for weekend furloughs. By the way, did you and General Frank Leavitt ever come to an agreement?"

"No, but we finally have a meeting scheduled after a months-long game of phone tag. The bombing here pushed it to the right."

"You look like death warmed over. I'm the one who should look sick."

"I came to talk to you about your mystery man, the one who approached you at your last hearing."

"Elliot Nichols?"

"That's the guy."

"Is he snoopin' around again?"

"Maybe. When you mentioned him before, you said he was 'rough-looking.' Can you be more specific?"

"He's plump and short."

"Bad teeth?"

"Oh, yes. How could I forget those nasty choppers?"

"Dark hair with gray streaks?"

"Bingo. You've seen him?"

"Yeah. I saw him right before you and I last met, but I didn't put two and two together. You sure his name is Elliot Nichols?"

"That's what he told me. I remember our exchange as if it happened two minutes ago."

"I'm not discounting your recollection. But he introduced himself to me as Rex Levine, and I've met someone else who may know him by another name."

"Blake, these reporters will try anything to get their story, and they aren't known for sophisticated spadework. He probably uses a different alias for each new acquaintance. Anything to slime his way onto the front page of whatever news outfit he works for."

"I'm not sure he's a reporter, Harry. Have you seen him since the hearing?"

"No, I haven't."

"And he didn't give you any contact information . . . any way to get hold of him?"

"Nope. I don't think I gave him much of a chance, though."

"Let me know if he contacts you again. I have a bad feeling about this guy."

"Why did he contact you?"

"I don't know," Blake said, standing up and walking toward the office doorway, "but I'm trying to find out. I'll let you know if I learn anything else." Blake stopped and threw a glance over his shoulder before exiting. "Harry, I want to be honest. I know a little bit more than I'm telling you, but what I know is highly classified and doesn't directly affect you—at least, I don't think it does. I'm sure you understand."

"Blake, I trust your judgment. You know that." Harry smiled and then gave Blake a stern look, wagging his finger at him in a parental gesture. "You remember what I told you last time?"

"Watch my back?"

"Get eyes in the back of your head."

Blake walked back through the conference room, nodded to Greta on his way out, and then stopped in the corridor to gather his thoughts.

Parker Johnson . . . Rex Levine . . . Elliot Nichols. He was getting closer. Now it was time to visit a funeral home, the last place in the world he wanted to go. Before leaving, though, he heard Greta hang up her phone, pick it back up, and dial a number.

"Clarence, it's Greta Williams in Harry's office. He'd like to meet with you right away. . . . He said you'd know what it's about."

41

Alexandria, Virginia

The funeral home was empty. That was bad for business but excellent for everyone without a financial stake in death. As Blake stepped inside and looked around, he found the place not much different than the pawnshop he'd visited a few days earlier.

There was a cheap aura of afterlife floating around like menthol cigarette smoke. The tan carpet—scrubbed over the years countless times with Amway products—was stained and musty. Blake noticed the vacuum cleaner overturned in the corner, its bloated, lint-filled dust bag barely visible beyond the string and mangled hair wrapped around the rotating brush. The seven-and-a-half-foot ceiling showed signs of water damage that would probably never be replaced for fear of asbestos exposure or, worse yet, the cost of remediation.

As Blake walked down the main corridor to the back of the building, trying not to touch anything, he hoped to find someone. When he reached the end of the corridor, he noticed an adjacent hallway that led to an office with lights on. He tapped on the door as he stood in the entryway, startling the unshaven young man with the long sideburns, who was sitting behind a desk covered with mounds of clutter. The young man's feet dropped from the desk when he saw Blake.

"Excuse me," Blake said, "can you help me?"

"What can I do for you?" the young man asked, reaching for the remote control, clicking off the screaming divorcees on *Judge Judy*, and then standing up with his hands in his front pockets.

"I need to know about a funeral that was held here for a John Smith."

"You mean a John *Doe*? We haven't had one of those in a while."

"No, believe it or not, this man's name was John Smith. According to the newspaper, his service took place a few weeks ago."

"I don't recall that one."

"Is the funeral director, or whoever runs this place, here?"

"Bob's out today. That's why his office lights are off."

"Silly me," Blake said, in no mood to be patronized. The emboldened young man had shaken off being startled and was sporting an attitude. "Do you have a record or list of the services? I just need to know who arranged for it."

"Yeah. We keep track of all the funeral services, but I can't hand that information out. People have privacy rights."

"Dead people don't have privacy rights."

"Maybe not, but the people who arrange for funerals usually aren't dead yet."

The young man was sharper and more rebellious than expected, but Blake was beyond impatience. "I'm sorry, what did you say your name was?"

"I didn't, but I'm Jack Gurode."

"Jack Gurode, I'm Special Agent Blake Hudson, FBI." Blake flashed his Department of Justice credentials—which made no reference to "FBI" anywhere—and lowered his voice an octave or two. "Let me be clear. I don't have time for your sassy comments. I'm working a murder case. Do you hear me? Am I getting through to you?"

"Yes, sir," the young man replied, now fidgeting.

"Now, are you gonna give me the information I requested, or do you wanna obstruct a federal investigation? Your call."

"I've got the book right here, sir. Hold on one second." The young man sifted through his desk clutter, grabbed a red binder, and thumbed through the pages. "What day did you say it was? Never mind. Here it is. John Smith. What is it you needed to know, sir?"

"Who arranged for it?"

"Right. The name is . . . let me see here . . . oh, yes . . . Elizabeth Martin." He tore off a small piece of notebook paper and scribbled on it with a pencil. "Here's her contact information."

"I appreciate your help," Blake said, taking the scrap of paper, reviewing it, and then sticking it in his back pocket. "I'll be in touch."

"Yeah, okay. Feel free to call us. No need to come back. You can grab a business card on the way out."

Blake, eyebrows still furrowed, stared at the rebel-cum-sycophant, who was reluctant to make eye contact. Although he'd received what he needed, Blake was still agitated.

"You should quit watching daytime television. It'll rot your brain."

"Elizabeth Martin, please," Blake said when the woman answered the phone.

"This is she."

"Ms. Martin, my name is Blake Hudson. I work for the attorney general of the United States. I need to talk to you about your ex-husband, John Smith."

"Okay. But I have to tell you . . . John just passed away."

"That's what I heard. I'm very sorry."

"Mr. Hudson," she said, "I hate to sound . . . how do I say this . . . heartless. But John and I divorced several years ago. I've remarried and . . ."

Blake realized that she was struggling to finish her thought. "I understand."

"I mean, I hadn't really spoken to the man for the last few years. He didn't pay much attention to the kids, and . . ."

"That's fine. I don't want to take much of your time. I just wanted to talk about his funeral, if I may."

"All right."

"It's my understanding that you arranged for the services. Is that right?"

"Well, the government paid for his burial and the funeral services, but, yes, I was asked to help coordinate. John didn't have much family to speak of."

"Interesting."

"I recommended a few Bible verses and hymns. I also told the funeral director about John's background—where he was from, what he'd done, things like that. I tried to cast it all in a positive light. You know . . . for the kids' sake."

"I understand."

"Wasn't easy."

"Were there many people at the funeral?"

"Not really. Mostly old colleagues from work. I'd say there were about twenty people there."

"Ms. Martin, has anyone from the FBI contacted you about his death?"

"Yeah, they called me."

"About what?"

"They called me to say he'd committed suicide and that there would be no need for a more in-depth investigation. Are you with the FBI?"

"No, I'm not," Blake replied. *But I do play an FBI agent at funeral homes.* "Well, to be clear, the attorney general oversees the FBI, meaning that the FBI director reports to him, but I don't work for the Bureau."

"Okay."

"This is a weird question, but did you notice anything unusual about those who attended the funeral?"

"No, I can't say that I did. I didn't know most of the people there, but John was always secretive about his work. As a matter of fact, until I read about his death in the paper, I thought he worked for the State Department."

"Really?"

"Yeah. One of his many lies." She let out a loud sigh. "As for the funeral, my main concern was just making sure the kids got through it."

"And did they?" Blake asked, feeling obligated to follow up.

"Yeah, I guess so. Like I said, John had always been estranged, but he *was* their daddy, so they had strong feelings for him. His death brought those feelings to the surface. They're going through that tough adolescent phase . . . you know?"

"I understand. And I know that seeing a loved one lying in a coffin will shake up an adolescent."

"Well, the children never saw him embalmed. It was a closed-casket funeral."

"Why was it closed casket?" Blake asked, debating whether to go further. He decided he must. "I thought John, uh, Mr. Smith had slit his wrists. That is something the undertaker or embalmer, or whatever you call him, could mask, right?"

"You see, that's why I assumed you were calling from the FBI. I've been waiting for someone to investigate this further."

"I don't follow you."

"*Lisa, go in the living room. Let me talk on the phone in private,*" she directed with her hand over the phone. She then put the phone back to her mouth. "Mr. Hudson?"

"Still here."

"John didn't slit his wrists. He . . . this is gory. I don't know if I should . . ."

"Please continue. I need to hear this."

"They told me he chopped off his right hand and then cut his throat with a knife."

"What!?"

"Yeah. It always sounded strange to me, but I just assumed the FBI concluded he'd cut his throat with his left hand. I would've thought, were he to do such a terrible act, that he'd cut off his left wrist and finish the job with his right hand. I feel strange thinking and talking about such crazy things, but he *was* right-handed."

"Have you told anyone else about this?"

"No, sir. The FBI called me before I had the chance to think more about it. And since I'd already spoken with them once, I just thought . . . well, I just thought they'd know better than me."

"Doesn't sound like it."

"To be honest, Mr. Hudson, I was more concerned about the life insurance policy. The kids were the named beneficiaries, and I was worried that a suicide would void the policy. But they told me that we'd passed the two-year window, or something like that, so suicide didn't affect the proceeds any."

"Is there anything else you can tell me?"

"I don't think so."

"Thank you for your time, Ms. Martin. You've been very helpful."

"No problem. Do you need me to do anything else?"

Blake thought about her question and became concerned about her safety. "No. I realize the nature of Mr. Smith's suicide is strange, but FBI agents are pretty thorough. I wouldn't think about it much more. Best to put this behind you."

"Are you sure?"

"Yeah, trust me. If you start coming up with outlandish theories about Mr. Smith's death, you never know if the insurance company will come knocking on your door claiming that some exclusion in the policy applies and asking for the kids' money back."

"I'm not going to say anything more about this."

"That's probably best."

42

Washington, DC

The next day, after spending too much time hold up in an obscure part of the Main Justice library, Blake waited until 8:30 p.m. to leave the office. Torrential rainfall provided him an opportunity to visit his old neighborhood. He had avoided his East Capitol Street residence since the day one or more assailants had attacked Judge. The risk of returning had been too great. But he needed the money he'd saved for this rainy day. His wallet, like Blake himself, was losing weight, and credit cards and ATMs were a no-no.

Returning from the library, he entered his dark office, turned on his desk lamp, retrieved his gym bag from the closet, and changed clothes. The building felt ominous at night as rain drops pelted his office window. He grabbed his black rain slicker, slipped it over his head, threw his gym bag over his shoulder, and punched his password into his phone to retrieve his voice messages.

"*First message:* Hudson, it's Henry Dalton. Give me a call."

"*Second message:* Mr. Hudson, this is Carry Strider from the Pentagon. I'm calling to confirm your meeting tomorrow with General Leavitt to resolve certain detainee issues. I'll send you a follow-up email with the specifics. Look forward to seeing you again. Thanks."

By the time he reached the National Mall on his trek home, the rain's intensity had increased. Other than the homeless contingent occupying the various park benches and wrapped in water-soaked blankets, Blake was the only person brave or unfortunate enough to challenge the elements. It had turned out to be a mighty storm.

As he continued walking toward the Capitol, he thought about the risk of returning to his house. His would-be killers could be staking it out. They'd expect him to come home. His Land Rover Defender, with slashed tires according to Amanda, was still parked nearby.

He had no idea what other surprises lay under the hood or within the brake lines, and he had no plans to find out. To get in and out of the house undetected, he'd need to be swift and elusive. And lucky.

His adrenaline racing, his legs voiced no protest to the steep incline up the north side of the Capitol. As he marched up the hill, he thought about the Capitol Summer House off to his right. In a matter of weeks, he'd transformed from hunter to hunted. Now, just a few blocks from home, he'd never been so lost.

––––––––––

The gym bag plopped onto the untended sod, and Blake scaled the wooden-planked fence that separated his backyard from the narrow alleyway behind his house. Jumping from the fence, he landed on the puddle-soaked ground, crouched down to grab his bag, and listened for any unusual sounds.

"Unbelievable," he mumbled under his breath as his hands searched his empty pockets. "Way to go, Hudson." Forgetting his key to the backdoor was unacceptable. His miscues were mounting. If he wasn't more disciplined, he thought, his errors would seal his fate.

He trekked across the small backyard to the house, swinging the gym bag over his shoulder. Like a pirate scaling a masthead, he ascended the wooden ladder that was affixed near the kitchen's exterior. He could hear splattering rain pelting against and running down the tin gutters at all edges of the roof. The sky was pitch dark, illuminated only by periodic blankets of lightning accompanied by the delayed crackling of thunder.

Once he reached the roof where he'd broken bread with Natasha, he walked to the brick chimney and grabbed the iron crowbar that lay against it. He walked back to the shingle-covered, square section of plywood that capped the rooftop entrance to the attic. After prying open the attic cover and busting the useless latch underneath, he tossed the crowbar aside and crawled down into the depths of the attic.

He had gained access to his house.

After opening the hatch that separated the upper space from the second floor, he wiped the spider webs from his face and closed the roof hatch. Then, with his legs dangling from the ceiling, he dropped down into his landlord's abandoned bedroom on the second floor. He unzipped his gym bag in the dark, pulled out his plastic red flashlight, and turned it on.

The room was barren except for the IKEA furniture, personal trinkets, and some scattered toiletries. The queen-size bed was covered with a dark-green bedspread, loosely draped over the mattress. An eight-by-ten photograph surrounded by a silver-plated frame was tilted upright on the adjacent nightstand. His skinny landlord was holding up a large red snapper, extending his arms toward the camera to make his fish appear larger on film; a light-haired woman with a gigantic smile was nearby, an empty bottle of Diet Snapple in her hand. The room was subsumed with the pungent odor of mothballs emanating from the closet. He could hear the cadence of water drops dripping from a leaky water faucet in the nearby bathroom.

After surveying the room, Blake removed his hood, tiptoed to the second-floor hallway, and waited at the stairwell, once again listening for any unusual noises. Hearing none, he walked down the steps, tiptoeing his way to the bottom, occasionally stopping and listening. Once he reached the bottom floor, he unlatched the hook on the door leading to his rented space and darted across the narrow hallway into his bedroom.

After shining the flashlight around, he focused its beam on his unmade bed. He threw aside the brown disheveled sheets and the navy down comforter, lifted the queen-size mattress, and reached underneath. He exhibited a sigh of relief when he saw the yellow-and-blue-makes-green Ziploc bag. It still contained both his official and personal passports, $2,700 in cash, three Susan B. Anthony dollar coins, and a 1933 Goudey Lou Gehrig baseball card, graded a six, worth as much as the rest of the bag's contents. Those who'd ransacked his house hadn't bothered to check his hiding spot.

As he continued staring at the Ziploc bag, his flashlight began to dim and, within seconds, the batteries died and the room was dark. It didn't matter, he thought. He was almost done and had the intended loot in his hands. A quick tour of the living room, and it would be time to go. Time was of the essence, and he realized that he couldn't stick around and reminisce.

Before leaving his bedroom, though, he stared at the area where he'd found Judge. With each flash of lightning shining through his bedroom window, he caught a glimpse of the dried blood and matted dog hair. The Pop-Tart wrapper remained, evidencing the methods of a madman, an unequivocal manifestation of evil. The sight made his stomach turn . . . his blood boil. He needed to move on. He couldn't allow his emotions to cloud his judgment or slow him down.

He peeked outside the door before exiting the bedroom. Nothing. No one. Each raindrop collided against the window and then trickled down; some raindrops merged with others and then traveled more quickly down the glass, out of sight. He then tiptoed to the living room.

Nothing had changed but the smell in the air. The stale smell of dog was a reminder of better times, times when his best friend was around to console any problems he might have. He longed to be back to a time when dog hair shed on the couch and rugs weighed on his mind. Now, his problems were incalculable, and both he and Judge were fighting to stay alive.

CHAD BOUDREAUX

He tossed the gym bag onto his shoulder. He could now see, with each lightning flash, the strewn papers on the living room floor, the memorialization of his life scattered across the hardwood. He focused on his answering machine sitting atop his desk.

Its red light was blinking.

He hesitated before mashing the button, afraid of what the messages might reveal. It seemed that each additional revelation led to another unexpected turn in a Byzantine course of uncertainty and danger.

Beep. "Hudson, this is Dalton. I have tried calling your office a few times. Give me a ring when you get this."

Dalton probably wanted to talk about basketball, Blake thought, but he could have some more information on Clyde Rothman's death. Rothman, he recalled, had mentioned that Dalton was instrumental in obtaining the file on Brent Olson.

He couldn't understand how his life had taken such a dramatic turn for the worse, especially in such a short period of time. He couldn't believe that someone, or *ones*, was hunting him, trying to kill him. He wished that he could have his life back . . . that Michael Gregg had never assigned him to Operation Scavenger Hunt . . . that he'd never met the late John Smith. Exasperated, Blake turned around to make his way back to the stairs. It was time to leave.

But before taking another step, he froze in his tracks.

With help from the last burst of lightning, he'd seen something . . . something in the darkness outside the large window overlooking the backyard.

Movement!

He focused his eyes on the window, but he could no longer see anything. Everything was pitch black. But someone was there. He was sure of it.

Then, with the next display of lightning, his body shut down. He felt his heart lodge in his throat as his brain tried to process what his eyes were witnessing.

Brent Olson was standing outside in the rain . . . the soldier's stoic, auburn eyes staring right back at him.

43

Brent's eerie stare, clenched teeth, and camouflaged clothing were cause enough for Blake *not* to open the back door. But the gun in Brent's hand was more convincing. Brent pointed it toward the brass door handle, indicating that he wished to be let in . . . posthaste. Blake stood hypnotized, evaluating his options, his stomach in knots.

He could bolt to the hallway, he thought, or break for the front door. Under either scenario, though, the odds of his escaping a bullet were negligible. Even if Brent chose not to shoot, Blake was still in peril. Brent would crash through the window or bust down the back door with limited effort. That was a given. This guy was the archetypical warrior. Obtaining access into a nineteenth-century house was child's play. Brent, Blake gathered, had probably mastered the art of breaking and entering as a toddler, before being potty-trained and learning to tie his size-three combat boots. His gesture that Blake open the door was nothing more than an offer to prevent unnecessary destruction; perhaps he wished not to draw the neighbors' attention to the impending havoc.

Given the lack of viable options, Blake decided to let Brent in. Better to face the challenge head-on, he realized, than be shot or attacked from behind. From the look in Brent's eyes, coupled with Natasha's discouraging message blaming Blake a few days earlier, Blake wasn't expecting a pleasant reunion. The mammoth creature sneering through the window hadn't stopped by for English tea or to catch up on old times. If Brent wasn't in cahoots with Nichols, then he—like Natasha—probably had pegged Blake as Benedict Arnold reincarnate. On the other hand, if he was on Nichols's payroll, then Blake had but a few breaths remaining. Either way, the news wasn't good. He prayed that this horrible episode would be over quickly.

The deadbolt clicked, and Brent kicked in the door. Blake flew backward onto his back but hopped back on his feet . . . his body crouched in a defensive position, his fists in the air!

He thought about Judge and tried to channel his anger. He would surely go down . . . but not without a fight!

"What's your problem, Brent!? Put the gun down!"

But his defensive maneuvering was no match for his predator. It only prolonged for a second the imminent beating. Brent easily deflected Blake's wild punches, charged forward, and, like a threatened rattlesnake, uncoiled and struck.

Still holding the gun with his right hand, Brent grabbed Blake's throat with his left and carried him to the built-in bookshelves. Brent had Blake elevated two feet from the ground. Blake stared into the madman's eyes. Despite all the fatalistic thoughts running through his mind, he was most alarmed by the calmness Brent displayed with his prey.

"Why'd you do it, Blake?" Brent growled.

"I don't know what you're talking about!" Blake said, fighting to breathe.

"Wrong answer," Brent said, increasing his grip on Blake's throat, lifting him a few more inches.

"Brent!" Blake pleaded, "let me expl—"

"I trusted you, Blake," Brent said. "But you let me down. You let us all down. Now I have a friend who is in a Pakistani prison, probably being tortured."

"Brent!" Blake gasped, "I—"

"I never leave a man behind. That's the code. There are no—I repeat, *no*—exceptions."

Blake could no longer utter a word. His face was turning a light shade of blue.

"Do you understand me?" Brent asked, not expecting an answer, his head tilted like a canine trying to decipher an unintelligible phrase. "Do you understand what you've done . . . the damage you've caused? Do you know what I do to traitors? Are you that stupid? Did you not think that I'd hunt you down and make you pay? Did you take me and my friends for fools?"

Blake stared back at Brent with his desperate eyes wide open, the strangulation exacerbated by the hopelessness. The lightning flashed in the background, followed by thunder. Blake wanted to answer Brent's many questions, but it was no use. He was losing consciousness.

"Here's what you're going to do, Hudson," Brent directed, his faint words of hope—hope that Blake would live—ringing hollow in Blake's limp body and oxygen-starved brain. "You're going to leverage your connections at the Defense Department and ensure that Jake is extracted from Pakistan. I don't care how you do it, but you'll make it happen." Brent shoved a torn piece of notebook paper in Blake's mouth. "My colleagues and I will be waiting for our authorization, travel plans, and equipment. Tell whomever you contact that we'll be expecting a call no later than tomorrow night. I won't tolerate any bureaucratic windbags getting in my way."

SCAVENGER HUNT

Brent released his grip, and Blake fell to the floor. "And here's your incentive," Brent continued, standing over his quarry, his gun leveled at Blake's head. "If Jake is extracted, you live; if not, then I'll come back for you. I'll track you down to the edge of the earth. You will *never* escape my wrath."

Blake spat out the piece of notebook paper and opened his eyes to see Brent walking toward the back door. He put his head down and gasped for air. A half-minute later, he gazed toward the backyard as another round of lightning lit up the sky, but he could no longer see his attacker. G.I. Joe had disappeared.

44

They had captured Jake Reid. Still stunned by that revelation the following morning, Blake closed the iron gate that separated his basement rental from the rest of the world and began walking toward the Capitol on his way to Main Justice.

The news, if true, put things in perspective. If Jake had never returned from the Pakistani mountains, that would explain the secretive group's disbandment. Whoever was running Scavenger Hunt would've balked at the prospect of terrorists parading around their newest hostage with grand pageantry and regional fanfare. That perverse dog-and-pony show, with Jake Reid as the show horse, could expose the operation. It didn't matter, Blake realized, whether that parade of horribles transpired; the mere possibility would be enough to trigger unmitigated panic . . . to cause the puppet masters to jerk the strings. To cut the loose ends and clean up the mess.

Blake ran his fingers through his hair, waved at a familiar face, and waited for the walk sign before crossing the street. Why had no one told him of Jake's capture? And why did Natasha and Brent believe the canard that Blake was to blame? The answer to those questions was simple. He was the patsy.

Despite all his problems, Blake's quest for resolution was taking shape. He had to assume he'd been set up. That would explain why John asked him to participate in the clandestine group in the first place. It would explain why he was never allowed to carry his weight in the outfit. Smith had never needed—had never wanted—a lawyer to provide legal advice for his missions. The core, underlying nature of the operation was illegal.

Blake was in serious danger. Unknown renegades were not only tracking him but also focused on expediting the death of the would-be squawker, the Justice lawyer who could reveal the key players in the unlawful operation.

SCAVENGER HUNT

As he walked on the sidewalk, his eyes scanned the houses, rooftops, parked automobiles, and pedestrians up and down the road. He remained cautious, but time was running out. To meet Brent Olson's demands, he needed to hustle.

Brent could snap Blake's arms and legs like dry spaghetti without blinking an eye. A lethal soldier, he'd spared Blake's life once, but his mistaken belief that Blake was a turncoat made a second act of mercy unlikely. Brent had stormed Blake's house like Omaha Beach and squeezed around Blake's neck the non-negotiable terms and conditions that dictated his fate. And Blake knew that testing the limits of Brent's retributive promises would be like playing Russian Roulette with a fully stocked cartridge of bullets. Meanwhile, all around him, professional killers wearing ominous masks were targeting people. They had murdered Blake's friends and colleagues and strangers tied to the operation. If he wasn't careful, he knew he'd be next.

He had to find the source, the mysterious man who kept popping up at every turn with a different name.

Elliot Nichols. Rex Levine. Parker Johnson.

As Blake kept walking, he knew finding that man wouldn't be easy.

The late Peter Karnes had told Blake's informant there was an "insider." The most logical candidates for "insider" were Michael Gregg and John Smith. Gregg had roped Blake into this mess, but since his death, things had only gotten worse. The local gumshoes had found Smith's fingerprints in Blake's house, but that evidence was no longer reliable. As morbid as it sounded, the chopped-off hand of a dead man could leave behind fingerprints. Blake couldn't be sure that Smith—*all* of Smith, that is—had broken into his home.

Maybe someone else in the secretive group was the "insider." Clyde Rothman had made it clear that several members of Scavenger Hunt had shady pasts ripe for extortion. It wasn't out of the question that Nichols would blackmail one of them. Blake, after all, hadn't known these people long. Maybe he'd misjudged their loyalty or motives.

That one of his Justice colleagues would conspire against him was the most troubling possibility. Could the "insider" be Rick, who had been snooping around the eighth floor, or Amanda, who wanted to know every detail of his time away from the office? Was Clarence Niles the "insider?" Clarence had tried to obtain access to Blake's office. What was he looking for? And what about Harry Mize, who'd suspiciously called Clarence after Mize's last meeting with Blake, or the attorney general himself? Kershing was the closest in rank to the vice president and had political aspirations himself.

As his shapeless thoughts coalesced, Blake knew that he couldn't expose the vice president until he found Nichols. And he couldn't find Nichols until he found Nichols's "insider," whoever that was.

Blake regretted how far his mind had wandered. Coming up with conspiracy theories implicating his closest colleagues was not moving the needle. He needed to prioritize his thoughts, or he was doomed. And as he worked to clear his mind, one thing came into focus.

He *had* to find Natasha Hensley.

As he approached the next intersection, Blake looked across the street.

And that's when he saw him.

A lanky, athletic man dressed in a dark-gray suit. He shared the same height and physique as the Phantom who'd followed him to the Metro station on Halloween night. The man was staring right at Blake and, like a menace, beckoning him with his finger. Blake turned away and began walking, but not before he noticed the shiny glare from the man's belt. A pistol.

Walking to the intersection of Independence Avenue and Sixth Street, Blake peered over his shoulder. The man had jaywalked across Independence and was marching toward him at a determined pace. He noticed the man wore in his right ear a receiving device, similar to that worn by the Secret Service, or the FBI agents on the attorney general's protective detail.

Within seconds, Blake could hear an automobile accelerating less than a block away. He had little time. He picked up the pace, walking so fast that he would pass a casual jogger. But it wasn't fast enough; the man was gaining on him.

As Blake neared Sixth Street, he could see two other men staring at him and coming his way, converging on him. He heard an automobile's tires in the distance screeching around the corner—heading toward him down Sixth Street.

He was being hunted in broad daylight!

Those after him were relentless—desperate. Innocent pedestrians walked all around him, most coming to or from Eastern Market. The walk signal began flashing once Blake reached Sixth, and he never broke stride upon reaching the road.

At that moment, he heard the car engine roar once again, and he looked to his right. A black sedan was racing for him! Blake stopped in his tracks . . . the car bearing down on him . . . and accelerating.

Standing in the road, and in the oncoming car's path, he tried to see the driver's face. But it was no use. The glare on the windshield shielded the driver's identity. He looked around and saw the goons approaching. He waited one moment longer and then he saw something else.

A mother and her small child! They were holding hands and walking from the other side of the street. *They don't see the car coming!*

Blake had no more time to think. In that brief moment, he charged toward the mother and her child, and, at the same time, caught a glimpse of a heretofore unseen Good Samaritan walking down the road with a bouquet of two-dozen red roses.

SCAVENGER HUNT

"Get out of the road!" the Good Samaritan screamed as he dropped the flowers and leaped over the curb and into the street, sprinting to save the child and his mother.

But Blake was their only hope. With the speeding sedan just thirty yards away and traveling at least fifty miles per hour, Blake dove and tackled the mother and child, the little boy's head crashing down to the pavement, the mother's back plunging into the ground. Blake's knees and elbows grated into the asphalt before his chin slammed against the curb.

Before the child could cry and the mother scream, the black sedan, in an instant, thrust into the Good Samaritan and catapulted his body into the air. The driver of the sedan then hit the brakes and skidded out of control into the intersection.

Just at that time, the driver of a mustard-yellow school bus traveling above the speed limit down Independence Avenue hit the brakes. But it was too late. The bus collided with the sedan, crushing in the right side of the vehicle and plunging it into a parked, lime-green hybrid on the side of the street. The sound of twisting metal and the smell of gasoline, radiator fluid, and burned rubber filled the air.

After a short pause, people from all around began wailing. The Good Samaritan lay in the middle of the street, not moving, making no sound. Blake jumped to his feet, noticing the look of terror in the woman's eyes below him. The child took a deep breath, gasping for the air that would soon generate a frantic scream of fear and pain. Blake surveyed his surroundings and saw that his pursuers had disappeared.

Vanished amid the chaos.

Blake stared back down at the two lives he'd just saved. "Are y'all okay?" he asked the mother. His question was met without a response as she turned over and tried to console her crying child.

Blake stared at the Good Samaritan and then noticed that several witnesses were rushing to his aid. He pulled out his phone and dialed 911. "There's been a terrible accident at the corner of Sixth and Independence, Southeast. At least one death and more injured. Send ambulances, fire, and police."

Without saying another word, he darted off toward the Justice Department.

Brent Olson was still waiting . . . plotting.

45

Twenty minutes later, his shirt was drenched with sweat, and he was out of breath as he reached the Main Justice building. Blake searched his pockets for his badge and presented it to a sandy-haired security guard whom he'd never met or seen.

The guard eyed him through his Oakley sunglasses before accepting the badge. "You running from trouble? You look a little flush."

"Doing fine," Blake said. "Just getting in a little exercise."

The guard looked at Blake and then at the badge several times. "In your suit?"

"Busy day," he said, still waiting for his badge. But the guard kept analyzing it like a forensics expert reviewing hanging chads on a voting ballot. "If not now, it won't get done."

"And your chin is all scraped up."

Based on the inquisition, Blake sensed the guard might deny him access to the building. But Blake couldn't allow that to happen. He *had* to reach his office. The consequences of failure were far direr than being detained by DOJ security guards. Brent Olson's demands were unequivocal, and the soldier wasn't known for making idle threats. Blake nevertheless decided he needed to play along . . . for now.

"Not used to jogging in my dress shoes and fell face first."

"Young man like you doesn't have running shoes?"

"Left my gym bag at home. It's been hectic around the office, and I just—"

"Make sure you have a nurse look at your chin," the guard said, scanning Blake's badge and handing it to him. After the green light flashed, he said, "Have a good day, Mr. Hudson."

Once inside the building, he walked to the stairwell, nodding his head and feigning a grin at acquaintances-turned-suspects along the way. Upon reaching the stairs, he began running at full speed until he reached the fifth floor.

He opened his office door and went straight to his framed college degree hanging from the wall. He took it down, turned it over, and pulled the tape from the large white envelope appended to the back. He grabbed his phone from his pocket and punched in the number.

"This is Blake Hudson. Is he in?"

"Yes, Mr. Hudson. He's waiting for your call."

"Thanks."

"Hello, Blake?" General Leavitt asked.

"Yes, General."

"After thinking over what you told me earlier today, I know why you've been so difficult to track down. Somebody has dumped some snakeheads in your Koi pond."

"They've certainly dumped something on me. It's been a rough stretch, that's for sure."

"You have the coordinates from your group's last assignment?"

"Yes, sir. One second. I have them right here."

"Just read them to me over the phone so we can get Olson and his team on their way." Blake complied.

"Thanks, Blake. Hurry over here so we can get this thing mapped out."

Blake rushed from his office, sprinted back down the stairwell, and exited at the opposite side of the building, far removed from the curious security guard. After reaching Tenth Street, it didn't take him long to flag a taxi.

He felt his phone vibrating as he lunged into the cab. "Take me to the Pentagon," Blake directed as he unlatched the device from his belt. At this point, he was no longer screening calls. He had greater worries than people listening in on his conversations.

"Blake Hudson."

"Hello, Mr. Hudson. My name is Katherine Myers. I work for the FBI."

"Hi, Katherine. How can I help you?" he asked. "I'm pretty busy right now."

"This won't take long. As you may know, one of our agents recently passed away, and—"

"Clyde Rothman was my friend," Blake interrupted. "I'm well aware of his death."

"I'm sorry. Did I see you at the funeral?"

"No, I didn't have a chance to attend."

"Well, it was nice. He had many friends."

"He was a great guy."

"It was such a horrible accident."

"Yeah," Blake said facetiously. "There seem to be a lot of car accidents lately, don't you think?"

"What do you mean? I don't understand."

"Never mind."

"I'm calling because, in assuming Clyde's responsibilities, I found a document stashed away in one of his books."

"Katherine, I'm not trying to be rude, but I'm really busy right now. Can you tell me how this affects me?"

"The document I'm referring to has your name and number on it. I called your office, but your assistant told me you were on vacation. I didn't know if you were waiting for a response, and, if so, how long it could wait."

"All right."

"So I hope you don't mind, but I asked her for your cell phone number. If you don't need this information, I was hoping you could explain to me why Clyde had this and why he may have kept it hidden away rather than in his other files."

"Is it just one document?"

"That's correct."

"Can you describe it to me?"

"Sure. It's just a log sheet that we keep for requests made for background information on federal employees. The log sheet I have in my hand notes requests made from the Office of the Attorney General—your office. It contains the initials of the requesters, but . . . someone, presumably Clyde, scribbled your name and number on it. I don't see your initials anywhere. Do you have a pending request that needs to be followed up on?"

"No, Katherine. I don't. I appreciate the call, though."

"Okay. I'm sorry I bothered—"

"Wait a second," Blake said. "Can you read me all the entries on the log sheet, along with the corresponding initials?"

"Sure. I don't see anything wrong with that."

After she complied with Blake's request, he rubbed the side of his face with his free hand. "Interesting. Can you please describe to me the protocol for documenting background file requests? I want to know more about the initials?"

Blake had one more question after Myers described the protocol, and her answer to that question sent a shiver down his spine.

He couldn't believe it.

"Katherine, I need you to listen to me! You need to shred that log sheet right now and never speak about this to anyone! You have no idea what's going on, but Clyde Rothman's death was not an accident! I hope I haven't gotten you in trouble, but you must do what I tell you! The nature of Clyde's death should be evidence enough for you to do as I say!"

Blake hung up the phone without awaiting a response. He reached for his wallet and then grabbed the top of the bench seat in front of him, pulling himself forward toward his driver.

"We need to turn around and go back to the Justice Department," he demanded, pulling out a one-hundred-dollar bill and holding it up. "*Pronto*, if you know what I mean."

––––––––––

". . . is on the phone. Wait! You can't just go in there!" the assistant exclaimed.

"Sorry. This is an emergency."

Blake didn't knock but just barged right in and sat down. Recognizing the expression on Blake's face, the person he came to see ended the call.

"I told him you were on the phone!" tattled the assistant, who'd followed Blake into the office.

"That's all right," the person behind the desk said, directing all attention to Blake. "You okay? What happened to your chin?"

"It's fine, but if I survive this dumpster fire you've ignited, I'm demanding hazard pay."

"What's that supposed to mean?" the person asked. "You look like—"

"Like what?" Blake snapped, wriggling in the leather receiving chair, waiting to speak until the assistant left the office and shut the door. "Like someone beat my dog to a bloody pulp . . . until he was unconscious . . . his ribs exposed!? Like someone killed my friends and colleagues!? Like I've been running for dear life the last few weeks!?"

"What's going on, Blake?"

"That's a good question. Why don't you tell *me*?"

"Tell you what?" the person asked.

"Don't feign ignorance. I'm about to catalog a laundry list of evidence for your indictment. I'm here to discuss it before I go public, before exposing your role in this criminal enterprise. Maybe I can help soften the blow. But if you want to play dumb, fine. I'll walk."

"You threatening me?"

"Those aren't threats."

There was a long pause, and then the person behind the desk broke. "I'm sorry, Blake. I didn't know anyone was in danger."

"Save your worthless apology. Say you're sorry to my dog. Say you're sorry to Clyde Rothman. He was murdered because of you!"

"What? Blake, I'm telling the truth. I didn't mean to hurt anyone."

Blake continued his scathing stare. He had found his mole, and he was confident the mole would provide him with the remaining puzzle pieces.

"Listen," the mole continued, "I'm just a lackey who reports information. I didn't murder anyone, and I *certainly* didn't play a role in whatever happened to your dog."

"I'm sure you meant to say 'Judge.'"

"Judge. Sorry."

"You expect me to believe you?"

"Blake, they're blackmailing me! Being a conduit of information felt like a small price to satisfy their demands. I never fathomed anyone would get hurt. Besides, it sounded like a necessary operation. It sounded like an effective vehicle to prevent another attack."

"You had me fooled. I figured a mole was monitoring my actions, but I couldn't find you."

"What changed?"

Blake considered revealing his source. "You asked for background files on me and others a few months ago, before this nightmare began. You didn't know, I guess, that the FBI tracks requests that come from our office on a log sheet."

"They wrote down my name on a log sheet, and you identified me from that." It wasn't a question but a statement of revelation.

"Not exactly," Blake said. "If that were FBI protocol, I would've solved this mystery several months ago. You see, I called my now *dead* friend, Clyde, who told me about the request for the files."

"Okay, but that still—"

"But the Bureau, I learned today, doesn't spell out the full *names* of persons from this office making requests. For instance, it wouldn't read 'Blake Hudson.' The log sheet only contains a person's *initials*. So it would read 'BH.'"

"I don't understand. If you knew of my request several months ago and knew that my initials were on some FBI tracking document, then why didn't you know earlier? My initials are different than everyone else's in this office, aren't they?"

"True, but because I've never laid eyes on an FBI log sheet, there were two factors surrounding FBI protocol that caused confusion. First, I was unaware of the first piece of the protocol: you're supposed to document *initials*, not names. And second, Clyde, apparently, was unaware of the second piece of the protocol: you're supposed to document the initials of a person's *name* not his title."

"I still don't follow you."

"It's simple in retrospect. And it makes sense why Clyde thought the attorney general himself had requested the files." Blake waited for a reaction that never came. "Don't you get it? Your initials are 'AG.'"

Tears began to pour down Amanda Gormon's eyes. She stood up to approach Blake.

"Sit down, Amanda."

"Blake," she cried, plopping back down in her chair. "I'm so sorry! *Please* forgive me! I'll do anything to make it up to you!"

"Don't worry," he said. "You'll have multiple opportunities to earn forgiveness. First of all, you need to tell me who put you up to this. Was it Kershing? Was it the vice president?"

"No, no. To my knowledge, the AG doesn't know anything about . . . did you just say the vice president!?"

"Let *me* ask the questions!" Blake shouted.

Amanda, cowering at his rebuke, said, "I've never spoken to the vice president."

"Peter Karnes? Anyone else from the VP's staff?"

"No. I've never heard of anyone named Peter Karnes, and I've never spoken to anyone on the VP's staff about this."

"Who then?" Blake probed.

"A guy named Parker Johnson. He called me and told me about this project several months ago. Told me I needed to . . . look, Blake, I never thought my actions would ever put anyone in harm's—"

"What did Parker Johnson tell you, Amanda?"

"That I just needed to monitor some things for him—look after the group and you in particular. He said I couldn't tell you anything about my or his involvement."

"Who else is involved? Clarence? Rick?"

"No, they aren't involved. Not to my knowledge, at least."

"Why was Clarence trying to get into my office?"

"I'm the one who asked you that question. I honestly don't know."

"Did you erase my files?"

"What?"

"You heard me! Did you erase the Operation Scavenger Hunt files on my computer?"

"No! Why would I do that?"

"Did you ask someone else to do it?"

"No. Absolutely not."

"Don't act so innocent, Amanda. I know it wasn't just Clarence in my office. You were in there rummaging through my desk drawers and my file cabinets," Blake said, acting on a hunch, not knowing if that were true.

She didn't respond, so he had guessed right.

"Amanda, what were you looking for in my office?"

"I was told to find any information on Scavenger Hunt," she said. "Blake, I did it for your own good!"

"That's an interesting angle on this," Blake deadpanned. "You were nosing into my business for *my own good*?"

"Johnson told me the operation had failed, that people would be asking questions. He told me I needed to find and destroy any documents you had. He said that people would be out to get you. He told me that you'd be in a lot of trouble if they found any documents in your possession that—"

"If you didn't erase my computer files, then who did?"

"I had no idea that your computer files *were* erased."

"You just assumed that the physical files in my office were all people would look for when the operation failed? Come on."

"I just did what Johnson asked. To the extent it matters, I pushed back at first on going into your office."

"And then?"

There was a pause. "And then I was threatened."

"Threatened through blackmail? Something in your past?"

"Correct."

"Do you have this Parker Johnson's contact information, his phone number?"

"I have an email address."

"Well, if you didn't erase my files, then Johnson has recruited someone else in the building besides you. Any idea who that could be? Someone in JCON?" Blake asked, referring to the computer experts that worked for the Justice Consolidated Office Network.

"No idea, but finding someone to erase your files would be easy for this guy. He wouldn't have asked me to do it; I don't know your password."

Blake didn't tell her that his password was underneath his keyboard and that she could've found it when snooping around his office. He knew she was telling the truth on this point. He remembered being at his computer when his files were erased. Someone had done it downstairs at the JCON desk. He would probably never find out who, but he agreed with Amanda. Given the other complicated shenanigans Parker Johnson, Elliot Nichols, or Rex Levine was capable of, co-opting someone from JCON would be a cakewalk.

"What do you know about Smith?"

"Never met him, but Johnson told me he was running the operation. I know he killed himself."

"Did Johnson tell you that?"

"Yes."

"So you never had any contact whatsoever with Smith?"

Amanda shook her head.

"What about the other members of Scavenger Hunt? Did you ever talk to Brent Olson or Jake Reid? Did you ever speak with Natasha Hensley?"

"No."

"Amanda?"

"*Honest*, I didn't."

"Do you know if any of those folks I just mentioned knew about Parker Johnson?"

"No, I don't. He never mentioned them to me. I only knew of the others—Natasha, in particular—from discussions I had with you."

"Do you know who broke into my house?"

"Johnson told me that Smith broke into your house."

"Yeah," Blake said. "I'm not so sure."

"Johnson called me right before it happened. He told me that Smith had gone off the deep end. That he couldn't find him. That he hadn't returned any of Johnson's calls. That he was saying and doing strange things. He told me he was worried about Smith. And then, a few weeks later, they found Smith dead. Johnson acted like he was devastated and told me it was a suicide."

Blake pursed his lips, shook his head, and issued a loud sigh of frustration.

"Do you want me to email Parker Johnson?" she asked.

"Not right now. We're going to the Pentagon. You don't understand how messy and dangerous this has become. Once we're done with General Leavitt and his team, then you can take me to Parker Johnson."

"Whatever I can do."

"Offer accepted. You're working for me now."

46

Given the traffic and the short distance from Main Justice to the Archives/Navy Memorial Metro station, Blake decided to take the subway. It would be a quick Metro ride to the Pentagon. But as he and Amanda passed the area where Harry Mize's life had almost ended, Special Agent Henry Dalton appeared out of nowhere.

"Hudson, how ya doin'?"

"Hey!" Blake replied, startled. "Doing fine, Henry."

"And haven't I met you once before . . ."

"No, I'm Amanda Gormon."

"Pleased to meet you, Amanda."

"Henry, I owe you a long overdue thanks for obtaining those files I needed," Blake said, trying to act casual and wanting to check the "Be Nice" box, get Dalton on his way, and drag Amanda by her blonde ponytail to the Pentagon. "Things are crazy right now, but I'd like to buy you lunch soon."

Dalton stood between Blake and the escalators leading to the subway. "You can start by returning my calls."

"Things have been hectic," Blake said, trying to mask his impatience. "Well, Amanda and I have to—"

"You know," Dalton continued, stepping closer, "it's pretty rude to just blow me off like that."

Blake, taken aback, tilted his head and scowled. Noticing the change in Dalton's tone, he became vexed. "Are you muscling up to me, Henry?"

"I think we need to talk. . . . It's in your best interest."

"Actually, a man twice your size believes it's in my best interest to be on time for his meeting. Not sure what's stuck in your craw, but if you'll excuse us—"

"Look, Hudson," Dalton said, grabbing Blake's arm, "I just need to ask you a few questions about Rothman. I'm working on his murder case."

"Thought it was an accident," Blake deadpanned, staring down at Dalton's hand.

"The coffee shop? Ten minutes max. Alone."

"Amanda," Blake said, rolling his eyes, "you can walk with us and wait outside."

The coffee shop was crowded when they entered. "I'd like to face the window," Blake said.

"Someone out to get you?"

"Yep. Just like the movies."

"What did you do?"

"You wanted to talk about Clyde?"

"Right. Rothman was—"

"Wait. How is it that Clyde's murder is tied to counterterrorism, Henry? That is your job, isn't it? Counterterrorism?" Blake asked, his eyes examining each passerby outside but never allowing Amanda to escape his view.

"Rothman died in a car wreck. Do you know anything about it?"

"I'm not answering any more questions until you answer mine."

"Did I do something to offend you?" Dalton asked. "I thought we were friends."

"I thought so, too, but friends don't interrogate one another against their will."

"It was the background checks."

"What about them?"

"My name was scribbled somewhere in Rothman's files. When they started the investigation, they came and interviewed me. Given the nature of the request and the circumstances surrounding his death, I took an interest in the investigation. That's how I got involved."

"I don't know anything specific about it."

"About what? . . . Why are you so concerned about people walking by?"

"You asked me if I knew anything about his car wreck. I don't. Someone cleaning out Clyde's office told me that he died in a car accident. A few hours ago Katherine confirmed it."

"Katherine?"

"Clyde's replacement."

"Why were you talking to Katherine?"

"What's with the twenty questions?"

"I'm an investigator, Hudson. I need to know what's going on."

"She found me the same way they found you. Clyde was a proficient note-taker. Realizing that I worked for the attorney general, she wanted to make sure we didn't have a pending personnel request."

"Did you?"

"No."

"She didn't tell you how it happened?"

"Nope. But since this is a murder investigation, I would lay money on his being run off the road, or perhaps the theory is that he was drugged or was a posthumous alcoholic."

"Or perhaps all three."

"Not surprising."

"Why? Do you know who could've done this?"

Blake paused for a moment. "No."

"Just a good guess, huh?"

"You have two minutes left."

"You seem pretty cavalier about all this. I thought you and Clyde were close."

"That's not fair, Henry. I've been lying awake at night mourning Clyde's death, hoping that I didn't have anything to do with it. But right now, I'm fighting my own battles. I'd be happy to discuss this further with you in a day or two."

"What can you tell me about John Smith?"

"He's dead."

"I realize that. Do you know how he could've died?"

"Are you investigating his death too?"

"Rothman pulled his file. It's probative."

"From what I hear, the FBI ruled his death a suicide."

"Lucky you, huh?"

Blake diverted his attention from the window and stared in shock at Dalton. "What did you say?"

"I find it interesting that you make a strange request for background files on, among others, John Smith. The request is made to Clyde Rothman. It just so happens that Smith and Rothman both end up dead, both dying peculiar deaths."

"Am I a suspect, Henry?"

"Hudson, you're now my primary suspect."

Before Blake could respond, a man stood up from a table in the rear of the coffee shop and began walking toward him. It was the same lanky, athletic man who had chased Blake into the road. Odds were, Blake gathered, he was also the Phantom. The man stopped behind Blake.

"So is his name Nichols, Johnson, Levine, or none of the above?" Blake asked.

"Who? The person behind you?"

"No. The man you're working for, Henry. The person who put you up to this."

"I don't know what you're talking about."

"Whatever. Are you aware that this goon behind me has been chasing me for the last several days, staking out my temporary residence?"

"That's what I asked him to do, Blake. That's what he gets paid for. He's FBI."

Blake looked over his shoulder. "So FBI, are you upset that your conspirator driving the sedan didn't kill me?"

"We have no idea who that was," the man replied.

"Right," Blake said sarcastically. "You speak into your little walkie-talkie thing here and unknown killers just drive out of nowhere?"

"Hudson," Dalton said, "unless you're willing to talk, I'm placing you under arrest for the murder of John Smith and Clyde Rothman."

"I expect my fate is sealed whether I talk or not."

Dalton looked at the FBI agent behind Blake.

"Go ahead," Blake continued, "arrest me. Don't forget to read me my *Miranda* rights. I haven't heard them since law school."

Dalton nodded his head, and the agent grabbed Blake's wrists and pulled them behind his back. Blake looked outside to see that Amanda had fled. While surprising, it didn't matter. He would never be able to meet Brent's demands. Worse yet, if his suspicions were correct, he'd be killed before Brent's deadline expired. But he had nowhere to run. The lanky goon—the infamous Phantom—was right behind him. Blake couldn't escape beyond his chair much less the table or the coffee shop.

"Hey, Phantom," Blake mocked, "after I die in a car wreck later tonight, make sure you soak me down with some single-malt scotch. I deserve better than the cheap stuff you gave the other victims."

The FBI agent turned Blake's wrists.

"Ouch!"

"Is that comfortable?" the Phantom asked, grabbing the handcuffs from his belt.

"Easy!" Dalton snapped at his cohort. "You do that again with a suspect, and you'll be picking up trash on the side of the road for a living."

The Phantom just smiled in rebellion. He had whom he wanted, and that's all that mattered.

But before he could snap the handcuffs, he screamed in pain and collapsed to the floor.

He'd been blind-sided, knocked over the head with a large, hardcover textbook that Amanda had picked up from a nearby table. All seven hundred twenty-five pages of American History had knocked the man unconscious. And before Dalton knew what was transpiring, she'd snatched a scalding-hot cup of coffee and thrown it into his face.

"Ahhhhh!" he screamed, falling to his knees.

Amanda grabbed Blake by the arm and rushed to the front door. Within seconds, they were gone.

———————

Chevy Chase, MD

The man studied his grisly face in the mirror. His features looked different than they did twenty years ago. And while the various surgeries over time had played a principal role in altering his appearance, age and cigar smoke had expedited the change. The lines were now distinct, staking out their permanence, the skin—especially around his eyelids—was heavier, more rough-hewn. The eyes themselves, always unremarkable, contained little hint of hope. They were more calculating than emotional.

He turned on the faucet and began rubbing his hands under the lukewarm water. These hands had carried several variations of guns and knives throughout the evolution of weaponry. They'd carried out the unspeakable acts of violence and exacting punishment that his profession required. They were once dangerous weapons in their own right, and they'd long been immune to sensitive touch. The hot water pouring over the joints in his fingers had a temporary soothing effect on his rheumatoid arthritis, a condition the corti-coid-steroids and biological drugs no longer treated. But he rarely, if ever, worried about discomfort. Mental perseverance, he believed, always conquered, or at least mitigated, the physical aches and pains.

And his calloused heart suppressed all emotional pain. At least until today. Today was different. Today his heart was betraying him, allowing old feelings to creep into his blood-stream. Such treacherous emotions were contraindicated to his hard-wired makeup. They were nothing but a weakness, a hindrance that would only cause more pain if indulged or allowed to take root. He turned the knob until the water was scalding hot. The steam was obscuring his reflection. His hands were turning red as he scrubbed them with the coarse bar of Lava soap. In the end, though, he couldn't wash away the feelings.

After turning off the water faucet, the man dried his hands on a cotton towel, stared again into the mirror, and sneered.

He walked from the bathroom and stopped at the foot of his king-size bed. For many years, it had known only one occupant. Nevertheless, he slept on one side, leaving enough room for his wife. But she never slept in this bed. She had never even been to this house. She had her own bed, a bed that he'd purchased for her a lifetime ago. A bed several feet underground. It was there, underground, where she'd been cured of her invasive cancer, the elements of her disease being absorbed into the coffin's padding. He lowered his head and made his way toward the staircase.

Once he reached the bottom floor, he approached an empty bedroom reserved for his daughter. He opened the door for the first time in several months. The cold room contained a twin bed, a red and white chest of drawers, and a closet with no door. All empty. There was nothing on the walls but the original pink paint.

This room was off-limits. He had promised himself that he'd never, *ever*, ruminate over its symbolism. Yet, now he was here—door wide open—doing just that. His heart was sub-jugating his mind. With all his might, he slammed the door shut, cursed his resolve, and stomped away to his study.

He marched straight to his desk and sat down. He opened the left desk drawer and retrieved one of several manila folders. The folder was marked, in bold type, PROJECT REELECTION and, in blue ink, A.K.A. OPERATION SCAVENGER HUNT. He pulled out a dossier from the folder. The first document was well worn.

ALIAS: PARKER JOHNSON.

PROFESSION: UNREVEALED; CLEARLY A GOVERNMENT OFFICIAL WORKING ON INTELLI-GENCE MATTERS.

CONTACTS: PETER KARNES (OVP)(DECEASED); JOHN SMITH (CIA)(DECEASED); AMANDA GORMON (DOJ)(TARGET).

INFORMATION: POSSIBLY KNOWN TO JESSICA MCWILLIAMS (TARGET)(CG. INTERN) (KARNES'S FIANCÉE; WHEREABOUTS UNKNOWN); RAYMOND LEACH (TARGET)(CONOPS, INC.) (KARNES'S FRIEND)(WHEREABOUTS UNKNOWN; LAST CREDIT CARD TRANSACTION IN PORT-LAND, OREGON).

He slipped the Parker Johnson document back in the folder and reviewed the next one.

ALIAS: ELLIOT NICHOLS.

PROFESSION: UNKNOWN; FORMER HOSPITAL EMPLOYEE IN TENNESSEE.

CONTACTS: ASSISTANT ATTORNEY GENERAL HARRY MIZE, III (DOJ)(POTENTIAL TARGET). INFORMATION: NO FUTURE UTILITY.

And then the final document.

ALIAS: REX LEVINE.

PROFESSION: GOVERNMENT CONTRACTOR, SPECIALIZING IN TELECOMMUNICATIONS.

CONTACTS: BLAKE HUDSON (DOJ)(TARGET). INFORMATION: I MADE MENTION I WAS WORKING WITH FBI; MADE REFERENCE TO FAMILY.

The man placed all three documents back into the folder. He had never asked for this. It had sought *him* out. He had taken cautious steps not to become too engaged, but he'd failed. His love for his then-new country had fallen only behind that for his family.

But things had changed. His wife had grown very ill. The lymphoma had spread. She had been at death's doorstep, being ushered inside by the Grim Reaper himself. And then men working for his newly adopted country, his colleagues, had approached him. They would do everything in their power to help his dying spouse, they'd said. And they'd honored their promise. They had made the best treatments available, medicines and procedures never sanctioned by the government they served. Money? No object. They never sent a bill. In the end, she'd lived an extra two years because of their efforts.

But it hadn't come without a price. They had forced him to turn his back on his daughter. He had to disappear into the shadows. The next few years of his life had been devoted to his new country, performing deeds that its leaders would never publicly acknowledge or condone.

He thought about the current operation—what he'd dubbed Project Reelection and its foot soldiers coined Operation Scavenger Hunt. Like many before it, the operation was of paramount importance. But since terrorists had captured Jake Reid, its secrecy had been in serious jeopardy, so he needed to take certain necessary steps. Al Thoorah would likely videotape Reid in custody, show him off to the world. Investigations would be opened; maybe they already had been. People would talk.

He needed to tie up loose ends. Most of those involved would live because he trusted they wouldn't talk. He couldn't kill everyone, so he would spare those with the worst transgressions. They knew he would destroy them if they squawked. The others wouldn't be so lucky. In the end, people weren't as important as the cause. Their lives were the expendable cogs in the overall machination, nothing more.

Had he forgotten that undeniable fact?

If not, then why had he chosen *her* for the project? Did he believe he could make an exception for her? That would've been a foolish thought, he realized. No. He had made an error, a costly one at that. Errant behavior was not his trademark, but he wasn't immune to its pervasiveness. He despised his emotions for casting their vote. They had been without suffrage for decades. They were staging an unprecedented coup, attempting to overthrow the totalitarian regime governing his heart.

He had been unable to resist the temptation to be closer to her. While he'd been optimistic that, once the job was completed, he could set her free, things hadn't gone as planned.

He stared at the safe. It hadn't been opened in years, but he'd never forgotten the combination. It was the birth date of the one he'd left behind. *Her* birthday. A date that remained seared in his mind. A date whose anniversary had become harder to forget with each passing year. As he rotated the dial, the clicking sounds served as a resounding warning to cease and desist.

But he continued—(three spins to the right) month; (two spins to the left) day; (one spin to the right) year—and pulled the lever.

SCAVENGER HUNT

Now that the safe was open, there was no turning back. The photograph was in fair condition, the center still creased where he'd folded it long ago. The colors were still bright. To the left of the crease, stood the man he'd once been. A younger man, ignorant of the world's hardest lessons. His nose had been much narrower, his cheekbones less refined. His grotesque teeth had become more stained with each cup of coffee and each cigar. To the right of the crease, there was a more beautiful sight. The two whom he'd once loved more than life itself—his wife and his gorgeous daughter.

After staring at the photograph for several minutes, Nikolai Loginov placed it to what remained of his heart. Not since his wife's death—and the subsequent staging of his own—had he experienced so much remorse. But Loginov's brush with tenderness and affection was short-lived; his heart was fighting off the coup and once again was taking marching orders from his brain. Yes, he'd made an error in choosing her, but he'd not make another in trying to protect her. Like before, the cause was just too great.

Loginov grabbed the dossier from his table and turned on the shredder. After feeding the dossier into the shredder's mouth, he focused his attention once again on the photograph. He nodded his head in recognition of what he felt compelled to do, and then the photograph was no more.

Before the shredder stopped humming, Loginov grabbed his cell phone and made his way to the leather chair at the far end of the study. He turned on the nearby lamp, sat down, and toggled through the catalog of phone numbers of those who'd recently called him. After finding the number he needed, he pulled a cigar from his coat pocket and lit the end. Once the smoke began to billow toward the ceiling, he grabbed another phone, this one secure and sitting on the table near his chair, and dialed the number.

"Hello," the soft, innocent voice answered.

"Natasha Hensley, please."

"Hi, Daddy."

47

Washington, DC

Two days later, Blake and Amanda were holed up at the Pentagon for the third straight day. They hadn't left DOD headquarters since their arrival, sleeping and showering in the facilities provided to them by General Frank Leavitt on behalf of the United States Armed Forces. Their participation in the planning phase of the extraction, billed as mission support, was nothing more than moral support bordering on loitering.

Blake was leaning against a conference room wall and staring at Amanda, who was seated at the end of the large table in the middle of the room. Officers pinned with colored ribbons were seated near her. The audio was almost up. There would be no video for this mission.

Blake remained anxious, replaying in his mind the tracts from Brent Olson's "Greatest Threats" album. Extracting Jake from Pakistan was crucial. And while Jake's safety didn't ensure his own, it was a condition to that end. No doubt about it. If Jake's life ended prematurely, Brent would ensure that Blake's did too. To make matters worse, this mission would be the toughest to date. The enemy was expecting a rescue attempt. The terrorists had never attempted, not even through clandestine means, to negotiate for Jake's release. This was personal.

"Audio's up!" a general barked.

Blake eyed the men and women in uniform at the table. In the end, convincing them to support the rescue operation hadn't required much arm-twisting. That's not to say they hadn't been reluctant at first. After Blake had explained that Jake had been captured on an enemy compound in Pakistan, the military brass had been dead set against any rescue mission. In fact, they weren't happy about the circumstances surrounding his capture. They'd rebuked Blake for being associated with an unauthorized cadre of renegade fighters, and they'd scolded him for being engaged in unsanctioned military activity.

But then Blake had uttered two words, two words that changed everything—"Brent" and "Olson."

After Blake invoked Brent Olson's name, they rolled out, vacuumed, and steam cleaned the red Pentagon carpet. The military muckety-mucks praised Blake for merely knowing the man. Major Olson was the topic of conversation at their private clubs, in their locker rooms, and at their exclusive dinner parties. He was *the* enigma. He represented all that was right with the United States Armed Forces.

To be clear, they didn't approve of *Jake Reid's* mission, but Major Olson was involved, so nothing else mattered. It was that simple. Major Olson had called in a favor, and Uncle Sam was sounding the bugle. *If he only knew,* Blake thought, *the power he wields around here, he could have had the entire Pentagon mobilized weeks ago without my help.*

"Central Command, this is Wildhorse. Do you copy?"

"Yes, Wildhorse. Loud and clear. Where is Muzzleloader?"

Muzzleloader, Blake knew, was Brent's codename for the mission.

"Muzzleloader's in position, sir. Awaiting orders."

"Give us an assessment, Wildhorse."

"Yes, sir. Fifteen enemy gunmen are guarding the small compound. Two guards on each side carrying AK-47s. The enemy has a fifty-caliber on the roof. Several armed men are patrolling the area."

"Analysis, Wildhorse?"

"Another walk in the park, sir."

"Roger that, Wildhorse. Stand by."

"Copy, sir. Standing by."

The men around the table gazed at one another. Amanda, Blake could see, had closed her eyes. Chaotic events were overtaking her like a category five hurricane. She was unaccustomed to losing control. Shocked by her valiant rescue at the coffee shop, Blake tried to reconcile his conflicting emotions toward her. In the end, there was no simple formula for working through conflict with friends; but he would forgive her when the time was right. Meanwhile, there was a simple formula for staying alive: Jake rescued equals Blake rescued. And that's where he channeled his current energy.

Blake flinched when a hand touched his shoulder. He turned around to find the hand belonged to the deputy secretary of the Department of Defense.

"I'm Don Travers," DepSec said. "And you are?"

"Blake Hudson, sir."

"Are you the one that organized this extraction?"

"I'm the one who requested it, sir," Blake clarified, looking up at the man's towering, slender frame, hooked nose, and almond eyes. His brown hair was trimmed tight, like that of his colleagues. "General Leavitt organized it . . . at the behest of Brent Olson."

"You're friends with Major Olson?" DepSec asked.

"I work with him. Yes, sir," Blake said, choosing his words carefully.

"And you're with which branch of the Armed Forces?"

"I work for the Department of Justice, sir. I'm a lawyer, not a soldier. But come to think of it, I've been more of a soldier than a lawyer over the last few months."

Travers's face betrayed his confusion.

"We were part of a group," Blake clarified. "A covert group created to—"

"Say no more," DepSec said, patting Blake on the shoulder once again. "Special times call for special measures."

"Yes, sir," Blake said, relieved that he wasn't required to explain the details.

"A friend of Major Olson's is a friend of mine."

Western Pakistan

The barrel of Brent Olson's M-16 machine gun was about to heat up. This wouldn't be a turnkey operation. He was loaded for bear, and things were about to get ugly.

Really ugly.

He'd once again have the advantage. His calmness never failed him when things got hot. When the world was on fire, he saw things in slow motion, heard important sounds that others couldn't, and blocked out the irrelevant noise . . . the guilt. His mind was clear, focused on only one objective—saving Jake Reid.

His heartbeat began to slow, his teeth began to grind, and his eyes took on a catlike form. His nostrils were flaring, preparing for the imminent scent of slaughter. In just a few minutes, Olson had transformed from a cautious soldier into a natural-born killer.

He would ask his Creator for forgiveness later.

Right now, it was time to settle the score.

Jake Reid hadn't eaten for days. He was losing a little hope and a lot of weight. He knew that—for better or worse—his days in this nasty, unsanitary cell were numbered. An operative had to realize that, once captured, the probability of survival was low, the chance of rescue even lower. But Jake knew he had an advantage that most prisoners did not. He had

SCAVENGER HUNT

Brent Olson on his side. Brent had often mentioned that he never left a man behind. Jake knew that his companion wouldn't forget about him. He was confident that, assuming Brent was still alive, the burly soldier would come to rescue him soon.

Jake struggled to his feet when he heard the enemy soldiers screaming from the roof. He could hear heavy, frenetic footsteps pouncing overhead. Something was going on. His stomach churned. He was utterly helpless. He could do nothing but wait and listen. As he focused his attention on the rooftop, he paid scant attention to the two guards beyond the bars that surrounded him. In their angst, they'd turned toward him and yelled foreign obscenities before exiting the building. He stood alone in the hot, windowless cell. And waited.

His adrenaline pumping, the sounds around him were familiar. Rapid machine-gun fire. More screams of agony. He heard a grenade explode, mortar fire, and ammo discharged from a .50-caliber. Bullets peppered the outside of the building that encased his cell. Shouts of anger and fear. Bodies were falling on the roof above him.

Chaos!

Amidst it all, he also noticed the silence that accompanies death. The screams were fading, emanating off in the distance. He thought about his precious, innocent little girl as he waited for his imminent execution.

Thanks for the entertainment, Mr. Reid.

It wouldn't be long until someone walked in and shot him. There was nothing he could do, nowhere he could run. He had never felt so vulnerable, at least not since that night in Alexandria, Virginia when he found Rebecca Ann. But all was not lost. He would be with her soon, holding her hand and singing children's songs in paradise.

He cowered in the corner of his cell. He heard something or someone crash into the door just a few feet away, and a man yelled out in intense, unrecognizable agony before his dead body crumbled to the ground, blocking the narrow line of sunlight underneath the door. Jake's heart sunk as he watched the small band of sunlight reappear, the dead body dragged to the side. He closed his eyes as he heard someone lifting the squeaky latch on the door.

And then he opened his eyes to see the door to the compound fly open.

The sun shone through the doorway and lit up his cell, blinding him. As he shielded the light from his eyes, he tried to peek through his fingers.

The figure walked into the compound and closed the door behind him.

"I was beginning to wonder if you'd come back," Jake said with a growing smile and a sigh of relief, holding up the shackles around his wrists, squinting at the man through the bars of his cell.

"I told you: I never leave a man behind," Brent said, blood dripping from his wounded right shoulder and off the razor-sharp tip of his serrated blade.

48

Washington, DC, one week later.

Hangar 6 was several hundred yards south of the commercial terminals of Ronald Reagan Washington National Airport. Because of her frequent travel on the FBI's Gulfstream V with the attorney general, Amanda knew the place well. It was where the "Who's Who" in Washington, DC arrived and departed without the hassle of long lines, screaming babies, and multiple identification checks.

Traipsing past the office for Signature Flight Support, she was thankful that she'd worn tennis shoes. She moved with caution on the moist dirt, leaping from one clump of crabgrass to another as if trying to evade land mines. Pressing forward, she neared the unmarked hangar, which resembled a cavernous barn. That was the place where she'd confront the man who'd caused so many problems for so many people.

Elliot Nichols, a.k.a., Parker Johnson, a.k.a., Rex Levine.

With the hangar in sight, she stopped and took a deep breath. Her mind insisted that she go no farther, that she run away and never look back. Her heart, on the other hand, was more cavalier, imploring her to face the music, trust Blake, and bring an end to this horrendous nightmare. In the end, unlike most times before, her heart won out. Her die cast, she continued walking to the hangar. She had to make amends for the pain that she'd caused.

Though startled, Amanda wasn't surprised to see two muscle-bound men wearing dark Roka sunglasses and tailored black pinstriped suits posted at the front of the hangar. Blake had warned her that the man with many names wouldn't show up alone. The two men stood motionless as she approached. She made a point not to stare, wondering if one of them was the notorious Parker Johnson, whom she'd only emailed and spoken to on the phone. As she reached the hangar, she peered past them into the large structure. She saw no one else.

"I have a five o'clock appointment," she said.

"He's expecting you," the man with fair skin and red hair replied. "We need to search you first."

Amanda looked at the man with the tanned skin and jet-black hair before responding. "Suit yourself."

Black Hair directed her to extend her arms as he patted her down. She could feel her body shaking. Black Hair then asked her to turn around as he finished his search.

"She's clean."

Red Hair turned to Amanda. "Walk with me."

Amanda complied and followed him inside. Black Hair stayed behind to guard the main entrance of the hangar.

She could see the hangar was no longer operable for its original purpose. It looked more like a gigantic storage shed for heavy equipment than leasing space for functional aircraft. Upon closer examination, she realized it was being used as a maintenance facility. It was loaded with airplane and helicopter parts, and tire stacks rose several feet high. White fifty-five-gallon drums, used to store solvents, paints, and other chemicals, were scattered throughout the space.

The percussion from Red Hair's boots echoed throughout the hangar. That echo was coupled with the creaking sounds of rickety metal caused by the wind outside blowing against the frame of the building.

Amanda was growing more anxious as they marched forward. Red Hair's stern facial expression was unsettling. He was all business. That he remained silent only made things worse; and although she couldn't see a firearm on his person, she gathered that he had one concealed. She guessed that Red Hair was current or ex-military by the way he walked. His mannerisms did nothing to rebut that theory. She glanced back over her shoulder to the front entrance, toward the light, and saw Black Hair still tending his post, facing the opposite direction.

No longer hearing Red Hair's footsteps, she turned her head back around. As her eyes readjusted to the darkness, she saw the silhouette of a man twenty feet away.

He was staring at her.

"Ms. Amanda Gormon. Or should I say, Amanda Cromwell? We finally meet in person," the ominous figure said as he stepped into a small ray of sunlight that had penetrated the rooftop, his heinous teeth revealed through a wicked smile.

"Yes," she replied, her knees trembling as she confronted the man whom Blake believed was an indiscriminate killer. "I believe you said your name was Parker Johnson."

"That's correct. I did tell you that my name was Parker Johnson. I apologize for lying to you. Of course, you know better than anyone the need for an alias."

Amanda remained silent.

"I'm remiss for not meeting you in person before today, and I'm sorry our first encounter has to be in this run-down place. I would've preferred a nice dinner in an exquisite restaurant."

"No objection here. My car is waiting outside."

Nikolai Loginov erupted with laughter that filled every inch of the hangar, a chafing cackle that sent shockwaves from one end to the other. "No, Ms. Cromwell, I think you and I both know that's impossible. We understand the gravity and sensitivity of the work we've been entrusted to carry out. It would be most unwise for our relationship to be revealed in public."

"I don't know what you mean."

"Oh, I believe you do. You are an intelligent woman, which is why I recruited you in the first place."

"And I guess your knowledge of my past had nothing to do with it?"

"Your past transgressions provided me with the leverage I needed, but you must admit, I've lived up to my end of the bargain. No one knows of your family history or the fact that you lied about it on your background forms. And if your cooperation continues, it will never become a matter of record."

"That was our deal."

"Of course, if you're here to tell me that you have second thoughts, then I'm sure the attorney general will be most unpleased to learn his most trusted advisor has a father on death row. The fact that he butchered three children and their parents probably won't sit very well. Of course . . . I could be mistaken."

"I had nothing to do with my father's sickness. I changed my name long ago and disassociated myself with that man. I haven't seen or spoken to him since I was in grade school."

"Then you probably shouldn't have lied about your family history during your background check. Last time I looked, that was a federal crime. If you, let's say, ever wanted to run for office or become a federal judge, being convicted of a federal crime wouldn't help you out too much. Again, I could be mistaken."

Amanda didn't respond. Despite his evil, the hideous creature in front of her was right.

His voice turned from sarcastic to curt. "Now what do you *want?*"

Amanda strove to maintain her composure. "I came to tell you that Hudson knows that I'm involved. He's ready to disclose the nature and the specifics of the operation. I need guidance."

The man chuckled underneath his breath. It was an odd response, and it troubled her. "Let me ask you a question first, Ms. Gormon," he said, using her desired name. He needed something. "Who else in your office knows about this *operation*, as you call it?"

SCAVENGER HUNT

Amanda could feel her heart beating. Something was wrong. That question was unexpected, especially at this point in the conversation. Why hadn't he asked about Blake's revelation of her involvement? Did he already know? Even then, why hadn't he questioned her about what she had implied—that she and Blake had spoken about the operation? Surely he didn't know that. Or did he?

But there was something else about the man's question that troubled her. Were she to answer it, she would become expendable. It was clear. He was closing down the operation and cleaning up the mess. He planned to kill her right here, right now. She had only one thought on her mind.

Don't answer that question!

"I know the answer to that question. Hudson told me. And I remember the names of those whom I've told. But before I tell you, I want to know why you just didn't recruit Hudson alone. Why go through me?"

"You always have to assume the worst with these types of jobs. You always need a scapegoat if they go wrong. To have a goat, you need someone who is clueless about what's going on. Mr. Hudson was my goat."

"That doesn't answer my question. Why bring me in?"

"You don't think I'd let my goat roam free, do you?" He paused for a moment to measure her reaction. "You're doing a fine job, Ms. Gormon. No need to be frightened. I'll speak with Mr. Hudson and explain to him how important he is to protecting our country. The job will be over soon, and we'll all return to our normal lives. Now, I just need you to tell me who else knows about this operation. And why is it that you keep looking around?" he asked while unbuttoning his suit coat, revealing the handgun wedged in the front of his pants.

Amanda panicked. "I have a live wire on me! I'm taping everything you say! Others are listening in!"

"Surprise, Surprise!" Loginov bellowed before breaking into a sinister laugh. "I know you're carrying a wire, but it's not live. You see, the person to your left, the one who brought you to me, has already confiscated the recording device for your wire. He tells me he's had a rather busy day."

"What are you talking about?"

"I was worried he wouldn't be back in time to greet you. Breaking into your house, locating the recording device, and then driving down Interstate-395 in rush-hour traffic can be taxing on a man. For being so smart, you have acted like a fool."

Amanda was speechless.

Loginov flashed a sinister smile. "Ms. Gormon," he continued, "I'm sure Mr. Hudson warned you not to talk of your plan over the phone. He would've expected your phone conversations to be monitored. The heart-to-heart you had with your mother was a very touching and revealing conversation. She gave you some good advice. If you'd followed it, you likely would be at home with her now."

"My mother doesn't know who you are!" Amanda screamed, panicked. "She doesn't know about anything that can harm you!"

"I'll make you a deal. You tell me who else in your office knows about my operation, and I'll promise that you, your family, and the pretty little girl you're looking after remain unharmed. Audrey is her name, I believe."

Amanda was devastated, her bottom lip throbbing. "You leave Audrey out of this! She's been through enough!"

"I've proven that I live up to my end of bargains. But I'm getting impatient with your unwillingness to live up to yours!"

Amanda thought about what to say. Despite her paranoia, she had the presence of mind to realize that any misstatement could be her last. "There is one other person who knows about the operation, and he or she knows how to find you if I'm not back in thirty minutes!"

Loginov reached for his gun. "I'll take my chances, sweetheart, and I'm sick of playing games." The gun was drawn and at his side. "You have five seconds to tell me—"

His verbal threat was interrupted by the sound of an empty fifty-five-gallon drum over-turning on the concrete floor. That event was followed by a single gunshot blast that pierced the side of the hangar forty yards away. Amanda, Red Hair, and Loginov all flinched before turning toward the calamity.

What they saw was surreal.

Someone was being tackled from behind by one of Loginov's hidden henchmen who sported a prominent scar across his jaw and cheek. The intruder hit the ground with Scarface crashing down on his back; the gun the man once possessed slid along the floor. Red Hair rushed over to pick it up. Scarface jumped to his feet, placed his right foot on the intruder's back, and then leveled a pistol to his head.

Loginov laughed. "In chess, we'd call this checkmate. In life, we call it truly fortunate . . . or unfortunate, depending on where you sit."

The man on the floor closed his eyes in anguish.

"Welcome to the party, Mr. Hudson. I've been expecting you."

49

"I couldn't have planned this any better myself," Loginov celebrated, "and I'm paid handsomely to concoct the most elaborate schemes."

"Yeah, this is turning out to be a great show," Blake responded.

"I guess your new friends are rubbing off on you. But they forgot to tell you that it takes a lot of training to stage a successful sting operation. Actually, I must give you more credit," he said, stepping back from the ray of sunlight into the darkness. "If everyone had listened to you, you may have pulled it off."

"I don't know what you're talking about."

"Agent Rothman's replacement, for instance. She decided it was a good idea to report your conversation. She didn't know of my network of reciprocal favors at the FBI. You spooked her when you said her life was in danger. Then, of course, Amanda decided she would call Mommy. That didn't help you any."

Blake didn't say another word. Everything he had to say was cliché. Something along the lines of "take her and not me" came to mind, but it would be of no use, just a sign of further weakness. There was no reason to further embolden the spirit of a madman. Loginov had outsmarted Blake handily, and now he was just playing games with his captured prey before executing him. He turned his head away from the darkness, toward the front entrance of the hangar. The sun was beginning to set.

But then he noticed it. Black Hair was no longer at the front entrance. And before Blake knew what was going on, he heard Amanda scream at the top of her lungs.

Blake turned his head to witness the unthinkable.

Black Hair was falling from above!

His body had barely fit through the hole in the rusted roof. During the free-fall, it never twitched or braced for the impending contact. Black Hair never screamed. All indications were that he was dead before the slack in the rope ran out, his neck snapped, and his body jolted to a split-second stop before careening a few feet back toward the rooftop, only to be thrust by gravity back down again until his corpse dangled no more than ten yards from the ground.

Before anyone could react, Brent Olson climbed through the hole in the rooftop, scaling down the rope that supported the lifeless figure hanging in mid-air. Olson lunged from the rope onto a steel, horizontal support beam in the rafters. He pulled out two handguns and began blasting.

Everyone else stood awestruck. Loginov reacted first, firing shots into the rafters. Red Hair rushed away to get a better shot at Brent, but Scarface stayed put. He turned around and fired six straight shots at Brent before cursing and trying to reload.

Blake watched as Loginov fled into the shadowy abyss. Capitalizing on his opportunity, Blake began crawling away. When he was a few yards from his captor, he stood up and sprinted from the crossfire and toward safety. With Amanda running behind him, they darted toward a covered turbine engine thirty yards from the center of the hangar.

Three heretofore hidden henchmen emerged from various points within the hangar. Wielding weapons, they began firing at Brent. Blake could hear the clinking sound of shell casings hitting the ground along with sounds of staccato gunfire. Many of their bullets penetrated the roof, causing more light to sneak through. More bullets ricocheted off the vertical support beam behind which Brent was reloading.

After emptying their chambers, the three newly-emerged henchmen sought to find more strategic locations. They wanted to surround Brent from below, not allowing him to hide behind the rafters.

But they wouldn't get far.

Soon after they turned to run, a red four-wheeler entered the hangar and roared toward them at a blazing speed. The two nearest the entrance never processed the two twelve-gauge shots fired from Jake Reid's Browning sawed-off shotgun that lifted them off the ground. Jake wasted his third shot when the third henchman jumped behind a stack of tires, rolled over, and then hopped to his feet in firing position. The man squeezed off three quick shots at Jake. But Jake had swung his body to the left of the four-wheeler, using the roaring machine as a shield. The shots punctured the four-wheeler but missed their target.

Jake lunged back upright onto the vehicle's seat, tossed his empty shotgun to the side, and then jumped off. As he hit the ground, Reid tucked and rolled. In an instant, he was back on his feet, wielding a pistol and sprinting out of sight. The ATV cruised forward to the rear of the hangar, decelerating before it rammed against the back wall. But Reid was no longer focused on the four-wheeler. He was searching for the man he'd missed.

Meanwhile, Scarface sought cover. Along with Red Hair, he continued firing shots in the air. Taking his chances, Brent leaped from the horizontal support beam. Flying through the air, he grabbed hold of the rope. Black Hair's lifeless body swung back and forth like a pendulum on a grandfather clock. Brent wrapped his legs around the rope and fell backward, his body suspended upside down.

Still swinging back and forth, evading gunfire, Brent began crawling down the rope headfirst. He pulled out a large knife and cut free the dead man at the rope's end, his body crashing to the ground. Brent, still hanging upside down from his legs, reached behind his back, pulled out his two guns, and unleashed rapid gunfire on the enemy.

Once the rope stopped swinging, deadened by Brent's weight, he flipped over backward and landed upright on the ground in combat position. Still dodging bullets, he sought cover, reloading along the way. After taking position behind a fifty-five-gallon drum, Brent leveled his guns and scanned his surroundings as if his head were on a turret. There was panicked movement throughout the hangar, but no clear targets remained in sight.

Jake was watching the action from behind a rusted fuselage when his target decided to make a break. This time Reid would not miss. He got a lock on the man, turned his pistol sideways, and then pulled the trigger. He would need only one shot.

There were only two henchmen left, not including Loginov.

Reid moved toward Amanda and Blake.

"What are you and Brent doing here, Jake?" Blake whispered loudly. "How did you find out about—"

"Stay put." Jake directed. "You should be safe here."

"Okay," Blake said looking back at Amanda, who nodded in agreement.

"I need to find Brent," Jake muttered to no one in particular. "I need to find *Loginov!*"

Elliot Nichols, a.k.a., Parker Johnson, a.k.a., Rex Levine . . . Loginov.

All gunfire ceased, ushering in an eerie silence. Smoke and haze filled the air. Blake then saw a figure in motion across from him. It was Brent, running behind large obstacles to the back of the hangar.

Someone fired two shots from where Brent had fled. Someone bellowed in pain and collapsed to the ground. The voice in agony, Blake knew, was not Brent Olson's.

Two scavengers remained: Red Hair and Loginov.

Without warning, Jake darted toward Brent, sprinting across the middle of the hangar. Someone fired more shots, and Jake hit the ground, rolling into attack formation. Blake noticed Red Hair firing shots at Jake from behind a fifty-five-gallon drum. Jake returned fire and then aimed his weapon at the drum and emptied his gun chamber. The drum, full of fuel, exploded, catching the enemy gunman on fire. Red Hair was in flames, screaming and flapping to the middle of the hangar, where he fell to his knees.

Jake located Brent, and they continued after Loginov.

It didn't take long for them to find him.

"And now for the coup de grace," Loginov said, walking behind Amanda and Blake, a gun pointed in Blake's side and Loginov's other hand grasping both Amanda's and Blake's hair, their heads compressed together. "Snap, snap. The party's over."

"This will not end on your terms, Nikolai," Jake said, reloading his firearm. "I guarantee you that."

"Jake, it's been a long time. Before this project, I thought you'd die of boredom in Mexico. You should thank me for saving you from small-town inertia."

"Not after what you've done to my family."

Thanks for the entertainment, Mr. Reid.

"You and I are wired the same, Jake. After all we've been through, we can never be fishermen."

"I didn't know what else to do after you betrayed me."

"Revenge is a dangerous incentive, Jake. And you seem to be fond of some facts more than others. You jeopardized our mission then, just like you have now. You can't expect others to take the fall for your miserable failures. And don't act like you were the choir boy. You had blood on your hands."

Jake's face turned a fiery crimson. "I'm about to have *your* blood on my hands."

"I just purchased the Cadillac of life insurance policies," Loginov said, referring to his two hostages. "Your threats don't frighten me. Your personal vendetta isn't worth more lives. Even someone with your death wish realizes that."

"I'll be the judge of that. And don't overvalue my feelings for those two. I came back to the States for one reason, and it wasn't to make new friends. My mission ends here."

"How did you know it was me who revealed your identity, Jake?"

"Natasha told me. Another girl whose life you undervalued. A true patriot who's been neglected for many years. Your own *daughter!*"

Blake's eyes went blank as his mind processed the stunning revelation. After catching his breath, he tried to turn and look at Loginov.

"I see," Loginov said. "She tied you and me together from my CIA file, which she stole from Langley. My Natasha is wilier than her old man," Loginov laughed with a hint of pride. "I was wondering why she was so angry on the phone. I guess she read the transcript of my interview with the inspector general's office."

SCAVENGER HUNT

"You'll be ruining no more lives, Nikolai. Natasha has been hard at work compiling an extensive record against you."

"My flesh and blood. I'm the victim of my own good judgment, no? Or should I say *genes*? I assembled the best of the best. Looks like that decision may come back to haunt me."

The barrel of the handgun in Blake's side was shaking. The latest disclosures regarding Natasha had her father growing anxious. That wasn't good news for Blake and Amanda. Time was running out. Jake was forcing Loginov to make a move. Blake turned to look at Amanda. Her brown eyes were staring straight ahead. She was preparing for death.

Blake's eyes focused back on Jake and Brent, who were staring back at him, each realizing they'd been reeled into the maniac's current. Each surmising of ways to swim out. Blake noticed the frustration on their faces. They clearly didn't have any answers.

It would come down to Blake. How much risk did he want to take? He knew he had to act. Loginov wouldn't be afraid to execute one of them and take the other as a hostage. Blake knew that he was the probable first victim, Amanda being easier to manage.

Fate had dealt the cards. It was Blake's play. He didn't have time to evaluate every potential scenario or balance risk versus reward. Loginov was about to pull the trigger. The banter among adversaries was drawing to a close.

He had to act.

With Loginov's gun in motion, Blake waited until the barrel was directly behind him. If Loginov fired a shot, Blake didn't want Amanda taking the bullet.

It didn't take long. He could feel the tip of the barrel once again buried in his kidneys.

He stopped thinking and winked at Jake and Brent. He then whirled around and plunged his left elbow into Loginov's sternum.

Blake felt the excruciating pain at the same time he heard the gunshot reverberate throughout the hangar. Before collapsing to the ground, he managed to knock the gun from Loginov's hand. As he curled up in a fetal position, he could hear Amanda scream before she broke free from the madman's grasp. She then scurried to the discarded weapon and picked it up.

While lying in a gathering pool of blood, Blake could hear the fleeing footsteps of the man who'd just shot him. Brent raised his firearm and was prepared to shoot Loginov, who was running to an inconspicuous exit door at the hangar's rear.

"No!" Jake shouted at Brent. "He's mine."

Jake led his fleeing target like a duck hunter leads a low-flying mallard. He fired a shot that missed. Then, standing stoic, he fired again, and again, until Loginov dropped to the ground, grabbing his left knee in pain. Jake walked to his wounded prey, his smoking gun out in front of him.

"Blake's been shot!" Amanda screamed, running to him.

"He shot me in the side," Blake grimaced. His face began to heat up like an electric stove burner. "Where's the gun?"

Blake snatched the handgun from her and labored to his feet. Then, favoring his wound, he marched toward Loginov, who was lying on the ground, groaning, and holding his left knee.

Jake peered over his shoulder and saw Blake approaching. Blake had the dilated eyes of a psychopath, and that concerned Jake. He hadn't considered it earlier, but Blake's hair was longer and disheveled, his face hardened and unshaven. The kid had lost weight, and the muscles and veins protruding from his arms were visible. It was a look not dissimilar from the one that Jake had seen in his Mexican mirror. It was the look of devil-may-care.

Unadulterated, reckless abandon!

"*Blake!*" Jake yelled, like a parent whose small child is about to toss the car keys in the ocean.

But Blake couldn't hear Jake, nor did he wish to.

"Do you think this is a game!?" Blake screamed at Loginov, blood oozing from his left side and dripping onto the floor. "Do you think you are God!?"

"Blake!" Jake screamed again as Blake drew closer to Loginov.

"Do you think you're leaving here alive!?" Blake asked, checking the gun's clip, noticing that five bullets remained. "You butchered my dog! You killed my friend, my colleague, and countless others! You tried to have your minions hunt me down and kill me! You made my life a living nightmare! And for what!?"

"You are nothing to me, counselor," Loginov taunted, continuing to focus most of his attention on Jake, whom he believed to be the primary threat.

"I'm about to mean *everything* to you, sick freak!" Blake wailed as he charged ahead, the gun leveled at Loginov's head.

Before he could pull the trigger, Blake had the palm of Jake's hand in his face; Jake's other hand was wrapped around his wrist. Blake's gun was pointed in the air.

"Put the gun down, Blake," Jake beseeched. "You don't want this man's blood on your hands. He's not worth it. You have your whole life ahead of you."

Infuriated, Blake remained resistant to Reid's warning. "Get out of my face, Jake! You don't know what this guy has done! He's a brutal killer!"

"Blake," Jake said, acting calm, "I'm sorry you were shot. I'm sorry about your friend. I'm sorry about your dog. But this—"

"What do you know, Jake!? I told you to get out of my *face*! I don't need your condescending apologies!"

"Blake," Reid said, "let it go. Listen to me. . . . Let it go."

SCAVENGER HUNT

"You let it go, Jake!" Blake said, trying to wrestle away from Jake, to finish the job.

Jake, losing patience, swiped his foot underneath Blake's legs. Blake crashed to the ground, his head slamming against the concrete floor below him.

Loginov, taking advantage of the commotion, tried to make his way to the ATV, which was idling against the back wall of the hangar. He knew that his only hope was to reach the four-wheeler, climb aboard, and speed away to safety. He had slithered about thirty yards before the size-fifteen combat boots of Major Olson stopped him.

"Where do you think you're going?"

"You have no qualms with me, Olson," Loginov said. "I've done you no harm. We needed you for those missions."

"When you mess with my friends, you mess with me."

Jake was on top of Blake, who was kicking to get free. "Blake!" he yelled. "Listen to me. You're going to listen to me. You asked me what I know, Blake. And I'm going to tell you."

"Get off of me, Jake!"

"Listen! The man who you want to kill is the same man who caused my daughter to be rmurdered."

Blake stopped fighting.

"Yeah," Jake said. "Loginov tipped off the men who had their way with my little girl. That monster right over there is to blame for . . ."

Thanks for the entertainment, Mr. Reid.

Jake pulled Blake's face to his own.

"They took her away from me, Blake," Jake whispered as his body began to shake, tears welling up in his eyes. "*He* took Rebecca Ann away from me. Do you understand?"

Blake closed his eyes, remembering the brutal pictures of Rebecca Ann Reid that Clyde had shown him on the Federal Mall, remembering the note that had been pinned to her mutilated body. THANKS FOR THE ENTERTAINMENT, MR. REID. He then opened his eyes and nodded. "You finish it then."

Jake released him, wiped the tears from his eyes, and hopped to his feet.

"Jake!" Loginov shrieked, now with abundant fear in his voice. "I had no idea your daughter would be harmed, and you know that! Don't try and pin her death on me!"

"Poor use of words, Nikolai," Jake responded, walking toward Loginov with his firearm brandished. "Very unfortunate, in fact."

"If I were you, mister," Brent counseled, glaring down at the helpless, wounded man under his foot, "I'd start saying my prayers."

Jake raised his gun to his nemesis's head as Brent stepped away.

"You're making a big mistake, Jake!" he screeched. "I didn't know!"

Jake said nothing as his finger inched closer to the trigger. He thought about his precious little girl. He still couldn't believe she was gone. He couldn't believe it was here, the moment he'd waited for every minute of every day since her death. He was about to write the final paragraph in the final chapter in the horror story he'd lived for so many months. He closed his eyes and felt the salty saliva trickle down his otherwise arid throat.

Thanks for the entertainment, Mr. Reid.

And then he heard someone say something behind him in a soft, controlled voice.

"Jake," Amanda said, her lips shaking. "It's not going to bring her back."

Brent and Blake, *shocked*, turned around and looked at Amanda, who had tears rolling down her cheeks.

Jake said nothing. He never turned around, his finger now nestled against the trigger.

Amanda spoke again. "It's not going to end the pain."

Jake squinted his eyes in agony, tears flowing down his face once again, his right arm and the gun in his hand shaking violently.

"He'll get off!" Jake pleaded with clenched teeth. "He owns the justice system! He owns everyone!"

"He won't get off," Amanda promised. "We'll make sure he's brought to justice. Of all our weaknesses, there's one thing we're good at. The law. The justice system."

Jake opened his eyes and stared at Loginov, who was curled up in a ball, cowering. "He'll walk!" Jake screamed.

"I'll make it my life's mission to guarantee that he doesn't walk, Jake," Amanda said. "On my mother's life, and that of a little girl named Audrey, I promise you."

Jake looked at Amanda . . . and finally lowered his gun.

Amanda sighed in relief and, for the first time in days, smiled.

But then, without warning, Jake raised his gun again and jammed it into Loginov's temple!

Thanks for the entertainment, Mr. Reid.

"Your life is over, *amigo*," he whispered.

"NO!!!!" Amanda screamed.

And then it was finished.

50

The black Suburbans drove through the Pennsylvania Avenue roadblock without being asked to stop for inspection. There would be no guards peeking through the windows; there would be no German Shepherds sniffing for traces of explosives. Everyone standing in official uniform around the gate knew the attorney general was cleared to pass without being subjected to White House security procedures.

Blake Hudson was sitting next to Attorney General Bill Kershing in the first of two bench seats in the back of the vehicle. Blake was staring outside the tinted window, toward the Treasury Building, sensing that Kershing was looking at him, trying to understand how this could have happened under his nose, trying to figure out what went so terribly wrong.

As they passed the White House on their way to the southwest gate, Blake noticed all the tourists stopping, staring toward him, and trying to get a glimpse of someone famous. Blake was reminded of his first meeting with John Smith at this precise location. That day felt like a lifetime ago. He thought about how his life would've turned out had he declined to be part of Smith's group.

"You'll do fine," the attorney general said.

"Have you taken care of the Henry Dalton problem? I don't want him trying to arrest me again."

"I told the FBI director that she'd better never again investigate any of my men without my express consent."

"And Dalton?"

"I'm giving him a service award."

"Why?" Blake asked, staring at Kershing.

"Because he saved your life, Blake. He went beyond the call of duty to protect your hide. The director told me that your friend at the FBI . . . what was his name?"

"Clyde Rothman."

"Rothman had indicated in his notes that you were in serious trouble. Dalton read those notes after Rothman died and stationed an agent near your house to protect you. Dalton tried to bring you in, but you were too sly for the FBI."

"Really? But Henry thinks that I murdered John Smith and Rothman."

"No, he doesn't. When you wouldn't cooperate, he believed he needed to bring you in for your own protection. Of course, with Amanda at your side, it was Dalton who needed protection." The attorney general stifled a chuckle.

"Why didn't they just tell me they were FBI?"

"That's what happens when you assign counterterrorism agents to a domestic security job."

"And Amanda?" Blake asked, knowing this was a touchy subject with Kershing.

"She submitted her resignation this morning. She'll be cleared of any wrongdoing."

"What's she going to do?"

"As of this Friday, she's going on a date with Henry Dalton."

Blake blinked hard. "You're kidding, right?"

The Suburbans drove into the most exclusive parking lot in the world. Blake could see the West Wing entrance to his right. "We should be back in thirty minutes," Kershing said to the driver as the vehicles stopped.

Blake walked in pain but in stride with Kershing, grabbing his wounded side as they entered the West Wing of the White House. Blake had visited before but never to meet with America's commander in chief. As Blake and Kershing approached the small security desk near the White House Mess Hall, Blake focused on what he had to do, what he had to say.

"We're here to see President Clements," Kershing announced to the secret service guard at the desk.

Before the guard could respond, however, the president's chief of staff emerged from the Situation Room and greeted them. "Hi, Bill," he said, shaking the attorney general's hand. "The president is expecting you."

"Todd, this is one of our best lawyers, Blake Hudson."

"Blake? Todd Whitehurst. Pleasure to meet you."

"The pleasure's mine, sir," Blake said.

Whitehurst escorted the two men down the corridor. As he continued reciting his speech in his head, Blake couldn't help but focus on the low ceilings and the current photographs on the walls, photographs showing President Clements campaigning in the battleground states of Ohio, Pennsylvania, and other areas in the so-called Rustbelt where voters had learned how to make politicians earn their vote. The president had no idea what he was about to hear, Blake thought.

Blake, as he oftentimes did, mused that the West Wing itself was an irony. This tiny, two-story office building constituted the nerve center of the most powerful nation in the world. Whereas the presidents, kings, and prime ministers of other nations worked in palaces and castles, the most powerful man in the world worked in a tiny, annexed wing with a dark-blue carpet.

After the three of them had walked up the carpeted stairs and down the second-floor corridor to the front entrance of the Oval Office, Whitehurst signaled for everyone to stop. President Clements was on the phone.

"Mary Beth, I love you more than you know, but you're not going to wear that skirt to our dinner tomorrow night. I'm not going to have you dressed like a tawdry sailor's fantasy in front of our most important donors. Talk to your mother about this. You know how important this night is to us. . . . I understand, but it's out of the question. . . ."

The president hung up the phone, turned his chair around, and cast his piercing blue eyes on the trio. "Come in, Bill. I've come to realize that it's easier to be the leader of the free world than it is to lead my children."

"Thanks for seeing us, Mr. President. We know you're busy. Let me get right to the point. I have Blake Hudson with me."

"Mr. President," Blake said, nodding in respectful recognition.

"Hello, young man. Welcome to the Oval Office. Looks like you had an accident."

"Unfortunately, that was no accident," Kershing said in a serious tone. "Blake has some important information to impart to you today, Mr. President. I'm here to support him, and once he says what needs to be said, you and I can discuss next steps."

"Well, let's get down to it. Have a seat."

"Mr. President," Whitehurst said, "I think we should probably walk outside for this discussion."

"Lead the way, Todd." The president of the United States rose from his leather chair and combed his hand through his thick, gray hair. "Blake, where are you from?"

"I'm from Austin, Texas, sir," Blake said as they stepped outside.

"So you're a Texas Longhorn?" President Clements asked, placing his hand on Blake's shoulder as he followed him out the door.

"Yes, sir."

"Mr. President, Blake is one of your political appointees," Whitehurst said, attempting to establish Blake's credibility with POTUS. "He's also one of the attorney general's closest advisors."

"That's certainly true," Kershing confirmed.

"He's handled and successfully resolved many sensitive problems for your administration in the past," the chief of staff continued, "and he has the utmost respect and confidence from everyone in the White House and the Department of Justice."

"Well, Blake, I expect nothing less from my appointees. Thank you for your commendable service," Clements said, closing the door behind him. "Please have a seat in any of the chairs here. You still need to be careful what you say on the patio. Thomas Jefferson is watching us." Clements pointed to the Jefferson Memorial, from which the statue of the third president was peering down on them from across the Ellipse. "Now, tell me what's on your mind."

"Thank you, Mr. President," Blake said.

He then took a deep breath, and began his story . . . a story that would crush any hopes of a Clements second term.

EPILOGUE

Baja Coast, Mexico

Leaning back in the plastic lounge chair and drinking an ice-cold Tecate under a Mexican sun, Blake realized that his tan would be quirky. The bandage wrapped around his mid-section would make it look as if he passed out in a tanning bed with a weight belt on. But he didn't care. He was too busy admiring the Baja Coast shoreline through his sunglasses and between his two big toes as the forty-four-foot yacht pressed forward. It had been an incredible trip from California, and Cabo San Lucas was minutes away.

Jake Reid asked Brent and Molly Olson if they wanted to navigate the rented vessel. After thanking Jake for the opportunity, they both declined. The two were huddled together near the yacht's stern like junior-high sweethearts in the back of a '57 Chevy. They had been holding hands since they woke up, not wanting to let go.

"You know, lovebirds," Jake said, adjusting his Yankees cap, "neither of you is going anywhere. You can let go of one another."

"Tend your boat, Captain," Brent replied with a smile.

"Blake, do you need another beer up there?" Jake asked, diverting his attention toward the bow.

"I'm good."

"Just let me know if you need anything," Jake said. "We wouldn't want you to lift a finger on this all-expenses-paid luxury cruise."

"My doctor prescribed a strict diet of rest and relaxation. You know that."

"You keep reminding me. But I've had hangnails worse than the pin-hole-sized gunshot wound you've been nursing for weeks."

Blake laughed and then pulled from his shorts' pocket the newspaper article he'd already read several times on the voyage.

Former CIA Operative and FBI Agent Arrested for Murder, Treason

Nikolai Loginov was arrested yesterday for the alleged murders of at least twenty people and for treason against the United States. FBI officials took Loginov, a former counter-intelligence specialist for the U.S. government, into custody after he sustained a gunshot wound to his left knee. Specifics of the incident leading up to his arrest were not revealed. A senior Justice Department official, speaking on the condition of anonymity, told The Washington Post *yesterday that prosecutors had ample evidence implicating Loginov in a wide array of illegal activity, and they expect a multi-count indictment to be forthcoming in the next few months. When asked how this information was obtained, the official stated that agents had been collecting evidence over the past few months, and they had received several good leads and lucky breaks in their investigation. . . .*

Blake crossed his arms and thought of Natasha Hensley.

"Blake, how many times are you going to read that article?" Jake asked.

"I'll keep reading it until I believe it. I still don't understand how Natasha gathered all this evidence."

"She's a remarkable creature, Blake. Relentless in her covert investigation."

"To think that she was hiding in the bushes the night I met my informant at the Summer House. There were so many odd things that happened that night. And what I really can't believe is that she reached out to Rick."

"They all risked their lives for you," Jake confirmed. "They must be some pretty good friends. After Natasha called Rick, he notified Clarence, who then got Harry involved."

"I had them pegged as primary suspects in all this." Blake turned to Jake. "When you spoke to Natasha, did she mention why she doesn't want to see me? I don't understand what's going on with her. She knows that I'm not to blame for any of this."

"Give her time. Like you, she's been through a lot. She can find you if and when she wants. I think I can understand what she's feeling right now. We both lost the driving force in our lives. It's like losing a soul mate who antagonized and comforted you at the same time. Hard to explain, but you should expect her to be a basket case for a while."

"What does that have to do with me?"

"You're a lot dumber than you look. You know that? Natasha has some wacky feelings for you. Get a clue. I know it's hard to imagine—an incredibly gorgeous, intelligent woman having feelings for a—" Jake started.

"Easy, buddy," Brent interrupted.

"You're right. You've proven your meddle. Cautious barrister turned fearless attack dog." Jake cringed after saying the last word. "Sorry, Blake. Bad choice of words."

"Don't worry about it. Judge has been on my mind since we boarded this boat. I know that a pet is not the same as a . . ."

"Say no more," Jake said. "Emotional pain is relative. I'd never diminish the hurt you feel for Judge just because I lost a daughter. Focus on positive things right now. We have an exciting two weeks ahead of us. Drink another beer."

Molly and Brent made their way toward the bow, and Jake picked up the CB transmitter and spoke in fluent Spanish, reading off the boat's coordinates and instructing his Mexican aide-de-camp to meet them on land a few minutes early. Jake noted that he'd made good time, and he wanted to make sure transportation and other necessities were ready when they arrived.

"What's going on?" Brent asked.

"We're going to dock a few miles from Los Cabos. There's a house there where we can freshen up. Should be there in ten minutes."

Blake raised the back of his lounge chair. His injury was feeling much better now, and he no longer needed painkillers to sleep. He nonetheless moved gingerly as he slipped his white T-shirt over his head. He then re-situated himself and grabbed his beer once again. He could see the shore in the distance. He also spotted the house Jake had referenced.

"Blake, are you feeling better?" Molly asked.

"I feel great right now. I'm anxious to get to shore, though, and I can't wait to see Amanda, Rick, and Clarence later tonight when they fly into Cabo."

"I look forward to meeting them . . . well, I know Amanda, of course," Brent said.

"Brent, when we get to the house, would you mind rubbing my neck?" Blake asked, feigning pain. "It's still sore."

"Blake, how many times do I need to apologize?"

Blake laughed. "You apologized enough when you stormed the aircraft hangar and . . . helped me out."

Blake, respectful of Molly's ears, decided not to be more specific when describing Brent's heroics.

"Brent could never hurt anyone," Molly responded, once again kissing her husband on the cheek. "He's just a big teddy bear."

"Yeah, Blake," Brent said. "You should be more sensitive to my feelings."

"I think I will just let that one . . ."

Blake's speech trailed off. He couldn't finish his statement. His eyes were homed in on a rock outcropping that was coming into sight. Setting down his beer, he glanced at the trio on the yacht, all of whom were smiling at one another, each aware of what was perplexing Blake.

He gazed again at the outcropping, trying to bring everything into focus. He spied two figures. One was seemingly taller than the other—one black, one white. One was sitting down. The other was clad in an orange and white sundress, which was flapping in the wind.

Blake walked to the bow and held the railing. The black figure rose from his sitting position—his tail wagging.

The sun-dressed figure was now in sight—her green eyes staring right back at Blake. Her auburn hair was blowing with the same rhythm as her clothes. She was breathtaking.

Blake forced himself to take his eyes off the outcropping. "Jake, you told me Judge was staying with a vet-approved pet sitter."

"I think you'll recognize the pet sitter I chose. She comes highly recommended."

Blake's feet hit dry ground before the boat was docked. And before he could get his bearings, he was forced to brace himself for impact. Judge was running at him, full speed ahead and eyes wide open. Not even thinking about his gunshot wound, Blake dropped to one knee to receive the large, loveable beast, who decelerated before impact. Blake grabbed Judge around the neck and rubbed his cropped ears.

"Judge! You're okay!" Blake couldn't let go. At this point, he could no longer control his emotions. He was encouraged to see that Judge's wounds were healing, his newly grown-in coat covering most of the scars. "Jake!" he yelled to the boat captain, "Judge is—"

"Judge is just fine, Blake," Natasha said. "But he's missed his best friend."

"Natasha," Blake said, standing up with his hand on Judge's head. "I was afraid you—"

"I'm sorry I accused you, Blake. I've done everything I can think of to make it up to you."

"Blake," Jake said, "I've been wanting to tell you this but couldn't. During the operations that Wonder Woman here was conducting behind our backs, she visited the animal hospital every morning to check on your mangy mutt."

"Is that true?" Blake asked.

"Well, at the time, he was the only one I could trust," she said, smiling and shrugging her shoulders.

As Judge meandered off toward the boat to greet the remaining passengers, Blake moved closer to Natasha. "I really, really missed you," he said. "I've been wanting to talk to you for—"

Before he could finish talking, Natasha lunged toward him, grabbed his head with both hands, and initiated a passionate kiss.

When the kiss finally ended, Blake ran his fingers through her hair and looked her in the eyes as their noses touched. "I hope you know Spanish," he said. "It looks like we're going to be here for a while."

"I'm actually fluent in Spanish," she giggled.

"Really?"

"Blake Hudson, there's a lot you don't know about me."

"I know," he said smiling. "That's what I'm afraid of."

ACKNOWLEDGMENTS

Thank you to:

My family, anchored by the love, steadfastness, and encouragement of my wife, Kristi.

Cortney Donelson, my esteemed editor, for her patience, spirit, rigor, timeliness, and commitment to excellent tradecraft.

Morgan James Publishing for giving me a chance.

My closest friends, those who know my best secrets and worst attributes yet handle them with gentleness. I want to give special thanks to Luis Reyes, who early on encouraged me to "see it through."

My earliest editors and colleagues from the US Department of Justice, including Ken Zwick, Ted Cooperstein, and Jeff Wadsworth.

Carole Sargent, the crown jewel of Georgetown University and provider of hope.

My mentors who wielded so much power while in government but who always chose love of country over themselves: David Margolis, Michael Chertoff, and John Ashcroft. References in the book to "thinking outside of the box but within the constitution" are drawn from the lips of Attorney General Ashcroft right after 9/11. That solid direction is forever etched in my memory.

The real-life scavenger hunters. You know who you are, but we probably don't. We don't deserve you.

ABOUT THE AUTHOR

Chad Boudreaux is a Washington insider hired by the US Department of Justice the night before the September 11, 2001 attacks—launching him immediately into counterterrorism work that earned him high accolades at an early age. His success in the Justice Department carried him to the US Department of Homeland Security, where his role as deputy chief of staff allowed him to work directly with Secretary Michael Chertoff, advising him on significant policy, operational, and legal issues facing the Department. He is currently the chief legal officer of a publicly traded, Fortune 300 company and America's largest military shipbuilder. Boudreaux leverages his unique, high-level experience in global security matters and his extensive legal expertise to craft breathtaking, insider stories of mystery and intrigue that are ripped from today's headlines and sure to shock his readers.

A free ebook edition
is available with the
purchase of this book.

To claim your free ebook edition:

1. Visit MorganJamesBOGO.com
2. Sign your name CLEARLY in the space
3. Complete the form and submit a photo of the entire copyright page
4. You or your friend can download the ebook to your preferred device

Morgan James
BOGO™

A **FREE** ebook edition is available for you
or a friend with the purchase of this print book.

CLEARLY SIGN YOUR NAME ABOVE

Instructions to claim your free ebook edition:
1. Visit MorganJamesBOGO.com
2. Sign your name CLEARLY in the space above
3. Complete the form and submit a photo
   of this entire page
4. You or your friend can download the ebook
   to your preferred device

Print & Digital Together Forever.

Snap a photo   Free ebook   Read anywhere